Knowing Me *Knowing* You

Brian Finnegan

HACHETTE
BOOKS
IRELAND

First published in Ireland in 2013 by
HACHETTE BOOKS IRELAND

1

Cataloguing in Publication Data is available from the British Library

ISBN 978 1 44479 294 7

Typeset in Caslon by redrattledesign.com

Printed and bound in Great Britain by Clay's Ltd, St Ive's plc

Hachette Books Ireland policy is to use papers that are natural, renewable and
recyclable products and made from wood grown in sustainable forests. The logging and
manufacturing processes are expected to conform to the environmental regulations of
the country of origin.

For Miguel

I listened, motionless and still;
And, as I mounted up the hill,
The music in my heart I bore,
Long after it was heard no more.

From 'The Solitary Reaper' by William Wordsworth

August 1983
The Visitors

Maggie takes a pull on her cigarette with puckered lips, and emits three perfectly formed rings of blue smoke. 'If your life was an Abba song, what would it be?' she asks, her voice puncturing the silence, like the pop of a helium balloon.

She's trying to ignore the insistent, buzzing headache at the front of her skull and the fact that her mouth is as dry as the Mojave Desert. It's probably something to do with the two bottles of her father's homemade wine she nicked from the garden shed yesterday evening – which seems a lifetime ago. It was 'absolutely vile', according to Dee, but they drank every last drop, passing one bottle and then the other between the four of them as the sun went down over the pointed tips of the pine trees on the eastern side of the lake.

Beside Maggie at the front of the boat, Daniel is silent. He hasn't opened his mouth since they woke up this morning, their hair strewn with leaves, gritty traces of soil in Maggie's mouth. Maybe it's because he's so quiet that she can't stop talking.

Charlie's saying nothing either, but he's hardly what you might call a chatterbox. He's taken off his windcheater, sweating with the exertion of rowing, and Maggie can see the flex and release of the muscles under his T-shirt as he pushes and pulls the oars through the soupy water, the rhythm bearing them relentlessly towards the shore and home.

She leans over the side of the boat to peer at her reflection. Even though it's muddled by eddies from the oars, she knows she looks different from yesterday.

She takes another pull on her cigarette. 'Bloody Hell,' she says. 'Don't all speak at once!'

'I'm just thinking,' says Dee, who's sitting behind Charlie at the prow of the boat. She'd plonked herself there when they'd got in, insisting she'd be the navigator.

A thin film of mist hovers just above the surface of the lake, mirroring a hazy white sky that will turn blue and cloudless before long. Even the birds are quiet. A twitter here or there as the oars cut soundlessly through the water's surface, not the usual cacophony that greets the dawn.

'Mine's "Head Over Heels",' says Maggie, and when nobody answers, she adds, with an exaggerated sigh, 'Anyone want to know why?'

'Because you're like the girl in it?' says Dee.

'Exactly!' Maggie laughs, the words of the song playing in her head. 'I'm a leading lady. Pushing through unknown jungles every day.'

'Mine's "Money, Money, Money",' says Dee, 'because I'm going to marry a millionaire. He'll have more money than Rod Stewart and we'll live in a mansion in Beverly Hills, with a maid and a gardener and a pool and a Rolls-Royce ...'

Maggie shifts her weight from one buttock to the other on the hard wooden seat. She's had a hundred conversations like this with Dee, stretched across their beds in each other's houses, flicking through issues of *Abba* magazine with their chins in their hands. Abba split up six months ago, but in letters Maggie and Dee wrote to each other, they swore to keep their love and devotion for them alive until the day they died. They've been Abba's number-one fans since 'Super Trouper' was number one on *Top of the Pops*. And that was yonks ago, long before Dee was sent away.

Charlie shakes his head. 'You're a lunatic,' he says to Dee, the corners of his mouth twitching. Any moment now he might crack a smile.

'Takes one to know one,' Dee retorts, shoving his shoulder.

Maggie wonders if something went on between them last night when they were at the rock pools on the other side of the beach together.

Originally she had come up with the idea for the Abba fan club because Dee had blurted that she fancied Charlie, the week she came home for the summer holidays. 'I'll tell him you fancy him,' Maggie had suggested, jumping at the idea of helping her best friend, but Dee had squealed, 'No! Please! Don't!' So instead they'd sat in the Coffee Bean, eyeing up Charlie and his twin, Sam, over mugs of hot chocolate, while Maggie tried to come up with some alternative plan.

Charlie and Sam Jones. Identical straight blond fringes, spot-free sallow skin and big white teeth, like Americans, although they'd moved to Sligo from Ballinasloe, which was the arse end of nowhere. Brand new in town since Easter, they'd already been snapped up for the grammar-school football team.

'I don't think they'll be into Abba,' Dee had said, when Maggie suggested her new strategy. 'Look at them. They're so *cool*.'

At the Coffee Bean, Charlie and Sam were already surrounded by girls who wore royal blue Mercy Convent uniforms when they weren't on school holidays, not muck-brown Ursuline ones, like Maggie's. Girls who had giggles that rang out like pealing bells, books clutched against their perfectly pert chests and hair that fell in bouncy, honey-coloured curtains down their backs, as if they'd all just stepped out of a salon. Girls who looked nothing like Maggie, with her bush of carrot-orange curls. Or Dee, who was at least a foot shorter than every other girl their age.

Dee had been right. Sam had given a derisive snort when Maggie had walked up to the twins and suggested the Abba fan club. 'Get lost,' he'd said.

Later, outside the Coffee Bean, Charlie, who had said nothing at all during the exchange, was waiting for them. 'Can I be in the club?' he'd asked, in a voice that was a little deeper than his brother's but also a little less sure of itself. Maggie linked her arm in his and said, 'Of course.'

They'd walked partway home with him, Maggie chatting about 'The Winner Takes It All' and how she knew all along it meant the absolute end, and that no matter how uncool people thought Abba were, no other band in the history of the world was as good, including The Beatles.

Typically, all Charlie's attention was on Dee, who was walking on his other side. She barely came up to Charlie's shoulder and she was a bit chubby underneath her oversized sweatshirt, her Levi's 501-clad bum sticking out from the bottom of it, like a Zeppelin (Dee's word, not Maggie's). But boys always went for her, much more than they went for Maggie.

'We'll call for you tomorrow,' said Maggie, when they'd got to the bottom of Charlie's road, which she did after breakfast the next day, even though from that day on it was plain as the nose on his face that Charlie had eyes only for Dee. He never said much, but most of the time he was taking her in.

Daniel's hand is flat, his fingers splayed on the peeling red-painted seat of the boat, almost touching Maggie's. Last night, when they were lying together on Daniel's PLO scarf, spread across the ground as a makeshift blanket, he had begun to cry. Maggie had put her arms around him and made soothing sounds as his body was racked with silent sobs. She hadn't asked him why he was crying, but she thought she knew. It was about his mother. The memory makes her want to reach over and put her arms around him again, to pull him close. She feels a surge of something, the same waves crashing through her blood that she experienced last night when they were doing it.

She catches his eye and sees that he's smiling, as if he's thinking the same thing.

It's funny. You couldn't call Daniel handsome, not in the way Charlie's handsome anyway. His black hair hangs lankly down over his eyes, which are too close together. His front teeth stick out a little over his bottom lip and his chin has more acne on it than hers but, bizarrely, when he first showed up Maggie was reminded for a fleeting moment of a man from one of the black-and-white films her mother likes to watch on Saturday afternoons.

'What do you think your parents will say?' he asks, reminding her that they are approaching the shore.

'I don't give a fuck,' Maggie replies, and grinds the butt of her cigarette out on the floor of the boat with her heel.

She's going to be in big trouble, though. The wine, the boat, the island were all at her instigation. She'd giggled as she untied the boat from its moorings, insisting no one would notice it was gone and they'd be back before anyone knew it. Then it had been her idea to stay the night, even though they'd told no one at home that they were going anywhere. They'd just disappeared.

At the time, buoyed up by the wine, she was thrilled by the recklessness of the adventure that staying on the deserted island would be, but now that Daniel has mentioned her parents, her heart is sinking.

'So, what's yours?' she asks him, in an effort to lift herself back up.

'My what?'

'You *know*. If your life was an Abba song ...'

'I'm still thinking,' Daniel replies. On the wooden seat, his little finger reaches out and touches hers. She hooks her pinkie around his, and squeezing tight, experiences an exquisite burst of happiness.

'Let's make a promise,' Dee pipes up. 'Let's promise that if Abba ever get back together we'll go to see them.'

'They won't get back,' says Maggie. 'Björn said it would never, ever happen. And Agnetha. I think they all hate each other now.'

'Never say never,' says Charlie, resting the oars for a moment.

Daniel shrugs. Suddenly the couldn't-care-less boy from England, who'd replied to their ad on the supermarket noticeboard because he had nothing better to do, is back. 'In ten years' time nobody will have heard of Abba,' he says.

'I'll still love them,' says Dee. 'In a hundred years I'll still love them.'

'When you're a hundred and fifteen,' Charlie quips, and half smiles again.

'I promise!' says Maggie. She feels it fervently.

'Me too,' says Charlie, stretching out the oars again.

'Me three,' says Dee.

'What about you?' Maggie asks Daniel, her finger still linked around his.

'Trust me. They'll be history,' says Daniel. 'But if they're not, I promise too. If you promise to shut up.'

Maggie guffaws. 'I'll shut up when you tell me what your Abba song is,' she retorts. 'You can't fool me, mister. You *definitely* have one.'

'That's for me to know and you to find out.' Daniel smiles again and his eyes are boring into Maggie's.

Maggie experiences the waves in her blood again, pushing out through her chest. She's never felt anything like it before. She turns and holds her hand over her eyes to shade them so she can see how close they're getting to the shore. It's about five minutes away, she figures.

Turning back to Daniel, she laughs again, even though a cold shudder has made its way up her spine. 'I think I know what it is,' she says. 'It's dead easy.'

'Go on, then,' says Daniel. 'Guess.'

She glances at the approaching shore again. She doesn't know that, after the boat reaches its mooring, Daniel will disappear from her life so completely, it will be as if he hadn't even existed. She doesn't know that she will never again be the Maggie who is on this boat in this perfect moment, trying to work out what Daniel's Abba song is.

Part One
SOS

1. Since the Day We Parted

The clock on the bedside table read 01:43 as Maggie Corcoran struggled out of the kind of deep sleep she hadn't had in months. Somewhere in the room her mobile phone was ringing.

Benny, who was curled up on the pillow next to her, lifted his head. If cats had eyebrows, he might have crooked one.

The phone stopped ringing the moment Maggie located it in her dressing-gown pocket, which was in a bundle under a pile of clothes on the armchair beside the chest of drawers. She'd just had time to read that the missed call was from William when the ringtone shouted again – she almost dropped the phone.

'Jesus, William!' she answered it. 'It's two o'clock in the morning.'

There was silence at the other end of the line and then a sob. 'Maggie,' William said, his voice like a lost child's, 'I think Rita's having an affair.'

Maggie pushed a clump of sleep-dense hair behind her ear and sank back down on to the edge of the bed. The carpet around her feet was strewn with clothes, shoes and balled-up tissues. From the corner of her eye she could see a discarded pair of knickers, like a wilted parachute.

'Maggie?' William said. 'Are you there?'

'Yes,' Maggie replied, trying her best to sound detached.

Benny stalked across the bed to sit beside her, his short tail curled neatly behind him, his one eye closed. He yawned, showing his wonky bottom teeth.

Poor Benny. She didn't know exactly what age he was, but the vet said somewhere around sixteen, which in cat years was over the hill and far away. He'd arrived at her door one day five years ago, with his right eyeball hanging out of a gruesome mess on his face. A fight with another cat, probably, the vet said. Since then Benny had been permanently at Maggie's side. She felt an affinity with him that she'd never had with another animal, and now his one-eyed, lop-sided predicament echoed inside her all the more.

'Can I come over?' William asked, choking up again.

Benny opened his eye and gave her one of his don't-even-think-about-it looks.

Maggie turned away and pushed a stray bra into a small bundle of clothes with her foot. 'Where are you now?' she asked.

'In my car, outside his house. She's in there with him, I know it.'

'In where? With who?'

'Roger Collins.'

Maggie tried to picture Roger Collins. Was he the heavy-set guy with the unkempt beard and the dog-hair-covered parka? Or that fellow from West Yorkshire with the stutter, the one who never stopped talking? Truth was, Roger Collins could have been any one of the men from the composting group, all of whom hovered around Rita Wilde as if she was the Madonna (the pop star, not the mother of Christ) of Decomposed Matter.

Maggie had gone along with William to the first few meetings and watched how all the men tried to second guess the nugget of composting wisdom Rita would bring forth next, hoping to impress her with their knowledge of how to get a fine grain, but for the life of her she couldn't fathom what they saw in the woman.

Benny stretched out and put the pad of one paw on her knee, his claws out.

Rita might have been the same age as Madonna, exactly ten years older than Maggie, but there the resemblance ended. She was like a cake that had been left out in the rain. As shapeless as the tent-like, rainbow-coloured clothes she'd probably worn to Stonehenge for midsummer 1970, she was one of those women who clung to a version of themselves they should have let go a long, long time ago.

Maggie had said something to this effect almost three months ago to the day, when William told her he was leaving to shack up with Rita in her probably patchouli-scented flat in Hackney.

William had snorted. 'Rita doesn't go around pretending to be something she's not,' he'd said, in a maddeningly even tone. 'She's the real deal.'

Trying not to raise her voice, Maggie had replied, 'What are you talking about? She's as real as an Oompa Loompa!'

William had greeted this with a look of disgust. He'd zipped up the case he'd been packing, then pronounced: 'Rita's more real than anyone I've ever known.'

It was like the final line in one of those awful West End ensemble plays about life in the suburbs, the kind William had been so keen on when they'd first moved to London.

The inference was that by comparison Maggie wasn't 'real'. That she wasn't honest. Her reaction to the accusation was like being caught in a tunnel in a crosswind: she'd tried to keep her balance, but felt like she was being buffeted from all sides. No matter what she said, how much she begged him not to go, her voice couldn't be heard above the roar.

He'd said, 'Goodbye, Maggie,' with awful, deadened finality and walked out of the front door with his suitcase, leaving her barely able to stand in the instantly silent hallway. Without warning, in the space of half an hour, everything she had imagined to be real and secure had been ripped away from her.

But William's goodbye had not been the last line in the play. Not by a long shot. The last line had been delivered by a doctor with a polar-white beard and Sigmund Freud spectacles, in an office that could have been a bank manager's, except for the light-box lined with mammograms of Maggie's right breast hanging on its wall.

The last line was: 'Stage Three A invasive ductal carcinoma, Mrs Corcoran.'

Or maybe it wasn't.

Maybe that was the last line of the first act, and there was a second act to come. For here was the real Rita now, having a real affair with a man in a dog-hair-covered parka. Possibly.

And here was the cancer-stricken woman's husband coming back to her, in her hour of desperate need.

Maggie stroked Benny's head and experienced an unexpected surge of purpose, a feeling she hadn't had in so long it was like coming upon an oasis after months of thirsty trudging across a vacant, dry desert. At the beginning, after William had left, she'd tried to come up with all sorts of strategies for getting him back, but she'd hit dead ends at every turn her mind took, until she'd just given up. But now, Rita, simply by dint of her unfathomable attractiveness to the opposite sex, had played right into Maggie's hands.

Or maybe the gods had thrown a dice. Maggie could tell her husband about the cancer now. In blind shock, she hadn't been able to bring herself to say anything to anybody about the diagnosis. It seemed like eternity, although it had been just over a week, since she'd sat in Dr Snow's office, gaping in silent horror at the offending mammograms.

Maggie could almost taste the sweet relief that would come with unburdening herself at last. 'Okay, William,' she said, into the phone, still trying to sound lackadaisical. 'Come home.'

2. A Shoulder You Can Cry

As Maggie pushed a bundle of dirty clothes into the bottom of the wardrobe, and cherry-picked the balled-up tissues from the floor, Benny kept watch from his perch on the bed, unblinking. 'Don't give me that look,' she warned the cat, leaning over to pick up a shoe. 'I'm not going to do anything stupid.'

Benny jumped off the bed and rubbed himself against her shin as he passed her on his way out of the bedroom, turning once to give her a disdainful one-eyed glance before setting off down the stairs.

In the shower Maggie tried to ground herself. There was no need to leap to conclusions. William himself might be leaping to conclusions about Rita. Maybe she wasn't having an affair. Maybe William was being paranoid … although, given his temperament, it was unlikely.

Brushing her teeth, Maggie rubbed a patch of steamed-up bathroom mirror clear with one hand. The woman staring back at her was foaming at the mouth and looked as if she'd aged ten years in a week. She tried to bring her thicket of hair under some control with the fingers of her left hand. But it was a lost cause. Since William had walked out, she'd let it go and it had grown out into the Jaffa-orange Afro she hadn't let take root since she was a teenager. She'd let her swimming go too, and the Bikram yoga she'd been doing every Thursday morning.

What was the point? It didn't matter any more. For all her exercise and diet consciousness, her husband had left her. And once the chemotherapy started, she'd lose her stupid hair.

She left it alone and dabbed some concealer under her eyes to get rid of her dark circles. She smeared gloss on her lips and brushed on some blusher to bring up her colour and make herself a little bit presentable.

Pulling on her dressing-gown, she went downstairs to put the kettle on. Benny, who had taken up his favourite position beside the toaster, observed her as she cleaned off the kitchen worktop, which was littered with debris from the Marks & Spencer's ready-meal she'd had for dinner, washed down with a full bottle of Chianti, which had been on special offer and consumed against Dr Snow's advice.

In the queue at Marks, she'd noticed another middle-aged woman unloading a meal for one and the same Chianti at an adjacent till. Her head was wrapped tightly in a washed-out scarf and her face had been deathly pale. She had had that inward look about her, as if she was completely in a world of her own, her shoulders hunched as she lined up her packages precisely on the belt. Then she'd noticed Maggie gawking at her and had half-smiled in recognition, not of who Maggie was but *what* she was. Someone just like her.

Maybe cancer was like having a baby. Once you joined the club, everyone else with it clocked you and gave you a knowing look.

The kettle was coming to the boil as William's car pulled into the drive, illuminating the hallway with its photographs of the family dotted along the walls. Pictures from various holidays with the kids over the years – Poppy at her first holy communion, Harry on the day of his graduation, flanked on either side by Maggie and William looking in the full of their health, proud and confident for the future of their family unit.

That photograph had been taken just over a year ago, and how unbelievably everything had changed since then. Harry was in

Australia on his year's youth visa. He hadn't been available on Skype for weeks. And Poppy, living in that awful squat, might never have been the freckled little girl in a communion veil, with a big smile and one missing tooth, her prayer book clutched in white-gloved hands.

Maggie went to open the front door, but at the same time William let himself in. He had surrendered his family, but not the keys to his family home.

'Hi,' Maggie greeted him, searching for something else to say but coming up short.

Benny, who had followed her to the door, let out a long, low miaow and darted up the stairs.

'It's late,' said William. 'I'm sorry.' He looked like death warmed up.

'That's okay,' said Maggie. 'Come on – the kettle's boiled. I'll make us a cup of tea.' She turned towards the kitchen but, sensing that William wasn't following, turned back again.

He was standing there, head bowed, shoulders heaving. 'I can't believe it,' he said, wiping his nose with the back of his hand. 'She told me she loved me.'

He was the author of his own fate, of course, and it wasn't lost on Maggie that he was crying over another woman, but the urge to comfort him was almost irresistible. 'I'll make a cup of tea,' she said again, then added, 'unless you want something stronger?'

'Hold me?' William asked, his voice miserable in the dim hallway.

It was what she had prayed for, wasn't it? What she had begged God for in the dark of her bedroom the night after getting her diagnosis, lying in a puddle of her own tears and snot, fear and isolation threatening to consume her until there was nothing left.

Her husband wanted her again – even if it seemed like now he wanted her more like a little boy wants his mother.

He walked towards her, arms outstretched, and she tentatively took him into her embrace. Bringing his face to her shoulder, she stroked his hair and whispered, 'It's okay. Sssh …'

William heaved another sob.

She'd tell him about the cancer in the morning, she decided, when he'd had a night's sleep. Until then, she'd be his shoulder to cry on. It felt right and good, as if the role she'd always played had been restored to her and the curtain was up on a new act.

3. Loser Standing Small

When she woke, it took Maggie a few seconds to become fully aware of what had happened the night before. When she'd climbed into bed with William, she'd experienced an overwhelming, gut-churning hunger for sex with him, something she hadn't felt since she couldn't remember when. She'd kissed him hard and ground her body into his, with a desperation she couldn't hide, but William hadn't responded. He'd cried again, his tears wetting her neck. And then he'd nodded off in her arms.

Still only half awake, with morning light tentatively peeping through the curtains, Maggie reached out for him and found his side of the bed empty. The yawning panic she felt every time she got under the duvet alone at night rushed back with such force that her eyes snapped open and she sat bolt upright.

Benny was sitting on the end of the bed, carelessly licking one of his paws.

Maggie rested back on the pillow and inhaled to the count of three with her eyes closed. She wasn't alone. William was home. He was probably downstairs making the diesel-strength coffee he needed every morning to get himself functioning. The idea of it gave her comfort – how quickly their old routines could be re-established.

Her eyes were closed for less than ten seconds before she realised the house was utterly silent. There was no hiss and clank of the coffee machine from the kitchen, only the sticky sound of Benny's tongue cleaning his paw.

She pushed the duvet back, her heart pumping dread through her veins.

'William?' she called.

She stood up and went to the bedroom door.

'William!'

She half-called his name once more on the way down the stairs. In the kitchen she stopped cold. There was a note on the table, anchored there by a half-drunk glass of orange juice. 'Maggie,' it said, in a rushed scrawl. 'Talked to Rita. Everything's OK. Didn't want to wake you. Will call later. X.'

Maggie slumped down at the table and read the note again. Angry tears pricked her eyes. He'd signed it 'X'. Last night he'd lain in her arms telling her she was the only one who understood him.

She put her face on the table, feeling the slightly cool texture of its unpolished wood against her cheek. From this vantage point she had a skewed vision of the smiling family photographs lined up on the wall of the empty hallway. The family she'd somehow lost.

Benny, sitting on the floor now, gazed up at her sideways.

You couldn't bring a cat for moral support to your first chemotherapy appointment, could you? It was probably against all hospital-hygiene rules.

Maggie lifted her head. Her chemo wasn't starting for another week. She didn't want to think about it.

Was it too early to call Poppy? The clock on the wall said 09:47, so it probably was. She didn't imagine they went in for early nights in the squat, or that anyone had to get up for something as bourgeois as a day's work. But hearing Poppy's voice would be proof that the photographs on the wall actually meant something, that they were still a family, even if they had all gone their separate ways. It might make Maggie feel like a mum again – needed in the way she had taken for granted all those years.

'Hey, Mum,' Poppy said, picking up after one ring. 'What's going on?' She sounded fresh as a daisy.

'I'm just calling to say hello,' said Maggie, and her chin wobbled dangerously.

'We're on our way out,' said Poppy. 'We're going to the anti-Israel protest.'

'The what?' Maggie asked. Her throat was constricting.

'Bloody Hell, Mum. You need to start reading the newspapers. There's a revolution happening. The people are rising up against the oppressors. We're claiming the—'

'Your father came back,' Maggie interrupted. 'Last night. But he's gone again.'

There was silence down the line and Maggie was filled with guilt. She had sworn to herself that she wouldn't get the children involved in the separation, wouldn't make them take sides.

'Mum—'

'He's gone back to her.' Maggie couldn't stop herself. Hot tears rolled down her face.

'Look, Mum, can I call you later? Orlando's waiting with the guys in the car for me …'

Maggie wiped the tears from one cheek with the back of her hand, flattening skin that had once been taut but now felt like old knicker elastic. 'Sure,' she said, 'call me later,' knowing it was unlikely this would happen.

For a second she thought Poppy had hung up, but then she said, 'Mum, you know the money you said you'd put into my account? I don't want to bother you, but …'

'Oh, honey, I'm sorry,' Maggie said, refilling with guilt. 'I completely forgot.'

'Could you do it today, on-line? Only if I don't pay up I'll be *persona non grata*. Everyone else has put their share in.'

'I'll do it now,' Maggie said. 'Two hundred, isn't it?' At least they were going to do something about decorating that awful house.

'Hold on for a second,' Poppy said. While Maggie held on, she heard her daughter shouting at someone – Orlando, probably, who looked like a down-and-out surfer, even though his father was the Earl of Something or Other. 'Give me a break, will you? I'm coming!

'I have to go,' Poppy said into the phone.

'Okay, honey.'

'And, Mum,' Poppy told her, before hanging up, 'Dad's being a total patriarchal prick. The sooner you get over him, the better.'

But that was easier said than done. And calling William a patriarchal prick didn't quite fit. Patriarchs were supposed to be powerful, imposing figures, weren't they? William had always been the needier one in their marriage, and she'd given him whatever support he required, not because he'd demanded it but because it had made her happy to keep him happy.

Maggie read through his note again, with its stingingly casual 'X' at the end. Three months after he'd departed, she still couldn't make any sense of it. Maybe Rita Wilde had special powers. Maybe, like a *Macbeth* witch in Birkenstock sandals, she'd cooked up a spell to lure him away. It sounded fantastic, but nothing else seemed plausible.

Maggie pulled off a piece of kitchen roll and dabbed her puffed-up eyes as Benny started circling her calves, miaowing in the strung-out way he always did when he wanted to be fed. She sighed and went to pull a portion of Sheba out of the press under the worktop. As she forked its pungent contents into the dish by the back door, Benny waited with his beady eye on her. He never quite trusted that he was getting the standard of food he expected until he tasted it.

Maggie returned his stare, squeezing up the aluminium carton. 'Save your breath,' she warned.

The cat put his head into his dish and began noisily to dig into his Rabbit in Delicate Gravy, instantly oblivious to anything else.

On the kitchen table her phone, on silent, vibrated. Maggie's heart gave a pathetically hopeful leap. Maybe it was William.

Instead, the screen said 'Blocked', which meant it was more than likely Oona. Maggie's sister was the only person she knew who withheld her number.

She hovered over the kitchen table, trying to decide whether to pick up the phone or not. Just as it was about to ring out, she grabbed it and answered.

'I thought you might be screening your calls,' said her sister, by way of greeting. There was never any 'How are you?' with Oona.

'Hi, Oona,' Maggie replied. 'I can't screen calls if I don't know who's calling. Your number is withheld.'

'Well, I'm not giving every detail of my life to all and sundry. There's no such thing as privacy any more. Everyone knows everyone else's business.'

'People's numbers used to be in phone books,' Maggie reminded her sister, wondering what she wanted. Oona only called when she wanted something. Otherwise she waited for Maggie to call her.

'Anyway,' said Oona, 'I was wondering if you could do me a tiny favour.'

'What kind of favour?' Maggie asked, knowing she wouldn't say no, and guessing it wouldn't be a tiny one.

'Can you take me to Ikea? I want to get a chest of drawers for the spare room.'

'Sorry, I can't today,' said Maggie, trying to sound apologetic. She couldn't think of anything worse than negotiating the Ikea maze. 'I'm working the afternoon shift.'

Oona let out one of her sighs. 'I don't understand why you let them make you work Saturdays,' she said.

'It's a library, Oona,' said Maggie. 'Saturday is our busiest day.'

'Well, it's not fair on you, that's all I'm saying. And I really wanted to get that chest of drawers today.'

'We could go tomorrow,' Maggie said. 'Libraries are closed on Sundays.'

'Oh, God, no,' said Oona. 'Ikea is Hell on Earth on Sundays with all those people who have nothing better to do than bring their entire families, like day-trippers. Are you working next Saturday?'

'No,' said Maggie. It was her one weekend off in the month. But, having said that, the doctor had told her she had to go on sick leave from the start of her chemo, so she'd be having weekends off for the next three months at least.

'It's settled, then,' said Oona. 'You can pick me up on Saturday morning, around eleven.'

'I suppose so.'

'We could make a day of it. Have lunch in the café.'

The thought if it made Maggie groan out loud.

'For God's sake, Maggie,' said Oona. 'It will be good for you to get out. You don't want to be fading away to nothing all alone in that house, like some sort of Miss Havisham.'

It was odd to hear Oona, who had never so much as picked up a book in her life, make a literary reference, but then Maggie remembered that the BBC adaptation of *Great Expectations* had finished last Sunday. She shuddered at the memory of the cobwebbed old-before-her-time woman's gruesome death.

'I'm not a Miss Havisham, am I?' she said to Benny, after Oona had hung up. Benny stopped eating his Sheba and then, without looking up, resumed where he had left off.

4. Don't Think about Tomorrow

Ruth looked at her watch and gave the vaguest of tuts as Maggie set her bag on the floor behind the reception desk, fifteen minutes late.

For a moment Maggie considered not bothering to give her the satisfaction of an apology, but then she relented. 'Sorry I'm late. The traffic was a bloody nightmare.'

The truth was that the nearer the time had come to leave for work the less she felt she could bear going in, and then, at the very last second, she'd realised she couldn't face the day at home alone, with nothing to think about except what was coming down the line, so she'd grabbed her bag and jumped into the car.

The traffic hadn't been bad. When Maggie had pulled into the library car park, she'd left the engine on, flicking through the CD that was playing until she'd found the track she wanted, 'Voulez Vous'. She'd sung along with the windows rolled up. It was the Abba song she always used to reboot herself when she felt she couldn't go on.

'That's okay,' Ruth replied, with a glare that said it wasn't. She pointed towards the returns trolley, which was so overloaded that books had tumbled to the floor in slipshod piles around it. 'Can you take care of these?' she asked. 'First thing.'

'Actually, I was going to set up Story Corner,' Maggie said.

Ruth gave her a studied smile and fingered the top of her rounded belly, like a man stroking the bonnet of his brand new sports car. 'Alison's doing story time today.'

It was the fourth Saturday in a row that Alison had made a beeline for the children's section and had bagged the only job in the library that Maggie really enjoyed. She loved reading to the kids, doing the characters' voices and bringing the stories to life. It reminded her of when she used to read to her own two, Harry laughing with delight at every little twist and turn, Poppy constantly asking questions, trying to make the story go the way she wanted, rather than the way the book told it.

'After you've sorted the returns, I need you to process the new arrivals,' Ruth added, indicating three towers of books teetering on the far side of the counter. She stroked her belly again and turned back to her computer, presumably to update her Facebook profile.

Since she'd got pregnant, Ruth had stopped actually working. Maggie now spent most of her three and a half days a week clearing up the mess that festered in book and paper mounds around her boss, who only moved from her swivel chair for toilet breaks. Ruth had been overweight before, but now she overflowed beyond the sides of the chair, her wide-set eyes and button nose making her look like a ginormous pregnant sloth.

Maggie checked herself. Judging from the slightly green pallor of Ruth's skin, she was ill again. The poor woman's morning-sickness phase had turned into all-day-long sickness, even though she was going on seven months. 'How are you feeling?' she enquired, and Ruth shrugged with the resignation of a woman who'd been languishing on Death Row for ten years with no hope of reprieve.

She'd be going on maternity leave at the end of the month and Maggie had applied to fill Ruth's position while she was off. She hadn't particularly wanted the extra hours, but the money would have come in handy. Although she had only herself to take care of, it was harder and harder to make ends meet. There'd been a few times when she was tempted to dip into William's account. It was still linked to hers on-line, but she knew he watched it like a hawk so he'd notice any transfer she made.

Taking the managerial job was out of the question now. She still hadn't told Ruth about the sick leave the doctor insisted on. Every time she tried to do it, a cold fear lodged itself at the pit of her stomach and she put it off for one more day.

Before tackling the returns, she made a quick detour to the kitchen for coffee, via Story Corner, where Alison was already sitting on a baby stool at one of the miniature tables, going through possible books for today. Once, when Maggie was passing as Alison read Roald Dahl's *Matilda* to the children, one of the little ones had put up her hand and shouted, 'You look like Miss Honey, miss!'

Maggie had to admit it was true. With her tidy nut-brown hair, always set back from her open-cheeked face with an Alice band, her pastel cardigans and constant string of pearls, Alison was the picture of a teacher for whom children brought apples to school. Sometimes Maggie brought her home-baked goodies. When Alison had exclaimed with pleasure, munching a fresh-from-the-oven brownie, Maggie had made another batch the following Saturday, just to bask in the glow of her admiration again.

Alison was an unlikely friend. She was some sort of distant relation of the Spencer family and lived in a house overlooking Hampstead Heath. The part-time hours in the library were her way of 'asserting her independence', she'd told Maggie, when she'd taken the job six months ago. Her husband was director general at London FM, so she certainly didn't need the money. Maggie guessed it was her only escape valve from her three-year-old twins, whom Alison called 'a handful', which was an understatement the size of the former USSR.

'Oh, Maggie, there you are,' Alison said, glancing up from the book she'd been skimming through. 'Ruth was worried you weren't coming in.'

'Poor Ruth,' Maggie said. 'She looks terrible.'

'I know.' Alison shuddered. 'I'll never forget how sick I was with the twins.'

'Coffee?' Maggie asked, wondering if she should confide in Alison. They met for lunch every so often and went for a drink sometimes after work, but hadn't really progressed to the confessional level of friendship yet. She'd kept the diagnosis to herself for so long now, though, that it was beginning to tick inside her, like an unexploded bomb.

'That would be lovely.' Alison smiled, standing up and straightening her pale pink woollen skirt.

In the shoebox that passed as a staff kitchen, Alison took one of two plastic seats as Maggie put the kettle under the tap. 'I'm so exhausted,' Maggie began, feeling her way rather than jumping in. 'I didn't get a wink of sleep last night.'

'Me neither,' Alison sympathised, although there wasn't even a hint of a dark circle under either of her eyes.

'William arrived out of the blue at two this morning.'

'Maggie,' Alison said, squeezing her hands together in her lap, 'I want to ask you a favour. If it's too big, please, please, say no, okay?'

Maggie clicked the kettle on. 'Okay,' she said, searching Alison's face, which was creased in a rare frown. Foreboding leaked like acid through her veins. Whatever Alison was going to ask, Maggie knew she wouldn't be able to refuse.

5. Memories That Remain

'I'm only asking because I'm at my wits' end,' said Alison, but her frown had smoothed out. 'Promise you'll say no if you can't.'

'Cross my heart and hope to die,' Maggie replied, her stomach growing more uncomfortable by the second.

'Simon and I are invited to a wedding in Vienna next weekend and we were thinking it would be a perfect break. We haven't been by ourselves together once since the twins were born.'

'I remember what that was like,' said Maggie. An unwanted memory came into her mind of hanging clothes on a line one summer's day when Harry and Poppy were still in Pampers. A splatter of mustardy bird shit had landed on the pristine white sheet she was pegging up, bringing with it the dull epiphany that all the things she'd imagined for herself as a girl weren't going to come true: she was trapped in an endless cycle of laundry and feeding and cleaning that would last so long it was impossible to imagine a different future.

'My sister was supposed to take the boys because the nanny has some family function back in Warsaw,' said Alison, 'but her hockey team's made it to the European finals, which are on in Antwerp next Saturday.'

'Antwerp is supposed to be beautiful,' said Maggie, in a listless effort to steer the subject away from what was coming.

'You wouldn't be able to take the twins for the weekend, would you?' asked Alison. 'I know it's a lot to ask. I wouldn't leave them with my mum – God knows what would happen – and Simon's parents are a bit ancient … You're the only one I trust,' she added, and Maggie was instantly caught between Heaven and a hard place. The Heaven was the flush of gratified pleasure she experienced at being told she was the only one Alison trusted with her children. The hard place was the children.

Maggie prided herself on the fact that children liked her, and that was because she liked children. But, even if she hated admitting it to herself, she had a hard time warming to Alison's twins. They were boisterous to the point of belligerence and both still in nappies. There was nothing worse than changing someone else's three-year-old's shitty nappy, never mind two of them.

'Of course I'll do it,' she told Alison.

'You will? Oh, Maggie, you're such a star! You don't know how much we need this break. The twins have me run ragged.'

'They're lovely boys,' Maggie lied, trying to keep her pleasure at being the trusted one on the boil, at being good and taking the children, rather than being bad and telling Alison where to go. 'It'll be a joy to have them.'

Maggie drove home from work with the radio blasting at full volume. It was all arranged: Alison would drop the boys over to her on Friday afternoon and pick them up late on Sunday. Her flight got in at 8.45 p.m.

Thirty-six hours later, Maggie calculated, she'd be checking in for her first chemo session.

'I so owe you one,' Alison had told Maggie, as they'd both clocked out from their shift. 'Seriously.'

Maggie had smiled. 'Don't be silly.' She felt good about helping Alison out of a bind, and it would be nice to hear kids playing in the house again. It might take her mind off the ordeal ahead.

As she came to a stop at a set of traffic lights on Chamberlayne Road, she flicked through the stations with her steering-wheel radio control. On London FM, the girl from *Glee* was belting out the chorus of 'Night Star'. The lights went green and Maggie lurched the car forward as a memory of Daniel ushered itself into her mind, the picture that always came: him sitting on the boat that summer's morning so long ago, his little finger curled around hers.

'Never known this feeling,' the *Glee* girl sang. 'Never cried these tears. Now I see the future. For a million years.'

Of all the songs in all the world, why had that stupid TV show picked this one? You couldn't turn on a radio or walk into a public space without being assaulted by it. Maggie reached to switch off the radio, then decided against it.

The first time she'd heard 'Night Star' was in 1989, the summer of her wedding. The rainfall that June had been record-breaking, even for Ireland, and it was belting down – it had sounded as if handfuls of gravel were being thrown at the windows of her parents' house – as she'd watched *Top of the Pops* alone, her mum and dad gone to their bridge night.

Mike Read had waxed lyrical about a new entry to the charts, introducing the up-and-coming Danny Lane to sing his 'Night Star', and then the cameras had panned across the studio to pick up Daniel standing on a stage, beginning to strum a guitar. She'd recognised him instantly. He looked almost the same as he had the last time she'd seen him, only he had grown into himself. The nose was perfectly proportioned, his square chin was devoid of spots, his teeth no longer protruded and his hair ... The devil-may-care greasy style had been replaced with a bleached-white buzz-cut, sticking up underneath the brim of a pale blue pork-pie hat that sat on the back of his head.

Maggie had watched in stomach-churning horror as he sang his chirpy love song, accompanied by an unseen band, and when he had finished, she'd flicked the television off with the remote control.

Her legs had been like jelly when she'd stood up, her heart walloping against her ribs. She'd lurched to the downstairs bathroom and leaned over the toilet bowl, retching and trying to block out the memory of the sour smell of disinfectant that had permeated the clinic in Manchester. But nothing had come up.

All through that summer Maggie couldn't get away from the song. In the weeks that led up to the wedding, it shot to number one and became the song of the season. Daniel was everywhere – on the cover of *Smash Hits* when she went to buy milk at the newsagent's; chatting amiably with Terry Christian on the couch at *The Word*, with barely a hint of the taciturn Daniel Maggie had known when she was fifteen; the video for his song, which bizarrely featured Daniel rowing a little red boat against animated waves, filled banks of television screens in the home-entertainment section of Coleman's Electronics.

Daniel's reappearance in her life, however remotely, had thrown Maggie into a storm of sleepless nights. She'd tossed and turned, composing letters in her head to him, which she'd thought she might send care of his record company. But what would have been the point? He probably didn't remember she existed.

Plus he was a pop star now, so what interest would he have in her?

Plus she was marrying William, whom she loved.

'Night Star' had come on the radio on the morning of her wedding, when she was getting ready for the church. Her mother, who was trying to do something with the bush of orange hair sticking out of the front of Maggie's veil, had stiffened, and Maggie had quietly walked across the room to switch off the radio.

The lead girl from *Glee* was belting out the closing lines now: 'Night star, my night star, we're standing on the shore. I want to know this feeling for ever more … for ever more.'

On the TV show the girl sang it with her face screwed up, like she was having her underarms waxed. Maggie couldn't understand why all the kids sang like that now, as if they were in excruciating pain.

Daniel had had one more hit, 'How To Be A Man', but then he had disappeared from the public eye, becoming pop's most famous recluse, bar Agnetha Fältskog. Every now and then over the years Maggie had heard 'Night Star' out of the corner of her ear and wondered what Daniel was doing. Thoughts of contacting him again would come to her, but she'd push them out of her mind. She didn't even know where she might find him.

Maggie turned from London FM to Radio 4 where a serious discussion about composting was in progress on *Gardeners' Question Time*. She blew a raspberry in disgust and switched off the radio, driving the rest of the way home in silence, the words of 'Night Star' repeating in her brain.

She was about to turn into her house when she noticed a purple Volkswagen camper van parked at the other side of the street. There was no mistaking it.

Maggie steeled herself as she pulled into the driveway. Sure enough, Rita Wilde, composting queen, was standing on her doorstep, looking like someone who had been dipped in glue and dragged through a flea market. Benny was next to her, rubbing the top of his head lovingly against her calf.

6. Here I Go Again

Christ! Now even the buskers were singing it.

At the bottom of the stairs, Daniel put his bike down and ploughed past the man standing just inside the entrance to the tube station, a ruddy-cheeked guy in faded jeans and a hoodie who hardly looked like your number-one *Glee* fan.

The song followed him out on to Ladbroke Grove in an oddly plaintive echo, causing him to wish he had a hoodie of his own so he could shroud himself.

'You were there. You were there. And I never needed anyone more…' The busker was a good baritone, Daniel had to give him that. At least his version sounded better than the one on *Glee*, which was almost unbearable to listen to. It was sung by the show's two main characters, a boy and a girl, and they'd taken away Vince's trademark reggae rip-off baseline, replacing it with a string section and a key-change in the final chorus that made it sound like a Broadway showstopper. Something about the girl's vocal, especially when she hit the high notes, made Daniel's stomach churn with sour discomfort. Her fervour reminded him of when he was writing the song so many years ago, with Maggie in his mind's eye.

Maggie … He tried to imagine her now. Married with kids, probably, middle-aged and overweight, living in Irish suburbia.

Although he didn't think of her every day, she had never quite gone away, even though it was a good thirty years since that summer.

Standing at the traffic lights, waiting for the green man, Daniel lifted his head for a hasty glance around. The busker's voice had faded beneath the din of traffic, but he was still worried someone might put two and two together.

Before now, recognition had been rare, and if people did pick him out in the crowd, they never got it quite right. 'I know you from somewhere,' somebody might say in a bar, and Daniel would exit stage left before his or her memory cells had had a chance to catch up. Or some woman of a certain age might stop in the street with a smile of vague recognition as he walked past.

But ever since the song had appeared on *Glee*, he had been recognised more and more. People were getting his identity right first time.

Daniel stopped at the shop across the road from the tube station to pick up some milk, and even though the man behind the counter smiled because he was a regular customer, he couldn't shake off the paranoia.

'Cold today, wasn't it?' the shopkeeper said, and Daniel nodded in silent agreement, averting his eyes. He didn't want to chat. He just wanted to get home, close the door and cut himself off from the world outside, which was encroaching on him again, making him more and more uncomfortable every day.

He had been only nineteen when he had signed away the publishing rights to 'Night Star'. How was he to know a TV show would appear twenty-six years later that recycled old pop tunes and made them global hits? How was he to know *Glee* would have its biggest chart-topper with 'Night Star'?

The bag lady was in her usual Saturday perch outside the library on the corner of Lancaster Road. She gave him a gummy smile as he crossed over to her, nodding hello. 'All right, love,' she said, from beneath her layers of scarves.

'All right, Annie,' Daniel replied, reaching into his pocket for the twenty-pound note he gave her every Saturday. 'How have you been?'

'Can't complain.'

In his other pocket, Daniel's phone began to vibrate. 'Excuse me,' he said to Annie, handing her the money and pulling out the phone with his free hand. The screen said 'Blocked Number'. 'You had anywhere to sleep this week?' he asked, ignoring the call. 'It's been a cold one.'

'Here and there, love. You know how it is,' Annie replied, as noncommittal as ever. Since he'd moved here just over a year ago he'd been having a variation on the same conversation with her every week. He was aware that, for reasons of her own, she wanted to give nothing away, and that suited him fine. He had his own reasons for keeping himself to himself.

Daniel shoved his phone back into his pocket. He was getting calls from unidentified numbers ten times a day now, which he routinely ignored. The first few times it had happened, he'd answered the phone to different journalists who wanted to ask him how he felt about the song being number one again. Now he had put a policy in place not to answer unidentified callers.

He waved goodbye to Annie and walked towards Portobello Road. There, the last of the market traders were taking down their stalls, the usual Saturday smell of half-rotted vegetables mingled with fried food pervading the air.

At the Westbourne Park Road junction, his phone rang again.

'Fuck off,' he mumbled, taking it out. But instead of 'Blocked Number', the screen said 'Jade'.

'Where are you?' she said, when Daniel answered.

'And hello to you too,' he replied.

'You're not home.'

'No. I'm not home, Jade. Why?'

'We're here, waiting for you.'

Daniel turned into Powis Gardens and looked ahead. Two-thirds of the way up two figures, one tall, one short, were standing outside the steps that led to his front door. He stopped on the corner and watched them. 'I'm not forgetting something, am I?' he said. 'You didn't arrange to come over?'

'Your son doesn't have to make an appointment to see you, Daniel.'

'I know he doesn't.' Daniel started walking again. 'But if I'd known you were coming …'

'You'd have baked a cake? Daniel. Where *are* you?'

'I'm walking towards you,' said Daniel. 'I can see you.'

'Good,' said Jade, and hung up.

'Hey, Noah,' Daniel said to his boy, when he reached the pair. 'How you doing?'

Noah dipped his head. He was wearing a DayGlo pink and blue baseball cap, its oversized peak sticking up, perpendicular to a long, pointed fringe of bleached hair that came to a sharp point over his left eye. His right eye was ringed with black makeup and his mouth was so glossy that Daniel wondered if he was wearing lipstick.

'Where *were* you?' Jade said, and looked at her watch as if Daniel had deliberately not turned up in time for a scheduled meeting.

'I had a session in Whitechapel,' he said, locking his bike to the railing.

'A session?' Jade said, perking up. 'Who with?'

Daniel smiled to himself. Jade never changed. She looked exactly the same as she had on the night he'd met her on the front step of that little bar in Santorini, except for maybe a hint of crow's feet around her brown eyes. The same soot-black Louise Brooks bob and fringe, the same smattering of freckles across her rounded nose. And the same thing she'd always had for celebrities. Wasn't that why she'd homed in on him in the first place?

'Maya,' he said. 'She's recording a new album.'

Jade rolled her eyes. 'Like *that's* going to go anywhere. You should do something of your own again, you know. That *Glee* song's never off the radio.'

'Leave it out, Jade.' Daniel put his key into the lock.

Jade checked her watch again. 'I can't stay long,' she said.

Something about the way she said 'I' sounded emphatic. She hadn't said 'we'.

Daniel turned to Noah, who was staring back towards Westbourne Park Road, his pimpled chin bunched up as if he was about to burst into tears.

At his feet, Daniel noticed for the first time, was a large gold-lamé carry-all.

7. A Sitting Duck

'Will you have a cup of coffee?' Maggie asked, turning on the tap to fill the kettle. She was trying to gather herself.

'Oh, no,' Rita replied, as if she'd been offered crack cocaine. 'Do you have any herbal or fruit tea? Chamomile would be lovely, or peppermint, if you have it.' She had taken off her purple poncho in a waft of a perfume that smelt faintly of basil and was leaning back on a kitchen chair, her yellow-stockinged legs stretched out in front of her. The voluminous mauve dress she wore was embroidered on the shoulders, with little bits of mirror glinting amid the rainbow-coloured threads.

Maggie couldn't help meeting her eye as she crossed the kitchen to look in the cupboard. She was smiling in the way Maggie imagined psychotherapists smiled at their patients – thoughtfully.

'I'm not sure what herbal teas I have, if any,' said Maggie, digging through boxes that had sat in the larder cupboard since Jesus was a boy. She put her hands on a faded pack of blackcurrant and ginseng. 'Will this do?' she asked, pulling it out.

Rita nodded, and gave another of her smiles.

Maggie could have kicked herself for smiling back. In the still of the night she'd twisted and turned with stomach-wrenching hatred for this woman. She'd sat up and shook her fists at the heavens, swearing vengeance on Rita Wilde through bitter tears. Yet here she was, grinning like some sort of village idiot.

She was seized with an urge to blurt, 'What are you doing here?' But instead she put a teabag into a cup and said, 'The rain was terrible on Monday, wasn't it? The reports said over a week's worth fell in twenty-four hours.'

Rita gave her a slightly confused look, which morphed into her default smile as Benny hopped up on to her lap.

'Awful,' she said, with the briefest hint of a wince, which meant Benny had his claws out.

The cat gave Maggie a fleeting glance as she put Rita's tea in front of her. Usually a comment about the weather was an opening gambit: the person returned an observation that you could improve on, and so on and so forth. It was an easy route into conversation, which Rita was clearly not interested in taking.

Maggie still couldn't figure out what William saw in her. Although there were few wrinkles around her saucer eyes, and none to be glimpsed under her low-hung fringe, her age showed on her chin, or lack thereof. Her face became her neck without interruption, except for the beginnings of two jowls that hung below the deep grooves of her cheeks. Fans of crimped black-and-silver hair were draped across her shoulders, in an attempt, Maggie decided, to deflect attention from the lack of lower facial definition, but nobody would be fooled. For all her herbal tea and reiki, gravity was having its way with Lovely Rita, Compost Maid.

'I wanted to talk to you,' Rita began, after a sip of her tea. Her voice sounded like a meditation CD.

Maggie opened her mouth to reply, but Rita's hand went up. 'I know how you must feel about me, and I don't blame you. Although you understand that we all make our own choices in life. We are all responsible for ourselves.'

There was a gap for Maggie to say 'yes', although she really hadn't a clue what she was agreeing to and her instinct was to give an emphatic 'no'. Still, she nodded.

'I'm worried,' said Rita, and reached across the table, her bangle-draped wrists landing dangerously close to Maggie's. 'I'm very worried.'

Maggie cleared her throat and pulled her hands into her lap. 'What about?'

'About William, of course,' said Rita, her voice suddenly not so meditative. 'He's behaving very strangely.'

'Is he?' said Maggie, attempting to sound innocent of the fact.

Rita picked up her tea and blew on it before taking another sip. 'I know he stayed here last night,' she said, her voice smooth again. 'He told me everything.'

Maggie's nails dug into her palms and she said nothing. There was an air of accusation about Rita, but it was hardly Maggie's fault that William had come running home, was it?

'Did he say anything?' Rita asked. 'About me?'

Benny, now firmly ensconced on Rita's lap, gave a wide yawn.

'He thinks you're having an affair,' Maggie said. 'With Roger Collins.'

Rita gave the lightest snort. 'Unbelievable,' she said, both hands stretching across the table now. 'He's been going on like this for the last fortnight, accusing me of all sorts of infidelities.'

There was another gap, a space for Maggie to give Rita some direction. But what could she say? *It's just a phase – he'll get over it?*

'Was he ever like that with you?' Rita asked. 'He never struck me as the jealous type.'

Benny fixed Maggie with his one eye, staring at her intently, as if he was trying to impart something.

Throughout their years together, William had never been possessive, had never questioned whether other men were looking at Maggie or vice versa. Now she thought about it, she had no idea whether that was a good or bad thing. Jealousy suggested passion, and Maggie would never have said that William was a passionate man. His lack of possessiveness suggested that he had felt secure with her, but on the other hand, if he was possessive of Rita, perhaps he was passionate about her in a way he had never been during their marriage.

Which was better? Security or passion? Which was love?

'I don't know what to do,' Rita said, and as Benny gave Maggie another lingering look it became clear what *she* must do to get William back once and for all.

But no. She couldn't do that, could she? It would be wrong. It would be lying.

Yet if Rita believed her she'd dump William so fast he wouldn't know what had happened. He'd be home within the week.

Dragging her eyes away from the cat, Maggie put her hands back on the table. She touched Rita's wrist, which felt skeletal for all her facial droopiness. 'I know what you're going through,' she said. She cleared her throat. 'He was always like that with me. If I so much as glanced at another man, he'd lose his marbles altogether.'

'Really?' Rita frowned.

'Oh, yes.' Maggie nodded. 'It was a constant problem.' She took a sip of her tea. 'Don't worry, though,' she added. 'He may have had his jealous rages, but he never got violent with me. I have that to be thankful for.'

Rita's eyebrows shot up under her silvery fringe. Her therapist's smile had properly vanished. 'You make him sound deranged,' she said.

Maggie smiled in a way she hoped looked jaded. 'Don't be silly,' she said, letting Rita's wrist go. 'He just has a few more insecurities than most men. You'll learn to manage him like I did.'

'But how?'

'Well, one strategy I always had was to get out of the house if

I saw that glint in his eye. You know – that look he gets when he's about to lose it.'

Rita stood up. Her hand went to the poncho on the back of the chair. 'I think I have to go now,' she said.

'Are you sure?' Maggie said, with a soothing smile. 'Stay and finish your tea.'

Rita was already pulling on her poncho. 'No.' Her discombobulated voice came from its environs.

At the front door, she stopped. Her eyes were large in her fleshy face. 'Thank you for being so honest,' she said.

Maggie suppressed a pang of guilt. 'Are you sure you're all right?' she asked.

Rita nodded and bit her lip. 'I've always thought we could be friends,' she said. 'We're very alike, you know.'

Alike? Maggie couldn't see how. As far as she could remember, she had never worn a poncho in her life. She was strictly a blue jeans and white T-shirt woman. At a push she wore a simple black dress with matching pumps for a night out. Rita, with her haphazard, clashing style, the waft of essential oils she left in her wake, was everything Maggie was not, and Maggie was glad of it. Except that her husband had chosen haphazard, clashing, essential-oily Rita above his blue jeans and white T-shirt wife.

'Maybe we could go for a coffee sometime, or for something to eat,' Rita wondered, her voice a needy question mark.

'Maybe,' said Maggie.

As Rita's purple camper van pulled away from the kerb, she added, 'In your dreams,' under her breath.

Benny was sitting on the doorstep beside her, calmly watching Rita drive away.

'Your daddy will be home before you know it,' Maggie told him, and closed the front door.

8. Put Me to the Test

'No,' said Daniel, shaking his head slowly. 'No way.'

Jade sat quietly, staring at the table, then looked up at him, her expression a cross between steely and pleading. 'I wouldn't be doing this if I didn't think you were ready for it,' she said.

Beyond the butcher-block counter that separated the kitchen from the living room, Noah was sprawled across an armchair, watching television while listening to his iPod through an oversized pair of lime green earphones. It was as if he was doing everything in his power to block out their conversation.

'You've got a proper set-up now,' Jade went on, taking in the kitchen and living room with a sweep of her hand. 'He's got his own room.'

'It's full of boxes and shit. I haven't had time to—'

'Daniel,' Jade cut him off. 'I want you to know that I trust you now. With Noah.'

Daniel let out a short, low laugh. 'I see what you're trying to do,' he said, shaking his head again. 'Pretending this is some sort of vote of confidence. You're his mother, for fuck's sake. You can't just dump him on me.'

'You're his father,' Jade snapped back. 'And I'm not *dumping* him.'

'But—'

'But what, Daniel?'

Daniel took a deep breath. It had always been a royal pain in the arse arguing with Jade. She was invariably right. Back in the worst days of their time together, he had devised a strategy to stop her winning every argument by simply refusing to answer any of her accusations. He'd learned to say nothing.

But saying nothing wasn't going to work now. She wanted to leave Noah with him. Indefinitely. Which was impossible. 'It's not suitable for him here,' he said. 'It's miles away from his school to start with …'

Jade opened her sack-like leather handbag and rummaged inside. 'It's only a bus ride,' she said, pulling out a little blue tin of Vaseline. 'Look, Daniel. This is the best thing for Noah right now.'

'How can it be the best thing for him?' Daniel said. 'His own mother throwing him out.'

'Because I can't cope with him,' said Jade. She rubbed the Vaseline on her lips, refusing to meet Daniel's eye.

Daniel glanced at Noah. The music was so loud in the boy's earphones that he could hear its insistent beat from across the room. 'What do you mean, you can't cope? He's fourteen, for Christ's sake. All teenagers are a handful.'

'They're not quite as much of a handful as Noah,' said Jade. She clicked the lid of the tin closed and sighed. 'Him and Rob are at loggerheads all the time. I'm worried about what's going to happen if it goes on much longer.'

'At loggerheads? Why?'

Jade's shoulders slumped a little. 'Rob can't deal with the gay thing and Noah insists on shoving it in his face.'

'Right,' said Daniel, nodding slowly. 'Noah's gay?' He glanced at his son. He hadn't been imagining it. The boy was definitely wearing lipstick. And the scant floral shirt hanging off his narrow shoulders looked like it had come from Miss Selfridge. He'd always been camp, ever since he was a four-year-old, pretending he was Christina

Aguilera, singing 'You Are Beautiful' with a tea towel on his head to replicate her hair.

'I don't know.' Jade sighed. 'He hasn't said anything.'

'Haven't you asked him?'

Jade's lips disappeared into a line. 'That's the one thing we can't do. We have to wait until he tells us himself.'

Daniel took this in. Then his mind alighted on Jade's Neanderthal boyfriend. 'So, let me get this straight. Loverboy is giving your son a hard time about being gay, even though you don't know if he is or not, and you're throwing him out.'

'I'm not throwing him out,' Jade replied, putting her Vaseline and her phone back in her bag, as if she was getting ready to leave. 'Noah just needs a break. Rob's on his back all the time.'

'Why can't you throw Rob out?' Daniel said. 'He's the one causing the problem.'

Jade zipped up her handbag. 'It's just for a while,' she said, 'to let things cool off between them.'

'A while? How long is a while?'

'I don't know.'

Daniel stuck out his chin. 'Typical,' he said. 'The first sign of trouble and you bail out.'

'I resent that,' Jade replied, sitting up. 'In all these years I've never asked you for anything. Most of the time you were so stoned out of your mind, you hardly knew he existed, and now you're telling me I'm a bad mother.'

'I didn't say that.'

'Well, that's what it sounds like.'

'I'm just saying you could have warned me.'

'If I'd warned you, you would have found a way to back out. I know what you're like.'

Daniel was doing his level best to stay grounded. Having a child with someone meant they were forever a part of your life. You were never free of them saying, 'I know what you're like,' when the truth was that Jade knew fuck-all about him, really.

She'd been a summer fling in Greece, at the beginning of the year-long 'trip around the world to sort his head out', after he'd split from his record label. A fling that had turned into her spending the rest of the year with him, in Cambodia and Vietnam, New Zealand, China and South America. The trip had had no itinerary, just a random selection of places to fly to. Likewise, the relationship was anchorless. Once they'd got back to England, it had had nowhere to go. It would have just fizzled out and eventually Jade would have become a distant memory, like the world trip itself, if she hadn't turned up at his door two years later with a toddler she said was his.

'If you know what I'm like, then you know you shouldn't be leaving him with me,' Daniel said. 'I'm no good for him.'

Jade got to her feet. 'Daniel,' she said. 'Your son needs you.'

Daniel stood up too. 'No, Jade,' he countered. 'He needs *you*.'

Both of them turned to Noah, whose eyes were fixed on the television. When Jade turned back to Daniel, she was biting her bottom lip and her eyes were damp. 'Please,' she said. 'Don't make this any harder than it already is.'

She went over to Noah, knelt down beside him and lifted one of his earphones to say something into his ear. Daniel watched as she kissed his cheek and he shrugged her off. 'I'll call you later on, okay?' she said, but Noah ignored her. He folded his arms and stared hard at the television.

'He hasn't had his tea,' she said at the front door. 'Get him something nice, yeah?'

Daniel still thought she wasn't going to leave without Noah. But then she had closed the door behind her and was gone, and the son he barely knew was still in the living room, the tinny sound from his earphones leaking out into the hallway. Daniel stood there for a minute, trying to make sense of it and work out what to do next.

'Get something nice for tea,' Jade had said. That was a start. He'd figure out the next step after he'd done that.

When he went back into the living room, Noah had turned off the television. 'What do you want for your tea?' Daniel asked, but Noah didn't even look at him, the noise from beneath his earphones drumming out an insistent beat.

'WHAT DO YOU WANT FOR YOUR TEA?' Daniel shouted.

Noah lifted one earphone. 'What?' The plucked brow over his one visible eye was raised and his head cocked, in a kind of challenge.

'I was going to order in pizza,' said Daniel. 'You want some?'

'What-ev-ah,' Noah said, sounding like a girl on an American teen sitcom. He popped his earphone back on and stared into mid-space, arms folded.

This wasn't going to work out. No fucking way.

Daniel took a breath and counted to ten.

The kid didn't want to be here. He could sleep on the couch for tonight and then …

Then what?

He rummaged through the catch-all kitchen drawer for a pizza menu. He'd take Noah back to Jade's tomorrow. Maybe he'd arrange to have the boy for a weekend every month to take the pressure off. He could manage that, couldn't he?

He found a menu and pulled out his phone. 'Pepperoni okay for you?' he called to Noah, knowing his son couldn't hear a word he was saying.

9. A New Day Dawning

Sunday dawned dull and chilly. Maggie pulled her dressing-gown around her waist and shivered as she opened the curtains to see a flock of crows flying against a slate-grey sky. Her head hurt from the bottle of wine she'd consumed the night before and her mouth tasted sour.

She didn't know what she'd been expecting. Well, she did. She'd thought Rita would break up with William and that he'd arrive on her doorstep again last night, surrounded by his bags, in tears, and begging to be taken back.

But there had been no sign of him, and as the empty night wore on, out of habit, she'd taken to the bottle of wine and her laptop rather than waiting in vain.

Maggie always thought she'd stay on Facebook for just a short while when she logged on to the Abbaholics Anonymous group, but it had sucked her in. She'd glance at the computer's clock and suddenly it would be three or four hours later. It was the perfect distraction.

She wondered if Facebook was an addiction. Of the 507 current members of Abbaholics, she was friends with more than half of them, in regular contact with at least fifty, and sporadically connected with the rest. They were people she had never met in real life, but when she was with them on Facebook in the evenings, chatting or cross-posting and commenting, she felt a kind of camaraderie that became more and more real as she got through her wine.

Over the years with William and the children she had sort of separated off, made herself an island with her family. Since William had left, she'd felt even more stranded. Facebook was like the mainland. She could dock there for a few hours and be one of the gang. And, generally, no one wanted anything from her, except her opinion on Abba, which she gave freely, being their number-one fan.

Most of the Abbaholics members valued what she said, and gave good comments back, but some were just plain crazy. Like Manuel DeSantos, a surprisingly good-looking middle-aged Spanish guy, who saw the most perverse sexual innuendo in Abba's songs and was forever going on about Agnetha's 'bum'. Or Agnetha Fältsgok, from Sweden who, although she spelled the surname incorrectly, seemed to think she actually was Agnetha. Her profile photograph, blonde with her face in shadow, could have been of anyone.

Last night the main topic of conversation was *Mamma Mia!*, the movie, and as she got through her bottle of wine, Maggie had half forgotten her desolation and contributed with increasing gusto. She'd liked the film when she'd seen it in the cinema, but now couldn't bear to watch the DVD version she owned because she felt it made a mockery of Abba's music. She couldn't understand how Benny and Björn could allow a beautiful, heartfelt song like 'Chiquitita' be turned into a comedy routine, or how they could have possibly okayed Pierce Brosnan's cringe-inducing version of 'When All Is Said And Done'. They'd really let themselves down with that one.

At least Meryl Streep hadn't made a dog's dinner out of 'Slipping Through My Fingers', although, to Maggie's mind, she'd chewed the scenery with 'The Winner Takes It All'.

Agnetha Fältsgok, who had been one of the members on-line and chatting in real time, claimed to have instructed Meryl about the finer points of singing 'The Winner Takes It All', while another member, Graham March, went on and on about the anomalies between the film's backing tracks and the original recordings. He was a bit of an Abba anorak, Graham. Lately he'd been on every night, talking about the differences between the vinyl recordings and the CD issues, particularly *Abba Gold*. He was always going on about *Abba Gold*, dissecting it song by song.

That was the trouble with Abba fans. Sometimes they took it all so bloody seriously.

In the shower Maggie lifted her face into the stream of hot water, in the hope of washing away her hangover. She squeezed some shower gel into her palm and began to soap herself, thinking of the day stretching out before her with nothing to do. There had been a time when a Sunday like this would have seemed an unattainable luxury. Now it filled her with fear.

There was always the option of taking the tube into the West End and having a wander. She hadn't done that in an age. Or she could stroll down to Portobello Road and browse the antiques market. Maybe have coffee with the Sunday newspapers in that organic café on Westbourne Grove …

She felt on the underside of her breast for the lump, remembering the morning she'd discovered it just ten days ago, having a Sunday-morning shower just like this one. It hadn't been sore and didn't react when she'd pushed it with the flat of her finger. She'd thought she'd maybe been imagining it, but had still made an appointment to see the family GP the next morning. And then things had accelerated so fast that she still couldn't quite believe it was all happening.

Dr Gilmore, instead of telling her she was jumping to conclusions in his time-honoured way, had referred her for a mammogram that afternoon.

The radiologist, circling his pen over a little constellation of specks in the lower part of the swirly white cloud that was the mammogram of her left breast, told her it was best to be safe than sorry and referred her for a biopsy the following Friday.

The nurse, who typed in her appointment for the biopsy, had advised bringing a family member or friend, but Maggie had given her a glassy smile. She refused to go there. She wouldn't tell anyone about it until it was real.

She'd felt guilty being pushed in a wheelchair into Radiology for her biopsy, as if she was fooling the crowd. There was nothing wrong with her; she felt absolutely fine. But then, in the middle of it all, when the monosyllabic doctor who was working on her flesh had put a blood-soaked piece of cotton wool into a silver tray on a stand beside the raised bed, Maggie knew why the wheelchair had been used. She wouldn't be able to walk back out when the biopsy was finished.

As the needles penetrated the centre of her breast, and then the space under her arms where her lymph nodes were, tears had rolled down the sides of Maggie's face. Up until that moment she hadn't allowed herself to connect with the journey she'd been placed on without warning. But, with a wave of dizziness, she realised she actually was on the cancer train, hurtling down the line. She was not just imagining it. The lump had been station number one, then the mammogram. This was station three, and the next would be her diagnosis, which the taciturn doctor had told her she'd have to wait for.

It had taken a week, during which she obsessively Googled nightmarish images of women with mastectomies, livid scars snaking across their flattened chests, and pictures of rows of prosthetic breasts lined up, all the while imagining that, with every second of every day, the disease might be spreading, cell by cell, invading the rest of her body.

And then the diagnosis had come: Stage Three A invasive ductal carcinoma. 'This means the cancer has spread to other tissue in the breast and to the lymph nodes under your arm,' the oncologist, *her* oncologist, Dr Snow, had explained.

Rubbing his white-bearded chin, he'd told her it was important to begin treatment as soon as possible. 'The cancer you have is aggressive so we're going to have to treat it aggressively,' he'd said. 'We'll use a course of chemotherapy to bring it under control over the next three months, before surgery. Then there'll be radiotherapy to eradicate any remaining cancer cells, if there are any.'

'Surgery?' Maggie had blurted. 'Are you saying I'm going to lose my breast?'

Dr Snow took off his glasses and squeezed the bridge of his nose with a finger and thumb. 'You should know that there have been enormous advances in the treatment of breast cancer over the past few years,' he said. 'Most women who catch it early enough go into full remission. You came in early, but I'm afraid your recovery absolutely depends on a mastectomy. There are excellent advances too in reconstructive surgery, and we can talk about that at a later date. But first things first. Now we must focus on your chemotherapy.'

Maggie turned off the shower. In the steamed-up mirror she could just about see the outline of her breasts. She tried to picture one of them gone, but it was beyond the realms of her imagination. Her breasts had always been the part of her body she liked. Although she was going on forty-five, they were still firm, still perfectly round in a 36DD bra. Men still checked them out. She remembered calling them 'tits' once, at the beginning with William, when they were having sex. 'They're not tits,' he'd told her reverentially. 'They're breasts.' The way he'd said the word, fulsome with the r almost rolling, had made her swell with pride.

William. She had to tell him. It couldn't be put off any longer.

Outside the bathroom door, Benny started up a plaintive, starved miaow, urgently nudging her left calf with his head.

'Give me a minute,' Maggie said, wrapping a towel around herself.

She'd call William now, she decided, and arrange to meet him tomorrow. It would be better to impart the news face-to-face. And maybe she could ask him to come to the first chemo appointment. He owed her that much, didn't he?

10. Leave 'Em Burning

Daniel figured that taking the boy back to his mother immediately might send Noah the wrong message, so he decided he'd do it first thing on Monday. Sunday they would spend together, doing father-and-son things.

The problem was, he didn't know exactly what things fathers did with sons. His own dad had hardly been a role model in that regard, preferring to shut himself up in his study for hour upon hour, leaving Daniel to wander around their empty house, or to sit alone with his guitar in his bedroom.

This morning Noah had appeared in the kitchen, his face pale and makeup-free, his fringe dry as bleached tumbleweed, poking out from beneath a purple hoodie emblazoned with the glittering slogan 'Born This Way'.

'Hey there,' Daniel said, as the boy took a high stool at the butcher's-block island. Instead of replying, Noah inspected the chipped black polish on his nails.

'You want some coffee?' Daniel asked, holding up a half-full cafetière.

Noah looked at it, raised his eyes to Daniel's and gave him a look of incredulity, with an almost imperceptible shake of his head.

'Tea?'

Noah shook his head again.

Daniel poured himself a coffee and took a seat at the island. 'I thought we could hang out together,' he said. 'Do something.'

Noah shrugged.

Daniel held off for a few seconds, then tried again. 'What kind of things do you like doing?'

Noah looked at him blankly and shrugged again.

'Jesus, man, give me a break, will you?' Daniel said. 'I'm really trying here.'

'You're a proper hero, ain't ya?' Noah said, from beneath his hoodie. He got to his feet and stalked back up the stairs.

Daniel supposed he'd deserved that. He'd spent little time with the kid over the years, only ever calling at Jade's now and then to see how he was getting on and giving her money by standing order every month for maintenance. The thing was, although Noah was his son, Daniel had never felt like the boy's father. He hadn't wanted to be a dad, and hadn't believed Jade when she'd told him the kid was his. But there had been no denying the child's genes. He was the spitting image of Daniel. The same almond-shaped eyes, the same dent in the middle of his little chin, the widow's peak in his already thick black hair. It was like looking at a miniature version of himself.

Jade hadn't made any demands when she'd turned up. It was only right that Daniel knew about his son. At the time Daniel had thought otherwise. What you didn't know couldn't mess with your head, and the last thing he needed back then was anyone messing with his head.

He didn't feel guilty about doing the bare minimum. God knows he was the last thing any child needed in its life. He'd spent most of the previous decade in a haze of weed, chain-smoking joints the way other people smoked cigarettes. Every time a chink of reality let itself in, he'd spark up another. It was the only way he could survive from day to day without tipping over into panic attacks that left him feeling as if the whole world was spinning out of control, even though he rarely left the dim rooms of his flat to see any of it.

He couldn't have looked after someone else then, and he understood why, from Noah's point of view, he didn't exactly come off with flying colours, even if he'd been clean for nearly two years now, and had got out of that murky, ganga-stinking basement to start again.

Emptying the rest of the coffee down the sink and rinsing the cafetière, Daniel decided to let the boy stay in his room for a while, rather than bother him. He sat on the couch and opened the Sunday paper to check what movies were on in the cinemas. He was separating the Review section from the thick bundle when a clear plastic bag containing the *Sunday Times Magazine* fell to the floor. Emblazoned on the front was a studio shot of himself when he was about twenty, at the height of his fame, his eyes staring intensely into the camera. He looked like a startled fawn.

'Where Are They Now?' the headline read and Daniel's heart plummeted.

He pulled open the plastic wrapping and rapidly paged through the magazine until he came to another picture of himself – this time more recent, a paparazzi shot of him unlocking his bicycle on some unidentifiable street, wearing the purple bicycle helmet he'd bought only a couple of weeks ago.

His heart began to race.

The article, again taking its lead from the resurgence of the *Glee* version of 'Night Star', was about pop acts of the eighties and nineties whose stars had waned and all but disappeared from public life. Unlike those who turned up on reality TV shows or were touring the nostalgia circuit, these pop stars continued to shun the limelight for whatever reasons of their own.

Danny Lane, otherwise known as Daniel Smith, is the ultimate pop recluse. Having had two major hit singles and broken

America by the time he was twenty, this reluctant celebrity did the unthinkable and turned his back on the music industry in 1988.

Lane was discovered by fledgling producer Vince David, and his song 'Night Star' defined what came to be known as the Vince David sound in the mid-eighties, with a string of acts such as Girls On Top, Nikita, Dean Anthony and Flare.

Lane was the only one of the stable to go transatlantic, and his departure signalled a downturn in David's fortunes for much of the nineties, before he became a television producer, and judge on ITV's *Fame Game*. The show, now in its eighth year, has provided David with global pop brands Carrie Chaplin and boy band Made Up, both of whom have scored number-one albums on four continents over the past twelve months.

The journalist had done her research. She confirmed that Daniel now earned his living providing backing vocals to various acts and could be heard on the current breakout hit from the West End musical version of *Rain Man*. She'd traced him to the flat in Hampstead through the voting register. She might as well have given out his old address.

Daniel looked at the photograph of him unlocking his bike again. Now he saw that it had been taken around the corner from the flat, on Pond Street, probably when he was last over there to collect his post.

Daniel read on and found that *Heat* magazine was mounting a 'Bring Back Danny' campaign. According to the article, his music had achieved a new status, with several current acts citing the one and only album he had released as an influence.

Anyone else might have been flattered, but Daniel hated that album and everything to do with it. To him, being famous was like having no skin, with all the nerve endings in his body exposed. It had been a constant irritant with nowhere to hide and everybody wanting something of him that he knew he couldn't give.

It had almost destroyed his life.

Daniel looked up to see Noah standing at the living-room door. His freshly applied eye makeup was heavy, black with a touch of yellow above the lids, and he was chewing gum.

'All right?' said Daniel, trying to keep the shake from his voice.

Noah blew a big pink bubble until it popped. The noise was like an explosion in Daniel's head.

'Jesus! Fuck!' Daniel shouted. 'Don't do that!'

Noah stood for a moment, his chewing halted, his face expressionless. Then he hoisted his still-packed gold carry-all, which Daniel hadn't noticed at his side, onto his shoulder and turned away.

'Where do you think you're going?' Daniel asked.

Noah replied by stretching out his free arm and raising one freshly painted fingernail.

'Don't show me the finger,' Daniel said. 'That's not cool.'

But already Noah had left the building, having slammed the front door behind him.

11. Only Emptiness

William was late, which wasn't like him. Usually he was neurotic about punctuality, aiming to be a good fifteen minutes early to incorporate any unexpected delays along the way. This had driven Maggie nuts when they were together. He was always rushing her out of the door when she wasn't half ready.

She sat and nursed a skinny latte, which she'd originally sent back to have transferred into a mug rather than drink it out of the polka-dotted cup it had come in, which had been as big as a soup-bowl and just as awkward.

The café had sanded floors and exposed-brick walls dotted with gilt-framed pictures of urban landscapes. Its waiting staff had been chosen from a conveyor belt of Brick Lane types, who studiously dressed as if they couldn't care less what they looked like – a gangly boy with *faux*-greasy hair and a ratty grey T-shirt featuring a faded picture of ZZ Top; a diminutive girl with oversized square-framed glasses, a perfectly symmetrical jet-black fringe, and a floral wrap-around apron that *Coronation Street*'s Hilda Ogden wouldn't have been caught dead in.

For a split second something about her reminded Maggie of Dee. Maybe it was her tiny figure, or the way she was so businesslike, licking her finger as she turned the page of the little notebook she carried to write down people's orders. She hadn't seen or even called Dee since her wedding last year, and as she watched the girl take another customer's order, Maggie felt a pang of regret for their dwindled friendship.

The girl put her notebook into her apron pocket and began to clear empty cups and used plates off the next table. Maggie wondered how old she was – maybe late twenties, early thirties – then stopped herself. Since the day she'd turned forty, this was a habit she'd got into, comparing herself against other women by years. She didn't remember doing it before and, anyway, she knew she looked good for her age. Her body was more or less the same shape as it had been when she was twenty-five, she had no cellulite, and her boobs …

Hot flames of fear fanned her ribcage. Who would she be without one of her breasts? She'd complained about men who eyed them, but secretly she was proud of it. Their glances made her feel secure in herself in some way, as if the appreciation validated her.

And what if, after all the side effects of chemo, getting rid of the sickened flesh didn't work? What then?

'Here you go,' the ZZ Top boy said, putting her coffee, transferred into a mug, in front of her.

'Thanks,' Maggie said. As she sipped it, she tried to force her mind down a neutral path.

She had picked this place because it had been one of her and William's haunts when they'd first moved to London and William had started work at the bank around the corner. She used to meet him here during his lunch hour.

Of course there had been no bespectacled girls and ZZ Top boys back then. The only thing the place retained was its name, Frankie's, that of the man who had owned it when it was a greasy spoon.

To further distract herself, Maggie took out her phone and logged into Facebook to check the Abbaholics group for updates.

The most recent post was from Agnetha F: 'It is true! Abba are coming together again! We will play for one concert only, maybe in Stockholm. I am very exciting!'

Nobody had replied to the post – none of the group members ever did, recognising Agnetha for the nut-job she was.

Underneath that, a new member from Canada called Joel Singleton had written a wall post: 'Excited to have found this fan page. My favourite Abba song is "Slipping Through My Fingers". It reminds me of my daughter, Carly, who is eighteen now and has fled the nest. It's a very sad song, but so true.'

Maggie clicked on his profile. His daughter was the same age as Poppy, and he was right. Looking back on it, her own children's childhoods had slipped through her fingers like sand. Harry had been such a happy-go-lucky little boy, always laughing and running around. Poppy had been serious and wide-eyed when she was little, which she'd got from William. She'd looked up to Maggie as if she was a goddess among mothers, regularly saying, 'When I grow up I'm going to be just like you.'

How she had changed.

Maggie did a quick search for Harry on Facebook now and opened his profile. It hadn't been updated since 4 January, although he'd been tagged in a few pictures that showed him partying with other twenty-year-olds in hardly any clothes, all sporting tans that suggested the thought using sunblock never crossed their minds. Poppy had deleted her Facebook profile altogether. Since she'd moved into the squat with Orlando, all Facebook activity had been relegated.

'It's so last-century, Mum,' she'd told Maggie, rolling her eyes. 'Everyone just tweets now.' As far as Maggie could remember, Facebook hadn't even existed in the previous century.

The time was coming closer and closer when she'd have to tell both of them about the diagnosis. She couldn't put it off much longer. In a way it was the thing she dreaded most, even more than telling William, or the chemo and the mastectomy. When they were little, she thought, she would have thrown herself under a bus to save them from any pain. She still would. They'd always be her babies, in a way. She couldn't bear to think of them frightened and upset.

The door to the café opened and Maggie looked up. Two young guys with Elvis quiffs and ripped jeans walked in, giggling. Maggie guessed they were gay.

Where was William? She was sure she'd said two o'clock. It was twenty past now.

She clicked back into the Abbaholics Facebook group and replied to Joel Singleton's post.

'"Slipping Through My Fingers" is about Björn and Agnetha's eldest daughter, Linda, who was seven at the time it was written. I often feel the same about my own daughter, Poppy, who is also eighteen. Where did the time go?'

The café doorbell rang again and William walked in. Even from this distance she could see that he looked as he did when he was going through one of his insomnia phases: his skin had the gaunt pallor it took on when he wasn't getting any sleep; the colour had even drained from his eyes.

'You look exhausted,' she said, as he sat down, unable to hold herself back. 'Have you been sleeping?'

William gave her an irritated glance and said, 'Hello to you too.' He turned to get the attention of the ZZ Top boy and, when he came over, ordered himself a large Americano. 'You want another coffee?' he asked Maggie.

'I shouldn't, but what the Hell?' Maggie replied, with a small smile. 'A skinny latte, but not in one of those huge cups.'

William shot her that look again. 'Same old Maggie,' he said.

When the boy had gone off to get the coffees, William took off his suit jacket and hung it on the back of his chair. He had always been thin and awkwardly angular, as if his joints were hinged differently from other people's, but Maggie was struck by a new narrowness to his shoulders and the knobbles of bone protruding on the wrists that stuck out from his too-short shirt sleeves. She wondered if Rita had noticed it too. Was she taking care of him?

'So, what do you want to talk to me about?' William asked, scratching the top of his head. He was lucky enough to have kept a full head of thick brown hair without a hint of grey, but it was uncharacteristically unkempt, as if he hadn't bothered to brush it after getting out of bed, and it had a greasy sheen.

'Well … a couple of things,' Maggie replied. She didn't know how to begin.

'Okay,' said William. 'I have to be back at the office at three, though.'

'That gives us barely half an hour, William.'

His eyes went hard. There was definitely something up with him, a kind of edgy energy.

'Have you heard from Harry this week?' Maggie asked. The children were a safe way to begin.

'No,' said William. 'Have you?'

'It's been almost a month since he Skyped. Maybe we should be getting worried.'

'Not about Harry. I'm sure we're the last thing on his mind.'

Maggie decided to change tack. 'Poppy and her friends are redecorating their squat, which is a good thing, I suppose. I wish she'd get a proper flat, though. I've emailed her links to a few nice places to rent, but I don't think she even looks at them. And she won't consider college.'

The ZZ Top boy put their coffees in front of them and William gave a tired little thank-you smile. 'The kids are all right, Maggie,' he said, turning back to her, but he didn't sound reassuring. Instead it was a barbed comment.

'What's wrong with you?' Maggie asked, a bubble of annoyance rising in her throat.

William snorted. 'What do you think's wrong with me?'

'I'm sure I don't know.'

William put his cup down on its oversized saucer. 'What did you say to Rita?' he asked, almost under his breath.

'Nothing,' Maggie replied, clamping her mouth shut the second the word was out. A hot flush rose from her neck towards her cheeks.

'Bullshit,' William spat. 'You fed her a cock-and-bull story about me being some kind of jealous psychopath.'

'I never said those words,' Maggie said. 'She came to me for advice, that's all. I tried to help her.'

William put both hands on the table. 'Seriously?' he said. 'You expect me to believe that?'

Maggie felt another stab of irritation, followed by one of panic. This wasn't going the way she'd expected.

'Well, you were certainly very upset over her affair with Roger Collins,' she said, trying to salvage something.

William leaned over the table, his face weary and exasperated. 'There *was* no affair. Rita and I are fine, Maggie.'

'But you still came running to me the other night.'

William went quiet. 'I'm sorry about that,' he said, after a moment. 'I shouldn't have done it.'

'That's not what you said when we were in bed together. You said I was the only one who understood you.'

'I was upset. I didn't know what I was saying.'

'So, it wasn't true, then?'

William's expression changed, as if something was dawning on him. 'Maggie, you and I ... We're not going to get back together. I'm with Rita now. We're happy.'

'So why is Rita coming to me, throwing herself on my kitchen table, telling me you're acting like some sort of maniac?'

'And why are you telling her I *am* some sort of maniac?'

Maggie blanched. Rita was the last thing she'd come here to talk to him about, but she couldn't stop herself ploughing forward. 'I still don't get it,' she said. 'I don't know what you're doing with that – that compost bag.'

William got to his feet and reached into his trouser pocket. 'Her name is Rita,' he said, throwing a fiver on the table. 'And you'd better call her and apologise for what you said about me. You'd better tell her it was a pack of lies.'

Maggie set her mouth in a line and shook her head. 'No,' she said. 'I won't.'

William stood still for a second with his back to her, and then his shoulders slumped. He turned around. 'She still half believes everything you told her,' he said.

Maggie was tempted to reply that she was delighted, but thought better of it and then of why she had arranged this meeting in the first place. 'Don't leave, William. Sit down. Please.'

William sighed. 'No, I have to get back to work.'

Maggie checked her watch. 'You still have twenty minutes. Please, William.'

William didn't sit. Instead his expression changed to one of pity as he looked down on her. 'I know this is hard on you, Maggie,' he said, 'but neither of us was happy, not for a long time. You need to let me go.'

'We really need to talk …' Maggie tried, but William was already walking out of the café. As the door closed behind him, its little bell tinkling, she wondered if what he'd said about neither of them being happy was true. She couldn't remember being *un*happy.

Slumping in her chair, she cursed herself for not bringing up the cancer immediately. If she had, William would still be sitting opposite her – at least, the William she'd known. Not the new, gaunt, angry man, who seemed to think of her as an inconvenience.

She wanted to be angry in return, but she couldn't muster it. All she knew was that she'd missed her chance.

12. Try Once More

'Your eleven o'clock's here,' said Connie, popping her head through the door of Dee's office.

'Tell them I'll be with them in a minute,' Dee replied, without looking up. She hated it when Connie announced appointments by coming into her office rather than dialling from the front desk. 'Make a pot of coffee, will you? And bring it through to the boardroom with some biscuits.'

'No problemo,' said Connie. 'And I've made your hair appointment. They can give you a nine a.m. slot tomorrow morning. With James.'

'Good,' said Dee, glancing at her PA. She thought, not for the first time, that Connie was putting on too much weight. She'd have to say something to the girl soon. In a way, Connie was the front window of Reddy Communications and first impressions counted for everything in this business.

'Oh, and, Connie, before you go today will you pick up something at Fallon and Byrne for me to take home for dinner? Maybe a couple of portions of Thai green curry. And a bottle of wine. Sauvignon Blanc.'

'No problemo,' Connie repeated, and turned to go. It was her current stock phrase and, like the weight, would have to go.

Dee leaned back in her chair and looked at the clock on her computer, which said 11:01. It was always best to leave a client waiting exactly three minutes. It was long enough to give them the sense that you were extremely busy and short enough not to leave them feeling neglected. And she didn't want this particular client to feel in any way neglected.

She stood up and went to the full-length mirror that she'd hung behind the door so that she could always check her appearance before she met a client. Today she'd chosen the vintage cream Dior suit she'd bought at Jenny Vander. Its tailoring suited her figure, accentuating the curves of her hips and chest. She checked closely to see that her makeup was okay, then took her hair out of its bun, shaking it free to let it hang in a wavy auburn line down her back. In her experience, men tended to respond better when her hair was loose.

She went back to her desk, sat down and checked the clock again. One minute to go.

When the recession had first kicked in Dee had thought her business was finished. PR people thrived in the good times, but when finances were tight, companies tended to cut out the middlemen. She had braced herself for decline, deciding that she would hold on to her biggest clients with reduced rates and increased love, while trying to pick up some low-hanging fruit to fill the gap and stave off letting go any of her six staff.

But then the unexpected had happened. A whole new market had opened up and fallen into her lap. With so many companies going into receivership, the banks had found themselves loaded with going concerns that they had to keep operational in the hope of selling them on – businesses they knew nothing about. With a good team managing, the banks could sit back and let the viable businesses keep going, with much-reduced expenditure. Part of the reduction in spending was the pulling of advertising, so those businesses needed a good PR company to keep them marketed.

And that was where Dee and Reddy Communications had come in. Her first contract had been with the Bank of Ireland, which now owned a chain of super-pubs that were hubs in Dublin's social circuit. She'd got it through an acquaintance, who was dating one of the bank's business managers. That contract had gone so well that she had entered a bulk-buy deal with the bank, whereby they gave her a number of businesses to look after at a lowered rate. Discount or not, it had meant Dee could take on two more staff. Her business was expanding while others were falling by the wayside every day.

Today's meeting was with two receivership managers from Allied Irish Banks, who wanted Reddy Communications to take on a portfolio of restaurants in the city. She'd already had several meetings with Don and Niall, determining the terms of the deal, and today's would be the final clincher, in which they would tie down the spend. Dee knew how much they wanted to pay. She was going in with a much higher demand. They'd meet somewhere in the middle, which was exactly where she wanted to be.

She looked at the clock on her computer again. Then her eyes alighted on the photograph of Joe that stood on her desk in a royal blue Georgian-style frame she'd bought at Urban Outfitters. He wore the quizzical half-grin on his chisel-chinned, handsome face that had made her fall for him in the first place. This thought brought on a rush of such hopelessness that her throat caught. She put her palms flat on the desk to get her bearings back. Her three minutes were up and there was business to be done.

She gave herself a moment, then got to her feet, smoothed her skirt, took a deep breath and plastered on a warm grin before opening the door of her office to go and welcome her new clients.

The meeting had gone her way. Don and Niall had played their usual game of good cop, bad cop, but she was well on to them, playing her placating part with smiling ease, and in the end they'd negotiated the terms she'd gone in with a view to getting, and a three-month get-out clause on both sides.

As they were leaving, Don shook her hand with vigorous enthusiasm. The pain that shot up through her arm, into her chest and back was razor sharp. She smiled hard to hide the wince, and instead of shaking Niall's hand, she patted his arm as she led him from the boardroom, telling him an anecdote about a restaurant owner who had stolen all the art that hung on his walls.

'How did it go?' Connie asked, when both men had left.

'All good,' said Dee. 'We got the deal.'

'I knew you'd do it!' said Connie, clapping her hands together. 'I knew it!' Her eyes were shining.

Dee realised Connie was proud of her. It made her want to cry for shame.

'Excuse me,' she said, and headed quickly for her office. Once there she sat and opened the drawer of her desk to take out a pack of Nurofen Plus. As she put two into her mouth and swallowed them without water, the tears she had successfully held back all morning leaked out of the corners of her eyes.

13. Freeze the Picture

Because Noah had simply walked out of the house while Daniel was there, he wasn't considered 'high risk' as a missing person. The sergeant on duty at Notting Hill police station had told him not to worry, that Noah would probably be back by the time Daniel got home. He'd said they'd alert the patrols in the regular areas where runaway kids congregated in central London, that one way or another Noah would be fine.

But that had been yesterday, and since then Daniel had heard nothing. Noah seemed to have disappeared into thin air. His mobile phone had either run out of juice or was turned off.

'I don't believe it!' Jade had shouted, when Daniel had called her last night. 'You had him for less than twenty-four hours and still you managed to fuck it up!'

'Is there somewhere he would normally go?' Daniel asked. 'A friend's house, maybe?'

'Noah doesn't have friends, Daniel. Not that I've heard of, anyway.'

'So where do you think he might have gone?'

'Jesus!' Jade cried, and Daniel felt her panic rise. 'He could be anywhere!'

'I'm going out to look for him,' said Daniel, although he hadn't the first clue where to start. Maybe around Leicester Square or Piccadilly Circus?

But Noah could have caught a tube or a bus to God knows where. In the vast stretch of London, the boy was just a tiny speck. It was a city you could be sucked into and never found again. It was a city where danger lurked around every corner, if you really thought about it.

Daniel tried not to think about it as he trawled the Strand, one of the places he'd always noticed homeless people hanging about. There were no kids to be seen, just a few older down-and-outs in sleeping bags in shop doorways. He asked a few if they'd seen Noah, and described him, but invariably they were half incoherent, shaking their heads, their palms outstretched for spare change.

He finally got a taxi home at about two a.m., having extended his search to Charing Cross and Trafalgar Square, and then up into Regent Street. His feet felt like two blocks of concrete, but his mind kept racing, imagining Noah cold and alone in some fetid back alley, clutching his gold carry-all. He read stories about kids going homeless all the time. He'd never imagined it might be his kid.

All through the night Daniel didn't get a wink of sleep. He was overwhelmed with guilt. It was his fault that Noah was on the streets. If he hadn't shouted at him, his son would be under his roof now, sleeping safely. Instead he was out there at the mercy of whoever might take advantage of a teenager whose father had failed him.

Just before dawn, Daniel found himself praying. He hadn't talked to God since he was fourteen, after his mother's accident, coming to the conclusion then that prayers went unanswered. The people you loved could be taken away from you senselessly, without rhyme or reason. There was no God.

But, with his eyes screwed shut, he heard himself say out loud into the departing darkness, 'Please, God, let him be okay. Let me find him, and I promise I'll take care of him. I'll be a good father.'

He was greeted by utter silence. Not even the sound of early-morning traffic outside.

Just before ten a.m. Daniel woke from a half-slumber to the sound of the doorbell. He lay under the duvet for a moment, slowly regaining consciousness until the loss of Noah hit him again. It was just the same as waking up all those years ago and remembering each morning that his mother was gone and would never be coming back.

The doorbell rang again, jolting him out of bed. He threw on his dressing-gown and went downstairs, hope flooding through him. It might be Noah.

Instead it was the postman with a large package from Amazon, containing the book analysing the songs of Bob Dylan that Daniel had ordered.

He was out of the shower and getting dressed, ready to go out looking for Noah again when his phone rang. As usual the number was withheld so he ignored it, but then just before it rang out, he remembered he'd given it to the sergeant at Notting Hill.

'Hello?' he said, catching it in the nick of time.

'Danny?' said an instantly recognisable voice. 'Is that you?'

Daniel closed his eyes. 'Vince,' he said. 'How did you get this number?'

'Danny, my boy! Long time no chat!'

'I'm hanging up,' said Daniel.

'Don't! I want to talk to you.'

Daniel held the phone away from his face. He should have known Vince David would try to worm his way back into his life. Putting the phone back to his ear, he said, 'Well, I don't want to talk to you, Vince, so fuck off.'

True to form, Vince ignored him. 'I think it's time you went back in the studio, mate,' he said, shedding the niceties in his usual way. 'You have a window, Danny boy. It might never come again.'

'My name is Daniel,' said Daniel. 'And I don't want a window.'

'C'mon. It wasn't that bad, was it? We had a good time, you and me.'

Daniel almost laughed. 'Goodbye, Vince,' he said, and hung up.

Just before he left the house, he called the police station to ask if they had any news of Noah.

'We haven't had any reports,' the man on duty said. Like the last guy, he tried to reassure Daniel that Noah would be found and that they would do everything they could to locate him. 'Most people reported missing usually come home within a few days,' he said. 'Wait and see.'

But Daniel couldn't wait and see. He got on his bike and made his way towards King's Cross. He remembered some Channel 4 documentary about homeless kids hanging around there.

14. Nothing We Can Do

'It just goes to show, Dolores, you never know what's coming around the corner,' said Dee's mother.

'I know,' Dee agreed, leaning towards her dressing-table mirror to check for lipstick on her teeth. This was a regular part of their weekly telephone conversation, the bit where her mother would list the deaths of people in the town, most of whom Dee didn't even vaguely know or remember.

'She was there one day, and the next she was gone,' her mother added. She said this as if it was a brand-new revelation on the nature of life and death, when in fact it was her standard response to the passing away of anyone she knew, or knew of.

'Her family must be devastated,' Dee said – another stock reply.

'They are, they are ...' Her mother trailed off. Then she added, 'Did I tell you about Matty Jones?'

'Who?'

'Matty Jones from Larkhill Road. You used to be friendly with one of his boys. Charlie. Was that his name?'

A memory as clear and precise as a high-definition television picture came into Dee's head. She was fourteen and sitting with Charlie on the rocks on the edge of the shore at Beezie's Island, taking her top off. She grimaced.

'Anyway, Matty Jones has been diagnosed with Alzheimer's,' her mother said, when Dee didn't respond. 'Although you could tell he had it before now. He's not half the man he was.'

'That's awful,' Dee said, the memory of Charlie still flickering at the edge of her consciousness.

'I don't know how much longer he'll be able to take care of himself,' her mother went on. 'It's a terrible disease.'

'Terrible,' Dee agreed, sitting down on the edge of the bed. She wanted to end the phone call now. It had been a juggernaut of a day, back-to-back meetings at which she had stood at the top of the room giving presentations, with barely time between to deal with the emails piling up on her smartphone. Plus her chest and back still ached. All she wanted to do was lie down and close her eyes.

'How are things with Joe?' her mother asked.

'Great,' Dee said, using the word like a gate to shut down any further enquiries.

'Are you sure?' her mother persisted.

Dee signed internally. At Christmas, when she'd been home for a couple of days, her mother had walked in on her when she was in the bathroom, in her bra and knickers, brushing her teeth. She'd gasped when she'd seen Dee's shoulder.

It had been a perfectly innocent bruise too. Dee had slipped on an icy patch a few days before and jammed her arm into a pillar. Her mother frowned and wrung her hands as Dee told her about the accident but, mercifully, she hadn't said another word.

Since then, though, in every telephone conversation, she had asked the same question in the same anxious tone: 'How are things with Joe?' It drove Dee nuts.

'I'd better go,' she told her mother. 'The dinner won't cook itself.'

'What are you having?' her mother asked and, before Dee could reply, added, 'We had shepherd's pie last night. Your father said it was the nicest he'd ever tasted.'

'Well, you always did a lovely shepherd's pie,' Dee said. Sometimes she felt sorry for her mum, who had to find pride in the smallest things after a lifetime confined to housework.

Her mother gave a self-conscious laugh. 'Your father said to say hello. He's gone out for his pint.'

Every evening, as regular as clockwork, her father walked into town after dinner for one pint of Guinness, getting home in time for the news at nine. Her parents thrived on habit.

'Tell him I said hello back,' Dee replied.

Her mother cleared her throat. 'It's been ages since you were home. We miss you, love.'

Dee refused to let herself be drawn into feeling guilty. She went home plenty, and, anyway, there had been no such words when she'd been packed off to boarding school, without warning or explanation, the minute she'd turned thirteen. And not to board just down the road at the Ursuline convent, where she'd already spent a year as a day girl and found some friends, but in a school a hundred miles away, in the wilds of Connemara. She'd got home from Kylemore Abbey one weekend a month, if she was lucky, and when the bleak time came to get back on the Galway bus on a Sunday afternoon, her mother never said a word about missing her. Now, as she approached old age, she never stopped saying it.

Downstairs Dee heard the front door open. Her heart rate picked up.

'I have to go, Mum,' she said. 'I'll call you next week, okay?'

'Dee!' Joe shouted. 'Where are you?'

She could always tell by his voice what kind of mood he was in. Tonight it lilted. She put her hand over the phone and called, 'Up here!'

She said goodbye to her mother as he bounded up the stairs. When he rounded the door into the bedroom he was carrying flowers. Not a cheap bunch from Spar, but a bouquet like the ones the women on Grafton Street sold.

'I'm sorry,' he said, pushing the flowers at her. He had an eager, puppyish quality that made her want to laugh, but she forced her mouth to stay pursed.

She sat on the bed with the flowers in her lap and looked up at him. He was almost panting with adoration.

'Joe,' she said, gripping the base of the bouquet, 'if it ever, ever happens again, I'm leaving you.'

'It won't,' he said, sitting down beside her. 'I swear.' The lilt was gone out of his voice and now he sounded miserable. 'I don't know what came over me.'

They sat there, saying nothing, and then Dee leaned over and rested her head on his shoulder. He was wearing the aftershave she loved, Allure Homme, and she had an urge to kiss his neck.

Joe put his arm around her. 'I love you,' he said. 'I don't know what I'd do without you.'

Dee closed her eyes and lay back on the mattress. He moved over her, pushed up her skirt and pulled off her pants, throwing them across the room. He wrenched down his own jeans and underwear and pushed himself against her, squeezing her left nipple through the material of her blouse, his lips flickering at hers, his tongue urging hers out to meet it.

Even though she was in pain from the weight of his body, she wrapped her legs around his waist and pulled him in close, biting her bottom lip and then his, a gasp escaping as he entered and filled her, then pulled all the way out and did the same again, sending sparks flying through her veins, igniting her heart.

When Joe was inside her, it felt like perfect symmetry. She could totally lose herself, yet be so intimately connected to him at the same time that it was as if their blood ran together. It was the polar opposite of loneliness.

'I love you,' she murmured into his ear, just before the surge inside her broke into a surf of pleasure. He shouted her name, the cords in his neck stretched tight, like thick ropes, his eyes boring into hers as he came.

Later, when they'd got their breath back and he'd nodded off, she inched herself from under his arm and went to have a shower. Beneath the hot hiss and steam of the water, she didn't hear him come into the bathroom after her.

'What do you want for dinner?' he yelled, through the glass shower door.

Dee's stomach lurched and flipped. Backed into the corner of the stall, her hands clutching at her face, she called, 'I brought home some Thai Green Curry!'

When he was gone, Dee dried herself off as gently as she could and stood naked in front of the mirror over the sink. The bruising was at its most livid now, veiny purple and brown blotches stretching across the top of her chest and right shoulder, and down her arm. She touched the bruise to the side of her breast and breathed sharply. But she knew that the pain would subside over the next few days. The bruising had to be at its worst before it started to fade. That was the pattern.

15. Long-forgotten Things

The beach was pretty much deserted, although Cassandra had passed a few lone men in the dunes. Normally she wouldn't venture on to the beach at night, where guys cruised each other in the wave-swept darkness, but after tonight's meltdown with Coco she needed a bit of headspace. In a few hours German guys would be laying out their towels, getting first dibs on the best spots for a day of swimming and checking out hot bodies, but for now Playa de Las Salinas was Cassandra's own private Idaho.

She sat down on the sand, which had retained some of the afternoon's sweltering heat, and breathed slowly, taking in the hint of eucalyptus in the air. When she'd first come to the Canaries, she'd loved that smell. It was the scent of the perpetual summer on offer, the scent of a promise of excitement and romance. A promise that was never kept, if you thought about it.

Seriously, what was Coco like? It was drama after drama with her. The kid thrived on adversity.

Tonight's freak-out had occurred, thankfully, after the show – not right in the middle of it, like last week. Some straight guy in the audience had shouted, 'Show us your dick!' during the finale and Coco had just about held it together until she'd got offstage. Then she'd burst into tears, screeching at the top of her lungs, not caring who heard, that she was going to 'murder that fucking bastardo'.

In the dressing room, Coco wouldn't stop going on about it at the top of her voice, which led to another fight between her and the other queens.

'My dear, please keep your undergarments on,' Madam Ovary had said, peeling off one of her false eyelashes. 'If I had a penny for every time a heterosexual of the male variety asked me to reveal my appendage, I'd be rolling in it.'

Coco rounded on her from her dressing-table, her face streaked with mascara. 'It's different for you! It's different for *all of you*!'

'Here we fucking go again,' sighed Diana, who was still corseted within an inch of her life. She never changed in the dressing rooms, arriving and leaving work in full drag. 'Get off the trans rag, sweetie.'

Coco had sat bolt upright, her tears stopping as instantly as they had started. 'What did you say?' she'd asked, her voice a growl.

Although Coco hadn't had her final operation yet, even the vague suggestion that she still had a penis between her legs was enough to send her into hysterics. Cassandra remembered them well, those oestrogen rushes. 'Ladies, ladies,' she had said, feeling it was time to step in and restore order. 'Calm down, for God's sake.'

'*Calm down?*' Coco had yelped, her eyes burning. 'Calm down?' Without warning, she had launched herself out of her chair and on to Diana, pulling at her wig. 'You fucking bitch! Take that back!' she screamed.

Phyllis, in her bra and knickers, had egged her on, screeching, 'Girlfight! Girlfight!'

Diana had given as good as she got, wrenching the sleeve of Coco's dress so hard that a loud rip echoed through the room, causing Coco to let out an ear-piercing scream.

'For fuck's sake,' Cassandra had muttered, putting her wig on its stand. Then she'd shouted, at the top of her voice, 'Stop it! This instant!'

The dressing room went silent and all eyes turned in her direction.

'Oooh, get *her*,' said Phyllis, but she'd looked chastened, as did the others.

Madam Ovary was still at her mirror, nonchalantly wiping cold cream from her face. 'That's right, dears. Do as Mama Cass says.'

Cassandra wasn't sure when they'd started referring to her as Mama Cass. When she'd started doing her routines at Flikkers Showbar she'd been just one of the girls. But somewhere in the past eleven years she'd morphed from drag queen into Queen Mother, from Cassandra Delight to Mama Cass – the one all the girls came to for advice or comfort. The undisputed backstage matriarch, even though Madam Ovary was a good fifteen years older and, well, more maternally built.

'It's not fair,' Coco had cried, her bright orange bottom lip out. 'Nobody understands what it's like.'

Cassandra had put an arm around her. 'I do, sweetie,' she said, making her voice a soothing purr. 'It's a hard time right now, but we're all here for you, aren't we, girls?'

There were a few murmurs and nods of assent, but Cassandra knew they all thought Coco was a royal pain in the arse, and blamed her for insisting she be taken on by Flikkers in the first place. Mama Cass had certainly put a foot wrong with that decision.

Cassandra's buttocks were going a bit numb sitting on the hard sand, so she stood up and brushed off her silk kimono dress. In the gloom she thought she could see the outline of a figure walking in her direction. A shiver made its way up her spine, despite the heat of the night, and she squinted in the dim light to make out if the person was a man or a woman.

A man most likely. Cruising. Women hardly ever walked on the section of the beach designated gay.

Cassandra looked out to the inky black sea again.

Mama Cass. The name hardly suggested glamour, did it? There was a time when Cassandra had said to herself she'd give up the job as soon as she started getting middle-aged. To her mind, there was nothing quite as sad as an ageing drag queen, or worse, an ageing trans woman masquerading as a drag queen.

When she'd first experimented with drag in her early twenties, she was learning to hide plain, shy Cassandra to become an exotic Amazonian diva. Nowadays when she looked in the dressing-room mirror at Flikkers, she caught glimpses of her mother the last time she'd seen her, when she was in her late fifties and beginning to sag.

Although she went to the gym every day, and kept her body lean and hard, the sag was always waiting for her in that dressing-room mirror. She was turning into the drag queen she'd promised herself she'd never be, but she didn't know what else to do. Putting on slap and lip-synching was the only way she knew how to earn her bread and butter. It was what had paid for her to be who she was in the first place, financing the treatment and operations that had turned her from the boy she had long forgotten into the woman she was always meant to be.

Up ahead, near enough now so that Cassandra could see it was a man, the figure in the darkness stood stock still. There was an odd hum in the air, like the static anticipation of an audience waiting for the orchestra to begin just after the conductor had tapped his stand. And then the man fell to his knees.

Cassandra started towards him and, as he sank down, found herself running, the heels of her shoes jamming in the sand.

When she reached him, she could hear soft moaning. Cassandra knelt beside him. 'Are you all right?'

The man was old, maybe in his late seventies, completely bald and gaunt in a Hawaiian shirt. A memory of her father came into her mind, also on a beach, turning to beckon her towards the water, his dark hair thick and wavy.

The man moaned and his eyes locked on Cassandra's, wide with silent desperation.

Cassandra looked around for help, but no one was about.

The old man made a cracked, high-pitched noise.

'Sssh,' Cassandra said. 'It's okay.'

Panic bubbled up inside her, but she forced it down, pressed her palms into the man's chest, pushed hard and counted to three.

She pushed again and a wheezing noise came out of the man's mouth. His eyeballs rolled back in his head.

Cassandra pushed again with her palms into his chest but he seemed to have stopped breathing altogether now. His pupils rolled back down and met Cassandra's again. His eyes were full of terror.

The thought that came into Cassandra's head was *You are not alone.*

She took the man's head on to her lap and leaned over to cradle it, stroking his cheek. 'It's okay,' she whispered. 'I'm here. I'm holding you.'

A breath so slow it seemed to go on forever came out of his mouth. His eyes, welded to Cassandra's, were calm now.

And then he died.

Cassandra pulled his head up to her chest and wrapped her arms around him, tears dropping on to his still face.

Again, the image of her father came into her head. Laughing on the sand at Rosses Point, running down towards the sea, standing in the shallow surf, his chest bare and hairy, calling, 'Don't be a chicken, Charlie! It's not cold!'

In April it would be ten years since her mother's funeral, the last time Cassandra had seen her father. Or spoken to him.

A man's voice drifted to her from the dunes, and then another, in conversation. She knew she should call for help, but she wanted to stay cradling the man's head to her chest. Just for a minute more.

She stroked the man's cheek again, and looked out to sea.

Life was short and ten years was far too long. Her father could die like this any day. And what would be left? A world of regret.

'*Hola?*' The voice came from above her. '*Está bien usted?*'

16. A Potential Threat

The atmosphere in Jade's kitchen was tightrope tense. Across from Daniel, Rob was drumming his thick fingers on the table. The sound went through Daniel's skull like a jackhammer.

'I don't know what else to do,' Jade said. 'He can't have just vanished into thin air.'

The dark circles under her eyes made her look as if she'd suddenly aged.

Rob stopped drumming his fingers and said, 'Fucking typical.'

'What's typical?' Daniel asked, his teeth gritted.

'Fucking pigs,' said Rob. 'They don't do nothing, man. Just sit on their fucking arses.'

Daniel swallowed and said nothing. Like Rob was someone to talk about people sitting on their arses. Since his forced retirement from the music business he had done nothing but sit and play video games. Jade said that Noxious Apparatus were re-forming for a tour, but Daniel couldn't imagine Rob getting off his backside to do it anytime soon. What the fuck was Jade still with him for?

Noah had been AWOL for three days now. Daniel had trawled King's Cross, Camden, Brixton, Whitechapel, Finsbury Park, Cricklewood and Kilburn looking for him, showing Noah's photograph to anyone and everyone, but getting no joy. He'd realised that he couldn't cover London's vast stretch alone.

At least the police were taking it seriously now. They'd fed the picture Daniel had emailed them through their system, and every police station in the Greater London area had been alerted to his disappearance. It should have been some sort of comfort, but Daniel had Googled 'missing persons+UK' last night and found that thirty thousand people were reported missing every year. Noah was just one more for the police to deal with.

'We could make a poster and flyers with his photo,' Jade said. 'Put it up everywhere. Hand it out at tube stations …'

Rob snorted. 'Like that's gonna help. Nobody ever pays any attention to those things. They just go in the fucking bin, man.' He started drumming his fingers again.

'We have to try something,' said Jade. She put her face into her hands. 'This is all my fault.'

'It's not,' said Rob, and eyed Daniel. 'It's his.'

Daniel got to his feet, his chair falling to the floor behind him. 'If it's anyone's fault, it's yours,' he barked. 'If you hadn't been giving him shit in the first place, Jade never would have brought him to live with me, and none of this would have happened.'

Rob stood up at the other side of the table. 'Fuck you!' he shouted, the veins in his neck standing out. 'What sort of a dad are you, man? Can't even take care of your own fucking son.'

The wind was taken out of Daniel's sails. He bent over, picked up the chair and sat down again. Rob was a Neanderthal, but he was right. Daniel had failed Noah, right from the start of his life. It was much worse than any failing of Daniel's own father.

At the top of the table, Jade was crying. Her eyes met Daniel's and he was instantly filled with the cold dread that had lurked at the corner of every moment since Noah had disappeared.

'What if something's happened to him?' she said. 'What if he's—'

'We'll find him,' Daniel interrupted. 'I promise we will.' But he didn't know how he was going to make good on that promise. On the table, his phone vibrated. 'Jesus, not now. The number display, as per usual, said, 'Blocked'.

'Answer it,' said Jade. 'It could be the police.'

But Daniel just watched the phone until it stopped. 'It'll go through to voicemail,' he said.

Jade sighed and stood up. 'I'll make another pot of coffee,' she said.

Daniel had never seen Jade as a homemaker. During the brief time they'd shared his Hampstead apartment, she'd cared about as much as he did about the place. They'd lived out of the boxes he'd barely unpacked and the few bags she'd moved in with.

Now her kitchen was something out of an interiors magazine featuring *faux* farmhouse design, with its big rustic oak table, gingham curtains and white-painted frying pans, stencilled with pictures of hens, hanging on the walls. In the midst of it, Rob looked utterly out of place, like a troll trying to fit into a doll's house. Across the table he was sulking now, his massive arms folded, forehead furrowed.

Daniel did his best to speak evenly. 'When Noah comes back I'd appreciate it if you stopped giving him a hard time,' he said.

Rob continued to sulk. 'You don't live with him, man,' he said. 'You don't know what it's like.'

'He's a teenager. All teenagers are annoying.'

'All that makeup. And the clothes he wears … and the way he goes on.' Rob flicked his chunky wrist as he said this in an oddly fitting expression of camp. 'It does my head in.'

Jade turned from the sink where she was filling the kettle. 'It's not his fault. He's always been like that.'

'The kid needs to man up,' said Rob. 'I only tell him for his own good.'

Daniel inwardly groaned. There was no way he was ever going to let his son come back to live with this dipstick.

But they had to find Noah before he could tell him that.

'Have you got a printer?' he asked Jade.

'Yes. Well, Noah has one, in his room.'

'We should make those posters you were talking about. We can start putting them up tonight.'

17. The Music Still Goes On

'Linda grew up to be a singer, just like her mom. Did you know she made her first album with Agnetha, when she was only seven? My daughter, Carly, loved to sing when she was little. Was Poppy a little singer too?' After Maggie had read his reply to her on the Abbaholics Facebook group, she clicked on Joel Singleton's profile. He had accepted her friend request, so she had access to his photographs. They showed a handsome forty-eight-year-old outdoor type, with a smiling, sun-kissed, lived-in face. In every shot he had a little blond stubble on his softly rounded chin, and a full head of straight flaxen hair. Several photos featured Joel with Carly, who was a female version of her father, a little too masculine in her features to be called pretty.

For his relationship status Joel had chosen: *It's complicated.*

That sounded interesting. Although he was three thousand miles away, and she had never seen him in the flesh, Maggie pictured herself in bed with Joel Singleton, his body writhing against hers, his blond stubble scratching her chin as their tongues wrestled …

She couldn't remember how long it was before William left that they'd last had sex. People said it was like riding a bike, that you picked up where you'd left off, but the leaving off had been so long ago she couldn't imagine it would be that easy. Still, she found herself imagining it more and more often, always with random men. She'd even found herself at the beginning of a fantasy about Dr Snow while she was sitting in his waiting room last week.

Maggie went back to Joel's update and replied: 'Poppy, like her mother, hasn't a note in her head. But that didn't stop her, or me, singing all the time back in the day. We made a total racket together! BTW, did you know that Linda did backing vocals on Agnetha's comeback single, "When You Walk In The Room" in 2004?'

She'd been browsing on Facebook since she'd got up, with Benny cuddled on the chair beside her, losing herself in other people's updates and clicking through to the links they posted. In the upbeat messages she wrote on people's walls, full of exclamation marks and positivity, she projected herself as utterly carefree.

She clicked through to the YouTube link she'd put with her post to Joel – Agnetha singing her cover of the Searchers' 'When You Walk In The Room'. It was a happy song, but the tears at the heart of Agnetha's voice gave it such a melancholy air that Maggie felt a lump rising in her throat. She pushed it down.

The song ended and the complete silence that ensued was interrupted by a short, sharp ring on the doorbell. From his perch on the arm of Maggie's chair, Benny turned in its direction. It was probably somebody selling something or, worse, a Jehovah's Witness. They tended to hit on her with some religious fundamentalism every couple of months.

Maggie decided to pretend she wasn't in.

'Maggie! Are you there?' came a voice through the letterbox.

Maggie breathed a sigh of relief. It was only Alison. Maybe she was dropping in on her way home from her library shift to see why Maggie hadn't come in yesterday.

'Coming!' she called, standing up and walking into the hall. When she opened the door, Alison was standing on the step, flanked on either side by a three-year-old twin.

'Oh, Maggie! I'm so glad you're here,' Alison breathed. 'I thought you'd forgotten.'

Maggie forced a smile. 'Of course not,' she said, covering for herself. Behind Alison two baby car seats were plonked on the driveway gravel.

A car horn blew, and Alison turned to call to the black four-wheel-drive parked outside the front gate, 'I'm coming!'

She turned back to Maggie. 'Our flight is at seven and the traffic is terrible. Simon's super-stressed out.'

Maggie looked down at the twins and back up at Alison as the promise she'd made to mind them for the weekend slowly made its way back from her memory banks.

'Justin's almost there with the toilet training,' Alison said, placing a stuffed hold-all at Maggie's feet. 'You just have to keep an eye on him. Jake's flying along, and he'll tell you when he wants to go for a wee-wee or a poo …' She looked down at the twin on her left, supposedly Jake, although Maggie couldn't tell them apart. 'Won't you, sweetie?' she said.

Jake, his little red nostrils caked with dried snot, gazed up at his mother passively. Justin was staring at her in the same vacant way.

'If you can get them to sleep for an hour in the afternoon, they'll be far less cranky come the evening. Oh, and there's some drops for Justin's eye in the bag. He's got a touch of conjunctivitis.'

Alison went silent and gave a little cough. It was a signal, Maggie realised, for her to speak.

'Come in, boys!' Maggie said, keeping her smile plastered on her face as she bent down to the children. 'Let me see if I have something nice in the kitchen for you.'

'They eat just about everything.' Alison smiled. 'But don't give them sugar whatever you do. It makes them crazy.' She held both hands forward and ushered the toddlers into the hall.

'Look!' Jake cried, his voice unnaturally guttural for a three-year-old. 'Cat!'

He went off chasing Benny, who let out a loud squeal of protest and darted into the sitting room. Standing at Maggie's knee, Justin began to whimper.

'I can't thank you enough for this,' Alison said, as her husband blew the car horn again. 'Call me if there are any problems. Not that there will be. They're good as gold, really.'

She leaned down to kiss Justin, then backed out of the door and down the driveway. 'Thanks for this, Maggie,' she said. 'I honestly owe you one.'

From the sitting room came a high, strangulated miaow. Justin, who was now sitting on the hall carpet with his fists in balls, began to wail at the top of his lungs.

18. No Escaping

The bottle of wine stood on the coffee table, the gourmet dinner Dee had picked up at KC Peaches was still in its packaging on the kitchen counter, and Joe's mobile phone kept ringing out.

She sat with her legs curled under herself on the sofa, listlessly watching *Come Dine With Me*. She'd long given up on being dressed up for the occasion and was in her pyjama bottoms with a grey hoodie. It was only nine thirty but her eyelids were drooping and she felt like hauling herself off to bed.

Tonight was the anniversary of the night they'd met. In some ways it held more significance for her than the other anniversaries – their engagement and their wedding, because even at the time she'd known it was momentous. Before that night she'd thought that falling in love at first sight was the stuff of songs and cheap romance novels.

She could still picture the way he'd walked over to her in the bar, the roll of his square shoulders, the ease with which he held himself. It had been an evening out with the Single Ladies Club, a small group of similarly unattached women who had banded together with a view to meeting men for prospective relationships when they went out pubbing and clubbing.

The Single Ladies Club had three rules:

1. No getting involved in chatter with each other about your personal lives and forgetting there were men in the building.

2. No shyness. If you spotted a guy you liked, you went up to him and said hello, egged on by a bit of sisterly support.

3. If you met a guy you weren't interested in, you introduced him to one of the other girls in the group.

It was all a bit of harmless fun, really, and Dee hadn't taken it as seriously as some other Single Ladies. But she'd joined the club without question. In her twenties and thirties, she'd had no shortage of boyfriends. One relationship would end and she'd be right in the middle of the next in the blink of an eye. The trouble was, most of those relationships had ended in the same way after the same amount of time – around six months.

Invariably the guy started getting on her nerves. She'd find him pouting if she was late for a date because of work. Or getting competitive with her if she was doing particularly well. Or finding ways to criticise her without really coming out and saying anything. In time she began to believe that all men had the same underlying, maddening insecurity.

Her quest to find a man with whom she might stay the course had ended abruptly when she'd turned thirty-nine, and not of her own accord. At the time she hadn't thought she looked anywhere near her age, but something about her aura must have changed, because guys were simply not interested in her any more. In the bars she had always frequented, she could barely get one to look at her, never mind give her the time of day.

The Single Ladies Club had been a suggestion of her friend Anna, who had spent most of her thirties in a relationship with a man who had dumped her for a younger model the second she'd turned forty.

Anna was having none of it. There was no way she was getting out of the relationships ring without fighting her corner.

'Total ride, six o'clock,' Anna had hissed into Dee's ear, as Joe had ambled towards them in the bar, but Dee didn't reply. She had a mental picture of a lion coming in for the kill.

'Oh … my … fucking … God … He's gorgeous,' Anna said. 'Bags first dibs.'

'Ladies, can I get you a drink?' said Joe, taking a space at the bar beside them, his eyes locked on Dee's. The other thing she'd never really got in cheap romance novels was the bit where the girl melted as the guy of her dreams entered stage right, but here she was, almost a puddle on the floor.

'I'll have a gin and tonic,' Anna said, putting the no-shyness rule into action.

'And you?' Joe asked Dee. 'I bet you're a Chardonnay woman.' The line was a bit left-of-centre cheesy, but the way he said 'woman' was full of appreciation.

In an effort to get a grip on herself, she countered, 'I'm a Guinness woman, actually. A pint, please.'

The conversation flowed easily. His surname was Dimare, which went perfectly with his ample dark hair and black stubble on olive skin, and he had his own successful business importing wines from northern Tuscany, the region from which his parents had come to Ireland. He loved wine, he told her, because it was a drink that involved all the senses. Like the best things in life, it improved with age.

He had laid on the smooth chat-up lines with a trowel, but there was something genuinely sweet about him. With his loosened tie and rolled-up shirt sleeves, he looked like a big-handed farmer awkwardly squeezed into a businessman's suit.

As he'd excused himself to go to the 'little boys' room' one of those hands lightly brushed Dee's wrist, and she knew then she would sleep with him that night.

'I think I'll leave you two to it,' said Anna, as he walked away.

'Sorry,' said Dee, grinning. 'I've completely bogarted him.'

'That's what we're here for.' Anna had smiled, picking up her drink. Before she disappeared into the crowd, she'd turned back to Dee and said, with a wink, 'I think he's a keeper.'

And that was exactly what he had turned out to be. After two months, he had taken her to Glendalough for a Sunday walk, got down on one knee and proposed. Two more months later they were married in the Tuscan town of Pietrasanta, where his parents had returned to live. As she walked up the aisle of the tiny medieval church, Dee knew that she'd met her destiny. Yes, it was straight out of one of those cheap romances, but it was true.

The sound of a car on the street outside made Dee's ears prick up, but it drove past. She flicked the TV channels to see if there was anything else on.

When they'd got home from Italy, Joe had changed almost instantly. Or maybe he hadn't changed at all: maybe he'd just felt on solid ground now that she had married him. They were bound together, so he could reveal all of himself.

One Sunday evening, long before she was married, Dee had listened to a radio documentary about abused women while she ironed her blouses for the working week ahead. She thought now of how she had shaken her head as the women being interviewed talked about being unable to leave their abusers, how they stayed and endured in the hope of things getting better, always believing their husbands when they said they'd never beat them again until it was almost too late. Until those women were almost dead.

And now, despite everything she knew to be right and true, this was what was happening to her. Every time she thought about leaving Joe, a precipice appeared in front of her and she felt dangerously close to falling into an empty void. She had spent her whole life building up the barricades around herself so the rug could never again be pulled out from under her feet, becoming the boss of her own company, an independent self-directed woman. Yet here she was, forty-two years old, and believing her husband when he came home with flowers and promised he'd never lay a finger on her again, taking him into her arms and comforting him while he wept because he hated himself for hitting her, for losing control of himself like that.

She loved him – hopelessly, impossibly, unconditionally. And, twisted though it was, she knew he loved her back in exactly the same way.

Dee switched off the TV and pulled herself off the sofa. She was just mounting the stairs to go up to bed when she heard his key fumbling in the door. She went down and let him in.

'Hey, baby,' he said, half falling into the hall. There was no dark edge to his voice, and Dee breathed a sigh of relief.

'You're drunk,' she said.

'No, I'm not,' Joe slurred. 'I've only had a few. Scout's honour.'

'You'd better have some water,' she said, as he followed her into the kitchen. 'We've Anna and Tom's wedding tomorrow and you don't want to be hung-over.'

'Fuck,' said Joe. He slumped down at the table. 'Forgot all about that.'

'That's not all you forgot about,' said Dee, letting the tap run cold for a few seconds. 'We were supposed to have dinner together tonight for our anniversary.'

Joe groaned. 'Aw, sorry, baby. I got caught up with one of the clients.'

'I was waiting all evening, Joe.' She took a glass out of the cupboard and held it under the tap. 'You could have called me.'

The glass was half full when he kicked the tendon at the back of her knee. It fell out of her hand, crashing into the sink as her leg went from under her and she fell.

Stunned, with her face wedged against the door of the sink

cupboard, she automatically tried to push herself up with her hands, but another kick landed in the side of her ribcage.

'No, Joe. Please,' she managed to get out.

'*No, Joe. Please,*' he repeated, his voice a sickening, high-pitched parody. He reached down and grabbed her chin, forcing her face around to his. 'Don't ever speak to me like that again,' he said.

Tears began to stream down Dee's face.

'Here we go with the waterworks,' said Joe, standing up. 'Always the same with you, isn't it?'

Dee squeezed her hands into tight fists and braced herself for what was coming.

19. Running the Gauntlet

Finding a space to park the car at Ikea was like trying to locate a needle in a haystack. As Maggie drove around the indoor section of the car park, her heart sank lower and lower. It was Saturday afternoon. She should have known the place would be jammed to the rafters.

In the passenger seat Oona was straining her head this way and that, looking for a space, shouting, every now and then, 'There!' and then, 'No, that's just a trolley space,' or 'I must have been imagining it.' She had phoned first thing that morning, reminding Maggie that she'd promised to take her to buy a chest of drawers.

'I'm not sure I can do it today,' Maggie had said. 'I have Alison's twins for the weekend and I don't think I'll be able to cope with them in Ikea.'

'Nonsense,' Oona had answered. 'We'll be in and out in no time.'

Maggie had made some more reluctant noises, but Oona had impressed on her the urgency of getting the chest of drawers. She'd lined up a handyman to build it tomorrow, so she really had to get it today.

'We can put the twins in the crèche,' she'd added, which gave Maggie less of an excuse to opt out, so eventually she capitulated.

At least now the twins were happily gorging themselves on Jelly Tots in the back. When Maggie had first tried to put them into the seats she'd spent forty-five minutes trying to fit into the car, they'd protested like prisoners being strapped into electric chairs. Jake's fists curled up and his face squished with red rage as Maggie tried to negotiate the buckle on a strap that was more difficult to solve than a Rubik's cube. At the same time, an unseated Justin tried to climb into the front of the car, his pudgy feet pushing against Maggie's arm.

Once she had Jake secured, he began screaming at the top of his lungs. The sound drilled through Maggie's skull as she tried to make Justin stop going as stiff as a board so she could lodge him into *his* seat. By the time the two of them were strapped in they were both crying, their wails oddly in harmony with each other, like twin ambulance sirens.

She knew she wasn't supposed to give them sugar, but once she'd got Oona into the car, she'd pulled into a garage and bought a supply of sweets to keep them quiet. At least she wouldn't have to deal with the double sugar rush when they'd been deposited in the Ikea crèche.

'Sorry, we're full,' said the girl in the crèche, when eventually Maggie found parking and she, Oona and the kids arrived on Ikea's main concourse.

'Maybe I should go back to the car with them and wait for you,' Maggie suggested to Oona.

Oona put her hand on Maggie's arm and breathed, 'Don't leave me.' She was looking wide-eyed at the crowds milling amid the soft-furnishing displays that signalled the beginning of the Ikea maze. 'I can't do it alone.'

Each of Maggie's arms was being dragged by a twin dying to launch himself into the mêlée of shoppers. She gripped their sweaty little hands hard, but Justin's fingers, greased with Jelly Tot saliva, slipped from hers and he broke away in a run.

'Justin!' Maggie cried. 'Come back!'

Justin didn't look behind him. He just kept going until he had disappeared beyond a clutch of people browsing Tullsta armchairs.

'Here. Take him,' she said, holding out Jake's arm to Oona. She broke into a run, but was immediately hampered by a flank of shoppers. Over their shoulders she glimpsed Justin climbing onto a bunk bed in a children's bedroom display.

'Justin!' she roared, but he kept going up the ladder.

'Maggie!' Oona shouted from behind her. 'I've lost the other one!'

Maggie turned in time to see Jake dart behind a corner-seat couch with a sign hanging above it, saying it cost only £399.

Her heart was pounding. The one most in danger was Justin on the bunk bed. She'd have to rescue him first.

'Don't just stand there!' she called to Oona, as she pushed through the crowd. 'Get Jake!'

By the time she reached the display she'd spotted Justin climbing, he'd disappeared. A girl in a yellow Ikea polo shirt was passing by with a customer in tow. Maggie grabbed her wrist. 'Have you seen a little boy?' she said, pointing to the bunk bed. 'He was there a second ago.'

The Ikea girl gave a distracted smile, like a nurse in a madhouse, and shook her head. 'You should report him missing at the information desk just beyond Kitchens,' she said.

'Kitchens,' said Maggie. 'Which way is that?'

'Follow the arrows on the floor,' the girl said, her smile fixed. 'Or take the shortcut through Bathrooms.'

'Maggie!' she heard Oona cry from somewhere amid a sea of sofas. 'Over here! Quickly!'

When Maggie found them, Oona was standing ashen-faced beside a white two-seater Hagalund sofa-bed on which Jake was sitting in a pool of Jelly Tot vomit. He let out a guttural whimper, then brought forth another projectile of multi-coloured puke.

Behind her, Maggie heard a gasp of indignation and a few murmurs of disgust. Willing herself not to care, she picked up the howling Jake and stroked his back. 'It's all right, baby. It's all right.'

'What about the other one?' asked Oona, her eyes wild. 'Where's he?'

'We have to go to the information desk and put out a call for him,' Maggie replied, still stroking Jake's back. 'It's just beyond Kitchens.'

'Kitchens? Which way is that?' Oona said, just before they heard a scream in the mid-distance.

Everyone turned in the direction of an arrow pointing towards Bedrooms. 'Oh, Jesus,' Maggie said, and began to run with Jake bawling in her arms. When she and Oona came upon Justin he was hovering on top of a Birkeland wardrobe, his face a picture of delight.

'Mama!' he gurgled, on seeing Maggie, and she was filled with a conflicting desire to assure all the gaping bystanders that she was not the child's mama, not by a long stretch, and to climb up the wardrobe and grab him.

'How on earth did he get up there?' gasped Oona, arriving on the scene.

'Mama!' said Justin again, and the wardrobe teetered.

'Move aside, people, move aside,' said another Ikea yellow shirt, this time a young man with multiple chins and mutton-chop sideburns.

On the top of the wardrobe, Justin's mood darkened. His bulbous bottom lip protruded and clouds seemed to pass over his forehead.

'Now, now, little boy,' said the yellow-shirt. 'We're going to get you down from there.' They might have been in a scene in a movie where a guy was standing on the edge of a skyscraper, threatening to jump while a cop with a megaphone tried to talk him out of it.

'Take it easy,' Yellow Shirt told Justin, flattening out the palm of one hand.

Justin looked at him, looked at Maggie holding Jake, then burst into a loud show of tears. His fists went up to his eyes and with it he relinquished his grip on the wardrobe's edge.

Everything seemed to turn slow-mo. Yellow Shirt let out a kind of strangulated roar and half dived towards the falling toddler, his arms outstretched. Oona's scream was ear-piercing as Yellow Shirt cushioned Justin from landing head first on the industrial-carpeted floor.

Just as instantly as he'd started crying, Justin was giggling. Yellow Shirt looked stunned.

'Are you all right?' Maggie asked him, leaning over to lift the child out of his arms.

'I think so,' he said, and let out a cry of pain as Justin's nails dug into his nose, to hold on for dear life.

In the Ikea café, while the boys sat in tiny chairs slurping cartons of juice, Oona bemoaned the fact that she still hadn't got her chest of drawers.

Maggie took a mouthful of bitter coffee. She was waiting for her heart to resume its normal pace.

'Couldn't we see if there's space for them in the crèche now?' Oona asked.

Maggie said nothing. Instead she rubbed her temples. She'd felt panicked when Justin was about to fall to his death from the top of the wardrobe, but now she was consumed by another kind of terror. There were too many people in the café making too much noise. Oona's voice was high, reedy and right in her ear. The whole building was packed with people, all talking, all pushing their way through so they could buy stuff.

Meaningless stuff.

What was it all for? Why did places like Ikea even exist? What was Maggie doing here when she was about to face a horrible death?

She looked at Oona, who was still going on, her voice blending with the background noise.

'I think I'm going to die,' Maggie said.

Oona stopped talking and stared at her in silence. 'No, you're not,' she replied irritably, as if Maggie had pointlessly interrupted her.

'I have cancer,' Maggie said. 'I found a lump on my breast.'

Again Oona stopped. Her eyes went large in her head and then filled. 'Oh, no,' she said, tears spilling over. 'Oh, no.'

To Maggie's left, Jake threw his carton on the ground and shouted, 'More juice!'

'Are you sure it's cancer?' Oona asked.

'More juice!' Justin chimed in.

Maggie was already regretting that she had blurted it out. She didn't want to talk about it. Voicing the dread only made it edge closer. Made it worse.

'I'm starting chemotherapy,' she said. 'On Tuesday.'

Oona continued crying, her face twisted. 'Granny died from breast cancer,' she said.

Maggie blinked and swallowed. 'That's not exactly what I need to hear right now, Oona,' she said.

'God! I'm sorry!' Oona burst into a fresh wave of tears. 'Oh, Maggie, I couldn't bear to lose you,' she sobbed.

In the Ikea café, while Jake bawled for more juice and Justin took up the cry, Maggie found herself putting her arm around Oona's shoulders and comforting her. 'It'll be all right,' she said. 'You'll see.'

And she tried to believe herself.

20. Could Be That Guy

The call came at eight a.m., while Daniel was giving out flyers to the rush-hour crowds at Euston, from a Sergeant Robinson.

'We found him sleeping rough in a doorway on Caledonian Road,' the sergeant said.

Daniel called Jade, who was flyering Victoria, and in a flood of relieved tears, she arranged to meet him at Islington police station.

They arrived at the same time, to find Noah sitting by himself in the station's waiting room. He looked tiny, malnourished and utterly alone, the high peak of his baseball cap askew, the fringe underneath it dirty. Jade had rushed over and thrown her arms around him, but he didn't respond. Then, as quickly as she had been hugging him, she was berating him.

'Why?' she cried. 'How could you do that to me? I've been up the walls, Noah!'

Daniel put a hand on her shoulder to tell her to back off, but she shrugged him away. 'I don't know what I've done to deserve this,' she said. 'I thought you might be dead!'

Before they left the station, Sergeant Robinson leaned over to Noah and said, 'We don't want to see you in here again. The streets are no place for a lad like you. Keep at home, with your mum and dad, okay?'

Noah didn't reply, but he shot a dirty look in Daniel's direction, the tip of his oversized teenage nose sooty black.

When they got out of the station, Daniel said, 'Let's go into that pub over there.' Jade and Noah followed him in silence.

The place was practically empty, one of those olde-worlde bars that were popular in the eighties, with fake old books lining shabby-chic shelves; it all looked bona-fide shabby now. Daniel ordered a pint of lager for himself, a vodka and cranberry for Jade and a Coke for Noah.

'Look, mate, I didn't mean to piss you off,' Daniel said, once they were settled.

Jade shot him a glance that asked, 'Are you out of your mind?' To Jake, she said, 'What your father is trying to say is that we know this is a hard time for you, and that we want you to be happy, but …' She eyeballed Daniel to take the reins.

'Maybe it's best for you to live with me for a while,' Daniel said. He took a mouthful of lager to fortify himself. 'It's not so bad, you know.'

'And you can come to me at weekends,' Jade finished.

'What if I don't want to live with him?' Noah said, almost under his breath, his chin touching the neckline of his grubby 'Born This Way' hoodie.

'Christ,' said Jade, losing her patience. 'Would you prefer to live in a cardboard box in some piss-stinking doorway?'

'Maybe,' Noah muttered.

Now it was Daniel's turn to give Jade a warning look. 'There's no pressure,' he said, before she could go on. 'If you don't like living at my place, we can sort something else out, okay? Just try it for a while and see how you feel.'

It was enough to get a mutter of agreement from Noah.

The box room took longer to clear out than Daniel had expected. When he'd moved in just over a year ago, he'd only half emptied the boxes that had stood packed for more than a decade in the basement flat in Hampstead. He'd moved here because he didn't want to be underground any more, because he had decided to start some sort of new life for himself in a proper house, with proper light and space and an entrance that wasn't down a flight of murky steps. But the moment he'd shut the door behind him, he'd reverted to his habitual ways, except, of course, for the smoking. Whatever else he did, Daniel vowed he'd never go back to being stoned twenty-four/seven.

Part of his avoidance of starting the new life he'd promised himself was leaving the boxes unemptied. He wasn't tied down to the promise as long as they were packed and ready to be carted somewhere else. But the aptly titled box room was going to be Noah's bedroom now, so there was no choice but to tackle them.

Noah helped, but in a desultory way, not taking any initiative. He just followed Daniel's orders, which made it even more chaotic since Daniel didn't know where to tell him to put anything. He wished he could do it by himself, but Jade advised that he should involve Noah in the making of his new home.

Daniel got his son to stack the boxes, some in the living room, some in the hall. He'd go through them later and find places for their contents. When the room was emptied, they put the new sheets and duvet cover they'd bought at Portobello market on the bed.

'I'll pick up a wardrobe and a desk, next week,' Daniel said. 'We can bring your computer from your mum's.'

He sensed a kind of loosening in Noah, even though the boy was still silent. Taking advantage of it, he sat on the bed and patted the space beside him. Noah hesitated, then sat down too.

'I want to apologise,' Daniel began. 'I was out of order shouting at you like that.'

Noah's head dipped.

'It's just that I … I don't really know how to be a dad,' Daniel continued, searching for words to explain himself. 'My own dad wasn't great at it, and my mum died when I was your age. So … Well, nobody gave me any lessons on how to do it.'

Noah was wringing his fingers, his chin still on his chest. 'How did your mum die?'

'She had an accident,' said Daniel.

'What kind of an accident?'

For a nano-second Daniel went back to Cardinal Newman. He was surrounded by a group of fifth-formers behind the bike sheds and Philip Ewing was right up in his grill, saying, 'Your mum fucking killed herself, you doofus!' He wrenched himself out of the memory. 'It was a car crash,' he said.

Noah shrugged, and with the movement his leg softly grazed against Daniel's.

The bolt of raw grief this sent shooting through Daniel's body was so intense, it made him want to jump to his feet and get out of the room. But he forced himself to stay where he was.

He'd been pushing away feeling anything for so long … pushing life away. But Noah might wake him up, make him unpack his boxes instead of staying stock-still and scared shitless.

21. Try to Go On

'What's going on?' Poppy asked, standing at the sitting-room door with her arms folded. 'Why's *she* here?'

It was a question Maggie had hissed at William, dragging him straight into the kitchen after he'd arrived with Rita in tow.

'She insisted on coming,' he said, gesturing with his two hands, as if it was beyond his control. 'What's all this about anyway?'

Maggie wanted to shout, 'I have cancer, you bastard!' But she got a grip on herself. She needed Poppy and Oona to be there before she said anything. She'd have to go through it again later with Harry on Skype, and twice was more than enough.

'Rita will have to leave,' Maggie had told William. 'This is family business.' But he'd looked at her as if she had ten heads and retreated to the sitting room without replying.

Now he and Rita were wedged side by side on the sofa, their knees touching and their heads cocked, as if they were the front row, waiting for the main attraction. The sight made Maggie feel nauseous with fury, as if she didn't have enough to deal with. But she smothered her anger. She didn't want to make a scene and cause Poppy any more upset than she had to.

She could still remember the exact moment Poppy had first asked her about death, when she had just turned six. It was St Patrick's Day and the two of them had been waiting for the bus home from the parade in Willesden Green. For some reason that Maggie couldn't recall, Harry and William weren't there. Out of the blue, Poppy had looked up at Maggie with wide, worried eyes and asked, 'Are you going to die, Mummy?'

Maggie's instant reaction had been to laugh and brush it off. 'No, sweetie. Of course I'm not.'

'But doesn't everyone die?' Poppy said.

'Well, yes, they do.'

'So, are you going to die?'

Maggie had found herself backed into a corner, as she so often did with Poppy. 'Well, I suppose so,' she said. 'But not until I'm very, very old.'

'Sandra's mummy died and Sandra couldn't come to school,' Poppy said. 'I don't think her mummy was old. Not like Granny.'

'Well, some people die when they're not so old,' Maggie said, relieved to see the bus coming. 'But that won't happen to me, okay?'

Poppy hadn't replied, but later that night when Maggie went up to read her bedtime story, she was crying under her covers. 'I don't want you to die, Mummy,' she'd sobbed over and over, while Maggie tried to comfort her, feeling at a complete loss.

Harry's fleeting childhood questions about mortality couldn't have been more different. He'd asked if everyone died, then shrugged and accepted the answer before running back outside to resume his football game.

'Well?' said Poppy, when nobody answered her, not moving from her position by the door.

'You must be Poppy,' Rita piped up, smiling her therapist's smile. 'It's nice to meet you at last. I'm Rita.'

'I know who you are,' Poppy said, crossing the room and flopping down on the free armchair. She turned to Maggie. '*Mum?* Just tell me what's going on.'

'Wait until your auntie Oona gets here,' Maggie said, trying to give Poppy a reassuring smile. 'She'll be with us any minute now.'

'I can't stay long,' Poppy said. She fingered one of the thick dreadlocks her beautiful, golden-brown corkscrew curls had matted into. 'We have a house meeting at nine.'

William pulled himself up out of the crook of the sofa and sat on the cushion's edge, frowning. 'Is something wrong?' he asked. 'Are your parents okay?'

Poppy paled. 'Is it Granny?' she said.

'No, sweetie, it isn't,' said Maggie, forcing another smile.

The doorbell rang and William jumped up. 'I'll get it,' he said, like he was taking control, even though he looked utterly bewildered.

When he returned he was followed by Oona, who glanced at Maggie and bit her bottom lip.

There were a few seconds of heightened silence before Rita piped up again: 'I'm Rita,' she said, getting off the couch to bring herself almost to Oona's height and putting her hand out. Oona flinched and squeezed her handbag to her chest. 'Oh … hello …' she said, her voice wavering somewhere between nerve-racked and ice-cool. She turned back to Maggie with a questioning look, then said, 'Have you told them yet?'

Poppy stopped fingering her dreadlock. 'Told us what?' she said.

Tears started leaking down Oona's face.

Maggie took a breath to prepare herself.

'About the cancer,' Oona blubbed.

Maggie couldn't believe her ears. 'Oona!' she snapped. 'I wanted to tell them myself.'

'Mummy?' Poppy began to whimper. 'Have you got cancer?'

Maggie sighed and sat on the arm of Poppy's chair. 'Yes,' she said, and closed her eyes.

When she opened them again, William was staring at her in mute horror. Poppy's face was in her hands and her shoulders were heaving.

'It's going to be okay,' she said. 'Really, it is.'

'How do you know?' Poppy wailed. Beneath her grief there was a note of grievance. 'You don't know *anything*.'

Rita disengaged her hand from William's to touch the tip of her dangling Cherokee Indian-feather earring. Maggie couldn't read her expression, but it certainly didn't come under the heading of sympathy. 'Oh … I get it,' Rita said.

'Pardon?' Maggie replied, confused.

Rita smiled. Not her therapist's smile, but that of a detective who'd just shrewdly deduced the critical clue. A new-age Jessica Fletcher in *Murder, She Wrote*. 'This is another of your stories, isn't it? To get William back.'

A dazed hush fell on the room as everyone gaped at her. William's jaw was nearly in his lap and Maggie had the fleeting satisfactory thought that Rita had just signed her own exit warrant.

William turned back to Maggie. 'Oh, my God,' he said, clearly horrified. 'Is she right?'

Maggie's blood ran cold. She looked from William to Rita and back again in disbelief. She knew now why she'd put off telling them all for so long. She had been afraid she might be proven correct: that she wasn't surrounded by a family in whose bosom she could safely rest but by a random group of people, accidents of meeting and birth, who knew nothing about who she really was and cared only for themselves when push came to shove.

'I'm tired,' she said, getting to her feet. 'I'm going for a lie-down.'

'Maggie,' William said. Now he looked baffled. 'You can't just walk away after dropping a bombshell like that.'

'Mum,' Poppy chimed in, her voice a squeak, 'don't go.'

Maggie was torn. Inside her a battle was raging between sitting down for Poppy's sake and getting as far away from them all as she could. She was raging and guilty and sick with disgust, but every conflicting thing she felt was underpinned with unavoidable, unquenchable fear. Could none of them understand what she had to face?

At the sitting-room door, Benny was looking over his shoulder at Maggie, as if to beckon her.

'I'll just close my eyes for half an hour,' she told the assembled company, and followed him.

As Benny padded up the stairs ahead of her, his stubby little tail curling in the air, Maggie tried to take some comfort from his unconditional, unquestioning love. He was only a cat, but in some ways she felt he was the only living thing on the entire planet that would be by her side at the terrifying end.

22. *Everything Comes Back*

His name was Felipe Lugo Ortega. He had two daughters and six grandchildren, and his wife, Agata, had survived him although she was nine years older.

She had thanked Cassandra over and over again, her wrinkled, skeletal hands shaking as she gripped Cassandra's, tears glistening in a pair of hazel eyes that hinted at the beautiful woman she must once have been. She didn't speak English, but her eldest daughter, Raquel, translated.

'She says she is very glad that you were with him. The worst thing is to leave this earth alone.'

Cassandra spent a couple of hours in their cluttered house, fighting her claustrophobia in the keen understanding that they didn't want her to leave. The other daughter, Teresa, kept offering more and more food, another cup of coffee, another glass of water, placing her hand on Cassandra's shoulder as if to root her to the too-deep sofa. The mother constantly held on to her left hand.

Cassandra recounted the story several times, making sure to tell them that Felipe was at peace when he passed away. She didn't mention the terror she had seen in the old man's eyes when she had first knelt down on the sand beside his convulsing body.

When at last they seemed ready to let her go, Cassandra stopped at the front door and promised she'd visit them again.

The old woman said something in Spanish and Raquel translated, 'I am not sure how to explain this, but what my mother says is something like, "You are part of our history now."'

'But I have enough with my own history,' Cassandra complained to Coco, when she got home. 'I don't want to be part of somebody else's.'

'*Madre de Dios*,' Coco said. 'You need to take a chill pill, little lady.' She was lounging on the apartment's tiny terrace in a hot-pink bikini top and a pair of tight denim cut-offs, her long, tanned legs crossed at the thigh. 'Is no big deal,' she added, gesticulating with magenta stick-on nails. 'All Spanish families are like this, talking about history, history, history. On and on and on.'

Cassandra sighed, and sat down opposite her. 'I think I'm still in shock,' she said. 'I can't get the old man's face out of my head.'

'I know what you need,' Coco said, getting to her feet and pushing her oversized sunglasses up to her forehead. 'One of Coco's marvellous margaritas.'

'It's four o'clock in the afternoon, Coco. I'll have a cup of green tea, thank you.'

'Suit yourself,' said Coco, and disappeared into the kitchen. 'Boring old woman.'

She often said things like this, but Cassandra knew not to be offended. Even though Coco had only moved in with her six months ago, bruised and battered and taking up the offer of refuge on the sofa-bed for a few nights, she was now like a piece of the furniture. She'd taken over the sofa-bed, along with more than her fair share of space in the wardrobe in the bedroom, and although Cassandra knew she should be crawling the walls with frustration at living with another human being after all these years – especially someone as unpredictably volatile as Coco – she found her presence oddly comforting.

When Coco came back to the terrace, Cassandra was eyeing the tiny patch of aqua blue water she could see between the tops of buildings. 'A sea view, that's what it said in the brochure when I was buying this place,' she said, taking her cup of tea. 'It said nothing about it being the size of a postage stamp.'

'What? The apartment?'

'No, sweetie. The sea view.'

'Then why you buy it?' Coco asked, sitting down and crossing her legs again. She'd made a large margarita for herself, complete with a cocktail umbrella and straw.

'Because …' Cassandra began, and her thoughts trailed away. She'd bought the place for security. It was a home she could call her own, somewhere she could grow old without being dependent on anyone else. Plus it had been all she could afford at the time.

She sipped the tea, which was too hot. What was it her mother used to say about a cup of hot tea on a hot day? That it was more refreshing than any cold drink.

Since the moment she had cradled Felipe Lugo Ortega's head to her chest on the beach, unwanted memories of her parents had kept invading her thoughts.

'Earth to Mama Cass. Come in, Mama Cass,' said Coco, bringing Cassandra back into the moment. 'This is no good. It's like I am living with one of those … What's the word? You know, from the movies … those zumbies.'

'Zombies,' Cassandra corrected her, with a soft laugh. 'I'm sorry, sweetie. I'm just a bit distracted, that's all.'

'Uh-huh,' said Coco, pursing her lips round the straw in her margarita. 'Distracted like a zumbie.'

Without warning Cassandra found herself welling up. She drank some more tea to halt it.

The first part of the show went swimmingly. It was Saturday so a fresh flock of newly arrived tourists had descended on Flikkers. Those who ventured in usually stayed for the whole show on the first night, and newly made fans would come back loyally night after night for the week, until their flights took them home again.

Cassandra wore her Frida 'Super Trouper' wig, a mass of tightly permed henna-coloured curls, and Diana joined her onstage, playing a particularly reclusive Agnetha for their 'One Of Us Knowing You Takes It All' routine, which condensed all of Abba's break-up songs into two minutes flat.

Audiences loved that one and would call for it every night that week if they'd seen it on the first outing, and although Cassandra had done it a million times, she always got a kick out of the whoops and cheers that filled the bar after it was done. Tonight, though, she felt numb, as if she wasn't really present at all. Throughout the performance, Diana kept shooting her questioning looks.

In the dressing room she was changing out of her Frida wig and combing out her own hair for a take on Dusty Springfield's 'Son Of A Preacher Man' when she was overcome with a wave of nausea. She rested her hot sweaty forehead on the back of her hands, laid flat on the dressing-table, willing the sickness away. But instead the feeling grew.

'Are we okay, dear?' Madam Ovary said, but Cassandra couldn't reply. She gripped the side of the dressing-table and made herself sit up straight, thinking that might help, but it made her feel worse. Her vision twisted and she had the sudden understanding that if she didn't get up and run away as far as she could, she would die, too, in Madam Ovary's arms, just as Felipe had died in hers.

'Coco!' Madam Ovary cried. 'Coco!'

Coco popped her head out of the toilet cubicle at the end of the dressing room. 'What?'

'Come quickly. There's something wrong with Mama Cass.'

In seconds, Coco was at Cassandra's side, holding her elbow. 'It's okay,' she said, to Madam Ovary. 'She just needs to sit.'

As quickly as it had risen, Cassandra's panic and nausea subsided. She slumped at the dressing-table and took up a tissue to dab at the sweat that was now ice cold on her forehead.

'Are you sick?' Coco asked. 'Do you wanna vomit?'

'No,' said Cassandra, breathing slowly. 'I'm not sick.'

'What is wrong, then?'

'I have to go home.'

'Wait for me. I go with you after the next song.'

Cassandra looked at Coco for a minute, not understanding, and then she said, 'No, I mean I have to go back to Ireland. To see my father.'

23. My Picture Clear

From her vantage point at the side of the stage, Dee could see a table full of women, clinking wine glasses and laughing, as if they didn't have a care in the world.

Maybe they didn't. Maybe their lives were like jigsaw puzzles with all the pieces slotted into place, each of their pictures a perfect whole.

'Oh, God,' said Leanne Ó Muireadhaigh, fidgeting beside her in a silk dress that showed far too much spray-tanned flesh for an afternoon event. 'Are you as nervous as I am?'

Dee nodded, with a strained smile. 'You'll be fine,' she said, wondering how a person who anchored her own television show could be so jittery over a bit of public speaking. She came across as ice cool every Tuesday evening on TV3, skewering politicians with questions they never seemed to see coming.

Usually, on occasions like this, Dee didn't feel nervous at all. In her years at Kylemore she'd had more than enough experience in debating teams to make her a confident public speaker, and whatever team she was on back then had run away with the debate. It was invaluable learning, really, as was so much of the education the Benedictine nuns had imparted, however austere it had been. Those debates had set her up for success in her business, given that so much of it was about selling a point of view.

But today she felt queasy at the thought of taking the microphone. Underneath her blouse a bead of sweat trickled from her armpit down the side of her left breast.

A hush descended in the room as the woman who co-ordinated the event, and had invited Dee to speak, walked out from the other side of the stage. She wore a rose-pink woollen suit that was too small for her, its jacket trussing her chest so that she resembled a stuffed turkey.

She tapped the microphone to check that it was working and then, with a little cough, began, 'Welcome to the fourth annual *Gloss* magazine lunch for successful women in business. It's so exciting to see such a number of intelligent, powerful, self-confident women here. This is, I believe, a gathering of the feminine brains and brawn that will be at the cornerstone of Ireland's emergence from recession, the women who will shape this country's prosperous future.

'We have a host of hugely inspiring speakers and great entertainment lined up for you, but first I want to introduce our host for the afternoon. She first came to prominence on Today FM, where she co-presented the weekend talk show, *Hot Gossip* ...'

'This is me,' Leanne said, batting her telly-box eyes at Dee and biting her lip. 'Wish me luck.'

Dee held up her hand and crossed her fingers. 'Good luck,' she said.

As Leanne tottered out on to the stage towards the podium, Dee wondered if she'd manage to make the same journey herself without stopping halfway and doubling up. The pain in her ribs was so excruciating, she found it nearly impossible to walk straight. She was just about managing to cover for herself at work by spending most of the day sitting at her desk, sending Connie to do anything for her that might involve the slightest movement.

Of course, the morning after he had kicked her at the kitchen sink, Joe had sat on the end of the bed, ashen-faced and swollen-eyed, and begged for forgiveness.

'I don't know what's wrong with me,' he had told her, and his eyes had seemed so big and vulnerable and frightened that Dee had found herself wanting to take him into her arms.

She'd resisted the urge for about five minutes.

Now, on the stage, Leanne Ó Muireadhaigh had begun her gushing introduction for Dee.

'We need women in this country like Dee Dimare,' she was saying. 'She's an example of true female strength in a male-dominated world, a powerful woman who has created a thriving business at the forefront of the Irish media industry, without compromising herself or her principles.'

They were only words. *Strength. Powerful. Principles.* They didn't mean anything. The speech Dee had prepared for today was a pack of lies.

She had promised to leave Joe if he ever hit her again, but she couldn't. She was weakened by love, lost to herself. Her outer shell presented a woman in control of her own life, but inside that person had vanished. All memory and trace of the girl who had left Kylemore Abbey at seventeen, determined to make her own way in the world without depending on anybody other than herself, had been erased.

When Joe had said, 'I don't know what's wrong with me', the same sentiment had echoed inside Dee. How had she become this person?

The truth was, they both needed help.

'Ladies, please put your hands together for Dee Dimare!' Leanne exclaimed.

As Dee picked her way carefully towards the podium, amid tumultuous cheers and applause, a little light bulb went on in her head.

They *both* needed help.

What part did she have to play in the violence of their marriage? Joe was a good man. She knew that was the bigger part of him. The side that was filled with rage was only a tiny bit of who he was, and God only knew where it had come from.

If they could get Joe's good side to face his dark side, the good side might win out. If they could find out why Dee allowed him to treat her the way he did, maybe she'd never allow him to hit her again.

Tonight she'd put it to Joe. She'd tell him that the only hope for their future together was if they went to a counsellor. She didn't think he'd disagree.

At the tables surrounded by the leading women of Ireland, the applause died down. Taking the microphone in one hand, Dee cleared her throat.

24. Hope for Tomorrow

Waiting for chemotherapy was surprisingly like waiting for afternoon tea in a genteel hotel. Maggie had expected the room to be a mix of sterility and desperation, but instead it was decorated with primrose curtains and mismatched sofas, and full of the low hum of casual chatter. She was surprised, too, by the variety of people there. Seemingly anyone could get cancer, from geeky guys in their twenties to blue-rinsed old ladies.

Beside her, Oona kept glancing at the exit. Maggie was beginning to regret asking her to come along. Her twittering and fretting were doing neither of them any good.

'If you want to go out for a walk or something to pass the time, I'll be fine here,' she said. A pile of outdated magazines on a dark mahogany coffee table beckoned her, topped by an issue of *Hello!*, with William and Kate on the cover. Maggie wished she could pick it up and escape into the world of celebrity royalty rather than think about what was imminent. Not the chemo itself, but the sickness afterwards.

'No, I'll stay,' said Oona, like she was making a resolution. She reached over and gave Maggie's hand a brief squeeze, and Maggie was seized with the peculiar self-reproach she always felt when her sister was being kind. Usually Oona was the needy one, a role she had played in their family from the moment they'd cut the cord. When

Oona was on the other side of the fence, being helpful instead of wanting help, Maggie felt undeserving.

She decided to read *Hello!* anyway. She leaned over to the coffee-table and plucked it from the pile. Underneath it there was a *Sunday Times Magazine* with Danny Lane's face staring out from the cover beneath the headline, 'Where Are They Now?'

Maggie threw *Hello!* aside and picked it up. The photograph reminded her of a Bob Dylan album cover that William had had in his collection when they were first married. It was black-and-white and had been taken in Daniel's heyday. He wasn't sporting the trademark pork-pie hat and blond quiff he had worn on *Top of the Pops*. Instead he was styled like a beatnik troubadour, in a black polo neck. The dark, silky curtain of fringe she remembered him having when she'd known him all those years ago hung a few millimetres above his poker-straight eyebrows. His face was pale, his eyes gazing into the camera in a way that made him seem to be looking at Maggie alone.

'Danny Lane,' Oona said, when Maggie returned to her seat with the magazine. 'God ... Do you remember him?'

Oona had been just ten years old that summer, slight and always sickly. Maggie had vague memories of her begging to come along with her and Dee, as the Abba fan club began to take up all their time, but she had done everything in her power to leave her behind. Oona was just a baby. An annoying, clingy baby, who never stopped whining and wanting to go home the minute she got to go anywhere.

After Daniel had been sent back to England, and everything had gone wrong, Oona had had no understanding of what was going on. Once, when Maggie was shut up in her bedroom, Oona had stood on the landing, crying. 'Why's the door locked?' she'd sobbed. 'Please come out.'

'Go away,' Maggie had shouted, and shoved her face into the pillow.

She didn't know if Oona remembered that. It was certainly the only semblance of a conversation they'd had about what happened, either then or now.

A nurse in a powder-blue uniform top and navy slacks came into the room with a clipboard. 'Mr Davies?' she said.

The boy in his twenties stood up. He was wearing a woolly bobbled hat, presumably to cover his bald head.

Oona leaned in to Maggie. 'He's so young,' she whispered. 'You know … to have it.'

Maggie nodded in agreement. But the boy was chatting amiably to the nurse as he followed her. He didn't seem in the least bit fazed.

Oona was staring into the mid-distance, ruminating. 'Chemo is like poison, isn't it?' she said. 'You know, to kill the … it.'

'Cancer, Oona,' Maggie snapped. 'It's not a dirty word.'

Oona welled up. 'Sorry.'

'I'm a bit freaked out, that's all,' Maggie relented, 'and I'm taking it out on you.'

'That's okay,' Oona said, wiping her eyes. 'I guess we're all a bit freaked out.'

Maggie flicked open the magazine to find the article about Daniel. There was a paparazzo picture with it, taken from far away with a telephoto lens, of him unlocking his bike from a railing on some street. He was wearing a purple bicycle helmet.

Even after all these years, and all the times his photograph had been in the paper, it was still a shock to see him.

'When are you going to tell Mum and Dad?' Oona asked, out of the blue.

'In my own good time,' Maggie replied, licking a finger and turning to the next page, which was dotted with pictures of other pop groups from the late eighties.

'I don't know why you won't let me say anything,' Oona said. 'I was on the phone to Mum last night and I felt terrible. She hasn't a clue.'

'Please, Oona, leave it for now, will you?' Maggie asked, not moving her eyes from the magazine. The last thing she wanted to think or talk about now was her mother.

'But it's not fair, Maggie. Mum and Dad should know.'

It had definitely been a mistake to ask Oona to come. The first choice had been William, but something about his reaction on the night she'd told them all had put her off. After Maggie had come back downstairs, Rita had hijacked the event with a raft of alternative-therapy suggestions and a speech about positive thinking that sounded like something out of *Dr Quinn, Medicine Woman*. William had gaped at her in awe, as if she had indeed discovered the cure for cancer. Even if he had come alone, Maggie knew she would have been getting William plus Rita on some level, and she couldn't have borne it.

Poppy had promised she'd come to the next chemo appointment. Orlando's parents had invited her to Lindsay Park for the first time, for an overnighter, which, according to him, signalled approval.

'Orlando's so happy about it,' she'd said. 'I *have* to go. You understand, don't you?'

Maggie assured her she did. She was glad at least that Poppy had stopped hysterically begging her not to die.

Harry had cried too, his chin mottling on Skype, which was hard to watch. She had wanted to reach into the computer screen and cuddle him, the way she used to when he was a little boy.

'I'm coming home, Mum,' he'd insisted, but Maggie told him she wouldn't hear of it.

'It's too far,' she said, 'And we'll keep you posted. If I need you to come, I'll let you know, I promise.'

'I love you, Mum,' he'd said, before they hung up. The last time Maggie had heard him so forlorn was when he had been saying goodbye to her before his first trip with the Scouts. He must have been nine at the time, during that phase when he was always telling her he wanted to stay with her for ever when he grew up.

'Mrs Corcoran?' The nurse was standing in the doorway to the waiting room, her clipboard in hand.

Maggie stood and so did Oona. She grabbed Maggie's wrist and looked at her as if they were both about to walk the green mile.

'You know what?' Maggie said to her. 'I'd love a newspaper. Could you go to the shop in the foyer and get one?'

Oona didn't hide her relief. 'I'll get you a chocolate bar too,' she said, forgetting that the doctor had advised Maggie to fast for a few hours both before and after the chemo.

The chairs in the treatment room were like something out of a spaceship, huge green-vinyl-cushioned things that you had to get into rather than sit on. The boy in his twenties was lying back in his, opposite Maggie's, hooked up to a chemotherapy drip, his eyes closed. His chalky face and head looked infant-like, without eyebrows or even a hint of stubble, and his spindly legs under his hospital gown were hairless too. She wondered what kind of cancer he had and what stage it was at.

He opened one eye and caught her staring at him. 'All right?' he asked, giving her a half-smile.

'Yes,' Maggie replied brightly, and then relented. 'No.'

The boy nodded. 'None of us is in here.'

'This is Stuart,' said the nurse, arriving beside Maggie's chair. She started prepping Maggie's arm for the drip. 'He's on his fifth visit to us, aren't you, Stuart?'

'Fifth time lucky,' said Stuart, with a wink that looked jaded.

He and the nurse were about the same age. In fact, they could have passed for brother and sister if Stuart had had hair.

'Are you okay with needles?' the nurse asked, and Maggie nodded. She shut her eyes as it entered her vein, biting her inner lip at the sting. When she opened them, the drip was attached.

She pictured the brownish liquid in the tube going into her bloodstream as an army of ants, marching through her veins to start hauling away the cancer cells. The thought was creepy and comforting at the same time.

Stuart was smiling at her. 'This your first time?' he asked.

'Is it that obvious?' Maggie smiled back.

'Yeah, you look a bit weirded out.' His lip, she noticed, was pierced with a gold ring almost as thin as a strand of hair. She wanted him to tell her it was going to be okay, this kid with a ring in his lip, but instead he closed his eyes and seemed to drift off. She shut her own eyes but was immediately assailed with an image of ants crawling through her veins so she blinked them open again.

The nurse was still at her side. 'It's okay,' she said, putting her hand on Maggie's arm. 'The first time is the scariest, but you'll be fine. I'll be back in twenty minutes to see how you're getting on.'

Oona walked into the room. 'You're not going to believe this,' she said, clutching the *Mirror* under her oxter. 'It's all over the papers.'

Maggie sighed. 'What is?' she asked.

'Abba are getting back together.'

Maggie's jaw almost hit her chest. For a second it felt like the world had stopped turning. 'What?' She grabbed the paper Oona was holding out.

The headline shouted, 'Abbatastic!', and underneath it in bold type Maggie read, 'Swedish supergroup announce reunion concert'.

She read on, still hardly believing her eyes.

Abba were re-forming for one concert only, in Stockholm on 30 July. All proceeds of the concert would go to the children's charity Unicef, and tickets would go on sale on 1 May.

Agnetha, from the Facebook group, had been right all along. Was she actually the real Agnetha?

Maggie glanced over at the *Sunday Times Magazine* cover, featuring Daniel, sitting on the table beside her chair.

The coincidence was too much. It was a sign.

They had promised each other, as they'd rowed home from the island all those years ago, Dee, Charlie, Daniel and her, that if Abba re-formed they would go to the concert together.

She looked across the room at Stuart who was gently snoring as the chemo went into his body, trying to save him. He was just a boy. He had everything to live for.

And so did she.

August 1983
Our Last Summer

Little waves are licking the side of the boat. Every so often a fish leaps in the water, a silvery back glinting in the pale morning light.

Pike. Daniel's grandmother says the lake is full of them. No good for eating. No point in catching them.

He has a fleeting memory of fishing for pike on the shores of this lake with his father when he was just little. Now it seems hard to believe it ever happened.

'If your life was an Abba song, what would it be?' Maggie asks. She's smoking a cigarette and blowing rings, even though she claims to have had her first only last night.

Daniel has never met a girl quite like Maggie before. He didn't fancy her at all when he first met her, with her shock of orange hair and her freckles and her legs that look too long for her body, but gradually he's found himself hanging on to her every word. She's a ball of energy, always in forward motion, always making the next plan and a plan after that.

Except last night.

After he had come, with his hands pressed into the ground beside her shoulders, his face squeezed tight with the most exquisite pleasure he had ever experienced, she went perfectly still, her breathing shallow, her green eyes wide and staring silently up into his. And then, like some sort of kid who'd fallen and cut his knee, he'd found himself bawling.

He thinks he has an Abba song now, even though he doesn't like Abba. He only responded to the ad for the fan club on the supermarket noticeboard out of sheer desperation to meet other people his own age.

Daniel loves his granny, but she's hardly the company he's used to keeping, and he's found himself unable to make friends with any of the boys who live nearby. They're all the sons of farmers, smelling of sweat and silage, and they look at him with naked suspicion.

'You're a Brit,' one had announced the first week he was there, his voice loaded with something Daniel couldn't identify.

'Yes,' Daniel had replied, and that had been the sum total of the exchange. The boy has ignored him ever since.

Daniel had come across the ad for the Abba fan club one day when his grandmother had driven him into town with her for the monthly supplies. When he'd mentioned that he'd like to join the club, she'd said he could use her bicycle to get in and out of Sligo. He could help her on the farm in the mornings and go off about his business in the afternoons, if that was what he wanted.

'I like Abba,' she'd said, peeling a potato. 'They sing proper songs. Not like some of the shite you hear on the radio nowadays.'

That's the thing about Abba. Old people like them. Girls like Maggie and Dee, who are – let's face it – hardly cool, like them. Charlie likes them, although Daniel can't figure out why. He can hardly figure Charlie out at all. He certainly isn't like any of Daniel's friends back in Hove. Charlie plays football – Maggie told Daniel he and his brother are the best players in the school they go to – but he never wants to talk about it and claims not to follow a team. When Daniel tries to pursue other topics, like how Hendrix played the guitar or Dylan wrote lyrics, or even albums by Duran Duran and Spandau Ballet, Charlie doesn't engage. He's like an outline in a colouring book that hasn't been filled in.

From the corner of his vision, Daniel can see a leaf stuck in the thicket of Maggie's hair. It makes him smile and he turns to catch her eye.

'What do you think your parents will say?' he asks.

He'd met Maggie's mother and father for the first time last week. Her dad's a policeman, big-chested and intimidating, his hair shorn tight into his brick-like head. Her mother is about a third the size of him and has little brown eyes, like a mouse's. They'd travelled up and down Daniel, from foot to forehead and back again, before she'd started asking him a hundred questions about himself, making him uncomfortable, clucking around him when he couldn't find a way out of telling her about his mum and what had happened.

She'd called him a 'poor motherless boy' yesterday, when he'd arrived to collect Maggie, which made Maggie throw her eyes to Heaven.

Maggie calls her mum 'Mother Superior' and rolls her eyes at just about everything she says. She'd clicked her heels together and saluted her when she'd said she expected Maggie home at nine on the dot last night, and no later.

Mother Superior hadn't a clue about the stolen wine and Maggie's big plan to go to the island.

'I don't give a fuck,' Maggie says, and Daniel laughs, feeling a thrill of illicit joy run through his veins. She has the power to make him feel all sorts of things he's never felt before.

Last night, when he'd started crying, she'd put her arms around him and said, 'Sssh', rocking him back and forth. He'd been full of gratitude to her. When his tears were finished, he'd felt something like happiness, which he'd thought he never would again.

The day after the funeral, his father had gone to bed and didn't get up for nearly a month. 'It's like that when somebody we love is taken away suddenly,' his granny had told him – she had come over from Ireland to stay for a while. 'Your dad has to grieve now. But it will pass as all things must.'

His father had got up eventually and gone back to work and life had gone on, but the grief didn't pass. At night Daniel could hear him crying through the walls of the house; after work he locked himself away in his study. The odd time they found themselves in a room together, his father didn't even look in Daniel's direction. It was as if he couldn't bring himself to.

On the first anniversary of the accident, Granny came back to stay for a few weeks. When her visit was over, she said to his father that she was taking Daniel back to Ireland for the summer. That it would be better for him there.

Daniel hadn't objected. Neither had his father.

'Look,' Maggie said last night, after he'd stopped crying. She'd pulled away from Daniel, pointing to the sky. 'There's only one star.' He'd dried his cheeks with the back of his hands and looked up. The star was so bright that it was perfectly reflected in the blackness of the lake beneath it.

Beside him, Maggie began to sing the Abba song about the air that night and the stars so bright, and three words had popped into Daniel's head, shining as neon clear as the lone star.

I love you.

He'd wanted to say it out loud, to shout it! But then he couldn't because he was seized by fear, and he wasn't quite sure what he was afraid of.

Maybe of losing her too.

On the boat beside him now, Maggie says, 'So, what's yours?'

'My what?'

'You *know*. If your life was an Abba song …'

Daniel reaches out and links his little finger with hers. 'I'm still thinking,' he says.

Out on the water another fish leaps. The sun has fully risen and is illuminating Maggie's hair from behind, surrounding her head in a halo of orange.

Daniel knows he will love her for ever.

Part Two
VOULEZ VOUS

25. Resistance Running Low

For the first thirty-six hours after the chemo, Maggie felt as if she was surrounded by static, cut off from the world in a place far away, a realm of cold sweat and shivers followed by heat so white she couldn't remain still. The only time she felt fully engaged was when she was leaning over the side of her mattress to vomit into the basin Oona brought up from the kitchen and took away every so often.

When Oona went to work, William and Poppy arrived, without Rita in tow, thank God. They sat on either side of the bed, making stabs at conversation. William told some story about a guy in a rival bank who'd been caught embezzling, and Poppy described the grandeur of Lindsay House and how down-to-earth Orlando's parents were.

Maggie couldn't contribute to the conversation and guiltily wished they'd both leave. All she wanted to do was black out.

She didn't like throwing up in front of Poppy either. The first time it had happened, after she'd retched hard into the basin and brought up a torrent of watery vomit, she'd lifted her sweat-soaked head and caught Poppy staring at her in naked horror. 'It's all right, honey,' Maggie had said. 'It'll pass.'

Poppy hadn't replied. She'd stood up and walked out of the room.

'Don't worry about her,' said William. 'She'll be fine.' But he had the same terrified look, and he fumbled before handing her a towel.

Maggie asked him to take the basin and dump its contents down the toilet in the en suite. When he was gone, she reached achingly out and stroked Benny's head. He'd taken up position on the pillow beside her from the moment she'd crawled into bed, and hadn't moved.

'You don't mind all this, do you?' she said. Her throat felt as if it had been sandpapered and the inside of her mouth was sore. Benny, stretching his head into the cup of her hand, gave a wide yawn and closed his one eye. Maggie lay back on the pillow and let her eyes close too.

She woke again, with a start, in the dead of night, thinking it was time to get up for work. Then a fresh wave of nausea rushed from her stomach and she leaned out of the bed to vomit again, but only dry-retched.

There was nothing to bring up. There was no work to go to. It would be at least five months before she could return to the library, the doctor had said. After three, Maggie's pay would be halved, according to the sick-leave terms of her contract. On the phone, Alison said, 'If there's anything I can do, just ask,' when Maggie had told her about the cancer. But she didn't offer to call over.

On the third day, Rita had turned up in Maggie's bedroom, like an apparition, in a tie-dyed sari. 'William gave me the keys,' she said. 'He's got back-to-back meetings today.'

'There was no need for you to come,' Maggie protested. 'I'm fine, honestly.'

'I won't stay long,' Rita replied, but she'd spent the whole afternoon sitting by the bed, knitting what looked like a scarf for a giraffe and occasionally getting up to make Maggie lemon and aniseed tea, which she said was the best cure for nausea, but tasted sickeningly like liquorice and was impossible to keep down.

At least Rita didn't talk much, which was a blessed relief, and the click-clack of her needles was kind of relaxing, reminding Maggie of her mother knitting as the family watched TV when she was a girl.

She had knitted as if her life depended on it, her mother, and Maggie and Oona had been the models to show off her handiwork to all and sundry. There were photographs of them at four and two, pudgy and red-cheeked in matching canary yellow jumpers, bobbled hats, scarves and mittens. Maggie had a vague memory of the jumper, with its little daisies embroidered around the neckline. Her mother had loved those little touches, robin redbreasts on the pocket of a knitted Christmas pinafore, Easter chicks on the sleeve of a baby blue cardigan. By the time she was eight, Maggie had grown to loathe and detest the knitwear with its stupid embellishments as much as her mother insisted on her wearing it to show it off. It grew into a constant battle of wills between them.

'I'm telling Mum,' Oona had said yesterday, after Maggie had been throwing up for what seemed like an hour. It had been her childhood refrain whenever she got wind that Maggie was doing anything she shouldn't – 'I'm telling.'

'Please don't,' Maggie had replied, barely able to find her voice. 'I'll call her at the weekend.'

Even though this was a lie, she knew she couldn't get away without speaking to her parents for much longer. William had offered to do it for her yesterday, and Poppy had wanted to know how 'Granny and Gramps' were taking it.

The truth was that if Maggie could have got away without ever telling them, she would. Although her father would take the news sitting down in his favourite chair by the fire, as silently unforgiving as ever, she knew the minute her mother heard, she'd be on the next plane to London, brooking no protest. She'd insist on taking care of Maggie's every need, and she'd do it within an inch of her life. To the outside eye, she would seem the perfect mother.

She came across as holier than Mother Teresa, and a better mother than the Divine Mother of Jesus herself, but it was all as fake as a rip-off Fendi bag. After a little wear and tear, the seams frayed and the true quality of the goods showed through. The contents started spilling out of its murky depths, and they made a horrible mess.

That mess was the last thing Maggie needed right now.

She fell asleep with the click-clack of Rita's knitting needles still in her ear, and when she woke up it was the next morning and she was alone, apart from Benny, who was still sleeping on the pillow beside her, his back rising and falling in a slow rhythm. She reached out to cuddle up to him and realised that she felt vaguely like her old self again. The queasiness was gone.

She sat up and took two pills from the packet on the bedside table, swallowing them with the glass of water Rita had left there. Steroids prescribed by Dr Snow to help with the side-effects.

Lying down again, she contemplated staying under the duvet all day, snuggling up to Benny, but after another little snooze she woke up fully, her legs restless and moving about of their own accord. Staying in bed would be too much like giving in, she thought. What had Dr Snow said about positive thinking being a big part of the process? She decided that from here on, unless it was absolutely impossible to get up, she wasn't going to spend her days languishing in bed. She was going to get on with her life, and she had plenty to do. Like finding Daniel and Charlie. And calling Dee. And figuring out how she was going to be at the top of the queue for four Abba tickets, come 1 May.

In the kitchen she opened a carton of Sheba and Benny miaowed with such high-pitched relief that Maggie wondered if anyone had bothered to feed him while she had been incapacitated.

'Poor baby,' she sympathised, emptying a portion of Tender Terrine with Duck and Goose into his bowl as he pushed past her hand to get at it. Its gamey smell, which usually she found slightly revolting, made her realise that she was ravenous.

She made herself breakfast of bacon, eggs, toast and coffee and wolfed it down at the kitchen table, wondering if her sudden blast of energy was connected to the steroids. She texted Oona, William and Poppy the same message: *Fine today. No need to come over. xx*

It was ironic. Before she'd got cancer, she'd wanted William and Poppy back home more than anything. But the other day they'd seemed a burden, and now the idea of them was too distracting.

The article in the *Sunday Times Magazine* had traced Daniel to a house in Hampstead. It hadn't given an address, but finding it would be easy. All Maggie had to do was look at the voting register, which should be on-line.

But first she decided to call Dee.

She was disappointed to get through to her voicemail. She'd wanted to hear the excitement in her old friend's voice when she'd revealed the big plan.

'You're through to Dee Dimare at Reddy Communications,' Dee's voicemail message said, in clipped, businesslike tones. 'I'm sorry I can't take your call now, but if you leave your name and number, I'll get back to you as soon as possible. Thank you for calling.'

'Dee,' said Maggie, clearing her throat. 'It's me, Maggie. Long time no talk … I guess you've heard the big news about Abba. Can you call me back when you get this?'

After stacking her breakfast dishes in the dishwasher, she went back upstairs and changed the sheets and duvet cover, feeling more energetic than she had in weeks. Then she went back to the kitchen, sat at the table and flipped open her laptop.

'There are no free results for Daniel Smith,' the electoral register website told her, so she paid the fee of ten pounds with her Paypal account. And there it was, his address: Flat 1, 14 Collin Gardens, NW3 2PL.

In all the years she'd toyed with the idea of contacting him, she'd never imagined he'd be so easily found.

26. Tumbling Down

The counsellor reminded Dee of the therapist in *The Sopranos*. Not to look at, but in the way she sat quietly, gazing at Dee, as if she knew everything about the inner recesses of her psyche without being told a word. Her office, too, was like the therapist's in *The Sopranos*, book-lined and oddly masculine, with brown-leather-upholstered armchairs and the scent of a sandalwood candle pervading the air.

Dee gave an apologetic smile and said, 'I don't know what's happened to Joe. He said he'd be here at noon.'

'Maybe he's stuck in traffic,' the counsellor replied, in her calm, even voice, but her expression was saying, 'Maybe he's decided not to come.'

Dee took out her phone to check if Joe had texted. She'd put it on silent on entering the counsellor's office, cursing him for not getting back to her voicemail.

There were two texts in her inbox, but both were from Connie, one looking for confirmation of this afternoon's meeting with the general manager of Copper Alley restaurants and the other asking if she wanted her to pick anything up for lunch. The one missed call in her 'Recents' folder was from Maggie, who had rung several times since leaving her first voicemail about the Abba reunion.

Dee kept meaning to call her back. She hadn't talked to Maggie since her and Joe's wedding, which now seemed like a lifetime ago.

She and Maggie had been thick as thieves as kids, but something had happened after the summer of the Abba fan club that Dee had never been able to put her finger on. Maggie had all but disappeared. There were no more letters from her in the girls' posthole in the hallway at Kylemore, and when Dee got home for a weekend, she couldn't persuade Maggie to step beyond the threshold of her parents' house, never mind get invited in.

There had been some efforts to rekindle the friendship in later years. After Maggie had married William and moved to London to set up her little nuclear family, she'd invited Dee to visit. It had been a weirdly uncomfortable weekend, full of disjointed conversations, Maggie trying too hard and then not at all. Dee remembered lying alone in the divan in the box room, listening to the muffled sounds of Maggie and William talking through the wall in their own double bed and having the distinct impression they were bitching about her.

'Would you like to wait until your husband arrives?' the counsellor asked, her manicured hands spread on the leather arms of her chair. 'Or would you like to tell me why you're here, from your point of view, to get us started?'

Dee looked up from her phone. 'I'm not sure,' she said. 'I don't think it would feel right without him.'

'I understand,' said the counsellor. 'But I'm curious. Why wouldn't it feel right?'

'Because ...' Dee began, and stopped. The counsellor had introduced herself as Martha and welcomed Dee into her office as if she was greeting an old friend, having spoken to her only briefly on the phone to arrange this appointment. It had been way too familiar. 'Because,' she went on, 'we arranged to come to see you together. My husband needs to be here to discuss the problem we have.'

'Problem?' said Martha, with a small smile. 'Most of us have them in the plural.'

Dee returned her smile and the room descended into silence again. Somewhere amid its books and sombre paintings of cloudy landscapes, a clock was ticking loudly, but she couldn't locate it. Her stomach rumbled, the aftermath of Connie's stomach bug, which had taken the office by storm and was lingering far longer than it should.

They sat saying nothing for a good three or four minutes. Then Martha uncrossed her legs and, taking a leather-bound diary from the desk beside her chair, said, 'Maybe we should leave this for another day. Let me see what I have available next week.'

'No!' Dee said, louder than she had intended. 'I mean, couldn't we wait for him a little longer? I'll pay you for your time.'

Martha crossed her legs again and interlaced her fingers in front of her chin. 'Since you're paying me for my time, maybe you'd like to use it.'

'Yes,' said Dee, even though she felt very uncomfortable.

'Maybe you could start by telling me how long you and your husband have been married.'

'A year,' Dee replied. 'It was a bit of a whirlwind romance.'

'So you had only known each other a short time before you married.'

'Yes. We got married six months after we met. Although ...'

'Go on.'

'Well, it seemed like we'd known each other for a long time the minute we met. We're very alike, Joe and I.'

'That's good,' said Martha, before lapsing into silence again. Then, she added, 'Of course, when people marry very quickly, it can sometimes be a shock to the system.'

'Oh, no,' said Dee. 'We settled in with each other right from the start. We get on brilliantly.'

Martha nodded. 'So why have you come to see me?' she asked.

Dee squirmed in her seat. This morning, as she and Joe had left the house, he had promised he'd be there – he'd even said he was looking forward to it.

In her bag, her phone bleeped. Hoping it was a text from him, she pulled it out and slid the unlock button. But it was another message from Connie. The Copper Alley people wanted to bring their meeting time forward to two o'clock.

'Maybe it would be a good idea to turn your phone off for now,' Martha said.

Dee threw it back into her handbag. 'Perhaps you're right,' she said. 'We should make an appointment for another day.'

'Of course.' Martha reached for her diary. 'I think I have a space free next Wednesday at the same time.'

She was flicking through the pages when Dee's stomach cramped. The pain was like a lightning strike, so forceful that she bent over and gasped, holding on to the arm of the chair she had just vacated.

Martha glanced up. 'Are you all right?' she asked.

'Yes,' Dee managed. 'Just give me a minute.'

'I'll get you a drink of water,' said Martha, crossing the room to a cooler beside the bookshelves. 'Please. Sit down.'

As Dee lowered herself back into the seat, the pain subsided a little, leaving in its wake a wave of dizzying nausea. 'It's just this stomach bug I have,' she said, taking the glass of water from Martha with a shaky hand. 'I can't seem to shift it.'

'Maybe you should see a doctor,' said Martha, standing over her. 'You don't look well at all.'

'I'm fine, honestly,' Dee said. The last thing she wanted was a doctor examining her, asking where the bruises had come from.

She couldn't wait to get out. Down the stairs and on to the street so she could breathe in some fresh air. She stood up once more, willing herself to calm down, but then another lightning pain shot through her stomach and she doubled over again. She was going to have to get to a toilet. Quickly.

And then a warm wet substance rolled down her inner thigh.

Across the room Martha was lifting the phone on her desk and dialling.

'Oh, God,' Dee heard herself say out loud. 'What's wrong with me?'

27. Somewhere in the Crowd

'Danny, my boy!'

The instantly recognisable voice made Daniel's entire body stiffen. He concentrated on locking his bike to buy himself some time.

'Fancy bumping into you,' said Vince, his arms outstretched as if he was beckoning Daniel into an embrace.

Daniel took off his helmet. 'Hey, Vince,' he said, wishing he'd picked any other lamppost to fasten his bicycle to. He should have known better. The Vince David Productions offices were literally around the corner.

In the flesh Vince looked older than he did on TV. He'd aged, but in the way that Sean Connery had aged. His face had got craggy, but somehow he seemed smoother at the same time. As always, he was dressed in white. White shirt, white jacket, white trousers, white shoes, and those infernal tinted glasses through which you couldn't see his eyes properly.

He clapped Daniel on the back. 'It's good to see you again, Danny boy!'

Daniel refrained from correcting his old manager. Throughout their time together, Vince had refused to call him anything other than the stage name he had created. It had been coined at their first meeting, in a narrow attic office on the top floor of a building on New Bond Street over a hairdresser's.

'Daniel Smith is a bit common-or-garden,' Vince had said. 'We need something cheerier. Something cheekier. Something that will make the girls remember you.'

Daniel couldn't recall exactly how they had come up with Danny Lane. He'd been a bit bamboozled by the meeting, not knowing quite what to think of Vince David, with his Cockney barrow-boy swing and his nut-brown tan – talking about the big-time, like Daniel had just hit it, even though less than twenty-four hours previously he'd been busking at Oxford Circus to make enough money to eat that day.

That was where Vince had spotted him. He'd stood silently watching Daniel belt out The Beatles' 'Strawberry Fields Forever', while Saturday shopping crowds milled by. When Daniel had finished the song, Vince had handed him a card. 'Come and see me tomorrow,' he'd said. 'I think you've got real talent.'

Eighteen months later, Daniel was number one on three continents, Vince had a whole stable of acts climbing up the UK charts, and the headquarters of Vince David Productions had moved across the road to another building on New Bond Street, taking up all four floors.

'Fancy a cuppa?' Vince asked now, pointing to the café on the corner. 'Or something stronger, maybe? I've a nice single malt in my office.'

'Sorry,' Daniel said, shrugging. 'I'm kind of in a hurry.' The truth was he had a good hour to kill before his meeting with Maya.

'Well, I'm glad I ran into you,' said Vince. 'I wanted to talk to you about something.'

Daniel looked at his watch. 'Can it wait for another time?' he said. 'I've got to go.'

'I had a call from the people at *I'm A Celebrity, Get Me Out of Here*. They want to know if you're interested in going to the jungle. I said I'd ask you.'

Daniel shuddered. 'Tell them I'd rather stick needles in my eyes,' he said.

'You're a funny man,' Vince said. 'A laugh a minute.'

'I'm deadly serious, Vince.'

'Plenty of people would give their right arm for the opportunity, you know.'

'Look, Vince,' said Daniel, itching to get away, 'I'm in a hurry.'

'So you said, son. So you said. But, listen, give it a bit of thought, will you? As I said, it's a great opportunity.'

Daniel was about to turn away but then he stopped. 'A great opportunity for who?' he asked.

'What do you mean?'

'I mean, what's in it for you, Vince?'

'I just want to see you get back out there. You were born to do it, you know.'

Daniel shook his head slowly, looking his old manager in the eye. 'We both know that's not true,' he said.

Vince had been the one to talk him down from the first panic attack. It had happened as he'd made his way through hordes of fenced-off fans on his way to do the sound check for a gig at Wembley, the first of a sold-out three-night run after the American tour in 1988. Daniel could still remember the girl. The flash of the braces on her teeth, the baby-blue anorak she always had on, with the fur-fringed hood. She seemed to know what his every move would be before he made it. She was always there, waiting quietly outside whatever hotel he was staying in. She never came up to him and never said a word, until that afternoon.

He had been running the gauntlet to the stage door, surrounded by a pandemonium of screams and a million fingers clawing at him through the fencing, when he saw her standing at the end of the line. She was calling his real name – not Danny, but Daniel – holding her arms towards him, tears and snot running down her ruddy-cheeked face.

'Daniel!' she'd cried, as he came near, her voice high-pitched. 'I love you!'

The world had stopped turning on its axis. The screaming had muffled out until Daniel could hear only the dull thud of his own heartbeat. He had been overwhelmed with the sensation that he was leaving his body and spinning away into space, the ground whooshing away from him. I'm dying, he'd thought, and then, with a sickening rush, he'd hurtled back into himself.

'I love you!' he'd heard the girl call again and realised he was lying on the ground, his face against tarmac. He'd looked up at her. The sun was high in the sky behind her illuminating the outline of her hair, so it was a bright orange halo.

'What?' he'd said, and then everything had gone black.

Vince had shouldered him on to the stage that night, where he somehow found the wherewithal to perform for thirty thousand teenage girls, all screaming for him so the music he made was almost drowned out.

On stage you couldn't see the crowd: they were just a sea of darkness, a wave of sound. At the beginning he had pretended to himself that he loved it, because it was amazing and special, and so few people got to be the one at the centre, universally adored. But the truth was that from day one it had scared him to the core. Although he was the one supposed to be in control, the entertainer pulling the strings, he had felt as if he was being swept up in chaos. He'd hated it.

After the third night at Wembley, he had known it was over. He just had to find a way to end it.

On the street a convertible car with its top down began honking. A guy crossing in front of it, wearing a sharp grey suit and carrying a briefcase, shouted, 'Fuck you, arsehole!'

The car sped off, a blast of Abba's 'Gimme Gimme Gimme' perforating the air as it passed. Since the reunion announcement their songs were everywhere again. They kept bringing back fleeting memories of Maggie.

'Danny,' said Vince. 'You're a talented man and you only get a comeback window like this once in a lifetime. You should be recording.'

'I'll think about it, Vince,' Daniel said, to humour him.

'If you change your mind while you can still make hay, you know where I am.'

As Daniel watched him walk away, the heavens suddenly opened, and heavy drops of rain began to fall.

28. An Image Passing By

Cassandra didn't know if she was imagining it or not but the Customs man seemed to be giving her suspicious looks. He'd beckoned her over as she walked through the 'Nothing to Declare' aisle, looking officially puffed-up in his navy blue uniform, and asked her to open her case. Cassandra had smiled at him, but he hadn't smiled back.

It didn't feel like a random check. In Playa del Inglés she never worried about passing, just went about her business without a thought, but since she'd landed in Dublin it was as if she'd reverted back to the time when she was waiting for her final operation and was so paranoid about being rumbled on the streets she'd barely left her apartment, except to buy food. And then she'd worn a big woolly hat and outsize sunglasses to shield her from curious eyes, no matter what the weather was like.

Once, in the very early days of hormone injections and makeup experimentation, before she'd grown her hair and could afford only a less-than-convincing wig, she'd been surrounded by a gang of boys at a bus stop, who'd jeered at her, yelling, 'Tranny,' in her face and pushing her to the ground, then run away, aping each other's hoots of laughter. She'd believed she was in real danger, that they were going to beat her senseless or, worse, kill her. Looking back, of course, they were only a bunch of stupid teenagers, but at the time the threat had seemed real. Possibly because she had taken her life into her own hands by deciding to live every day as a woman.

That attack, or skirmish, or whatever you wanted to call it, had happened in Dublin. Maybe it had gone deeper than she'd supposed because now she understood why she thought people standing around the baggage carousel might be giving her sideways glances. Gran Canaria was a warm and safe cocoon; coming back to Ireland felt like exposure to the elements.

Her bag, lying open on the bench, looked exposed too, its perfectly innocent contents pieces of incriminating evidence. The underwear she took pride in never scrimping on had become sleazy proof that she wasn't who she appeared to be.

'Did you pack this bag yourself, ma'am?' the Customs official asked, poking through her things with his blue latex-gloved hands. The way he said ma'am sounded emphasised.

'Yes,' Cassandra replied. She imagined her voice sounded like a lumberjack's.

The man looked up sharply. 'Are you here on business or holiday?' he asked.

'I've come home to see my family,' Cassandra replied. 'In Sligo.'

Now she was growing impatient with the petty bureaucracy. What sort of a job was it, feeling up other people's knickers and asking them pointless questions?

'Well, have a safe journey onwards,' the Customs man said, closing her bag. He smiled now, friendly and open. 'Welcome home.'

In the arrivals concourse she took her mobile out of her handbag, wondering how much it would cost to call Sam in Ireland. Was it the same tariff as if she was calling from Spain?

She'd tried him a couple of times before leaving, but his phone always rang out and there was no voicemail so she couldn't leave a message. She thought of texting, but it didn't seem right. After all this time, it was too casual just to drop a message that she was coming home. *Hey, brother, I haven't spoken to you in ten years, but do you mind if I stay with you for a week?*

Maybe he had a different phone now.

She scrolled through her contacts, found the number she had for him and called it again, her hand shaking.

'Sam Jones, how can I help you?' he answered immediately.

'Sam,' said Cassandra. The sound of his voice had sent a bolt to her stomach.

'That's me.'

'It's me. Cassandra.'

'Who?'

'Cassandra. Your sister.'

Silence echoed down the line. Then Sam said, 'What do you want?'

Cassandra swallowed and clenched the phone. 'I'm home,' she said. 'I'm calling from Dublin airport.'

Another silence. Then: 'You're not planning on coming here, are you?'

'Of course I am. That's why I'm calling. I was wondering if I could stay at yours for a bit.'

'Why?'

'Because I need a place to stay.'

'No, I mean, why are you back?'

'Because I want to see Dad.'

Sam didn't reply. Behind him, Cassandra could hear a man shouting something about 'next week's order'. 'John!' Sam called back. 'Will you take care of that?' He came back on the line. 'Listen, Charlie, or whatever you call yourself nowadays, don't come home. Dad doesn't want to see you.'

'Look, I just need to know if it's all right for me to stay with you for a few days.'

'No,' said Sam. 'I don't want my kids around you.'

Cassandra's throat caught. She hadn't seen his boys since they were toddlers. They were in their teens now.

'I'll leave you and your kids alone,' she said, refusing to cry, 'but I'm going to see Dad, and you can't stop me.'

Cassandra hung up and breathed slowly. All around her people were greeting new arrivals, their eyes lighting up with happy recognition, with love. Even the people holding cards with names written on them were waiting to welcome someone. There was no one for her.

As hard as it was to scale the blank wall of Sam's implacable anger, it was ten times worse with her father. He had loved her so much when she was his son, his little buddy, but had turned a cold, hard back on her when she'd become her own woman.

Maybe coming home hadn't been such a good idea after all. On the departures floor there were booths selling tickets for charter flights returning to Gran Canaria today. She could get on one and forget she had ever thought of home and reconciliation.

But what would she be going back to? The most important people in her life were here.

29. Take a Chance

Flat One was in a basement under three storeys at the end of a row of huge white-fronted houses that must have once belonged to well-to-do London families. Although the street was typical Hampstead, neatly trimmed and shiny as a new penny, number fourteen had a skip outside it, half full of rubble, and there were tufts of yellowing grass growing around the edges of the bank of steps that went up to the ornate entrance. Maggie pushed open the creaky wooden gate to the basement and made her way down the stairs to the flat's front door. As she descended she thought she detected a movement behind the net-curtained window that looked out on the steps.

There was no bell or knocker so she tapped on the door with the knuckle of her index finger twice and waited. There was no answer, so she knocked again, a little less tentatively this time.

'What do you want?' came a voice from behind the door, a woman's.

'I'm here to see Daniel Smith!' Maggie called.

There was a shuffling behind the door, the click and drag of a chain, and then it opened a crack.

'Who are you?' said the woman.

Maggie could just make out that she was dark, maybe Middle Eastern. 'I'm a friend.' She wondered if that was still true after all these years. 'An old friend.'

'That's what they all say,' said the woman. One of her eyes, Maggie noticed, was a slightly different shade from the other – it was the colour of golden syrup.

'Is he here?' Maggie asked.

'Why should I tell you?' said the woman. 'I ain't his personal assistant.'

It seemed like an odd thing to say and Maggie didn't know how to reply. The woman's face was wedged between the door and its frame, surveying her intently.

Then she understood. With Daniel's song all over the radio, there must have been reporters looking for him, or fans. She smiled at the woman, who didn't smile back. 'I'm not from the press or anything like that,' she said. 'I actually am an old friend, I can assure you.'

'Don't matter anyway,' the woman said. 'He don't live here no more.'

'Oh,' Maggie said, disappointed. 'When did he move out?'

'I don't know, do I? I ain't his personal assistant, I told you.'

'Do you know where he's gone? I need to find him. It's important.'

The woman cackled. 'You and a million others,' she said.

Without even knowing she was going to play the C-card, Maggie blurted, 'I have cancer, you see. I wanted to tell him ...' She stopped.

The woman's golden-syrup eye glinted in the basement's half-light, and then she pushed the door to take off its security chain. 'Come in, then,' she said, and turned to make her way back into the flat.

Inside it smelt of fried food. It was so murky that Maggie bumped into a chair as she followed. A black cat, which had been sitting on it, let out an enraged miaow and darted into the gloom.

'Sit down,' the woman said. As Maggie's eyes adjusted to the dim light, she saw that her hair was a frizzy mass of black and grey curls. She was wrapped from neck to foot in layers of coloured woollen garments, jumpers, cardigans, scarves, even a pair of legwarmers under her knee-length skirt. The flat was stifling and Maggie wondered how she could breathe.

'I'm Maggie,' she said, extending her hand. 'Maggie Corcoran. Although when Daniel knew me, I was Behan. Corcoran is my married name.'

The woman took this in without expression and didn't introduce herself in return. Instead she lowered her woollen-clad body into a large armchair beside a plug-in radiator and said, 'I had cancer too. Only nobody never called it cancer back then. They was all afraid of saying it.'

It was still true. Beyond Maggie's diagnosis, only she had uttered the word. Not the consultants, not the nurses, not the patients at the clinic. The illness that must not be named. 'Are you better now?' she asked the woman.

'Yeah. They zapped it with that chemotherapy and radiation. Only thing is I ain't been able to keep warm since. Don't matter what time of year it is.'

Maggie made a sympathetic sound. She was beginning to regret playing the C-card, if that was what she'd been invited in for – a nice chat about cancer.

The woman, fixing Maggie with her mismatched eyes, said, 'He moved out about a year ago. Gave me the place to stay in, rent free.'

'Where did he go?'

'Didn't say. Keeps himself to himself, that one. Don't tell nobody nothing.'

'Have you seen him since?'

'A couple of times. Came to collect his post. I got another pile for him there.' She pointed to a bundle of envelopes on a stool by the door.

Maggie had an idea. 'If I wrote him a note, would you give it to him next time he collects his post?'

The woman shrugged. 'All right.'

Maggie opened her handbag and took out a pen. 'Do you have a piece of paper I can write on?' she asked.

The woman leaned over and searched a shelf under the dark wood coffee table that stood between them. 'There,' she said, handing Maggie an empty brown envelope. 'You can write on the back of that.'

As she wrote, Maggie was acutely aware that the woman would read her note once she was gone. There was no way of sealing it.

Dear Daniel, I don't know if you'll remember me. I'm Maggie Behan. We knew each other for the summer in 1983, in Ireland. We were part of an Abba fan club together.

She stopped. There was no way he didn't remember. Nobody forgot the person they'd lost their virginity with. But she didn't know how to phrase it without sounding stupid, without giving the woman in wool too much information.

We all made a promise back then that if Abba ever re-formed we would go to one of their concerts together.

She stopped again and glanced at the woman, who was leaning in slightly, all agog. She continued writing.

As I'm sure you're aware, Abba are re-forming for one concert only in Stockholm. I have four tickets and, if you get this note, I would like you to consider coming along. It would be lovely to see you again after all these years.

Saying she was in possession of the tickets already might be an incentive, and despite what the papers had said yesterday about them being more precious than gold dust, she was going to lay her hands on four by hook or by crook.

She added her phone number and email address, and signed the note, '*xx, Maggie*', before folding it and handing it to the woman, who immediately opened it and started reading.

'You'll be sure to give it to him?' Maggie repeated, a few minutes later, as the woman held the front door open for her to leave. At that very moment she felt as if her life depended on it.

The woman gave a noncommittal shrug. 'Sure.'

30. Misconceiving

There was a strangely exposed privacy to the curtained-off cubicle. Voices milled about outside – a couple of female nurses discussing a holiday one had taken, a man ordering X-rays on a phone, a confused old woman in the cubicle next door asking an orderly, 'Where am I?' Yet for all the activity beyond the curtain that surrounded her gurney, Dee felt cut off.

'A miscarriage,' the doctor had told her. 'You were approximately six weeks pregnant.'

'Miscarriage'. It sounded like something out of a news report – a miscarriage of justice – not something to do with her body.

The painkillers they'd given her exacerbated the disconnection; there was nothing but a kind of fuzzy numbness in the lower half of her body. She pictured static on a television screen.

Dee didn't know whether she'd passed out in Martha's office or not. Her journey to the hospital was hazy too. She had vague impressions of a man smiling down at her, telling her to breathe.

She remembered giving Joe's number to a nurse who asked for her next of kin on her arrival at the hospital, remembered being prepped for an IV drip in the same cubicle she was lying in now, remembered being told by an Indian doctor that she was miscarrying, but beyond that there was another space of nothingness.

She looked down at her stomach, which had a hospital-green blanket tightly tucked over it, and tried to imagine that she had been pregnant. That there had been a baby growing inside her.

The cubicle curtain swished open and the same doctor who had told her about the miscarriage walked in, closing it behind him. 'Ah, Mrs Dimare,' he said. 'You're with us again.'

Dee pulled herself up on the gurney's raised back with her hands. 'Hello, Doctor,' she said. She hadn't a clue what his name was.

He picked up a chart from the end of her bed and looked through it, then examined the machine her arm was hooked up to, which had orange numbers and graphs in ever-changing motion on its various screens.

'We'd like to keep you in tonight, for observation,' the doctor said.

Dee's first instinct was to say no, but she held her breath and instead asked, 'Has anyone contacted my husband?'

The doctor gave her a smile that looked more like an expression of sympathy you might get at a funeral. His teeth, contrasting with his skin, looked white and too large for his face. 'I'm not sure,' he said. 'There has been no answer on his phone.'

He pulled a plastic chair over and sat down. 'Mrs Dimare,' he began, 'we found extensive bruising on your body. On your left vertebrae, upper chest, shoulder and arm. Would you like to tell me where it came from?'

Dee held her breath. This was it, she understood. She could tell the doctor about Joe and a machine would be set in motion. He would be obliged to report it as assault, the police would get involved and the whole thing would be taken out of her hands. She imagined the relief of not having to manage it, of letting go. And then she said, 'I tripped and fell down the stairs.'

The doctor looked at her squarely. 'The bruising to the vertebrae is more recent than to your upper body. I would say there is a period of two weeks in between.'

Dee dragged her eyes away from his and focused on the pattern of floating feathers on the curtain surrounding the cubicle. She knew she was being given a choice. The miscarriage was probably a direct result of the kick Joe had given her on the kitchen floor. But she couldn't tell this stranger the truth. It would be like feeding Joe to the lions. And she wanted to talk to him, to show him the consequences of his actions. She'd lost a baby. She didn't want to lose her marriage too.

'I fell twice,' she said. 'Once when I was running for a bus. Then I fell down the stairs.'

The doctor didn't reply. She knew he didn't believe her, but she didn't care. Her marriage was none of his business.

'Mrs Dimare,' he eventually said, 'what happened to you is very serious. I want you to know that I am here to help. Is there anything you are not telling me?'

Dee had no idea where she mustered it from, but she gave him a wan smile. 'Honestly,' she said. 'There's nothing else to tell.'

The doctor stood up. 'We'll keep you in overnight,' he said before leaving the cubicle. 'I will check back with you in the morning.'

Dee's room had a view of the Dublin mountains from its high-up window. As dusk descended they turned from green to blue to dark purple, and then were swallowed by inky darkness.

There was still no word from Joe. Dee was beginning to wonder if, like the mountains, he'd disappeared into the night too.

Feeling was beginning to leak back into her lower half, twinges of pain in her abdomen, a need to get up and go to the little en suite toilet every fifteen minutes.

She didn't draw the curtains on the window. In between toilet visits, she lay under the blankets, looking out at the dark sky. There wasn't a star to be seen, not a hint of moonlight.

In all these years, before Joe and after, she had never thought of babies in any real sense. Of course she had vaguely imagined being a mother, wondered if the time might come when she would want to reproduce, to do what every woman was supposed to do. But the biological clock had never nagged her, and if it was in the background ticking away somewhere, she hadn't been aware of it.

Her mind cast back to a night when she and Joe were on their honeymoon. He had leaned over to her one night at dinner and said, with a twinkle in his eye, 'Let's go home and make babies.' Dee had been surprised at the feeling of elation this elicited. It was the first time in her life that the actual idea of making a baby not only seemed feasible to her but appealing – exciting, even. She remembered trying to picture what a little boy or a little girl she and Joe produced would look like as they walked to their hotel. She'd come up with nothing.

Dee pushed the blankets off the bed and pulled up the hospital nightdress they'd given her. She placed her two hands on the warm, slightly sweaty flesh of her belly and felt. There had been a tiny human life inside there, created by her and Joe. A little boy or a little girl.

A gaping grief opened up inside her, so wide she thought it might consume her, and she began silently to cry, tears wrenching from her body in painful gulps that she forced herself to smother, in case anyone might hear.

31. Falling Apart

On leaving Daniel's old flat, Maggie wandered towards Hampstead Heath. She hadn't been to the Pavilion Café in years and, since it was such a mild, dry day, she decided to treat herself to lunch and cake in its gardens. Her appetite, killed for a few days by the chemotherapy, was back at double the force, driven by the steroids.

The walk took longer than she'd expected so by the time she reached the café she was out of breath. Thankfully, there were just a few other people there – a woman with a cute child in its buggy and an elderly couple leaning into each other in deep conversation – so she got a seat immediately.

By the time the waitress came, Maggie was breathing normally again. She ordered a mozzarella, prosciutto and basil sandwich on focaccia, and tea, and sat back, turning her face to the spring sun.

There was little more she could think of to do to find Daniel. Although there were several Danny Lane fan groups on Facebook, he didn't have a profile, either under his real or stage name. Google had thrown up page after page of results when she'd searched both of his names, but none had any information about his current whereabouts. She could write to his old record company, she supposed. Surely they'd have his address to post royalty cheques to him, if that was the way it worked. But it was unlikely they'd give it out to some random woman, and what could she say to impress on them the importance of helping her? That he was the first guy she'd ever had sex with?

Her only hope was that he'd call for his post between now and July, when the Abba concert was scheduled.

The sun felt unseasonably hot on her skin. Maggie closed her eyes and ran her fingers through her hair. She felt some of it come out in a weird, painless way, and when she opened her eyes, she was holding a small clump of orange curls.

At the end of the chemotherapy treatment, she had been given a blue swimming cap-like hood, with frozen gel inside it. The idea was to wear it for an hour after each treatment to help curb hair loss. But the thing had sent throbbing, ice-cold pain to the stem of her brain, and she'd only managed to keep it on for ten horribly uncomfortable minutes. The consultant had told her that some people were lucky enough not to lose their hair through chemotherapy, and Maggie had determined that she'd be one of them.

She looked at the cluster of hair in the palm of her hand. All through her life she had hated those tight, wiry orange curls. Apart from the unavoidable colour, her day revolved around the impossibility of styling it, how it bushed out after being washed, how it hurt like hell as she tried to run a comb through it. It grew so fast that she had to go to the hairdresser every second week to get it cut back tight into her head, like the endless pruning of a shrub.

She'd hated her hair with a vengeance from the moment she was old enough to become aware of it, but now that she was losing it, grief overwhelmed her. Without it, she wasn't sure who she would be.

When the waitress arrived with her sandwich, Maggie was crying. The girl stood by the table and gave her a sympathetic smile, which made Maggie sob harder. She could just about bear feeling sorry for herself; other people feeling sorry for her made her feel ten times worse.

She cried while she ate her sandwich, its flavours mingling with the mucus running down the back of her throat. She cried through the slice of chocolate cake that followed it, all the time avoiding touching her head in case more hair came away and she was left in the café with bald patches.

The old couple and the woman with the child, along with others who had arrived while she was eating, kept glancing at her, but no one came over to see what was wrong. If the shoe had been on Maggie's foot, she wasn't sure she'd have interrupted either. Crying was private. When people broke down in public places, it was hard to know how to react.

She was dabbing her eyes with a balled-up tissue and chewing the last bit of tear-drenched chocolate cake when she heard her phone ringing in her bag. She lifted it on to the table and pushed its contents around, searching, hardly able to see through her puffed-up eyes.

Maggie's heart sank when she saw the name on the display. She couldn't talk to her mother. Not now. Not in this state.

She put the phone down beside her teacup and waited for it to go through to voicemail. She signalled for the waitress to bring the bill, and while she was waiting for it, her phone bleeped to say her mother had left a message.

'Maggie.' Her mother's voice sounded far away. 'Oona's told us everything. You're not to worry. I've booked a flight and I'm arriving on Saturday.' She paused and Maggie heard her clear her throat. Then she added, as if she was formally commiserating with someone at one of the funerals she went to, like other people went to the cinema: 'I'm sorry for your trouble.'

32. Something Going On

'It's kind of like being back at school, isn't it?' said Jade. She was sitting on a plastic chair beside Daniel, her knees pressed together at the hem of her pleated tartan skirt.

She had insisted on Daniel accompanying her. 'You said you wanted to be a good father to Noah, and this is part of it.'

Considering that Daniel had never met a teacher or principal for the duration of Noah's education, he thought he was getting in on the action at too late a stage and, what was more, he wasn't comfortable around schools. This one was a modern building with a glassed-off central courtyard filled with all sorts of tropical-looking ferns, but it had the same combined smells of chalk-dust and floor polish, the same sense of menace beneath the orderly rhythm of learning that his own school had had back in the day.

He hadn't gone in for the sports that ensured popularity back at Cardinal Newman, nor had he fitted in with any of the other groups that the kids at school had naturally divided into. The best he could do was half hang about on the fringes with a gang who liked to think of themselves as outlaws. The furthest they got to committing crimes was smoking joints cobbled together with tiny bits of hash they'd nicked from their older brothers, talking about the tattoos they were going to get and slagging off Adam Ant.

In the food chain of bad boys, they were minnows compared to the sharks of Philip Ewing and his cronies, who had ruled the handball alley and the back of the bicycle sheds as if they were Masters of the Universe.

Daniel smiled to himself. He'd looked up Philip Ewing on Facebook one night a few years ago when he'd smoked too much weed. The bastard still lived in Hove and had grown into a fat, balding, middle-aged man whose status said 'single'. A far cry from the long-haired git in the studded leather jacket who had attempted to make Daniel's life hell the year after his mother had died.

The door to the headmaster's office opened and a girl in the school's bottle-green uniform walked out, her hair tumbling out of plaits and stockings bunched around her ankles. 'He told me to send you in,' she said, eyeing Jade and Daniel as if they had committed some heinous offence.

The headmaster introduced himself as Chris, shaking Jade's hand first, then Daniel's. He looked ironed and starched, his thin hair parted at the side and plastered to his skull, his tie a poker-straight line against a pristine white shirt. 'Thank you for coming in,' he said, as they took the two seats before his desk.

From beyond the office window the raucous shouts of the playground started up.

'How is Noah doing at home?' the headmaster began.

Daniel frowned, feeling oddly defensive. 'He's fine.'

'Well …' said Jade, giving Daniel a sideways glance '… that's not exactly true. There have been some problems.'

'Go on,' said the headmaster. He folded his hands in front of his mouth.

'It's hard to explain. Over the past few months, maybe a year, it's like he's turned into a different person.'

'He's come to live with me,' Daniel interjected. 'There were some problems with his mother's boyfriend.'

'It's not just that,' Jade said. 'He ran away. He was gone for nearly a week, sleeping rough.'

'That's part of the reason I asked you to meet me,' said the headmaster. 'Noah's absenteeism for that week was unexplained. That is, Noah refused to say why he was not at school.'

'Well, now you know,' said Daniel, hoping this was the end of it. 'It won't happen again.'

The headmaster unfolded his hands. 'Please don't misunderstand me,' he said. 'I'm not criticising either you or Noah. I've called you in because I'm worried about Noah's welfare at this school.'

The words 'this school' had an air of conclusiveness about them that Daniel didn't like. Jade glanced in his direction, clearly picking up the same message. 'How do you mean?' she asked.

'I've been aware for some time now that Noah is being quite severely bullied.'

The noises from outside the office window had intensified. Daniel could hear whoops and shouts and high peals of girls' laughter.

'There is a policy in place at the school to tackle this kind of behaviour,' the headmaster continued. 'We've done our very best to implement it, but unfortunately we've been unsuccessful.'

Daniel struggled to take this in. 'So, what are you saying?' he asked. 'Noah's being bullied and you can't stop it?'

'Quite frankly, yes,' said the headmaster. He cleared his throat. 'The problem isn't during school hours. We can monitor what's going on during class and break times. It's outside school hours that we're worried about. Noah is being targeted.'

'But who's doing it?' Jade asked. 'Can't you suspend them or something? Or talk to their parents?'

'If we take disciplinary action, I fear Noah will suffer the consequences. As I said, we cannot protect him outside school hours.'

'So what do you suggest we do?' asked Daniel. 'Get the police involved?'

'I don't think that would be helpful. We're dealing with a very belligerent element here. I think, for Noah's sake, it would be better if you transferred him to another school.'

Jade shook her head. 'But it's the middle of term,' she said. 'I had to put him on a waiting list to get into this school in the first place.'

'I've explained the situation to the head teacher at St Bart's in Bayswater and he's willing to take Noah in. It's a smaller school with a liberal ethos. I think he'll do well there.'

'So Noah is the one who has to change schools, even though he's not the one causing the problem?' said Daniel. 'That doesn't strike me as fair.'

'Unfortunately Noah is part of the problem,' the headmaster replied. 'I've spoken to him on several occasions about his refusal to wear the school uniform, the way he dresses – his hair ... the makeup ... He's making himself a target.'

Daniel breathed evenly. Pinned to the wall behind the headmaster's desk was a large timetable marked in a pattern of highlighter-pen colours that must have made sense to 'Chris' and his staff, but would be utterly alienating to anyone else. That was the trouble with the school system. It had no space for those who didn't subscribe to its convoluted set of rules, those who didn't fit in.

He pushed his chair back and got to his feet. 'Thank you for letting us know,' he said.

The headmaster stood up too and took a sheet of paper off his desk. 'Here are the contact details for the head teacher at St Bart's,' he said. 'I think you'll find him very accommodating.'

As they sped away through the corridors, Jade was running to keep up. 'Slow down,' she said, but instead Daniel picked up his pace.

'We're finding Noah *now*,' he said. 'I don't want him in this dump for another second.'

'That's not a good idea,' said Jade, but Daniel wasn't listening.

You'd think that things might have progressed, that schools would be able to prevent kids being bullied nowadays. Or at least protect them. But, no, it was the same as it ever was. And that head teacher, Chris, with his tidy desk and not a hair out of place, he was worse than any bully. Washing his hands of all responsibility.

Jade stopped trotting and shouted, 'Daniel! I said no!'

Daniel halted in his tracks. 'What?' he said. 'You think we should leave him here? You heard what the man said. He's being *targeted.*'

'We should discuss it before we talk to Noah.'

'Discuss what? He's not safe here.'

'The money, for starters. St Bart's will cost a fortune.'

Daniel started walking again. 'You know we don't have to worry about that,' he said.

'And what about what Noah wants?'

'What do you mean, *what Noah wants*? Noah will want to go to St Bart's.'

Behind him Jade stopped again. 'I wouldn't be so sure about that,' she said.

33. Defences Breaking

'She's staying with you, Oona, and that's the end of it,' Maggie said, into the phone. She was sitting on the bed, propped up by pillows, with Benny at her feet, staring at her as if he was telling her to be firm in her resolution. Oona was the one who had told their mother about the cancer: she could put her up.

'But you have a whole house,' Oona replied, her voice reed-thin. 'It's not fair.'

This was not the first time she had bemoaned Maggie's great luck at having a 'whole house' rather than just a one-bedroom flat. In Oona's imagination, life had given her the bum deal while Maggie had had everything handed to her on a plate. The husband, the children, the house – the whole package.

Their mother still referred to her as 'Poor Oona', as if she had played no part in what had befallen her. But hadn't she backed out of her engagement to Derek at the last minute all those years ago, even though he was a good, kind man? And hadn't she enough money squirrelled away in the rainy-day savings account she was always going on about to put a deposit down on a house if she wanted to? She'd get a mortgage, no problem. She owned that flat outright, her job with Brent Council, which she'd had since the dawn of Christendom, was secure, and she was on the top pay grade.

'Put her in Harry's room,' Oona said. 'She'll be no bother.'

Maggie decided to try another tack. 'Please, Oona,' she begged. 'You know what Mum's like. She'll be fussing over me like a hen with an egg. I don't have the energy for it.'

At the other end of the line Oona went quiet. Maggie could almost hear the turning of the cogs and wheels in her sister's head.

'My spare room isn't nearly ready,' Oona said eventually. 'I never got that chest of drawers in Ikea.' Her tone was slightly accusatory.

'The old chest of drawers is fine,' Maggie said, trying to picture Oona's spare room. She hadn't been to the flat in so long she could hardly remember its proportions.

'No,' Oona said, and Maggie pictured her folding her arms and pursing her lips, the way she always had done when they were kids and Maggie had tried to persuade her to do something out of her comfort zone. 'My flat's far too small. We'd be on top of each other, and you know what my claustrophobia's like. You have plenty of space. You'll hardly know Mum's there.'

Maggie glanced at Benny. She could have sworn he'd rolled his eye.

But it was true. Oona's kitchen was so minuscule you'd hardly swing a newborn kitten in it, and her living room, packed in every corner with mementoes from her weekends in Paris and Barcelona and Vienna, with her similarly permanently single workmate Mary Alice, was built for one person only. A couple would end up murdering each other in cold blood if they had to share it.

Maggie sighed. 'God knows how long she's planning to stay,' she said, resigning herself.

'At least there'll be someone to look after you properly,' said Oona. 'It's exactly what you need.' Now she sounded like she was doing Maggie a favour.

After they'd hung up, Maggie realised she hadn't said a word to Oona about losing her hair. She'd come home from the café and headed straight for the shower, where more clumps had come loose and clogged up the plughole. As she was drying herself afterwards in the bedroom, she'd almost laughed at her reflection in the bedroom mirror, then begun to cry once more. The top of her head looked like an orange and scalp-pink patchwork quilt.

In her dressing-gown and slippers, she'd gone through the house and taken down every mirror. The one in the bathroom was part of the cabinet above the washbasin, so she covered it with a towel, determining to wrench it off the wall when she had the energy. She didn't want to see this shrinking version of herself. She wanted to remain intact in her imagination.

At the end of the bed, Benny got to his paws and arched his back in a languid stretch. Then he padded towards Maggie and crawled on to the warmth of her lap, curling his body around a few times until he found a comfortable position. She gave him an absentminded stroke.

She'd have to get Harry's room ready, and clean the house from top to bottom. Her mother would be on her doorstep in three days' time and she was the kind of woman who'd wear a white glove to inspect for dust, if it was socially acceptable.

Maggie thought about getting off the bed and fetching bed linen out of the airing cupboard to start on Harry's room. But she couldn't face it. Instead she decided to start her search for Charlie. It was by far the preferable option.

'Sorry, baby,' she said to Benny, lifting him off her lap so she could get up and retrieve her computer from the top of the chest of drawers. He gave a plaintive whine and went to find himself a spot on the pillow next to her.

A Google search for 'Charlie Jones' brought up a former *EastEnders* actor and a dead American sportscaster. He had no obvious Facebook presence either. There were 264 Charlie Joneses listed and none of the ones with photos even slightly resembled the Charlie Maggie remembered. She considered sending messages to each of the Charlies without photos, asking them if they were the same Charlie who had once been in her Abba fan club, then decided that was too ridiculous. How did people find each other in the days before Facebook? They picked up the phone.

She did just that and dialled International Directory Enquiries, looking for Charlie's parents' number.

'We have no listing for a Walter Jones Slugo, Ireland,' the operator said.

'No,' Maggie told her. 'It's Sligo. S-L-I-G-O.'

'Hold the line,' the operator said, and then an automated voice gave out the number, asking at the end if Maggie wanted to be connected directly.

'Yes,' Maggie said, delighted. However difficult it was to find Daniel, at least she'd come up trumps with Charlie almost instantly.

Charlie's father picked up on the third ring.

'Hello!' he shouted. 'Who is this?'

'Mr Jones, I don't know if you remember me. I'm Maggie Behan. I used to be a friend of Charlie's.'

'Who?'

'Maggie Behan.' It felt odd to be using her maiden name.

'What do you want?' The old man sounded a touch aggressive, which was not how she remembered him.

'I'm trying to get in contact with Charlie,' Maggie said.

She waited while Mr Jones broke into a fit of coughing at the other end of the line. 'Charlie?' he said, when he'd cleared his throat, and then repeated, as if to himself, 'Charlie.'

'Yes,' said Maggie. 'Do you have a phone number for him? Or an email address?'

'Charlie,' the old man said again, and this time Maggie thought she heard a forlorn note in his voice. 'I don't know where he is.'

34. Closed Your Mind

'Oh, God,' Cassandra groaned into her mobile phone, 'I can't figure out what to wear.'

At the other end of the line she could hear the sound of ice being crushed in the liquidiser on her kitchen worktop all the way back in Playa del Inglés. Coco was making one of her margaritas.

Above the grating noise, Coco shouted, 'Did you bring your red dress? The one that makes you look like Kim Basinger in *LA Confidential*. Oh, and the blue heels!'

'I'm not going for tea with Imelda Marcos,' Cassandra said. 'I'm going to meet my father for the first time in ten years. I need to look … well …'

'Old?' Coco supplied.

'Coco!' Cassandra snapped. 'I'm being serious here.'

'Maybe a little too serious, Mama C.'

'What's that supposed to mean?'

'You are a beautiful woman, remember? Your father should be proud of you.'

Cassandra sighed and sat down on the bed. On the wall above it was a painting that didn't know what it was, either an abstract landscape or a still life. Just like the nondescript paintings on walls of a million magnolia-painted hotel rooms skirting the edges of towns across the planet.

'Maybe I should wear my black halterneck,' she said. 'Something a little more conservative.'

'You are not going to a funeral.'

'No.'

'Then you should dress in something that makes you look happy, not like some sad old lady.'

In the end Cassandra chose a cream linen trouser suit, which she accessorised with a fuchsia silk scarf.

In the taxi that bore her from the hotel to the house she'd grown up in, her stomach lurched with every bump in the road. As it rounded the corner at the bottom of the hill, she had an urge to shout, 'Stop!' at the driver and tell him to go back. She could face her father tomorrow or the day after that.

But then she swallowed and resolved herself. She'd put it off for ten years. She wouldn't put it off for one more day.

Standing outside the house, she tried to repeat to herself the mantra she'd chanted from the day she'd begun her hormone treatment: 'You are a beautiful woman.' The mantra she'd taught Coco after she'd turned up, beaten and bloody, at her flat, like a terrified bird, sure her brothers would find her and kill her. 'You are a beautiful woman.'

Cassandra wondered if the key, which she'd kept in her purse all this time, would still fit the door, but decided not to chance it.

She pressed the bell, which vaguely rang inside the house, and immediately heard some movement. The blurred shape of her father appeared through the door's frosted glass, shuffling slowly towards her.

When he finally opened it, she couldn't believe her eyes. He had shrunk to half the size he had once been. Gone was the handsome, square-jawed, silver-haired father, who had stood strong and erect beside Cassandra as her mother's coffin was lowered into the ground a decade ago and in his place was a bent old man, liver spots showing through the sparse strands of grey on the top of his head.

When the priest had delivered his last blessing that bleak day, her father had turned away from the grave and walked off without saying anything. Cassandra had gone after him and tried to link his arm against the harsh wind, but he'd shaken her off.

'Please, Dad,' she'd begged. 'Mum wouldn't want you to be like this.'

He'd stopped and turned to her, his eyes wet and bitter. 'You broke your mother's heart,' he'd said. 'You killed her.'

Now, on the doorstep, he looked up into Cassandra's face and said, 'Can I help you?' There was not a flicker of recognition.

'Dad,' said Cassandra. 'It's me.'

Her father frowned, not understanding. 'I think you have the wrong house,' he said, retreating into the hall and pushing the door closed.

Cassandra reached out to stop it with the flat of her hand. 'Please, Dad,' she said.

'Go away,' said her father. 'I'm not your dad.'

Still holding the door ajar with her hand, Cassandra searched her father's face through the crack at the side of it. He looked utterly nonplussed.

Cassandra steeled herself. She hated having to do it, to use the name. But it was the only way. 'I used to be Charlie,' she said.

'Charlie?' The old man's voice faltered.

Cassandra tried not to cringe. 'My name's Cassandra now,' she said.

There was a moment of heavy silence and then her father started to cough. 'No,' he said, backing away from the door. 'Go away.'

'Dad,' said Cassandra, pushing the door fully open, 'I've come a long way.'

'Go away,' her father repeated. He fell, spluttering, against the wall and began to slip down.

Cassandra stepped into the hall and bent to help him.

'Go!' her father cried, pushing at her hands. His voice was filled with panic.

'Please, Dad. Let me help you up.'

'No!' her father wheezed. 'Leave me alone!' He whipped his head back, away from her, and it hit the wall with a dull thud. Then he lost consciousness.

35. Broken a Feather

'I think that looks absolutely stunning,' said the woman at Cancer Hair Support, who had introduced herself as Ginny. There was a Scottish lilt to her accent, so Maggie didn't know if she'd meant Jenny.

Maggie surveyed her reflection in the huge mirror, which was surrounded by lights, like those in a star's dressing room. Throughout her teenage years her heart's desire had been to have long, straight blonde hair with a flick at the front, just like Agnetha's. Now the woman looking back at her had exactly that style, and it looked as ridiculous as Maggie had thought it might. She'd only asked Ginny for it on a whim.

Behind her in the mirror, Oona and their mother stood gaping, like a tableau of women at a wake. They looked at once horrified and as if they were thoroughly enjoying themselves.

Maggie felt slightly hysterical. Before Ginny had started fitting the wigs, she'd removed what was left of Maggie's hair with electric clippers, then wet-shaved it to the scalp.

'What do you think?' Maggie asked her mother and Oona, trying to stop her hands trembling as she touched the wig at both sides.

'It's gorgeous!' her mother replied, too enthusiastically. She'd aged heavily since the last time Maggie saw her, which was three years ago when both of her parents had arrived unannounced for a weekend of what her mother called 'shopping and shows'. It was to do with her weight, which she still watched like a hawk. She'd spent most of her adult life starving herself to fit into a size ten, and tutting behind the back of anyone who even verged on overweight. But now that she was in her mid-sixties, she could have done with a bit of fat on her bones. It would have fleshed out her face, which had caved in at the cheeks, and wrinkled around eyes that looked too wide for her head. She still kept her hair the same colour, two shades darker than Maggie's Tango orange – her constant chignon had been sophisticated when she was younger, but now it made her face look even more emaciated.

She had kept her impeccable sense of style, though. The lilac blouse she wore with its collar turned up was cut to show off her angular body, and the double string of pearls around her neck shone with the exact same shade as her cream linen trousers.

Oona said nothing. Her eyes met Maggie's in the mirror and Maggie could have sworn she saw a hint of annoyance in them. 'I'm not sure,' she said to Ginny. 'I don't think I'm meant to be a blonde bombshell.'

Ginny gave a small, high-strung giggle. 'We might try something in auburn,' she said. 'Or how about brown? A lot of people go for brown.' She took the blonde wig, fitted it carefully back on to its polystyrene-head stand, and went off in search of some more choices, leaving Maggie to stare at her naked skull in the mirror.

Sometimes you saw women who had lost their hair to cancer and they were arrestingly beautiful, like Sinéad O'Connor in that video where she bawled her eyes out over some man. But Maggie looked, for want of a better word, flat. Without her carrot curls, she was undefined. Unidentifiable.

'The wigs they have these days are very realistic, aren't they?' her mother said, in soothing tones, taking the seat beside Maggie and surveying her in the mirror.

Oona nodded and sat down too, on the chair in a corner of the room. 'They are,' she agreed.

'I remember the wig poor Bernie Elliott had,' her mother continued. 'She looked like a poodle.'

'Bernie Elliott?' said Oona. 'Wasn't she married to the man who owned the corner shop?'

'God rest her soul,' said Maggie's mother, blessing herself with a vague representation of the cross, a movement made so many million times it was a reflex rather than a genuine expression.

'Here we are,' said Ginny, arriving back with a different wig. 'Why don't we try this one?' The wig she fitted on Maggie's head and brushed into shape was the shade of instant coffee granules. When she was done, Ginny stood back with a satisfied grin and, pointing the hairbrush, said, 'That's more you, I think.'

It wasn't bad in that it had the lustre of real hair, but its colour made Maggie look paler than the Bride of Frankenstein.

'Do you have something in orange?' Maggie asked. 'Nearer my real colour?'

'Orange?' said Ginny, with another of her nervous titters. 'No. We don't get much demand for orange.'

'That's okay,' said Maggie, taking the wig off. 'Maybe I won't wear one after all.'

Beside her, Maggie's mother gave a slight, surprised laugh. 'But you have to wear a wig,' she said, staring at Maggie's gleaming scalp in the mirror. 'You can't go around like that. What would people think?'

'That I have cancer, Mum,' Maggie wanted to say. But she held herself back. There was always a delicate balance with her mother, which she was in danger of tipping, from the frying pan to the fire. 'I'll take the blonde one,' she told Ginny.

'Are you sure?' Ginny asked. 'I can check the catalogue for red.'

'I'm sure,' said Maggie. She had no intention of wearing the wig, but it might be fun to take it to the Abba concert. Dee, who had always wanted to be Frida to Maggie's Agnetha, would get a good laugh out of it. If she ever returned any of Maggie's calls.

When they got out on to the street, it was drizzling. Oona put up her small turquoise umbrella with a frill around the edge. 'I'm famished. Let's get lunch somewhere nice. Make an afternoon of it.'

They might have been shopping for wedding dresses.

'Oh, that would be lovely,' their mother said, but then she hesitated and bit her lip. 'Maybe we should get Maggie home, though. She must be exhausted.'

The judder of annoyance Maggie suppressed morphed seamlessly into guilt. It was a perfectly caring and innocent thing for her mother to say, so why was she reacting like that? 'I'm fine,' she said, although her mother had been right: she was exhausted. 'Honestly.'

Her mother's high forehead was mottled with a worried frown; her too-wide eyes were searching Maggie's. 'Are you sure, love?' she said, and Maggie experienced another pang of familiar confusion. Sometimes she wondered if she was imagining the whole thing. Maybe her mother didn't mean to make her feel bad.

What had Rita said that day about taking responsibility for yourself? Perhaps, Maggie thought, it was time to grow up and put aside her childish distrust of her mother, time to take responsibility for her own feelings and not blame her mother for them. After all, people couldn't *make* you feel things, could they?

'Well?' said Oona. 'Are we going for lunch or not? It'll be bucketing down any second.'

'We're going for lunch,' Maggie said. 'I'm starving.'

36. Silence Ever After

They went into the greasy spoon on the corner, which was hardly what Oona might call 'somewhere nice', but was at least near enough to get indoors before the rain turned from drizzle to deluge. The mugs of tea the waitress put in front of them were so strong you could have trotted three mice on them.

Oona had asked for a green salad with the dressing on the side, after scanning the menu, which didn't offer salad of any sort whatsoever. The waitress told her she'd check in the kitchen for some lettuce, but that she didn't hold hopes of 'the chef' having any dressing. Their mother had hummed and hawed for ages, exclaiming about the vast number of calories she imagined there might be in an All-day Full English Breakfast, then declined to order anything to eat at all. Maggie wanted the breakfast, but decided instead to have a tuna sandwich and a glass of water.

In the short distance from the Cancer Hair Support place to the café, her woollen hat had soaked up enough rain to feel like a swollen, damp sponge clinging to the bare skin of her head. She longed to take it off, but there were people at every other table in the place. She imagined them all turning around to stare at the pink dome of her skull in fascinated horror, and her mother's mortification at the spectacle.

Oona poured a minuscule drop of milk into her tea and, stirring it carefully, launched into a tale about some new intrigue in her office. Maggie had heard a variant on the same story so many times over the years that she felt as if she knew all the players, even though she'd never laid eyes on them. Their mother nodded and made sympathetic sounds, although Maggie guessed she wasn't actually listening.

Maggie's phone bleeped to say she had a message.

'She's never off that thing,' Oona said, indicating the phone with her teaspoon as Maggie extricated it from her jeans pocket.

'Really?' their mother replied, sipping her dark tea with the slightest grimace. 'I'm glad we didn't have them when I was your age.'

Maggie bristled. It sounded like a dig.

The message on her phone was that she had missed a call from Dee. Strange, it had been on full volume the whole time she was getting the wig fitted but she hadn't heard it ring. She checked the date and time. Even stranger, it had come two days ago.

'Excuse me,' she said, picking it up to hit the return-call button and went to the café door for some privacy. She looked through the window at north London in the rain as she waited for Dee to answer.

'Maggie.' Dee's voice came on the line, just as Maggie was sure she was about to go through to her voicemail for the umpteenth time. 'How are you?'

'I'm good,' Maggie replied, then embellished, 'I'm great.' She'd decided that when she eventually got through to Dee she wouldn't mention the cancer. She didn't want to go into it with her. Not yet, anyway. 'And how are you?' she asked.

'Oh, you know. Crazy busy at work. It never ends.'

'And Joe?'

Dee's voice was chirpy. 'He's in great form. He sends his love.'

They shot the breeze for a few more minutes, Maggie watching people pass under a multitude of different-coloured umbrellas as she gave updates on Poppy and Harry, without mentioning anything about William's departure or Rita. That could come later too.

Dee replied she had no news, and talked about the snow in Dublin, which had ground the city to a halt.

'So, you wanted to talk to me about some big plan?' Dee said, when the small-talk petered out.

'It's exciting, isn't it?' said Maggie, turning to glance at Oona and her mother, who were deep in conversation, their heads bowed towards each other.

'What is?'

'You know. Abba. Getting back together.'

There was a pause, then Dee said, 'I suppose so. I haven't really thought about it that much.'

'But don't you remember? We made a promise when we had the Abba fan club. That we'd all get back together for their concert.'

Dee let out a hollow laugh. 'Oh, Maggie. That was so long ago. I don't think the others would remember. I certainly didn't.'

'I'm getting tickets for the four of us,' said Maggie. 'It's in Stockholm, on July the thirtieth.'

'Have you told Daniel and Charlie?'

'I'm looking for them. You don't have a contact number for Charlie, by any chance?'

There was silence at the other end, then Maggie heard a woman's voice in the background.

'Listen,' said Dee. 'I have to go.'

'Okay,' said Maggie. 'But are you in?'

'In?'

'Coming to the Abba concert?'

'I don't know.' Dee's voice sounded as if it was disengaging. 'I'm not sure.'

'You *have* to come,' said Maggie. 'We promised, remember?'

'Look, Maggie, I really have to go,' said Dee. 'We'll talk again soon, yeah? Give my love to William and the kids.'

37. Just Like a Child

The walls of the box room had been plastered with pictures of Lady Gaga, expertly hiding behind the mask her costumes made. Daniel understood the appeal, especially to kids like Noah, but he'd seen it all before – had allowed himself to be a kind of alien creation in the service of fame. Still, Lady Gaga had taken it to such extremes that there didn't seem to be room for the slightest hint of a human soul behind the slick marketing machine. She was like a robot from a mass-production line, spouting messages about the power of individuality.

Noah was sitting on his bed, leaning against the headboard with his knees up to his chest and his headphones on. He'd dyed his hair soot black and cut one side of it short, leaving the other to cover the entire left side of his face. On his exposed cheek there was a red-raw graze.

'All right?' said Daniel, handing him a mug of tea.

Noah lifted his headphones off and hooked them around his neck. 'Yeah,' he replied, pushing the long side of his hair behind his ear and taking the mug.

Daniel perched on the edge of the bed. 'So, what was in the bag?' he asked.

'This 'n' that,' Noah said, leaving his mug on the bedside locker. 'You know, school stuff.'

'You think there's any way we'll be able to get it back?'

Noah shrugged. 'Dunno.'

Daniel took a sip of his tea, which had gone lukewarm. 'So, run by me what happened again,' he said.

'I told you,' said Noah. 'They followed me and grabbed my bag.'

'Who are "they"?'

'Just some guys from school.'

'Do they have names?'

Noah stared Daniel for a second, then looked away. 'It was just some guys,' he said.

'Did they push you?' Daniel asked.

'No, I tripped.'

'Are you sure?'

Noah rolled his eyes. 'Jesus, Daniel,' he said. 'Stop with all the questions. I'm fine, okay?'

Daniel swallowed another mouthful of tepid tea. 'It's stealing, them taking your bag like that. Those books don't come cheap, and I'm sure there was other stuff in there, personal stuff.'

Noah said nothing.

'We could go to the police. If you had names.'

Noah's chin jutted out. 'We're not doing that,' he said. 'No way.'

'Why not?'

'It's not like it was when you were a kid. It's not like you can go telling tales and everything will be sweet.'

'I don't think it's any different now. There have always been bullies, Noah. That's nothing new.'

Noah set his mouth in a line.

'What about St Bart's?' Daniel asked. 'Have you given it any more thought?'

There was no reply.

'It's a great school, Noah. You'd be much happier there.'

'How do you know where I'd be happier?' Noah snapped. 'You don't know anything.'

'So, you're telling me you're fine with the way things are? With being chased after school and pushed over?'

'I told you, they didn't push me!'

'Okay, okay, they didn't push you.' Daniel sighed. He'd spoken to the headmaster at St Bart's, had agreed to the fees for the rest of the school year, plus the following year in advance, which he could more than afford with what was coming his way in royalties. He'd brought home leaflets about St Bart's extensive arts curriculum, and shown Noah the website. The place even had an 'Individuality Programme', where students were encouraged to find creative ways to express their identities. Daniel couldn't understand Noah's flat refusal to contemplate moving there.

'Just tell me why you won't even think about it,' he said.

'Because I don't want to go to that stupid dump,' Noah retorted. 'It's like a total cop-out.'

Now it was Daniel's turn to throw his eyes to Heaven. 'I don't get it, Noah,' he said. 'How is going to a school where you won't be bullied a cop-out?'

Noah flopped back on the pillow. 'You're such a coward,' he said.

Daniel resisted jumping to his feet. 'What's that supposed to mean?' he said.

'Go figure it out,' Noah muttered, and shoved his headphones back on.

This was Noah's signal that the conversation had ended, and Daniel almost went with it. But then he thought about his promise to himself to be a good father, and knew he couldn't leave it at that. They still hadn't resolved what they were going to do.

He went to the bedside table and pulled the headphone jack out of the boy's iPod docking station. 'Noah,' he said, raising his voice to be heard. 'You're going to St Bart's, and that's that.'

Noah gaped as if he'd been physically assaulted. 'You can't make me, Daniel,' he said.

Anger started creeping up through Daniel's chest, like acid reflux. 'Please don't talk to me like that,' he said, keeping his voice on an even keel. 'Show some respect.'

Noah's face hardened and he gave a derisive snort. 'Respect?' he said. '*For you?*'

Daniel nodded, still trying to rise above his mounting anger. 'Yes, for me,' he replied. 'I'm your father.'

'You're pathetic, Daniel, that's what you are,' Noah said, examining his nails.

Daniel's temper exploded. 'Stop calling me Daniel!' he roared. 'Who the Hell do you think you are?'

Noah's gaze inched away from his nails to meet Daniel's and his voice didn't fluctuate. 'I know who I am,' he said. 'And it's nothing like you.'

Daniel couldn't keep eye contact. 'Christ,' he said. 'I've had enough of this.'

'I don't hide away like some little mouse,' Noah went on.

Daniel's fists, which had been balled up tightly by his sides, fell loose. '*Don't* change schools, then,' he said. 'Have it your own way.'

'I will,' said Noah, and plugged himself back into his iPod.

Daniel turned and walked out of the room, shutting the door quietly behind him. Halfway down the stairs he stopped and thought of going back up there and insisting on St Bart's again. But it was pointless. He couldn't make the boy do what he didn't want to do.

At the bottom of the stairs Daniel went to the front door, opened it and turned his face up to the sky to breathe in a lungful of London air. Across the cloudless blue expanse above him the thin white line of a jet-trail was drawn. He imagined the speed of the invisible plane and the people inside it, all hurtling towards some unknown, far-away destination.

38. Still Another Mile

Maggie felt only a little depleted after the second chemo session, but the following day, after the breast-care nurse had come to the house to give her the blood platelet injection, her whole body seemed to go into shut-down.

If her mother hadn't shouldered her up the stairs, she wouldn't have been able to make it to her bed. At sixty-eight and a foot smaller than Maggie, Mum wasn't even out of breath doing it.

Maggie had looked into her eyes as they slowly took each step, her stomach roiling like a trawler in the eye of a storm, searching but coming up short. Still, the feel of her mother's arm around her, clutching Maggie's waist hard and fast, had made her less afraid. She couldn't remember when she'd last felt her touch.

Cocooned in her duvet, half dozing after bouts of vomiting, Maggie had waking dreams of bumping into Daniel in the street, watching his face light up as she told him about the concert. Her mother came to and from the room, bringing thin chicken broth and making her drink just a little, filling the Brita water jug by the bed, putting new cases on the pillows and taking away sweat-soaked ones.

Maggie was grateful. She'd never imagined allowing her mother to take care of her again. She'd pushed her away, knowing in her heart that she wasn't forgiven and would never be. She could bear her father's silence much more easily than her mother's artificial fawning. It was more honest.

But last night, when Mum had come in to check on her, Maggie had wondered if it was artificial after all. 'Thank you, Mum,' she'd whispered, barely able to form the words.

Her mother had reached out and stroked her temple. 'Get some sleep now,' she'd said.

As she'd nodded off she'd thought that maybe the cancer was bringing positive things into her life too. For all those years she'd been avoiding her mother, she'd also wanted her love again. Now that wish seemed to have come true.

In the morning, Maggie woke up feeling vaguely human again. Her energy was still completely zapped, but the sickness was gone and her head wasn't pounding. When her mother came in with a cup of tea, she pushed the duvet aside and said, 'I'm getting up.'

'Are you sure that's wise?' her mother asked. 'You're still very pale.'

'If I don't get up now, I'll never do it.' At some point during the days of being unable to achieve anything, Maggie had vowed not to let the treatment steal more time than was absolutely necessary. She did not want to be bed-bound. And the steroids helped.

They had breakfast together in the kitchen, which was sparkling like the set of a Flash ad. No sooner had her mother scrambled some eggs than the pot she'd used was stacked in the dishwasher.

Buttering a piece of toast, her mother was going on about Poor Oona. 'If only she could find herself a husband,' she said. 'It's not right that she's alone at this time in her life.'

'Oona's perfectly happy, Mum,' said Maggie. 'She lives the life of Reilly.'

'That's easy for you to say.'

The gratitude Maggie had felt last night began to ebb away.

'At least you've got your family,' said her mother, her eyes glittering. 'Oona has no one.'

This was too much. Maggie couldn't bite her tongue. 'Look around, Mum,' she said. 'What family are you talking about, exactly?'

Her mother went quiet, sipping her tea, then said, 'Don't start upsetting yourself.'

The two forkfuls of scrambled eggs Maggie had swallowed began to feel like curdled cement in her stomach.

'William called over last night, while you were asleep,' said her mother. It might have sounded as if she was changing the subject, but Maggie suspected she was doing anything but. 'He's beside himself with worry.'

Maggie pushed back her chair. 'I think I'll go to bed,' she said. 'I don't feel well.'

'Eat a little more, love, please. You need to keep up your strength.'

But Maggie couldn't stomach it. Not the scrambled eggs, which had turned jelly-like on her plate, or her mother's implication that William was somehow a wronged party.

In her bedroom, the nausea receded and slowly Maggie began to regret her retreat upstairs. She felt trapped, stymied from getting on with her own life in her own house. But from the kitchen she could hear the theme tune to *The Archers* above the sound of crockery clinking in the sink. She couldn't bear to go downstairs again.

She decided to escape instead into the world of Facebook and Abbaholics. Benny, who had remained in a deep sleep while she was downstairs, woke as she powered up her laptop, sitting propped against her pillows. He stalked over and tried to get between her and the computer.

'No, Benny!' she said, pushing him away, but then, seeing his disappointment, relented and took him under the crook of her arm. His purring started up immediately, like a little warm engine, and gave her some consolation.

Strangely there hadn't been a word from Agnetha Fältsgok on the Abbaholics page since the day it had become global news that Abba were re-forming. Maggie wondered again if she was the real Agnetha after all. Was she now busy getting ready for the big reunion? Given the blanket silence from Björn, Benny and Frida about the forthcoming plans, had she been told to keep schtum?

Activity was at an all-time high with lots of the other Abbaholics, though. People were posting the numerous bits of unofficial news that had leaked since the official announcement – how the reunion had come about; who was designing costumes; what songs would make it to the playlist ... There were links to newspaper articles, of which there were lots of new ones to browse every day, but all of it was conjecture, really. Since none of the Abba members had talked to the press since the day the concert had been announced, the whole thing had the air of a huge surprise waiting to be sprung.

People were also exchanging messages on the group's wall about tickets, looking to see if anyone had any inside information about getting them before the official on-sale day, or how to get to the top of the queue. The rumour going around the group was that there would be an allocation of only two tickets per person, to stop touts buying in bulk.

One way or another she was going to have to get four. Dee might have been ambivalent about the concert when they spoke. Maggie mightn't have found Daniel or Charlie yet. But, even though her energy was almost depleted again and now she wanted to sleep, she vowed to herself to do everything in her power to get everyone back together for that concert, if it was the last thing she did.

39. Breaking Her Way

From a vantage point behind the tall rubber plant by the lift doors, Cassandra watched her twin brother. He was standing by the white baby grand that sat incongruously at the entrance to the hotel's piano bar, shuffling from one foot to the other.

In the years since she'd seen him last, he'd put on a fair bit of weight and his hair had receded at the front, making his long forehead seem out of proportion with his rounded face. Even at this distance she could see his cheeks and nose had a high colour that rose from the neck up.

It was hard to imagine him as Sam the soccer star, whom every girl in town had once swooned over. Outside the gates to their house, gaggles of them would hang out after school or on weekends, waiting for him to come out so they could accost him. Now he looked like any other middle-aged man in a pair of chinos and a striped shirt stretching too tightly across his belly.

He'd called Cassandra's mobile this afternoon and asked her to meet him. Cassandra had suggested Hargadons bar in the centre of town, but Sam had replied with an emphatic 'No': he'd come to the hotel instead. She knew it was because he didn't want to be seen with her. He didn't want any unsuspecting locals coming up to them, wanting to be introduced.

She stayed watching him for a few seconds more, gathering herself for what lay ahead. Then, clutching her handbag, she strode forward.

'Sam,' she said, almost upon him before he clocked her. She held out her hand, not sure if that was the right way to greet him. 'How are you?'

He took it, faltering. 'Hello,' he replied, but his voice was formal, as if he was greeting a complete stranger. His eyes, too, seemed to be having a hard time taking her in.

'Shall we?' Cassandra said, indicating two seats and a table just inside the entrance to the bar. Sam looked around, then followed her.

'What would you like to drink?' Cassandra asked.

Sam sat down. 'I'm not here to drink,' he said, looking directly up at her. 'This won't take long.'

Cassandra took the seat opposite. 'They have table service,' she said. 'We can order when the girl comes over.'

Sam ignored her. 'Look,' he said, under his breath. 'I don't know what you're doing here. But I think you should go back to where you came from.'

Cassandra felt a prickle of intense irritation. Throughout their childhood Sam had been the boss, the one who had told her what she could do and when she could do it. The alpha twin, born first and biologically determined to be top dog. Cassandra knew that fulfilling her own destiny had been the ultimate challenge to his self-appointed authority over her. It had been the moment when they separated, and more than anything, it had been her assertion of independence that had made him turn away from her. That was what stuck in Sam's craw.

'I'm not going anywhere, Sam,' she said, turning to beckon the server who had just hovered past their table. 'I'll have a gin and slimline tonic,' she told the girl. 'My friend here isn't drinking.'

'Give me a pint of Carlsberg,' Sam said, looking daggers at Cassandra.

As the girl walked away, Cassandra sat back in her chair, crossed her legs and folded her hands on one knee. She surveyed the freshly applied chocolate-brown paint on her nails. 'Why didn't you tell me about Dad when I called you the other night?'

Sam eyed her. 'Because it's none of your business.'

'He has Alzheimer's, Sam. I think that's my business.'

'You fuck off for ten years and now you're suddenly St Charlie, back to save us all? Don't make me laugh.'

'I'm his daughter, Sam. I have a right to know. And my name is Cassandra.'

Sam gave a bitter grunt. 'Not to me, you're not. You're Charlie, pretending to be … to be … I don't know who the fuck you're pretending to be. You're a freak.'

Cassandra closed her eyes for a second. She had not come home to have this fight with Sam again. She'd come to make it okay with her father, and that was what she was going to do, no matter what her brother did or said.

'They told me at the hospital that he refuses to have home care,' she said, as the girl put their drinks down on their table. Cassandra gave her room number, then turned back to her brother. 'The doctor said he's not going to be able to take care of himself for much longer.'

'He's got me and Delia to look after him,' Sam said.

'He needs his family, Sam.'

'And what are you saying? That Delia isn't family?'

Cassandra took a breath. 'No,' she said. 'Delia is family. Of course she is. And the kids too. Look, all I'm saying is that I've decided to stay for a while to help with Dad.'

Sam shook his head. 'No way,' he said. 'You're the last thing he needs.'

'That's not true.'

Sam stood up, his pint untouched. 'Go home, *Charlie*,' he said. 'You're not welcome here.'

As he stalked away, roughly pushing past two women who stood near the hotel's front door, Cassandra had a memory of when they were children. They were in the back garden, going up and down the cement path on a pair of matching red tricycles. Ahead in the race, Sam had fallen off his bike into the grass. Instead of crying he'd lifted his little blond head and laughed.

Cassandra couldn't remember the last time she'd seen him smile, never mind laugh. She leaned forward and picked up her drink. In the end, he hadn't stopped her taking control of her own life. And he wasn't going to stop her doing what she had to do now, either.

40. Found You at Last

Benny sat on the kitchen table, his tail curled underneath him, and watched Maggie work, his one eye flickering as it followed the movements of her fingers on the laptop's keys. Every now and then his paw swiped at her right hand, and she shoved it away. 'No, Benny! Get off the table, for God's sake.' But the cat didn't budge from his spot and Maggie was only intermittently aware of his presence.

With much persuasion, she'd managed to get Oona to take their mother to Kew Gardens for the day, so the house was miraculously free and mercifully quiet. She had spent the last hour, set up with a pot of coffee and a pack of chocolate HobNobs at the kitchen table, searching for both Daniel and Charlie on-line.

She was coming up less than short.

There was absolutely nothing to indicate where Daniel was living now, so she gave up that search. The article in the *Sunday Times*, which she'd torn out in the chemotherapy waiting room, said that he'd been a backing singer on the original soundtrack recording for the *Rain Man* musical, so she looked that up. She hoped to find out where it had been recorded, in case Daniel did other work there, but there was nothing about that either.

She did find an info@ email address for the record company, so she fired off a missive, asking for Daniel's contact details, but didn't hold out much hope of a reply. Why would a music company send out such information to a random enquirer?

A quick Google search for 'Daniel Smith+backing vocals' brought up one other result, a failed *Song for Europe* entry in 2009 called 'Crazy Lover' sung by an act called Maya. Maggie typed the title into YouTube and came up with a video of a short, bouncy woman with a shrub of black curls and a catsuit that was way too tight, belting out a song in a high-pitched voice. She sounded like a little girl yelling in a playground. When the camera panned out, there were three barely decipherable singers with microphone stands, clicking their fingers in unison to the beat, in pure Eurovision style.

Maggie clicked on the enlarge button to make the video fill her screen. Although this blurred the picture, she could just about see someone who might possibly be Daniel in the middle of the singers. But she couldn't decide if it was actually him. Maggie let the video play out, watching the backing singer closely every time he came into view, trying to remember the physical presence of Daniel in her mind's eye.

She closed the window and looked at her desktop for a moment, then opened Google again and typed in 'Maya+Eurovision'.

A website for Maya came up. Although her stab at Eurovision seemed to be the pinnacle in her career, Maya was still selling her wares. She'd released an album and an EP since then, and at the bottom of the page there was an email address: bookings@mayamusic.co.uk

Maggie copied the address, opened Outlook Express and pasted it into a new email.

Dear Maya
My name is Maggie Corcoran, née Behan, and I am an old friend of Daniel Smith, who I believe was a backing singer on your song 'Crazy Lover'.
I am trying to locate Daniel to ask him to come to

a reunion. I'm wondering if you would have an email address for him or any other contact details. I know, given Daniel's fame, that I might seem like some sort of stalker, but I genuinely knew him before he was Danny Lane, and I would really love to get in contact with him again. If you could get back to me, one way or the other, I would be most grateful.

Clicking on 'send', Maggie took a HobNob from the half-eaten packet and bit half of it off. The kitchen clock said it was two twenty-five and Oona had said they'd be back by four, so she had a good hour and a half of freedom. Maggie could stick on some Abba and dance around the kitchen naked, if she wanted to. The thought was delicious, having the house so totally to herself. Not so long ago her days had stretched out into numb infinity because she was on her own here. But now, with her mother around all the time and Oona arriving to natter over dinner after work every day, she felt hemmed in.

She turned her attention back to the computer, to pick up the search for Charlie. Just as with Daniel, there had been absolutely nothing about him, no matter what search she tried, but she'd had an idea. Charlie's twin brother, Sam, would definitely be able to tell her where he was. She typed 'Sam Jones+Sligo' into Google and the top hit that came up was Sam's Tool Hire, Sligo.

It had to be him. There couldn't be more than one Sam Jones in such a small town. Maggie picked up her phone and dialled the number on the website.

A woman came on the line. 'Hello, Sam's Tool Hire, can I help you?'

'Can I speak to Sam Jones, please?' Maggie replied.

'Can I tell him who's calling?' the woman asked.

'An old friend. Maggie Behan is my name.'

'Hold the line, please.'

While Maggie waited, she wondered if he'd remember her. 'An old friend' was hardly the right description. Throughout their teenage years, Sam had looked on her and Dee with barely masked contempt.

'Hello?' It was a man's voice.

'Sam,' said Maggie. 'I don't know if you remember me. Maggie Behan?'

'Of course I do,' Sam replied, but his voice certainly didn't sound like that of a man delighted to hear from an old acquaintance. 'How can I help you?'

'I'm trying to get in contact with Charlie,' Maggie said.

'He's not here.'

'I know,' said Maggie. 'I spoke to your father, who said he hasn't a clue where Charlie is. And I can't find him on Facebook. It's like he's disappeared off the face of the earth.'

Sam said nothing in reply to this, so Maggie pressed on: 'I was wondering if you had any contact with him?'

'No,' said Sam. 'None.'

'It's just that I'm trying to find him to come along to the Abba concert in Stockholm in July. You've heard about it?'

'Look, I have to go. I'm busy.'

'We're re-forming the Abba fan club we had when we were teenagers.'

'Goodbye,' said Sam.

Just before he hung up, Maggie managed to squeeze in: 'If you see or hear from him, please tell him to contact me.'

When he'd gone, she realised she hadn't given him any contact details, so she pressed re-dial on her phone. The receptionist sounded reluctant as she took down Maggie's number.

41. Trying to Conceal

'What gas mark should I set the oven at?' Joe asked. He was down on his hunkers scrutinising the cooker's dials, wearing a navy butcher-striped apron. Dee couldn't help smiling to herself. They were constructing the dinner entirely from Marks & Spencer ready-meals. There was hardly any need for aprons.

She picked up the dauphinoise potatoes and squinted to read the instructions, which were maddeningly printed in the smallest font-size possible. 'Gas mark five for thirty minutes,' she said. 'We might as well put the parsnip chips in at the same time.'

'Right,' said Joe, pushing the oven's ignition button so it began clicking. 'Hand over those potatoes, young lady.'

Dee had expected him to object to having Connie and her new boyfriend over to dinner, but he'd been enthusiastic. Excited, even. He was being so good. Trying to make it up to her in whatever way he could.

The morning after the miscarriage, he'd arrived at the hospital at seven a.m. and, although it wasn't visiting time, barged his way in. She'd woken to find him sitting on her bed, sobbing.

Dee had instantly started crying too and for the next ten minutes the two of them had sat in silent grief together. At some point, his hand had made contact with hers on the bedcover and he had held on, like a man trying to save himself from drowning.

When eventually he spoke, he'd said, 'I'm so sorry,' and repeated it over and over again. 'I'm so sorry. I'm so sorry.'

A nurse had come in to take Dee's temperature and blood pressure. She hadn't said anything to Joe and had glanced at him only once, her face studiedly blank. Dee wondered if the nurse, who had seen her bruises, was quietly judging Joe as she pumped up the blood-pressure armband.

By the time she had finished and gone, Dee had recovered enough to ask, 'Where were you, Joe?'

'I'm so sorry,' Joe repeated.

'But where were you? I waited for you in the counsellor's office. Why didn't you call? Or text, even?'

'The Tesco guys.' Joe groaned. 'They took me completely by surprise.'

'What do you mean?'

He'd told her that Tesco, his biggest suppliers, had turned up at the office claiming they had made an appointment to review their account yesterday afternoon. He'd taken them to lunch to smooth over his unreadiness.

'I kept trying to get away so I could call you, but they wouldn't give me a moment,' he'd said. 'The lunch went on and on, and we had a few drinks, and then we went to a bar … And then … You know, how these things go.'

Dee wasn't convinced. 'How come you forgot such an important appointment?' she asked. 'It's not like you.'

'I don't know,' Joe replied. 'I honestly don't know.'

He'd sat there, still holding her hand, for another minute, then asked, 'How are you feeling?'

'There's still a bit of pain, but nothing like it was.'

Tears had started rolling down Joe's cheeks again. 'And the baby?' he said. 'How many months was it?'

'Six weeks,' Dee said. She felt drained, even though she'd only just woken.

Joe had lowered his head. When he'd looked up again, his eyes were agonised. 'I did it, didn't I?'.

'We don't know that for sure,' Dee said, feeling her usual helpless urge to comfort him, even though it was the truth. She was full of conflicting feelings, sorrow, blame, anger, fear … but the one coming out on top again was sympathy. Who knew what in Joe's background made him behave as he did? Maybe this was the shock he needed to wake up to the fact that it couldn't go on like this.

She had squeezed his hand. 'We could try for another baby, when we're ready.'

'Yes.' He had nodded emphatically, his eyes wet. He reached over to put his arms around her. 'I promise, on my life, I will never, ever hurt you again.' His muffled voice came from the shoulder of her hospital gown.

Later, as he was gently helping her into the car to bring her home, Dee had smiled for the first time in what seemed like an age. He had clicked the door closed and gone around to the driver's side.

Watching him through the windscreen, Dee had decided that this time it was true. She believed him.

'Will you have red or white, Sean?' Joe asked. 'Or would you like a beer?' He was being the perfect host.

'I wouldn't mind a beer if you have one,' Connie's boyfriend said. He was twenty-seven – 'A year and a half younger than me,' Connie had told Dee, when they'd started going out, as if it was an age gap of epic proportions – and he had one of those big faces that looked as if he was about to agree with what you said before you came out with anything.

'I'll have white,' Connie said. 'No, red … no, white. God! I can't make up my mind.'

'Why don't you try the white?' said Dee. 'It's a really nice Sauvignon

Blanc. I think you'll like it.' Connie was nervous, she knew. It was the first time she'd been invited to Dee's for dinner and it was clear she was all out to make a good impression, dressed to the nines with too much makeup, her copper mane pinned back with a glittery grip.

'Okay, the white, then, thank you.'

Connie shot Sean a sideways glance as he was about to drink the beer Joe had capped for him by the neck. He quickly took the bottle away from his face and began pouring it into a glass. 'Pardon my manners,' he said, and Connie's admonishing frown turned into an indulgent smile.

Joe had brought a beer to the table for himself and, following Sean's lead, poured it into a glass, although Dee knew he preferred to drink it from the bottle.

'The branding for the Copper Alley restaurants is wonderful, isn't it?' said Connie, taking a sip of her wine.

Dee smiled at her. 'Let's not talk shop,' she said. 'We deserve a little break, I think.'

The branding for Copper Alley was, in truth, all wrong. The receivers had insisted on using a graphic designer they'd employed for some other campaigns, probably because he was cheap. Dee would have her work cut out convincing them not to use his designs, but she was confident she could make them see that her way was the right way to proceed, and she had a great designer in mind.

'I'll drink to that,' said Sean, raising his glass. 'We all deserve a little break.'

'This is delicious,' said Connie, lifting a forkful of her starter. 'Is that nutmeg I'm tasting?'

'Yes.' Dee nodded. 'There's nutmeg in there.'

'You're a lucky man, Joe,' said Connie. 'Dee's such a wonderful cook.'

Joe laughed as he swallowed his beer. 'Yeah, right,' he said. 'A *wonderful* cook.'

Dee nudged his elbow and laughed too. 'Put a lid on it, mister,' she said. 'It's not like you're Gordon bloody Ramsay.'

Still laughing, Joe turned to Sean. 'Seriously, I don't know what her mother taught her.' He pointed at the starter with his fork. 'It's Marks & Spencer ready-meals for you VIPs, but generally we only ever eat takeaway in this house.'

Maybe it was his use of the third person – 'her' – but something about this struck Dee the wrong way. Topping up her water glass, she noticed that Connie was staring straight at her, saying nothing.

'She's very good at reading the instructions on a package, though,' Joe added.

Connie cleared her throat. 'I expect, with the amount of work we have on at the minute, you don't get much time for cooking,' she said to Dee, and then turned to Joe. 'Our mothers didn't teach us to be successful businesswomen and perfect housewives at the same time, you know.'

Joe seemed to consider this and then he smiled, his eyes twinkling, at Dee. 'I guess they didn't,' he said. 'But your mother did a great job one way or another.'

Dee accepted this as an apology and the conversation moved on. But for the rest of the evening she couldn't help noticing that Connie didn't once look in Joe's direction.

42. *Too Hard to Handle*

Jade waited until Noah was safely out of the room before she stopped smiling and sat down on one the stools at the kitchen island.

'Daniel,' she said, 'I'm getting really worried.'

Daniel, who hadn't paid Jade much attention in the commotion of Noah's return from his weekend at hers, loaded down with his desktop computer, saw that she was pale. 'What's going on?' he asked, taking the seat opposite her.

'I saw some texts on Noah's phone. He left it in the sitting room the other night when he went to bed, and I went through his inbox.'

'Seriously, Jade, that's not kosher.' Daniel didn't like where this might be going. 'The boy deserves a bit of privacy.'

Jade's eyes were big brown ovals beneath her fringe. 'The thing kept beeping all weekend,' she said. 'He'd read the texts and then look miserable, but he wouldn't say who they were from. I think he left the phone behind on purpose so I'd see them.'

'What did they say?'

'They were terrible,' Jade said, tears in her eyes. 'Calling him a faggot. Saying he likes to do awful things to little boys. Telling him they'll get him and teach him a lesson.'

'Who are *they*?' Daniel asked. He was feeling sick.

'That's the thing. All the texts were from a blocked number. There's no way of knowing who's doing it.'

'Noah must know.'

'If he does, he's not saying. He refuses to discuss it.'

Daniel thought for a moment. 'I'll get him a new SIM card,' he said. 'That way they won't have his number.'

Jade gaped at him as if he'd lost his mind. 'Do you think just because they don't have his number that Noah's going to be safe? We have to go to the police, Daniel.'

Daniel shook his head. 'Both Noah and his headmaster think that would make things far worse. They're probably right.'

'What are we going to do, then? A new SIM card isn't enough.'

'I'll talk to him,' Daniel said. 'There's still a place open for him at St Bart's.'

Noah didn't answer when Daniel knocked on his bedroom door. 'Can I come in?' he asked.

There was a barely audible 'No,' so Daniel turned the handle.

Noah was stretched out on his duvet, looking up at the ceiling. He didn't acknowledge Daniel's presence.

'Can I sit down?' Daniel asked.

Noah shifted his legs, giving him room to sit on the edge of the bed.

'Your mum told me about the texts you've been getting—'

'She shouldn't have looked at them,' Noah interrupted. 'It's none of her business.'

'Well, I agree that she shouldn't be looking through your texts. But what's in those texts is her business. It's *our* business.'

Noah shifted on to his side to face the Lady Gaga poster on his wall that said, 'Shine in your own way.' His shoulder heaved and Daniel felt the atmosphere in the room shift. 'Look,' he said. 'Your mum and I only want to help you.'

'You can't,' Noah said to the wall. He was definitely crying.

Daniel had an urge to lie down beside his son and put his arms around him. Instead he reached out and awkwardly rubbed Noah's back. 'It's okay,' he said, knowing it wasn't okay and that nothing he could say would make it okay. There were bullies in the world, and there always would be. And kids like Noah would always be the kind who attracted them.

'Are you still dead set against St Bart's?' he asked.

Noah shrugged Daniel's hand away and shifted further towards the wall.

'Noah,' Daniel said gently, 'please, let me help you.'

Noah turned his head around on his pillow to face Daniel. His eyes were puffed up and his cheeks streaked with mascara. 'There's nothing you can do,' he said.

'At least tell me who's doing this to you.'

Noah shook his head. Two fat tears rolled out of the corners of his eyes.

'Please,' Daniel begged, 'I can't bear to see you like this.'

Noah turned back to the wall. 'Go away,' he said, his voice catching. 'Just leave me alone.'

Back in the kitchen, Jade had made a pot of tea. She poured a cup for Daniel as he took a seat. 'Well?' she said. 'How did that go?'

'He won't go to St Bart's. He won't tell me who's been texting him … He's up there crying and he won't let me do anything to help him.'

Jade got to her feet and made for the stairs.

'Leave him alone for a few minutes,' Daniel said.

Jade's shoulders slumped and she stopped. 'It's awful,' she choked. 'First Rob … now this … It's all my fault.'

'How can it be your fault?'

'If I hadn't encouraged him. If I'd just told him to try and fit in instead of allowing him to have his hair whatever way he wanted, or letting him use my makeup …'

'I don't think it would've made any difference what you did,' said Daniel. 'Noah's a law unto himself.'

'That's true,' said Jade, and gave a short laugh. 'He's always been like that. Even when he was a little baby, he used to grab my necklace, and instead of putting it into his mouth he'd try to put it on.'

Daniel laughed, too, at the image of a tiny jewellery-strewn Noah, but his mirth was followed by regret. 'I missed out on all that.'

'It's the here and now that matters,' said Jade, pouring herself some tea.

'But what if I had been around, taken responsibility? Maybe he wouldn't be having these problems.'

Jade set the teapot down. 'Daniel,' she said, 'maybe he would have turned out exactly the way he has no matter what you or I did. The thing is, we have to work out what to do now.'

'I have an idea,' said Daniel.

'Go on.'

'We could talk to the parents of the kids who are giving Noah a hard time. See if we can reason with them.'

Jade sighed. 'But we don't know who they are.'

'Well …' said Daniel, warming to his plan. 'There's a way of finding out.'

43. Something in the Air

Standing outside the bar, Cassandra gathered herself. She didn't know why she was so nervous; it wasn't as if anyone would know her. She could have a drink alone, or maybe strike up small-talk with a local – anything other than staring at the four walls of her hotel room for another night, or listening for a millionth time to the piano-lite version of 'My Heart Will Go On' in the hotel's piano bar.

Of the handful of pubs the receptionist had recommended, she'd chosen this one because the girl said it got a 'colourful crowd'. When Cassandra had been a teenager it was a haunt for the lowest of the town's life, a kind of forbidden den of vice on the corner of a grimy alley, but since then it had been taken over by new owners and its clientele was made up of art students and musicians, if the receptionist's description was anything to go by. The kind of crowd who wouldn't all turn to stare the minute a stranger walked in.

She took a breath and opened the door.

At the front there was a small open area dotted with Formica-covered tables and mismatched chairs, and it was so packed that getting past it to the bar looked like being an army manoeuvre. Nobody even glanced in her direction as she negotiated it. It took her the guts of five minutes, during which she wondered why she was doing this to herself, before she got through the crowd and shouted at the barman above the din of reggae music for a glass of Chardonnay.

'Where have you been all my life?' said a man who was sitting amid the chaos on a barstool. He had rusty dreadlocks that looked dirty, and a pair of equally muddy eyes that travelled from Cassandra's breasts down her body and back up again.

Long before she had begun her transition, Cassandra had been annoyed by women who complained about guys talking to their breasts and not to their faces. They were lucky, she'd thought, to have men admire their beautiful women's bodies. But now that she understood how it felt to be sized up, like a piece of meat, it made her feel slightly ill.

She didn't bother replying.

'Cat got your tongue?' the man asked, and Cassandra gave him a tight smile.

'Get me another pint, will you, darlin'?' a voice shouted, from somewhere in the crowd, and then into vision squeezed Pauline Feeny. Cassandra had grown up next door to her. Now she was a forty-plus-year-old woman with pink hair and a nose ring.

Cassandra jerked her head away to concentrate on the barman, who was taking his goddamn time with her drink.

The guy with the dreadlocks stretched out one long arm and pulled Pauline in beside him. He whispered something into her ear and the two of them started laughing.

Mercifully, the barman was coming with Cassandra's wine. She paid him and, as she turned away from the bar, accidentally caught her old neighbour's eye.

There wasn't a hint of recognition in Pauline's smile. 'Sorry,' she said, moving to let Cassandra past. 'It's rammed in here tonight.'

Cassandra smiled back and made her way towards the seating area at the front of the bar, breathing a sigh of relief. If Pauline's non-reaction was anything to go by, she was safer than she'd thought she'd be, given that this was such a small town and she was bound to bump into plenty of people from her past.

Luckily she was in the right place at the right time to jump into a seat in a corner when two girls, who looked like a pair of clean-cut American tourists, got up to leave. Cassandra took off the little red bolero jacket she'd agonised over wearing and sipped her wine. She surveyed the crowd. They were all of a certain age, late thirties or forties, but had a definite Bohemian edge. She couldn't remember Sligo being like this when she was young. It had been such a narrow, homogeneous place, where even wearing a pair of sunglasses in summer set you apart.

'Excuse me, is anyone sitting here?' said a voice to Cassandra's left. She turned to look into the face of a man with sandy stubble and a pair of round, wire-framed glasses. He was pointing to the stool just vacated by the second tourist.

'No, it's free,' Cassandra said.

'Do you mind if I sit down?'

'Of course not.' Cassandra smiled. He was not unlike an older, more filled-out version of John Boy Walton.

He took the seat and put his pint of Guinness on the little table. 'It's busy in here tonight,' he said.

'Do you come here often?' Cassandra replied, and then, realising what had come out of her mouth, gave a little laugh. 'Sorry, I didn't mean that like it sounded.'

'Once in a while,' said the man. 'You couldn't call me a regular, though.'

They dissolved into silence. Then the man asked, 'You're not from around these parts, are you?'

Cassandra took a sip of her Chardonnay. 'Well, not exactly. How about you?'

'I'm a blow-in,' he said. 'I've only been here ten years.'

Cassandra laughed and they both went quiet again. Then John Boy Walton said, 'What's your name?'

'I'm Cassandra. Cassandra Jones.'

'Sounds like a movie star's name.'

'I can assure you I'm not a movie star.' Cassandra smiled. 'And do you have a name?'

'John,' he replied, and Cassandra nodded, grinning.

'What's so funny?'

'Oh, nothing.'

'No. Go on, tell me.'

'Well, when you sat down I thought you looked like John Boy Walton.'

'Ah,' said John, with a sage nod. 'A *Waltons* fan.'

Cassandra had a fleeting memory of sitting on the floor with her back against her father's legs as he sat in his armchair, watching *The Waltons* on Sunday afternoons. 'I suppose I am a fan, although I haven't thought about it in years.'

'Remember Corabeth Godsey?' said John. 'And the Baldwin sisters?'

'I used to love Grandma Walton,' Cassandra said. 'She was so cranky but she had those really twinkly eyes.'

John looked directly at Cassandra. 'She was the best, all right,' he said.

As he spoke, a man with a grey beard and bushy eyebrows appeared out of the crowd. 'There you are, man!' he said to John. 'We're all down the back. You want a pint?'

John held up his half-drunk Guinness. 'Great stuff. Same again.'

He stood up to go and his glasses flashed at Cassandra. 'Nice meeting you,' he said.

'Likewise,' Cassandra replied. She watched him walk away, feeling an odd sense of loss.

She was lifting her glass to her lips when John reappeared. 'Listen,' he said, 'I know this sounds like a total cliché, but can I have your number?'

Cassandra took her phone from her bag. 'What's yours?' she asked. 'I'll text you so you'll have mine in your phone.'

44. She's Extreme

It was surprising how quickly a routine took hold. Maggie's chemo appointment had moved from Tuesdays to every second Thursday morning. She took to baking the day before and bringing in muffins or flapjacks for the staff, who welcomed her with increasingly familiar smiles. Then she'd get her bloods done, to make sure her white cell count was high enough for the chemo, which, so far so good, it always was.

There was an hour to kill while the bloods were in the lab so she'd walk out of the hospital and wander the streets of Chelsea.

During her fourth chemo date, Maggie's mobile had gone off while she was pointlessly fingering the bras in Marks & Spencer. The clinic was on the line to tell her to come back, that she was good to go for treatment today. 'You're not supposed to go shopping in the middle of your appointment with a drain in your arm,' the nurse had reprimanded her.

'Oh, I'm really sorry. I'll be back in ten minutes,' Maggie replied, not feeling in the slightest bit apologetic.

She flouted the rules because, no matter how many batches of brownies she brought in, the clinic had a terrible, negative, fearful air hanging above it. Everyone sat there, staring grimly ahead at the terrifying unknown. Maggie couldn't help thinking of all the hundreds of patients who had occupied its sofas and chairs before her, wondering if they had come to the last station on the cancer train.

The minute she got home after the treatment she'd take to her bed, bringing only a big jug of water, a glass and a basin to vomit into, telling her mother not to let anyone disturb her. She preferred to be alone, to be violently ill in private.

She'd stay in bed on Friday, Saturday and Sunday, getting over the side-effects, and allowing herself a lie-in on Monday morning, but come eleven o'clock, no matter how she was feeling, she forced herself to get up. She'd shower to wash away the sweat and sickness of the past few days, and strip the linen off her bed to put it in the washing machine on the hottest cycle, telling herself that she was one session down, one more towards the end of her ordeal. She didn't allow herself to think beyond that, to the mastectomy, to the final prognosis. She'd reach those stations on the cancer train later.

In the past eight weeks as the chemo nuked her cancer cells, something else had been happening inside Maggie too.

'Where are you going?' her mother had asked this afternoon, poking her head out of the kitchen door when Maggie was pulling on her coat.

'Out,' Maggie said.

'Out where?'

Something about her mother's stance, the thinning of her lips, the narrowing of her eyes, made her look like a prison officer. 'That's none of your business,' Maggie found herself saying, and the minute it was out of her mouth she felt a surge of childlike delight.

Her mother's forehead bunched up and she followed Maggie down the hall. 'You know what the doctor told you,' she said. 'You need your rest.'

'I'll be back soon,' Maggie replied, and closed the front door behind her with a satisfying click. She'd only intended going to Queen's Park and back, to stretch her limbs and get a bit of fresh air, but she felt as if she was setting off on a journey around the world.

Looking death in the face, while you felt so ill that you literally couldn't move, had a liberating flipside. It showed you that most of the things you thought were important actually weren't. That knowledge gave Maggie a sense of freedom she hadn't felt in years, freedom from being tied down by rules created by other people – people like her mother, who showed no signs of ever going home to Ireland, no matter how often Maggie said she was fine now and didn't need her any more.

Of course, the steroids might have had something to do with her new-found sense of liberty, but Maggie didn't care. Instead of going to Queen's Park, she hopped on the number six, which conveniently came to a halt just as she was passing the bus stop on Kensal Rise.

On the bus she sat watching London go by, deciding she'd let it take her into Oxford Street, where she'd maybe have a cup of coffee, or browse in John Lewis. The day was hers to do anything she liked.

The bus stopped and a woman with her head wrapped tightly in a magenta scarf got on. She smiled as she passed Maggie's seat, making her way to the back. Suddenly Maggie was overcome by the opposite of freedom, a sickly claustrophobia. The thought of Oxford Street, teeming with shoppers, didn't seem so inviting after all.

She let her eyelids fall, telling herself to breathe, but the bus came to a sharp halt and her chin bumped against her chest, jerking her eyes open again. She looked out and saw it had stopped at traffic lights. On the pavement a man was unlocking his bicycle from a pole.

He had a purple bicycle helmet. Just like the one Daniel was wearing in that paparazzo shot in the *Sunday Times Magazine*.

The guy unlocking his bike looked up, as if he had become aware of Maggie staring at him through the bus window.

It was him! She was absolutely sure of it! She'd studied that photograph a thousand times, and the resemblance was unmistakable.

Instinctively her knuckles went to the window and rapped, but he wound his lock around his bike without noticing. Maggie pulled herself to her feet, her claustrophobia forgotten, as the bus started moving again. She jammed a finger on the bell.

The next stop was less than a minute further on. She jumped off and began to jog back in Daniel's direction.

By the time she reached the place where he'd been unlocking his bike, he was gone. She was so out of breath she could barely stand straight. Leaning over, she spotted him cycling away from her on the other side of the road.

'Daniel!' she called. 'DANIEL!'

His bicycle turned a corner and he was gone.

45. Unknown Jungles

As Daniel turned his bike on to Elgin Avenue he thought he'd heard someone shout his name. He put his head down and pedalled hard.

As he cycled, visions of the worst of it went through his mind – never being able to walk on the street without being chased, the impenetrable walls of pleading and noise and flashing lights that greeted him every time he stepped out of a car. It had been a circus, with Vince as the master of ceremonies and Daniel on the flying trapeze. But when he'd looked down, there was no safety net. There was only a void into which he was always on the verge of plummeting.

When he'd told Vince he was leaving, he'd tried to explain why, even though it was almost impossible to put into words. 'It's like I don't exist any more,' he'd said. 'It's like I've been taken over by Danny Lane.'

'But you *are* Danny Lane,' Vince had argued.

Daniel had stood his ground. 'I'm not,' he'd said. 'Danny Lane is someone else. All those people out there think they own him. Maybe they do. But they don't own me.'

Stopped at traffic lights, he remembered Vince shouting at him, his face red and livid. 'You've got what everyone wants!' he'd roared. 'You're fucking famous!'

'But I don't want it,' Daniel had replied, never so sure of anything in his life. 'It's not what I thought it would be. It's like standing outside yourself and watching yourself all the time, making sure you play the part right.'

That was true, but what Daniel couldn't explain back then was the out-of-control sensation he had when he wasn't standing outside himself, an increasing occurrence. Then he had understood that the grabbing hands and screams and pleading were real, and it had felt as if he was going to be ripped apart and torn into little pieces until there was nothing left.

No Danny Lane.

No Daniel Smith.

No one.

Vince wouldn't have understood anyway. To him, fame was Nirvana, not Hell on Earth.

Daniel reached Noah's school gates just before four o'clock, in time to lock his bike to a signpost and watch the first trickle of students leaving. He positioned himself just around the corner at the junction before the gates so he had an adequate view without being seen.

It was about twenty minutes before Noah emerged, alone. Daniel watched him shrug his schoolbag on to his back, look left, right and over his shoulder. He'd shorn the long side of his hair so that it seemed to have been attacked with a Stanley knife. It stuck out at all angles on one half of his head and, as of Monday, the whole mop had been bleached ash-white again.

As he made his way across the road to the bus stop, three boys in school uniforms came sauntering out of the gates behind him.

'Hey, No-*ah*,' the fatter and taller of the three called, his voice a shrill tease. 'Where do you think you're going?'

From his angle, Daniel could no longer see Noah, who must have been waiting at the bus stop. As the three boys advanced across the road, he turned the corner, staying close to the wall so he could see what happened.

He still couldn't make Noah out. The three boys were facing into the bus stop with their navy-uniformed backs to the road, the fat one hunched over. Daniel made out the word 'faggot', and began to approach them. But just as he did, Noah made a bolt for it. He rounded the corner at the other end of the block, the three whooping boys in hot pursuit.

When Daniel got around the corner, Noah and his tormentors were nowhere to be seen. He was breathing heavily and wondering where they could have disappeared to when he heard another whoop, from up ahead. He started running again, but hadn't got far when he came across a tiny alleyway to the side of what looked like an empty house.

Noah was on his knees, the contents of his bag strewn on the ground around him. The fat boy was holding him by his bleached hair, forcing his face towards the crotch of his school uniform.

'You like sucking dick, No-*ah*?' he was saying, while the other two doubled over with laughter.

'He prefers little boys!' said one of the others, taking a break from his hysterics. 'Noah likes tiny widdle-peepees, innit!'

Daniel had followed Noah today in the hope of at least seeing who was bullying him, and maybe, if the timing was right, having a man-to-man word with them. He'd try to make them see sense before finding out who their parents were. Instead he found himself launching his whole body at the fat boy.

'What the fuck?' shouted one of the other two, as Daniel's fist made hard, painful contact with the bully's face. The pair jumped on him from behind, but the force of his rage was enough to shake them off. He could hear himself screaming, but he didn't know what words were coming out of his mouth. And then he saw Noah's face, gaping up at him in abject horror.

He stopped, his fist still in the air, his other hand pinning the fat kid against the red-brick wall.

The boy's stare was venomous as Daniel let him go. 'Is this your daddy, No-*ah*?' he mocked.

Noah said nothing.

The other two started laughing again, not so hysterically, though. It was like the flat clack-clack of a pair of magpies.

'Shut the fuck up!' the fat one roared at them, then put his face right into Daniel's. 'You don't know what you just did, mate,' he said, in a dull growl.

He pulled away, flicked his chin and the other two followed him out of the alleyway. 'See you very soon, No-*ah*,' he called over his shoulder, as he turned the corner.

On his knees, Noah was gathering up the scattered contents of his bag. Daniel bent down to help him.

Noah pushed him away. 'What the fuck did you do that for?' he asked, on the verge of tears.

Daniel didn't know how to reply. He was sorry it had happened the way it did, but he wasn't sorry he'd laid into the fat kid.

Noah pulled himself up and wrenched his bag from the ground.

'Noah,' Daniel said, 'I couldn't stand by and let them do that to you.'

'You've only gone and made it ten times worse!' Noah cried, his face twisted with wet anger.

Daniel reached his hand out to touch his son's shoulder. 'We can sort this out, mate,' he said.

Noah shrugged him off and started walking. At the corner to the alleyway he stopped and turned back. 'I wish you weren't my father,' he said. 'I fucking hate you.'

46. Living without Aim

'Just smell that,' Joe said, with his nose in his glass. He breathed in deeply. 'It's exquisite.'

Dee swirled her glass and raised it to her nose. The wine had a deep berry-like bouquet, with little grace notes of cinnamon. 'Lovely,' she agreed.

It was a Pinot Noir, the most expensive bottle from the menu that had been handed to them by the restaurant's sommelier. Joe had insisted on ordering it.

'Happy birthday to the most beautiful woman in the world,' he said, extending his glass over the table.

Dee clinked hers against his and smiled. 'Thank you,' she said. 'This is perfect.'

He'd booked Patrick Guilbaud's without telling her, greeting her after work with a champagne aperitif and telling her to put her best dress on.

'And that's not all,' he said, reaching into his pocket and pulling out a small package tied with a scarlet ribbon. 'This is for you.'

Inside was a green leather jeweller's box and inside that, on dark blue velvet, sat a tiny emerald droplet on a chain so fine it looked like a glittering strand of golden hair. Dee gasped with pleasure. 'This is too much,' she said.

Joe stood up and came to her side of the table. 'Here, let me help you put it on,' he said.

It was so light that Dee couldn't feel it on her neck. Browsing the menu, her hand kept going to the emerald to make sure it was still there.

For starters they both ordered pea tortellini with crispy chicken and truffle dressing, which sounded divine. Dee chose fillet of salmon for her main course, while Joe plumped for the roast duck breast with *foie gras*. When the waiter had taken their order, and the sommelier had topped up their glasses, Joe said, 'We're not only here to celebrate your birthday.'

'No?' said Dee, with a knowing smile. 'What else could there be?'

'Only the best goddamn rebranding of a business since Steve Jobs came up with the iPod.'

Dee laughed with pleasure. Copper Alley had been all over the papers this morning, with food reviewers and business columnists waxing lyrical about the revamp. Her clients at the bank had spent last night at the launch fêting her for her savvy, telling her they'd never again question a decision she made, and toasting her with as much of the free booze as they could consume. She knew it was all a load of bullshit and, come Monday, they'd be tallying up the books and telling her she'd have to cut pointless corners on the budget for their next project together.

'I guess I did a good job.' She smiled. There was no need for false modesty.

'You blew it out of the water, baby,' said Joe, raising his glass.

He looked happy, she thought. The haunted look he'd had in his eyes since she'd woken up to find him sobbing by her hospital bed was gone. And, sipping her wine, she recognised that her own haunted feelings had evaporated too.

The waiter arrived with their starters and Joe dug in. She loved the peasant-like manliness with which he shovelled food from his plate to his mouth, which contrasted almost comically with the way he appreciated his wine, sniffing it delicately and savouring every mouthful.

'What are you thinking?' he asked, and the way he said it sent a little erotic shiver to Dee's centre.

'Nothing much,' she said. 'Just that ... well, this is nice.'

Joe held his fork in the air, midway between his plate and his mouth. 'I think something has changed,' he said.

'What do you mean?' Dee asked. Bizarre as it seemed, with the meal and the emerald that hung around her neck, the thought that he was about to dump her flitted across her brain.

'I don't know ...' Joe said. 'I just feel closer to you. Like we've come through the worst together.'

'I know,' Dee said, and she did, because it was true. He had accepted responsibility for what he had done. His remorse seemed weightier, his contrition more real, as if he'd come to a conclusion about himself and there was no turning back.

Joe put down his fork and cleared his throat. Now he looked as sweetly nervous as he had on the day he'd proposed to her by the lake. 'Do you think we could try again?' he asked. 'For a baby.'

Dee thought back to her devastation on that black night alone in the hospital bed. She had never fully wanted a child, but the loss of one had opened a yearning in her so strong that it had become the first thing she thought about in the morning and the last thing on her mind at night.

Joe was simply putting it into words.

47. *Comfort and Compassion*

The house looked perfectly neat and tidy, but only the slightest scratch to the surface revealed years of neglect underneath. Finding just a bottle of bleach in the sink cupboard, Cassandra went to Tesco and bought a basketful of cleaning products. Her mother had been house-proud to the point of obsession. She'd be turning in her grave now at the state of the oven, which was thick with black, sticky grime, or the encrusted ridges of the taps in the bathroom.

'There's no need,' her father protested, when Cassandra had rolled up in a taxi and emptied her bags of shopping on to the kitchen worktop. 'You're making a big fuss out of nothing.'

But Cassandra could see the relief in his eye. He was an old-fashioned man, living alone for the best part of a decade in a house without a woman's touch. Cassandra assumed Sam's wife did her bit every now and then, but if memory served correctly, Delia was hardly a housekeeper at heart.

She got to work on the bathroom first, using an old toothbrush to scrub every nook and cranny, pouring a half-bottle of Cillit Bang down the toilet to help shift the layers of brownish dirt welded to the bowl. Her father loitered on the landing as she worked, saying nothing.

'Go down and read the paper, Dad,' Cassandra told him. 'Or watch television.'

But he refused to budge.

While she was scrubbing the sides of the bath, strands of hair hanging over her sweaty forehead, he poked his head round the door and said, 'What's your name again?'

Cassandra wondered if it was the Alzheimer's. But then she figured it was perfectly normal for him to forget, given that he had only met her once since her name-change. 'Cassandra,' she replied.

Her father repeated the name. 'Cassandra.' It was as if he was trying it for size.

It took her the best part of the day to finish the upstairs rooms, which had cobwebs in every corner and dustballs on the carpets.

She took a break at lunchtime and made ham and tomato sandwiches for both of them, which they ate in silence, sunlight streaming through the kitchen window and landing on the picture of John F. Kennedy that had hung beside the dresser for as long as Cassandra could remember. At dinnertime she asked her father if he wanted steak or chicken. She'd bought both options in Tesco, trying to remember what his favourite meals were.

Her father lit up. 'Steak,' he said, with the air of a man about to be fed after a famine.

'Do you want chips with it or mash?'

'Chips,' said her father. His attention wandered to the kitchen window and he went quiet. 'Your mother used to make lovely chips,' he said after a minute.

Cassandra was overcome with sadness. After the rejection at her mother's funeral, she'd turned away from her father without looking back. In all the intervening time, between then and now, she'd only thought about herself and how she'd been hard done by. She hadn't imagined his loneliness.

'They were the best chips in Ireland,' she said, deciding to forget the oven fries she'd bought and try to replicate her mother's crunchy on the outside, floury on the inside hand-cut chips.

*

'This looks lovely,' said her father, when she put his dinner in front of him. He cut into his steak with supreme concentration, then chewed it slowly, briefly closing his eyes. 'You're a very good cook,' he added, after swallowing.

'Thank you,' said Cassandra, with a little flush of pride.

'What's your name again?'

'It's Cassandra, Dad. I'm your daughter.'

Her father frowned. 'I don't have a daughter,' he said. 'I have two boys.'

Cassandra put her fork on her plate. If, with the Alzheimer's, he had forgotten, how was she to explain the change to him? She decided to go for the simple approach. 'You have a daughter now,' she said, as gently as she could.

He looked at her in confusion and then, as it dawned on him, his mouth turned down at the corners. 'My Charlie,' he said, and sounded lost.

'Cassandra,' said Cassandra. She felt like crying.

Her father stared at her, then looked down at his plate. He picked up a chip on his fork and bit off the end. 'These are just like your mother's chips,' he said.

After she'd washed the dishes, she promised her father she'd be back tomorrow to do more cleaning, and that she'd cook the chicken for dinner. He half protested, then looked happy to acquiesce.

Instead of ordering a taxi, she walked across the town to the main Dublin road and the hotel, stopping on the way to buy the *Sligo Weekender* to go through its small ads. She'd have to find somewhere short-term to rent, and soon. It was stupid wasting her money on a hotel room. What she had in the bank would only last her so long before she'd have to think of what to do next – go back to work at Flikkers or find something to tide her over here.

Cleaning houses was exhausting work and by nine o'clock she found herself verging on sleep as she watched television, propped up with pillows on her hotel bed. She roused herself to take off her makeup and do her Eve Lom treatment. She cleaned her teeth and was putting on her nightdress when her phone buzzed with a text.

It was from John – she'd keyed in his name as 'John Boy' after their conversation about *The Waltons* that night in the pub. *Hi there, how r u?* he said.

I'm good, and u? she texted back.

Good here 2. Was wondering if u'd like to go out for dinner or a drink at the wknd?

I'd absolutely luv 2, Cassandra texted, then worried that she'd sounded desperate.

Great!! Sat nite, then?

Cassandra noted the double exclamation mark with relief. *Perfect,* she typed.

I'll call u on Sat 2 arrange.

Talk then.

Goodnight Cassandra.

Cassandra smiled to herself, wondering if this was a *Waltons* reference. *Goodnight John Boy,* she texted back.

48. Dead End Street

When Maggie and Poppy arrived, there were three other people waiting outside the Ticketmaster outlet. Maggie was relieved, having had visions of a queue extending all the way around Leicester Square and down to Haymarket. They were early so they had a good chance of bagging four tickets when the shop opened at eight o'clock. Better, anyway, than the precariousness of trying to get to the top of the queue on-line.

Dressed for a night of exposure to the elements, she wore a sheepskin hat and a waterproof windcheater over a thick woolly jumper, a T-shirt and a thermal vest. Poppy, on the other hand, wore a faded-to-grey T-shirt, featuring a barely discernible CND logo, a short skirt, a light camouflage jacket, red leggings and her ubiquitous Doc Martens. Her dreadlocks stuck out at the top of her head, tied up in a twist of mustard muslin. 'This is ridiculous,' she muttered, for the umpteenth time, as Maggie handed her one of the little folding stools William had bought years ago, when he was in his birdwatching phase.

Maggie didn't reply. She set her Tesco bag-for-life on the pavement. It held a flask of strong black coffee, to keep her alert, and a tin of buttered scones that she'd imagined convivially sharing with their queue-mates, as they chatted about Abba through the wee small hours.

Their queue-mates were not convivial. At the very top, on a similar folding stool to Maggie's, sat a man in an anorak with his hood tied so tightly she could see only a small part of his reddish face. He was keeping himself to himself. Two bleached-blonde women were standing up, completely unprepared for the night ahead in halter-tops and denim skirts that gave about as much coverage as two strips of dental floss. They were lighting cigarettes as Maggie and Poppy took their places and when Maggie said hello, they turned to give her a once-over, then leaned towards each other, muttering.

Maggie couldn't remember the last time she'd been in the West End at this time of night. Years and years ago she and William would go to shows together and then for a drink or two before catching the last tube home. The Hippodrome was the big club of choice in those days, but she'd never been. By the time she'd arrived in London, her clubbing days were already over. She'd thought at the time that she was supremely grown-up, married and already pregnant, with a husband who worked in a bank and a mortgage on their very own three-bed mid-terrace, but looking back on it she had been barely older than Poppy was now. Twenty-one and a bit.

She and William had been married within six months of them finishing college, making good on everyone's expectations, including her own. At the wedding reception, her father had brought himself to make a speech of such brevity that it had passed between the time Maggie dipped her fork to her dessert plate and brought to her mouth a piece of the madeira wedding cake, which her mother had insisted upon – his main point being how delighted he was that the Behan family was joining up with the Corcorans. After all, he and William's father had been friends since they were boys in school together, so it was a fitting union. Earlier that day, after walking her up the aisle and handing her over to William, he had had the air of a man relieved that the deal was finally being sealed.

'Hookers,' Poppy mouthed, flicking her eyes in the direction of the denim dental-floss girls and Maggie turned to take them in once more.

Surely not. What would prostitutes be doing in a queue outside Ticketmaster? 'Are you sure?' she asked, under her breath.

Poppy replied out loud, 'What do you think, Mum?'

Maggie didn't say it, but she had been thankful when Poppy had arrived home with her rucksack on Monday night and, bursting into tears, revealed that it was all over with Orlando. 'I hate him!' she'd sobbed, as Maggie's mother made a cup of tea and Maggie opened a Tupperware box of leftover flapjacks from the batch she'd baked for the nurses the Thursday before last. 'I never want to see him again.'

'What happened?' Maggie had asked, taking a seat beside Poppy at the table and stroking her hair.

Between sobs, Poppy had bitten off a chunk of flapjack. 'You wouldn't understand.'

'Try me,' Maggie urged.

Poppy had given her a despairing look. 'He doesn't believe in a woman's right to choose.' Fresh tears had welled.

'A woman's right to choose what, honey?'

'Abortion.' Poppy sniffled.

Maggie had stopped stroking her daughter's hair and her hand jerked away. It had felt like one of those movies where the action stopped and the actors froze. The familiar surroundings of the kitchen had fallen away, and there were just the two of them – Maggie and her mother – suspended in space, neither of them looking at the other. Maggie could hear the thud of her own heartbeat.

'See?' said Poppy. 'I knew you wouldn't understand.'

Maggie had caught her mother's eye. She didn't know what she was seeking there. Reassurance, maybe? But her mother was clearly exasperated. She glared at Maggie as if she had made some huge *faux pas*.

'What's going on?' Poppy had looked at each of them.

'You're not pregnant, are you?' Maggie asked.

'God, no,' Poppy had replied, as if she'd never heard anything so preposterous. Then she'd started crying again. 'I can't believe Orlando is such a patriarchal Fascist pig.'

'Excuse me for a moment.' Maggie's mother walked quietly out of the kitchen.

'He goes on and on about feminism and equal rights,' Poppy went on, oblivious to Maggie's discomfort, 'but when it comes down to it, really what Orlando wants is to control my body. He's a dictator, just like every other man on the planet.'

Since that outburst Poppy had barely left her room, only talking in gruff monosyllables when she came downstairs for the meals that were put in front of her. But still Maggie was glad to have her home. As long as the focus could be on Poppy, Maggie and her mother could co-exist in the same space without speaking the words that were bubbling just beneath the surface.

Today, after Oona had point-blank refused to come with Maggie to queue outside Ticketmaster, Poppy had jumped at the chance.

'Are you sure?' Maggie had asked her.

'Of course I am,' Poppy replied, pulling her Docs on, like a convict who'd just been reprieved. By the time they were on the tube, she'd been complaining about the futility of the exercise.

About ten minutes after they'd taken their places outside Ticketmaster, the two dental-floss girls stubbed out their cigarettes and ambled away, leaving them second in the queue. Throughout the night, fifteen more people arrived. Maggie counted them, surprised at the small number, but increasingly relieved too. With sixty-five thousand tickets on sale, she was sure to get the measly four she needed.

When she offered the man in the anorak a cup of coffee and a scone he refused, silently shaking his head. Beneath his hood, Maggie couldn't make out his expression. The woman who was now in fourth place behind Poppy was happy to take the offering, and stood holding the plastic cup in both hands to warm them.

'Would you like to sit down for a bit?' Maggie asked her, proffering her stool, but the woman said she was fine. She wore plaid trousers and a padded olive-green anorak, her hair perfectly shaped to her head like a black dome. She was too old to be standing in a West End queue at dead of night, Maggie thought, but then again, seeing Abba perform was a chance in a lifetime.

'I'm so excited about the concert,' Maggie told her, leaning past Poppy, who had been heavily involved with her phone for most of the time so far. 'I never got to see them when they were together, did you?'

'Oh, I did,' said the woman. 'In 1979, at Wembley.'

'They came to Ireland in 1979 too,' said Maggie, 'but I was too young and my parents wouldn't let me go all the way to Dublin.'

'I'll never forget it,' said the woman, munching the scone Maggie had given her. 'To this day, it was the best concert I ever saw. I always tell my husband the same thing. The best I ever saw.'

She might have been a bit on the dull side, but at least the woman – Mavis, as she introduced herself – was someone to talk to, or rather listen to, as the hours dragged by through dawn and towards opening time, with Poppy barely lifting her head out of her phone, except to complain that she was cold.

Maggie kept trying to steer the conversation back to Abba as Mavis regaled her with punchline-free stories about her grown-up children, laughing away as if she was sharing hilarious anecdotes.

'And the minister was late!' she shouted, over the noise of a man driving a green street-cleaning machine, spraying the gutters. 'So we couldn't start the service until one o'clock!'

Maggie laughed along automatically, as the guy beside her jumped to his feet, knocking over his fold-up stool.

'It's opening,' Maggie said to Mavis, who shut her mouth instantly and eyed the young man rolling up the shop's metal shutter, like a tiger stalking prey.

'About time,' said Poppy, putting down her phone. 'I'm literally frozen solid.'

'I told you to wear something warmer,' Maggie said, and Poppy squeezed her eyes shut in annoyance.

When the shop was ready for business, Maggie stood behind the man in the anorak, and Poppy stood behind her. Anorak Man carried out his business in a low whisper, counting out dirty notes that he'd unrolled from an elastic band. Then it was Maggie's turn. She smiled and said, 'Good morning. Can I have two tickets to Abba at Friends Arena in Stockholm, please?'

The guy, unshaven and unkempt, looked like he might be nursing a hangover. He started typing into his computer.

'Sold out,' he said.

'But that's impossible,' said Maggie. 'It's not even five past eight.'

The guy looked at her through bleary eyes. 'Believe me,' he said. 'It's possible.'

49. A Kind of Fear

Daniel woke up in foul mood. Even before he got out of bed he found himself groaning with fury at the sound of the car alarm that had been intermittently going off somewhere since yesterday evening. He flung off his duvet and stomped into the en suite to take a shower, stubbing his toe on the door jamb as he went. 'Fuck!' he swore, pain shooting through his foot. 'Fuck, fuck, fuck, fuck, fuck, FUCK!'

It had been a week since Noah had last opened his mouth to speak. Although the boy had reverted to spending most of his time in his bedroom, the atmosphere in every corner of the house was discordant and heavy. Daniel tried to tempt him downstairs by cooking meals he liked, or issuing invitations through his bedroom door to the cinema or to go shopping in the West End, but nothing was working.

When they did bump into each other, on the stairs, in the hall or the kitchen, Noah looked at Daniel as if he was something he'd found on the sole of his shoe. Then he'd retreat to his bedroom without a word.

Daniel didn't know if the bullying had escalated since his intervention. From the little he saw of Noah, there were no physical signs to say so. He'd emailed the headmaster, telling him what had happened and asking for the names of the boys involved, but the reply he'd received was noncommittal and lacking in information. 'Considering the families involved, it is my opinion that trying to negotiate with them is absolutely the wrong approach,' he'd written, reiterating his advice that Noah should relocate to St Bart's.

Daniel thought of following Noah again, then tailing one of the boys home without intervening in whatever bullying might take place, but after what had happened the last time, he dismissed the idea.

In the shower he cursed again – the shampoo bottle was empty – and washed his hair with a bar of soap, berating himself. 'You stupid prick. You fucking dickhead.'

In the kitchen he filled the kettle, flicked its switch on, and then, resting one hand on the countertop, told himself to take it easy. He'd have a strong cup of coffee and restart the day in a better frame of mind.

Upstairs he could hear Noah shuffling around, getting ready for school. Maybe today was the day the silence would be broken.

Taking a seat with a pot of coffee and a cup, Daniel listened for his son's footfall on the stairs. When it came, he straightened his back and waited, getting ready to say, 'Good morning,' with a smile.

But Noah didn't even come into the kitchen, and the sight of him passing through the hall on his way to the front door made Daniel jump to his feet. He'd dyed his hair pink, the exact shade of candyfloss.

By the time Daniel got to the hall, Noah had already shut the front door behind him. Daniel pulled it open again and ran down the steps to the street, still in his slippers. 'Noah!' he bellowed. 'Come back here this instant!'

Noah stopped without looking back, stood there briefly, and started walking again.

'Oh, no, you don't,' Daniel said, breaking into a run without caring that he'd left the front door hanging open, or that his slippers were getting soaked on the wet pavement.

'*What?*' Noah shouted, turning just as Daniel caught up with him. His lips were painted the same shade as his hair, the outline exaggerated so they looked twice the size. Just above them on the right-hand side he had drawn a beauty mark in the shape of a heart.

'You're not going to school looking like that,' Daniel said.

Noah stared at him in silence, then turned on his heel to start walking again.

Daniel ran in front of him. 'Are you out of your mind?' he yelled, as Noah came to a halt. 'You're bringing this all on yourself, looking like that!'

Noah folded his arms and cocked his head. 'Bringing what on myself?' he asked.

'I heard what that guy was saying to you in the alleyway. Calling you a faggot and telling you to – to …'

'To what?'

'You know what.' Daniel took a breath. 'Jesus, Noah, if you don't want people to kick the shit out of you because they think you're gay, then don't go around looking like you're gay.'

Noah didn't blink. 'Maybe I *am* gay, Daniel.'

'Are you?' It was out of his mouth before Daniel could stop it. He'd forgotten Jade's insistence on not asking.

'Are you?' Noah counteracted.

'What do you mean, am I?'

'Are *you* gay, Daniel?'

'Of course not.'

'You might be. You ain't had a girlfriend in years, Mum said.'

Daniel did a double-take. It was true about the lack of girlfriends, but that was because he'd sworn off women. He saw that there was the faintest trace of a curl on Noah's upper lip and understood he was being diverted. 'Come back to the house, Noah. Take the makeup off, at least,' he said.

Noah shook his head.

Daniel stood his ground, his arms folded in an echo of Noah's stance, and then grasped that there was nothing he could do to stop the boy making his own mistakes. 'I can't protect you unless you help me, Noah.' He sighed.

The trace of curl disappeared from Noah's lip and he looked fleetingly like the little boy Daniel had once half-known, even in the heavy makeup. But then he hardened his eyes. 'Who said I need you to protect me?'

Daniel flung his hands in the air. 'I give up,' he muttered, and moved out of the way to let Noah go to school.

Walking back to the house, he tried to imagine the conversation Jade had had with their son, when she'd mentioned that he hadn't had a girlfriend in years. It wasn't right that she talked to Noah about things like that. He was only fourteen, for God's sake. And it wasn't anyone's business but Daniel's.

50. *The Music Still Goes On*

Back in the kitchen, as Daniel poured the dregs of his coffee down the sink, he was assailed by futile guilt. He'd let Noah go to school dressed as he was. He'd just told his son that he couldn't protect him.

What kind of father did that?

His mind darted back to the day he'd come home from school after Philip Ewing had cornered him behind the bike sheds, telling him that the car accident had been no accident, that his mother had killed herself.

He'd dropped his schoolbag on the floor in the kitchen, then walked down the hall and straight into the forbidden study. His father had looked up from his desk. Instead of being angry at the intrusion, his face was a blank.

'Is it true?' Daniel had demanded. 'Did Mum kill herself?'

Since the funeral, his father had seemed to diminish in stature. His jaw was thinner, his shoulders were narrower, his lips turned inwards in his pallid face. His eyes alighted somewhere beyond Daniel's shoulder. When they returned to him, they were watery and cold. 'Don't you ever say such a thing about your mother again,' he said. 'Ever. Do you hear me?'

A lump rose in Daniel's throat but he resisted the urge to turn and run. He repeated, 'Is it true?'

His father rose to his feet and pointed at the door. 'Get out,' he said.

'Please, Dad …'

'I said get out!'

Daniel had been unable to stop himself running then, slamming the door behind him before taking the stairs two at a time. He threw himself face-down on his bed, willing himself not to cry because if he did he wouldn't be able to stop.

It was never spoken about again. His father became more and more withdrawn, so much so that Daniel blamed himself. If he had never brought home the horrible lie that Philip Ewing had told him, maybe his dad would have started wanting to be around him again.

Looking back, Daniel saw that this was ridiculous. It wasn't his fault that his father had retreated into a grief-stricken world of his own. Still, that moment in his study had been like the final nail in a coffin. They'd grown more and more apart, until one day, when he was seventeen and had just finished his A levels, Daniel had packed a bag, knocked on the study door, and told his father he was moving to London.

In the decade before his father had quietly passed away, they'd spoken to each other maybe six or seven times. Daniel had seen him only twice, visiting him on self-invented sufferance in that bleak house, where he'd remained alone to the end of his days. He'd vowed the last time never to go back again, as he had watched his dad squirm, clearly wanting to be rid of him.

At the end of the day, who knew if his mother had killed herself or not? It was a one-car collision with a wall. Her neck had broken when her head hit the windscreen and she'd died instantly. There had been no suicide note. No final farewell for Daniel, or a letter saying she would be looking over him as he grew up, telling him she loved him. Daniel could still vaguely remember her cuddling him and saying it. Almost every day you heard on the news about people dying in car crashes, about another life being snuffed out, and another. It was almost mundane.

Daniel had not had breakfast yet and felt a bit peckish. He considered going to the little café on Portobello Road for a full English, but then decided to have some toast and marmalade at home. He popped two pieces of bread in the toaster, put the kettle on for more coffee, and switched on the radio.

Of course an Abba song was playing – 'Mamma Mia'. There had been a lull in Abba-mania since the reunion announcement, but now that the concert was ever more imminent all the music stations had reverted to playing their hits back-to-back, day in, day out. You'd think it was the second coming of Jesus Christ.

An image of Maggie with her orange hair popped into Daniel's head, the way it did every time Abba came on the radio. The final bars of the song petered out as he was buttering his toast.

'*Mamma Mia!* We can't get enough Abba these days,' the DJ said, his voice bright with practised enthusiasm. 'We've got one Hell of an Abba competition coming up next week, people, so stay tuned in to hear all about it! In the meantime, here's another blast from the past. It's tipped to shoot straight to numero uno when it's officially rereleased next week. This is Danny Lane's smash 1988 hit, "How To Be A Man", remixed into a totally kick-ass dance tune by hot Brixton DJ outfit, Funk 'n' Further.'

Daniel dropped the butter knife.

It couldn't be.

The opening guitar riff played and then his own voice, almost unrecognisably clear and young, so naïve, floated out of the radio – '*A boy might think he's a man. He might do whatever he can …*'

Daniel lunged and wrenched the radio's plug out of the socket. He stood in the reverberating silence of the kitchen and tried to make sense of it.

Vince! That bastard!

He yanked his phone out of his pocket and searched for Vince's number.

'Hello, Vince David Productions,' a woman with an annoyingly nasal voice answered. 'How can I help you?'

'I want to talk to Vince – now.'

'I'm not sure he's available. Who can I say is calling?'

'Daniel Smith,' Daniel said, and then, on second thoughts, added, 'Danny Lane.'

The line went dead for a few seconds and then Vince's voice rang out. 'Danny, my boy!'

'What the fuck, Vince?'

Vince was oblivious. 'Great to hear from you! How have you been?'

'I just heard "How To Be A Man" on the radio. The DJ said it's going to be rereleased.'

'Isn't it fantastic? They've done great things with it.'

'You can't just remix and rerelease it like that,' said Daniel. 'I don't want it out again.'

'It's got a whole new lease of life!'

'You're not listening to me, Vince. I said I don't want it rereleased.'

The chirpiness disappeared from Vince's voice. 'I'm afraid that's not your decision to make, Danny, my boy,' he said. 'The record company owns the rights to the song. They can license them to whomever they like.'

'But ... I thought you owned the record company.'

'What's the big deal, Danny? Why not make hay while the sun shines?'

Daniel closed his eyes and squeezed the bridge of his nose with finger and thumb. 'I have no say in this, do I?'

Vince declined to answer. 'They're crazy for you again,' he said instead. 'You'll make good money from the remix.'

From the hallway he heard the doorbell ring. 'I have to go,' he said.

'Why don't you pop into the office for a chat, yeah? You should really think about recording another album. Or even a new single.'

The doorbell sounded again.

'I'm hanging up, Vince.'

'Just think about it, will you?' Daniel heard him say, as he pulled the phone away from his ear and pressed the hang-up button. He flung it on to the kitchen table and went out into the hall, just as the doorbell started up once more.

'All right, all right, I'm coming,' he said.

On the doorstep stood a diminutive woman, in a narrow grey business suit. She had long chestnut hair pulled behind one ear. 'I'm telling you there's no one home,' she was barking into her phone.

She stopped and looked up at Daniel. 'Mr Smith!' she exclaimed. She shoved her phone into the bag that hung from her shoulder, and stuck out her hand. 'I'm Joanna,' she said, flashing a smile. 'Joanna Brady.'

'How can I help you?' said Daniel, still reeling from his conversation with Vince.

'I'm from the *Daily Standard*,' said the woman. 'I was wondering if I could talk to you for a few minutes.'

'No,' said Daniel, his pulse speeding up again. 'Please go away.'

'I won't take up much of your time. I just wanted to ask you about being back in the limelight, how it's been for you ...'

'Go away,' Daniel repeated, stumbling backwards into the hall. He grabbed the door and slammed it shut.

In the stillness of the hall he could hear the thump-thump of his heartbeat and, above it, the journalist calling, 'Mr Smith! Please open the door!'

Daniel leaned against the wall, trying to let the cold hardness against his skull bring him back into himself.

The door's letterbox opened and through it Joanna Brady's clipped voice came loud and clear: 'Mr Smith. We'll get our story, one way or the other. It would be far better for you if you just co-operated.'

51. More Open-hearted

Cassandra wished Coco was there to tell her she looked like Kim Basinger.

She'd spent the whole afternoon trying to find something suitable to wear, wandering from shop to shop, repeatedly going through the process of stripping to her bra and knickers in overheated dressing rooms, scrutinising her reflection in various combinations of clothes and always finding herself wanting.

The dresses she wore in Playa del Inglés were bright and revealing; the prints went with the holiday style of the place, the party atmosphere of its endless summer nights. Those clothes had suited her too, the new Cassandra, with her freshly minted body. She'd wanted bright. She'd wanted revealing. She was celebrating and wanted to show herself off.

Now she found herself wanting to hide. Well, not hide exactly, but to fit into the style of the town, which wasn't zebra- or leopard-print or rhinestone-encrusted, which wasn't cut too high or too low. Yet none of the clothes she'd tried on seemed quite right. It was like she was negotiating her body all over again.

In the end she'd chosen a 1940s-style navy sailor-collar dress that tapered just below the knee, finding a narrow white belt in the same shop to tie it at the waist. It had a classic look, but accentuated her figure. Well, that was what she'd told herself in the dressing room. Now she wasn't so sure.

She'd arranged to meet John for wine and tapas at a place called Source. When he'd suggested it, Cassandra had smiled. Spaghetti Bolognese had been an exotic dish while she was growing up. Now the locals were dining on tapas and quaffing fine wines.

Sligo had certainly changed for the better. Yet Cassandra still found herself flung back in time. When she was a teenager, even though she'd tried her utmost to conform with how she appeared to the world, she'd always felt that eyes were on her, that people were nudging each other as she walked past them on O'Connell Street. In retrospect, she knew this was a figment of her imagination, that no one had questioned who she was back then – that they wouldn't even have thought to do so. Yet now she was imagining the same reactions again. The same eyes flickering suspiciously in her direction, the same nudges and murmurs as she passed by.

John had shaved off his sandy stubble and was waiting fresh-faced at a table for two when she walked into the tapas bar. He stood and went round to hold out a seat for her. Any other woman in the place might have taken this tiny act of chivalry for granted, but for Cassandra it was affirmation. It was unquestioning acceptance. 'You look very nice,' John said, as she took off her coat and sat down – more affirmation.

'Thank you,' Cassandra said, feeling a hint of her old shyness creep up. 'You look good too.'

He was wearing a sky-blue checked shirt, open at the collar, and a pair of cream chinos; his blond hair was parted carefully and combed to the side. Without his stubble he looked even more John Boy-ish. Cassandra wondered what age he was. In his mid-thirties, maybe. Too young for her, really, yet there was a kind of maturity about him, a hint of life experience beneath the boyish looks.

A waitress came and took their order, giving Cassandra a little time to settle in before she had to attempt proper conversation. In the taxi from the hotel, she had wondered what they'd talk about. It was unlikely they'd have anything in common.

'To your health,' said John, raising his glass when their wine was poured.

Cassandra lifted hers. 'Yours too.'

'So, what's a nice girl like you doing in a dump like this?' John said, as plates of tapas began to arrive.

'It's not a dump.' Cassandra laughed, looking around. 'I think it's lovely. This used to be a butcher's shop when I was growing up, you know.'

'You grew up here?' John asked.

'Well, sort of.'

'What does that mean?'

'It was a long time ago,' said Cassandra, picking up her fork. 'I did most of my growing up after I'd left.'

'And when was that?'

Cassandra dipped a chunk of *patatas bravas* into its accompanying spicy sauce. 'Tell me about you,' she said. 'What do you do for a living?'

John didn't seem to recognise that she'd batted his question away. 'I'm an ordinary common-or-garden handyman. Nothing to write home about. And what about you? What do you do?'

'I work in a bar,' said Cassandra. 'In Gran Canaria.'

'I've never been there,' said John. 'What's it like?'

Cassandra met his eye. 'Nothing to write home about.' She smiled.

The conversation began to settle down and flow. John, it transpired, was a writer in his spare time, and was working on a second novel. 'The first is under the bed,' he told her. 'I won't bore you with the details.'

'Please do,' Cassandra said.

So John had told her bits about the plot of the book he was working on now, which he described as a 'Chandleresque detective story set in the wilds of Donegal'. 'He's dealing with a serial killer and horizontal rain,' he said.

He didn't ask her any more questions about her past. It was as if he'd picked up on the message she'd sent him at the outset, and respected it.

On a bathroom break, Cassandra breathed a sigh of relief. On the rare occasion she'd dated guys in the Canaries, she'd responded to questions about where she came from with little bits of fiction. She had unshackled herself from her history so she'd felt free to rewrite it. But now she was at the heart of what had gone before and she didn't know how to negotiate the story.

At the end of the evening John took her back to the hotel in a taxi and told the driver to wait as he left her at the door.

'Are you sure you wouldn't like to come in for a nightcap?' Cassandra asked, thinking she sounded hopelessly old-fashioned, like Doris Day flirting with Rock Hudson.

'I think I'll call it a night,' John responded.

'That's okay,' said Cassandra, a little disappointed. Maybe the chemistry hadn't been what she'd thought it was. 'I had a lovely time, thank you.'

'Me too,' John said.

'Well, goodnight,' said Cassandra, turning to go inside.

'Cassandra?'

'Yes?'

'Can I see you again?'

Cassandra smiled. 'Of course,' she said, as John leaned in to bring his lips to hers.

52. Game Is On Again

Monday morning came, and Maggie felt worse than she had at any time since her treatment had started. It wasn't that the chemo was any more difficult to recover from than it had been after the four previous sessions. It was no better and no worse. She just didn't feel there was anything to get up for.

No tickets to the Abba concert to be had for love or money; no interest from Dee in going; Daniel within a hair's breadth one minute and vanished into the faceless muddle of London the next; Charlie nowhere to be found.

Maggie didn't know what she'd been thinking when she'd pinned all her hopes on a stupid reunion of people she didn't even know now, on a concert she should have realised she'd never get to. It was all an impossible fantasy.

This morning, her mother had popped her head through the door and said she wanted to go shopping for a new summer coat, which was a relief. She'd hardly left the house, except for mass on Sundays, in the past two weeks. Downstairs Maggie could hear Poppy moving about. She was probably still in the same CND T-shirt and leggings she'd been wearing since she'd come home, her face pale, her dreadlocks unwashed and pungent.

She moped about the house all day, every day, constantly complaining about what she was now calling Orlando's 'betrayal'. To listen to her, you'd think that Orlando had raped and pillaged an entire village of virgins, instead of having had a mild disagreement with Poppy over reproductive rights.

And the girl's bloody phone never stopped bleeping and ringing, mostly with texts and voicemails from Orlando, trying to get her to come back to the squat, as Maggie had been repeatedly informed.

'Why don't you call him?' Maggie asked. 'You could meet and talk it out.'

'Christ, Mum,' Poppy replied, with a maddening pout. 'You don't get it, do you? I can't be with a man who doesn't respect my autonomy as a woman.'

For all Maggie's annoyance, which she was careful to mask, she felt sorry for her daughter too. Poppy pretended to be hard and strong, but really she was a softie at heart, and she was pining for Orlando.

In the middle of Friday night, when Maggie was lying in a spasmodic sweat, having had her platelet injection earlier on, Poppy had come into her room.

'Mum,' she'd whispered, 'can I sleep with you?'

Maggie had woken from her half-dream with a start. 'What, honey?' she said.

'I'm feeling a bit lonely,' Poppy replied, her voice small.

Benny gave a sleepy cry of complaint and jumped off the pillow as Maggie shifted over, her stomach lurching. Poppy shuffled in beside her, cuddling up. The touch of her T-shirt against Maggie's skin felt abrasive, but she stroked Poppy's head and said, 'Go to sleep, honey. It'll be okay in the morning.'

Poppy needed her, and that was good. She had all but made Maggie redundant as a mother from the moment she'd turned thirteen. But with the intense heat Poppy's body was creating in the bed, all Maggie wanted was her out of it.

'Mum?' Poppy said, after a while, wrenching Maggie out of the sleep that had eventually come. 'Do you think Orlando loves me?'

'I don't know,' Maggie whispered, keeping her eyes shut. 'Do you love him?'

Poppy didn't answer, and after a few moments, Maggie heard little sobs. 'Don't cry, honey,' she said.

'Oh, Mum,' Poppy sniffled, 'I miss him so much.' And she went on crying.

When Maggie had woken that morning, Poppy had been back in her own bed. She'd come to again at noon to see her daughter hovering over her.

'Did you call Orlando?' Maggie asked, trying to bring herself back to life by inching up on her elbows.

Poppy gave her one of her glares. 'I told you, Mum. I'm not calling him,' she said. 'I don't know why you keep going on about it.'

Maggie lay back. 'Could you make me a cup of tea, honey?' she said. 'I'll try a bit of toast with it.' She wasn't sure she'd keep it down.

She listened to her daughter flump down the stairs and wondered if she'd been like that when she was Poppy's age, so changeable, so prone to stormy weather.

Now she could hear Poppy singing along to the radio in the kitchen at the top of her voice, a song that sounded at once familiar and foreign.

A waft of frying bacon drifted into the room and Maggie's stomach rumbled. Her nightdress was stuck to her skin as she pushed aside the quilt and put her legs over the bed, but she was so hungry her shower would have to wait. Benny lifted his head, yawned and got up to follow her. They went downstairs to the kitchen.

'I'm up,' she said to Poppy, who turned from the frying pan and miraculously smiled. She'd changed her clothes, and was wearing a pair of jeans and a washed-out purple T-shirt.

'Would you like some breakfast?' Poppy asked.

'Yes, please,' said Maggie.

The song on the radio segued without a DJ interlude into Abba singing 'Honey, Honey', and Poppy hummed along as she put more bacon into the pan. She didn't have the most melodious voice in the world, but Maggie was reminded of her as a little girl, swivelling her hips in the sitting room with her fist held to her mouth in approximation of a microphone as she sang along with her S Club 7 CDs.

'You're in a good mood,' said Maggie. 'What's going on?'

'What do you mean?' Poppy replied, but she had a twinkle in her eye.

'Is it Orlando? Have you talked to him?'

'No, I haven't,' said Poppy, pushing the bacon around the pan. The aroma made Maggie's stomach rumble again, audibly. 'I'm just in a better mood, okay? It has nothing to do with Orlando.'

'Okay,' said Maggie. On the radio, 'Honey, Honey' came to an end and a DJ began to speak.

'Mum,' said Poppy, taking the pan off the heat, 'I have some more stuff to collect from the squat.'

Out of the corner of her ear, Maggie heard the words, 'Four tickets.'

'Could you give me a lift?'

'Sssh!' Maggie said, and Poppy shot her a wounded look.

'Accommodation at Sweden's famous super-luxurious Absolut Ice Hotel and a thousand pounds spending money,' the DJ was saying. Maggie got to her feet and turned up the volume.

'To enter London FM's amazing and totally exclusive Big Fat Abba Competition, all you have to do is tweet, write on our Facebook wall, text or call our hotline to say why you deserve to see Abba in Stockholm this August. And remember, Abba-maniacs, the winner takes it all!'

The opening strains of 'Mamma Mia' kicked in, as Poppy put two plates of toast and bacon on the table. 'You haven't a snowball's chance in Hell of winning those tickets,' she said.

Maggie sat down again. 'You know my friend Alison?' she said.

Poppy shoved a whole rasher into her mouth. 'No,' she said, chewing. 'Why?'

'She works with me in the library,' said Maggie, digging into her own breakfast with renewed vigour. 'Her husband is the director general of London FM.'

53. Your Darling Fiddle

Dee thought her mother would be over the moon when she told her that she and Joe were trying for a baby, but instead she was greeted by silence.

'That's nice, dear,' her mother said eventually.

'Nice?' Dee said. 'Is that all you can say?'

'Well,' her mother replied. 'I mean ... well ...'

'Well, what?'

'Are you sure it's the best idea?'

Dee rolled her chair around from her desk so that she could look out of the window at the sky. It was clear blue, not a cloud in sight. 'Of course it's the best idea,' she said. 'Why wouldn't it be?'

'Well, your career for one thing,' her mother said. 'Babies take up a lot of time, you know. How will you run your business?'

'I'm not even pregnant yet,' Dee countered. 'I can figure all that out if it happens.'

'You're not as young as you used to be, Dolores. Having children later in life is a lot harder than it is for girls in their twenties and thirties, and there can be more—'

'Mum,' Dee interrupted, and swung her chair back to her desk. 'I have to go. I've a meeting in ten minutes.'

'All I'm saying is you should think about it,' her mother said.

'We have thought about it, Mum. Honestly, I thought you'd be happy for me.'

'I *am* happy for you,' her mother said, but she sounded miserable.

'And you'd be a granny,' Dee said, feeling like she was cajoling a difficult child. 'That'd be nice, wouldn't it?'

Her mother faltered. 'I hadn't thought about that,' she said, which was a barefaced lie. All through the years that Dee had hopped from relationship to relationship, never settling down, there had been an unspoken disappointment that she hadn't taken the anticipated route by getting married and producing a clatter of grandkids. At one time she had been less forgiving of her mother, when her refusal to fulfil these expectations had felt gratifying, like exacting quiet revenge, but she had long come to understand that her mother didn't deserve that. It was Dee's father who had insisted on boarding school, who had brooked no argument and remained steadfast in his decision, no matter how much Dee had begged not to be sent away. Her mother had simply not argued, because she couldn't. It wasn't in the nature of their marriage.

Now when Dee remembered those horrible winter Sundays, waiting outside the station for the Galway bus to open its doors, their breath billowing in clouds in the freezing cold, she could feel her mother's loneliness along with her own. Her mother had smiled, brushed Dee's coat down, making sure she was well turned out, and never showed an iota of what was going on inside. But her hug had lingered and tightened. She could clearly picture her mother's forlorn figure waiting at the station door all those Sundays until the bus turned a corner and was out of sight.

'You could come to Dublin as often as you liked to see the baby,' Dee said. 'And we'd come to see you too, so that she'd get to know and love her granny.'

In the background of her mother's kitchen the theme tune to the hourly radio news kicked in. 'Oh, that would be lovely,' her mother said, and Dee sensed that that was a declaration in an argument she was having with herself.

After she'd got off the phone, Dee buzzed Connie and asked her to go out to get a couple of salads from Cornucopia for her lunch. Then she called Joe's mobile.

He picked up after one ring, and sounded genuinely delighted to hear her voice. 'How's the most beautiful woman on the planet?' he asked.

'I'm not just a pretty face,' Dee said, with a giggle. 'I have an exceptional brain too, you know.'

'Oh, I forgot.' Joe laughed. 'You're one of those intellectual feminists, aren't you?'

'A strident one.' Dee laughed back. 'I'm burning my bra as we speak.'

'To what do I owe the pleasure of this call?'

Dee groaned. 'I just told my mother we were trying for a baby. She was hardly jumping for joy.'

'It's a bit early, isn't it?' said Joe. 'To tell her, I mean.'

'I suppose so. But I thought she'd be happy. God knows she hinted at it for long enough when I was single.'

'Give her time,' said Joe. 'She's probably worried you'll be disappointed.'

Dee picked up a pen and surveyed it. 'I don't think I will be,' she said. 'I have a really good feeling about this.'

'Me too,' Joe said. 'And I can't wait to try again.'

Dee giggled once more, like a schoolgirl. 'Neither can I,' she said.

'I should come over there now. We could lock the office door and try on your desk. And on the floor. And on the sofa.'

'Joe!' Dee protested. 'You'll put me off my work, and I have so much to do!'

'I've got a better idea,' Joe said. 'I'll book a room in the Clarence and meet you there in half an hour. We could pretend we're having an affair.'

Dee suppressed another laugh. 'Seriously,' she said. 'I'm hanging up now.'

'C'mon, baby. You know you want it.'

Dee squeezed her legs together, a warm feeling flooding through her. 'Okay,' she whispered, as if someone might overhear her. 'The Clarence in half an hour.'

'That's my girl,' Joe crooned, and Dee felt that melting again, the one she'd had on the very first night she met him. It was like she was a fiddle, and he was the only one who knew how to play her.

Hanging up, she buzzed through to Connie again to tell her not to get the salads after all, but Connie had already left the building.

54. *Trying to Conceal*

Hotel rooms were like blank canvases on which you could portray yourself any way you liked. The furniture, the bed linen, the pictures on the walls, everything was designed to be fit-all, tasteful, yet devoid of personality. A hotel room gave away nothing about your past.

It suited Cassandra, but at the same time left her feeling a bit at sea. Its anonymity allowed her to stay in the uncomplicated here and now with John. Yet, without her familiar things, the trinkets she'd gathered to feather the little nest that was her apartment, it was as if she had shed a part of her identity. Half of her dearly wanted John to sleep beside her in her own room, to see who she really was.

'A penny for your thoughts,' he said, a sleepy smile playing on his face.

'Oh, nothing,' Cassandra said. 'I was miles away.'

John inched over in the bed, opening his arms to her. His smell was musky, a mix of faint, sweet aftershave and spicy dampness. 'This is lovely,' he murmured, while Cassandra snuggled into the crook of his neck. She felt the muscles of his arms contract as he held her close.

This was the feeling everyone talked about, the feeling that had eluded her all her life. In her mind she tried to put words to it, but none came. It was as if all her life she had been one separate organism, part of the world yet separated from it, drifting and absolutely alone at the same time. When John was making love to her, when he was inside her and their eyes were locked together, amid their breathing and sighs and the rhythm of their bodies she felt surges of what could only be described as possibility. She thought maybe she could be loved for, not despite, who she was.

It had been this way all weekend, this feeling of connection she knew existed but had never thought she'd have for herself. He'd arrived on Friday night and they had barely come out from underneath the duvet since, except to shower together or push the room-service tray out of the door.

His stubble had grown over the two days, making him less and less John Boy-ish as the hours went by. On the first morning Cassandra had redone her makeup in the bathroom, afraid of showing herself completely unmasked to him, but now her face was naked. The paint she used to mark herself as a woman was gone, but for the first time since her transition, she felt absolutely herself without it.

'You're beautiful,' John said to her, as he had maybe a million times over the weekend, and their bodies began to move in rhythm again. Cassandra believed him. She was beautiful. They were beautiful together.

She breathed in the smell of him, taking it as deep into her lungs as she could.

'You okay?' he asked.

'I'm perfect,' she replied.

He squeezed her to him again. 'I feel like I've known you for years,' he said. 'It's weird.'

Cassandra laughed. 'Weird?' she said. 'Where did you learn to be such a smooth talker?'

John laughed too. 'No, what I mean is, it's weird that I know nothing about you, yet it's like I *know* you. You know?'

'I know,' Cassandra said.

'And you know absolutely nothing about me.'

A little disturbance registered itself, like a pebble thrown into a still pond. 'I like that,' Cassandra said. 'You're my international man of mystery.'

'But don't you want to ask me any questions? Like where I was born, or who my family is?'

Cassandra hid her face in the soft hairs of his chest. Outside the room she could hear a muted conversation in the hallway. A peal of laughter.

'Well, I know you grew up here,' John continued. 'You told me the restaurant we had our first date in used to be a butcher's shop, remember? And I know you live in the Canaries now, with your friend Coco. So what happened in between?'

Cassandra closed her eyes. The feeling that had eluded her all her life had not actually eluded her. She had held it at bay because of this. If she allowed herself to feel it, allowed a man to feel it with her, there would come a time when he would have to know who she used to be.

She pulled herself away from him and sat up. 'I'm starving,' she said. 'Let's order the pancakes with bacon and maple syrup.'

John leaned on one elbow. 'Have I done something wrong?' he asked.

'No,' Cassandra replied. 'I promise. You haven't.'

He looked at her and his sky blue eyes, without his John Boy Walton glasses, glistened. 'You don't have to tell me anything, if you don't want to,' he said. 'You can be my international woman of mystery.'

Cassandra knew instantly that when she looked back on it she would pinpoint this as the moment in which she fell totally and utterly in love with him.

Part of her felt like getting out of the bed, opening the hotel-room door and running as far away as her bare feet would take her. Instead she let him put his arms around her again. The feeling she had held at bay for all those years was too good to let go, just yet.

55. Get the Chance

Every day, for a week and a half, Maggie hadn't stopped texting and calling to leave messages on the London FM hotline, telling them why she deserved to win the Big Fat Abba Competition. She entered as many times as she could via their Facebook page too, and she didn't hesitate to use her unique selling point.

'Thirty years ago, three childhood friends and I vowed we would reunite if Abba ever did. I never could have imagined then that I would now be battling cancer, bald but determined. I am also determined to make good on that promise we made. Winning those tickets would make a childhood dream come true,' she said, leaving it open as to what kind of cancer she had, and whether it was terminal or not.

And it was true. No one knew whether she'd be given a reprieve or if the cancer would turn out to be terminal. At her last check-up, Dr Snow might have said that things were coming along 'nicely', that the treatment was 'significantly shrinking' her tumour, but he'd also added that until the course was finished, and possibly not until the mastectomy was done and the radiation treatment complete, they wouldn't know if she was 'out of the woods'.

He had emphasised 'possibly'. For all his reassuring professionalism and sympathetic smiles, Dr Snow was not God. The medical people did what they could. They unleashed the full force of their chemical compounds in the battle against the further invasion of Maggie's cells by a hostile force, but they couldn't predict the outcome. War was like that. You never knew who was going to win until the final battle was over.

Maggie was on the sofa, entering the competition on Facebook again with her phone, when her mother walked in. She was pulling on a pair of leather gloves, even though it was warm outside.

'What is it, Mum?' Maggie asked, without looking up from the phone.

'I'm going to twelve o'clock mass.'

'Okay,' Maggie replied. All the days rolled into one in the fortnight between her chemo sessions. She'd forgotten it was Sunday.

'It's the Feast of the Ascension,' her mother added.

'Is it?' Maggie said, pretending to concentrate on her phone. She had a fleeting memory of parading through the streets of Sligo town just after her first holy communion, all the girls in their white dresses and a priest at the top of the procession, saying monotone prayers through a megaphone. She had been so devout back then, with her little altar to the Virgin Mary on the windowsill of her bedroom and her white prayer book with its picture of Jesus surrounded by adoring children, one little girl sitting on his knee, staring enraptured at his halo.

Even though her dedication to Jesus and Mary had waned as she'd got older, and instead of going to mass on Sundays she'd started sneaking off to hang out by the river with Dee or whoever was available, she'd believed in God and the whole religion thing right up to when she was fifteen and her mother had told her they were going to the clinic in Manchester to have the baby 'taken care of'.

She could remember as if it was only yesterday her mother leaving her bedroom and locking the door behind her. Maggie had lain on her bed, staring at the ceiling dry-eyed, trying to make sense of it.

It was against God, wasn't it? Abortion. It was murder. A mortal sin.

But her mother, who had pride of place right behind the parish banner at the top of the May procession, was insisting on it. She wasn't in the slightest bit worried about Maggie's eternal soul, or even her own.

Maybe she didn't believe in all the stuff she said she believed in. Maybe it was all made up to keep people in step behind the priest and his megaphone.

'You should come to mass with me,' said her mother now, still unmoving from her spot by the sitting-room door. 'It might do you good to say a few prayers.'

Maggie almost laughed. 'Mum,' she said, 'I haven't gone to mass in twenty years. I'm not going to start now. You go. I'll make lunch for when you come home.'

'Well, if you won't pray for yourself, I'll pray for you,' her mother said. 'God hears us, you know. He listens.'

There were a million things Maggie could have said to this, but she bit her tongue. It would mean having to bring up Manchester and the whole sorry unmentionable thing. And that was what it was – unmentionable. From the moment she and her mother had boarded the boat back to Ireland, where everybody bar Maggie's father thought they'd just gone to Dublin for a mother-and-daughter treat, it had never been spoken of again.

Her mother lingered a few seconds more, then retreated out of the front door, without saying another word.

Maggie shivered and went back to Facebook to type in another ticket appeal on the London FM page.

As part of her campaign she'd popped into the library yesterday on the off-chance that Alison was working, so she could drop a hint about getting her husband to fix it. She couldn't ask outright.

'Actually, I really hate Abba,' Alison had said, when Maggie had waxed lyrical about Abba over coffee in the staff room.

It was the perfect opening for Maggie to tell her how much she adored them and how much it would mean to her to be able to go to the concert with her childhood friends.

'Well, you should definitely go,' Alison said, with an encouraging beam. 'It will be nice for you to have something to look forward to.'

'Well, the tickets are like the Holy Grail. Nobody can get them.'

Alison took a sip of coffee. 'I'm sure it's not that hard,' she said.

'London FM's running a competition,' Maggie went on. 'And, can you believe, it's for four tickets? Exactly the number I need.'

Alison put her cup down. 'And you want me to talk to Simon?' she said. 'Is that it?'

Maggie cringed and nodded, biting her lip.

Alison broke into a smile. 'Of course,' she said. 'I'll see what I can do.' Then she started going on about her problem finding a new kindergarten for the twins.

56. Age of No Regret

Joanna Brady hadn't lost any time. On her *Daily Standard* 'No Biz Like Showbiz' page, beneath another speculative story about the big Abba reunion concert – this time reporting from an 'official source' that there was in-fighting between the two female singers over what songs would take top billing – there was a half-page 'exclusive' about recluse Danny Lane.

'Lane Still Shunning the Limelight,' the headline read. The article continued: 'With Danny Lane's remixed single "How To Be A Man" shooting straight to number one, *Fame Game* judge and mega-producer Vince David says he wants the retired pop star to record a new album. But Lane, real name Daniel Smith, is hiding away in a west London mansion, refusing all media access.'

The article went on to reiterate the usual story about Daniel's retreat from the public eye to live the 'life of a hermit', ending, 'Typically, Lane was unavailable to comment.'

Daniel folded the café's newspaper and put it aside, shaking his head at the tabloid absurdity of a 'hermit' living in a 'mansion', like his mid-terrace was anything of the sort. If that was the worst Joanna Brady could do, he was relieved. Bar the mention of west London, this was the story the tabloids had been telling about him intermittently for years.

Without taking off the hat and sunglasses he'd taken to wearing, he ordered his usual from Sylvia, the waitress who always served him at the Castle – eggs Benedict with ham and a large Americano. Then he took out his MacBook. He preferred to be doing something in the café, rather than just staring into space. That way, people were less likely to disturb him.

Before he'd gone to school this morning, Noah had quizzed him about the song, asking about its provenance, saying everyone was talking about the video. Daniel had watched it once, and couldn't bear to let it play to the end. A souped-up montage of clips and photos of him from the days when the single was first in the charts, it made him look as if he was singing in synch with the heavy drum-beat Funk 'n' Further had laid under the track. He even looked as if he was saying, 'Funk to the Further,' the annoyingly catchy refrain that came at the end of each chorus.

'It's pretty cool,' Noah said, and Daniel felt he should be glad his son was actually talking to him, and had returned to some semblance of normality, even if he had shaved off his eyebrows so that he resembled a teenage cancer victim with shocking-pink hair.

Although Noah still shared nothing about school, it seemed to Daniel that things had calmed down. There were no more cuts or bruises, no lost books or bags, and Noah had even made noises about joining an after-class drama group that had started up.

Sylvia put his coffee in front of him and Daniel flipped open his MacBook to log on. His eye was drawn to the little red dot that said there were seven new emails in his inbox.

All but one were spam. The one that wasn't was from Maya. Daniel guessed it was a reiteration of her request that he go on tour with her up north for two weeks in August, which he'd declined when he'd agreed to meet her in the West End that day he'd bumped into Vince. Even more determined to say no – now that the second song was number one, there was no telling who'd recognise Maya's back-up singer and blow his cover – Daniel opened the email.

Hey Daniel, How goes it with you? All good I hope.
I got an email from a woman called Maggie Behan, who claims to be an old friend of yours. She was looking for your contact details, but I thought I'd better get your permission before giving them out.

Daniel shut the MacBook.

Outside the café two women were standing and chatting, one with a toddler in a buggy. The toddler, a little girl judging by the length of her strawberry curls, caught Daniel's eye and lifted her head to stare at him with unabashed curiosity. Daniel shifted his gaze away.

Maggie.

He had a fleeting memory of her laugh, which was more like a cackle, high and dry. The freckles dotted all over her face. The way she blew smoke rings like a professional.

And then he went back to the memories he never visited. Maggie's father barging into his grandmother's house. His granny shouting behind the front parlour door: 'Daniel's not that kind of boy!'

And then he was back in Hove, back in the still, empty rooms of his father's house, and it was as if he had conjured Maggie in his imagination. As if she hadn't been a real flesh-and-blood person.

Alone in his bedroom he wrote love songs for her. With guitar chords and words he tried to re-create the island, to bring himself back there, to smell the scent of the first fallen leaves under his body, to feel her arms around him and hear her whisper over and over again, 'It's okay … It's okay …'

The song he wrote was 'Night Star'.

He'd sent letters to her every week, as he'd promised he would on the station platform, her parents flanking her on either side, like prison guards. As his grandmother ushered him on board the Dublin train, her papery cheeks were wet with tears. In every letter he wrote the three words he'd desperately wanted to say that night, over and over again.

In the emptiness of his father's kitchen, where the acoustics were the best in the house, he'd recorded himself singing 'Night Star' on his cassette player and then posted the tape to her.

But there had been nothing in return.

No letters with Irish stamps addressed to him dropped through the door and landed on the carpet, which was now vacuumed once a week by a cleaning lady instead of his mother.

Slowly as September turned into October, and the months inched towards a Christmas with no tree or turkey or family games, he'd accepted that it had just been a summer fling. That it had meant nothing to Maggie. He made a New Year resolution to stop writing. To forget her.

And eventually he did. She had retreated to the back of his mind, only to be spontaneously exhumed every now and then as a vague reminiscence that made him feel the tiniest pang of loss.

And now here she was again. Real flesh and blood.

Maggie.

He opened his laptop and reread Maya's correspondence from the beginning. She'd pasted the text of Maggie's email beneath her own. All Maggie said was that she'd known him before he was Danny Lane, and she was trying to get back in contact.

Sylvia smiled and said, 'It's beautiful today, isn't it?' as she put Daniel's breakfast in front of him. 'I love days like this, when you can really feel the start of summer.'

Daniel gave her a distracted look, then clicked reply.

Hi Maya, All good with me, and with you too, I hope.
Please, on no account, give out my details to this woman.
Yes, she knew me in the past, but it is a relationship I
have no wish to resume.
Regards,
Daniel

57. A Concealed Attraction

Cassandra lingered at the sitting-room window and watched her father destroy the back garden. He'd insisted on going out to do some weeding and was on his knees, the grass staining his grey trousers, using a trowel systematically to rip up the bedding plants Cassandra had bought in the garden centre and planted yesterday.

It was part of her effort to brighten the place up, along with all the little improvements she'd made to the house, and although she supposed it was her father's dementia that made him mistake pink and purple lobelia for weeds, part of her wondered if he was doing it on purpose, to hurt her.

She tapped at the window to get his attention, but he didn't turn in her direction. Instead he held one of the plants in the air, looked at it with disgust, then flung it on the pile that was building in the middle of the garden path.

She picked up the duster and the can of Pledge she'd brought with her into the sitting room. Her plan for the day was to polish every wooden surface in the house to a healthy shine. She knew better than to go outside and confront her father. The first time the doctor had spoken to her about the Alzheimer's, he'd said that many sufferers became aggressive in the early and middle stages, that the mildest-mannered people often displayed uncharacteristically violent tendencies.

That was true of her father. One minute they'd be playing poker – so far he'd retained a comprehensive knowledge of the rules of the game – and the next he'd be flinging his cards across the room, roaring at Cassandra, calling her every name under the sun.

It was always a shock. Her father had never been one to yell.

'Far too soft-hearted for his own good,' her mother had often said about him. He might have been a big man, the traditional bringer home of the bacon, but Mother was the undisputed boss. On pay-day she rubbed her red-knuckled hands dry on the front of her apron and held them out to take Dad's full wage packet. He got a small spending allowance every fortnight and the rest of the money was put to use elsewhere.

Cassandra had a memory of her father crying on the night his own mother had died, sitting in the dark kitchen with fat tears rolling down his cheeks. Cassandra had been six at the time, and wanted to get up on his knee to comfort him, but she remembered her mother saying to her father, clear as day, 'What are you crying for?'

Looking back on it, the house had been divided into two camps. Sam was Mum's favourite, the two of them thick as thieves because they were so alike, tough-skinned and tenacious. And Dad, quiet, soft and sensitive, had had his clear favourite too.

That was why he was so hurt at the funeral, why at the lunch afterwards in the hotel he'd told her in a low voice he would never accept her the way she was, that even looking at her made him sick to his stomach.

Cassandra glanced out of the sitting-room window and saw that her father was standing with the trowel hanging at his side, glowering at her, the front of his trousers grubby with two dirty green patches. She turned away again.

Sometimes it was like it used to be. They were friends once more, quietly understanding each other without having to say much, and Cassandra tried to believe he had forgiven her, that he accepted and loved her again, the way he once had. But then he'd forget her name, or where he was, and she'd remember that his acceptance of her was part of the dementia. It wasn't real.

The disappointment she felt when he turned on her, or looked at her in the way he was staring at her now, didn't taper away. It was a fresh rejection every time. It made her understand over and over that she'd never be accepted back into her family.

Twice on the street, when she'd been out shopping, she'd seen Sam coming in her direction. She'd held her breath, readying herself to say hello to him, but on both occasions he'd crossed to the other side of the road, putting his head down. She'd wanted to call out to him, 'Sam! Please talk to me. You're my brother!'

But she couldn't. She knew he was ashamed of her. If he stopped to talk to her on the street, someone might notice, put two and two together, and then the truth would fly like wildfire around the town.

Every day she thought of leaving. Of going back to her own apartment in the Canaries and her job, to the comfortable life she had created for herself.

'It's terrible here without you,' Coco had complained on the phone last night. 'Madam Ovary. She thinks she's the big boss of us all now. And the girls, they keep saying, when is Mama Cass coming back?'

When indeed? Cassandra knew she was going to have to make a decision very soon. Her money was running out.

She'd already been to see the manager of the county nursing home, St John's, who had agreed to put her father on a waiting list for free care and admit him when things became unmanageable. Until then, home nursing was available four days a week. Cassandra was sure Sam and Delia could manage the other days between them. So, really, if she wanted, she could leave right now, instead of facing her father scowling in the back garden for one more minute.

But someone else held her here.

Over the years, after she'd fully come into her own as a woman, she was pursued by and had been with several guys, but nothing had ever come of it. After two dates, she'd find herself reluctantly agreeing to a third. At the third, she'd smile and internally calculate incompatibilities. She rarely, if ever, agreed to a fourth. She'd figured she was a slow learner. She was learning to love herself, and that was the most she could do.

And now she'd met John. In the last place she'd expected it, love had appeared. She couldn't run away from it any more than she could run away from herself.

58. Mother Says

'Would you like a cup of tea, Mrs C?'

Maggie lifted her head, her eyes adjusting to the dim curtained-off light in her bedroom. 'Orlando,' she said, her mouth slack with sleep. 'What time is it?'

'It's one o'clock, Mrs C,' Orlando replied. His hair was tied in a dirty-blond knot on the top of his head, and he wore a loose white sleeveless T-shirt and three-quarter-length baggy shorts that dipped in the middle, Gandhi style. Maggie both hated and was comforted by the way he called her 'Mrs C'. On one hand it made her feel like one of the old biddies in the snug of the Rovers Return, when *Coronation Street* was in black-and-white, and on the other it had the warm ring of familiarity, which had been sorely missing from the house for what seemed like eternity.

Benny was sitting at Orlando's feet, regarding Maggie. Since Poppy's boyfriend had moved in, the cat had moved from his sentry position on the pillow and now followed Orlando's every movement. At first Maggie had felt slightly aggrieved by the abandonment, but now she was happy for Benny. Orlando was a new friend for him. The last few months with just Maggie for company had been no cat picnic.

'I think I'll get up for a while,' Maggie said. She didn't feel as whacked as she usually did on the Sunday after her chemo. Dr

Snow had explained that they were changing to a different type – she couldn't remember its name – which wasn't as aggressive as the chemo used during the first six sessions.

She was two-thirds through the course now. 'Only two more to go, Mrs C,' Orlando had winked when Maggie arrived home from the hospital on Thursday, causing Poppy to give him a sharp sideways look.

Maggie couldn't understand their relationship. If Orlando said white, Poppy said black. He was a born optimist, finding something to be joyful about in every situation, while Poppy had grown pessimistic to the core. The chemo, as far as Poppy was concerned, was only a gateway to more suffering. She bemoaned Maggie's impending loss of a breast, calling it 'mutilation', as if the doctors had decided to do it on a misogynistic whim.

She'd brought Orlando home with her last Friday. 'The squat is over,' she'd told Maggie. 'It was a total dump anyway.'

Slowly, as the weekend progressed and Orlando didn't leave, Maggie realised that Poppy intended him to stay.

'It's just for a while,' she said, when Maggie confronted her. 'Until we find something else.'

Maggie didn't object. Orlando regularly left his boxer shorts on the floor of the main bathroom, and he had a habit of surreptitiously picking his nose, but it was impossible not to like him. And Poppy was a million times easier to deal with when he was around. There was no more crying in the small hours of the morning, no more asking for cuddles while Maggie fought the night sweats.

But other people in the house were not as happy about Orlando's arrival. The day after he had unpacked his bags, Maggie's mother came into the kitchen and said, 'I want to speak to you, Margaret.'

When Maggie was a kid, if her mother was punishing her for some infraction or other, she had always called her 'Margaret'.

Her mother sat down at the table and held her two hands in front of herself, as if she was getting ready to pray. 'That boy is having intercourse with your daughter under this roof,' she said.

For a second Maggie didn't know what boy she meant. And then Orlando's laughter rang out from the back garden. She tensed inside. Was it wrong to let Poppy sleep with him? She'd always thought it was better that her daughter had a steady boyfriend, considering how free and easy the whole sex thing was nowadays, and given Poppy's own propensity towards radicalism. It seemed a good thing that she wasn't out having anonymous sex with every Tom, Dick and Marxist Harry.

'It's different nowadays, Mum,' she said gently. 'It's normal for girls Poppy's age to …' She didn't know quite how to put it. She couldn't bring herself to say the word 'sex' to her mother's face.

Her mother glared, then shook her head very slowly, her lips pursed. 'It's a sin,' she said. 'You of all people should know that.'

The hairs on the back of Maggie's neck pricked. 'What do you mean?'

Her mother stared at her, unmoving. 'You know exactly what I mean. Tell that boy to go. You don't want what happened to you to happen to Poppy.'

It was the perfect opportunity. After all these years her mother was bringing up that which could not be talked about. But Maggie sat dumbly at the table, unable to find any words to retort with.

In bed that night she'd come up with all sorts of smart replies. 'What happened to me won't happen to Poppy because you forced me to go to that clinic with you, Mother.' Or: 'Poppy won't get pregnant because she's educated about sex. What chance did I have?'

But it was too late. Maggie had the feeling that her chance had come and gone, that her mother would never broach the subject again. She didn't think she had the courage to go there under her own steam.

*

She had a shower, dried herself, then put on a white cotton dressing-gown and followed Orlando and Benny downstairs. There was no sign of her mother anywhere. She must have gone to mass. Maggie decided to have her tea sitting in the shade of the oak tree at the end of the garden. She hadn't been on Facebook for ages. There should be plenty of interesting conversations going on with the Abbaholics group.

Orlando set up a table and chair under the tree for her and Poppy carried out a tray with tea and buttered toast on it, squinting up at the sun. 'It's too hot,' she said, putting the tray down. 'I hate summer in London.'

Maggie glanced up from her laptop. 'Thanks, sweetie,' she said.

As Poppy trudged back to the house, the Abbaholics Facebook page flickered to life on the screen.

Since the concert had been announced, ninety-eight new members had 'liked' Abbaholics Anonymous and Maggie had diligently sent them friend requests from her own profile.

People were posting the usual guesswork. Denise Whooley from Melbourne wrote: 'I have it on good authority they will be doing the mini-musical *The Girl With the Golden Hair.*' Whether or not the 'good authority' Denise cited was a figment of an overactive imagination, there were 211 'likes' for her news, and a slew of comments below about it being definitely true and mentioning other Abba musicals, *Chess*, *Mamma Mia!* and *Kristina*, which Maggie had queued up all night for front-stalls tickets to see when it had played for two nights only at the Royal Albert Hall a couple of years ago, and had been sorely disappointed by.

She posted a comment saying as much, then clicked into her messages to see if Joel Singleton had written.

Sure enough, there he was in her inbox, his little blond thumbnail beaming out of the screen.

Hi Maggie, The Abba song I keep coming back to is 'When All Is Said And Done', which is about Benny and Frida's divorce. It's so much less bitter than 'The Winner Takes It All', which was about Björn and Agnetha's divorce, and that's why I like it more. It's about wishing your ex-partner happiness rather than being angry that they've moved on. What kind of divorce was yours? A 'Winner Takes It All' or a 'When All Is Said And Done'?

It was a good question. Although neither she nor William had broached the subject yet, Maggie wondered how it would pan out. Did she thank William for all the memories and not blame him? Or was she a loser standing small? Thinking about it, even though William was calling in regularly to check on how she was, he hadn't been on her mind in ages, not in the way she used constantly to think of him anyway.

Beneath his divorce question Joel had written another message: *Are you going to Stockholm for the concert?*

As Maggie took this in she watched her mother arrive in the kitchen and look out the garden window, without seeming to see her. As if she was an invisible woman.

She went back to her computer: *Yes, I am going to Stockholm*, she replied. *I can't wait.*

She hadn't been able to bring the Abba fan club together. She hadn't even been able to get tickets. But nothing would stop her going to that concert.

59. Love Is Strong Enough

Stupidly, there was a police roadblock where Leeson Street met the canal, so traffic had come to a standstill. Dee reached over to the passenger seat, picked up her phone and then put it down again. She was itching to call Joe to tell him what the doctor had said, but at the same time she was reluctant.

Flipping through the stations on the car stereo, she came upon Abba belting out 'Take A Chance On Me'. They were never off the radio these days.

It was one of those songs that made her mind flicker back to a specific moment in time so profoundly she could almost smell the sun-cream she'd been wearing as she lay on a rug in the back garden of Maggie's house on a sweltering summer's day not unlike this one. They'd been wearing bikinis they'd bought in the newly opened Sligo branch of Dunnes Stores and reading out the 'Dear Cathy and Claire' page in *Jackie* magazine to each other.

Maggie's idea to reunite the Abba fan club was utterly cock-eyed, as had been all the plans she'd made when they were kids, but now, as the sun belted through her car window to the strains of Agnetha and Frida's high voices, Dee wished she'd been more enthusiastic about the whole endeavour. Even if there wasn't a chance in Hell that they'd get to the concert, she shouldn't have been so ambivalent when it was suggested, in memory of their closeness that summer if nothing else.

The car in front of her inched forward. As Dee took her foot off the brake to follow suit, her mobile phone buzzed to life on the seat beside her. Bringing the car to another standstill, she picked it up and saw there was a message in her inbox from Joe: *Missing you like crazy*, he'd texted. *See you later*.

He was being over-attentive, the way he always was after an incident. Dee couldn't call it violence, exactly, but the air in the bathroom when he'd grabbed her wrist last night had turned uncomfortably hostile. She'd found herself jerking away from him, almost tripping into the shower stall in the expectation of being hit, but instead Joe had smiled and picked up his toothbrush, saying, 'Whatever you want, baby,' as if there had been no argument about going to visit her parents.

Maybe he'd stopped himself before he tipped over, and surely that was a good thing. It meant he was making an effort to keep his new leaf turned over, that he was stopping himself before he lost control.

Before she went to sleep, she'd kissed him and said goodnight, deciding to give him the benefit of the doubt. He was working on himself, and for their marriage to work she had to support him. Sometimes that was what marriage was, her mother had told her once. Hard work.

Yet the first thing she'd felt when she woke up this morning was dread. His body beside her, rising and falling as he sleep-breathed, was oppressively hot. She couldn't get out of the bed quick enough.

The morning sickness didn't help. She'd been hiding it from him, waiting until she'd had her doctor's appointment so the pregnancy could be confirmed. She couldn't quite believe it had happened so quickly, especially at her age, and she didn't want to give him false hope.

But here it was. The diagnoses. The prognoses. She was six weeks pregnant, due on 15 March next year. Dee couldn't get her head around it. Only a few months ago she hadn't really imagined becoming a mother.

She pictured Joe's face on telling him. In her mind's eye she saw him light up with joy, but the thought didn't bring her happiness. Along with the certain knowledge that a new life was growing inside her, something else had been conceived. She couldn't put her finger on it exactly, but it felt like a stone, hard, round and shiny, sitting in the pit of her stomach.

She made herself a cup of tea and waited in the kitchen for Joe to come home, telling herself to cop on. This was supposed to be one of the happiest moments in her life. In *their* lives. She had to let go and enjoy it.

When he walked through the door, Joe instantly picked up on her energy. 'Are you all right?' he asked, his eyebrows knitted with concern. 'If it's about going to see your folks, I've cancelled the golf.'

This news momentarily distracted her. Last night, Joe had been adamant that he couldn't miss the tournament.

'Joe,' she said, 'I've been to see the doctor.'

The knot in his forehead deepened as he took a seat. 'Is there something wrong?' he asked.

Dee's heart beat in her ears, as she said, 'Joe, I'm pregnant.'

His reaction was what she'd thought it would be. He jumped up and threw his arms around her, then jerked away as if he'd done something rash and dangerous. 'How are you feeling?' he asked.

'Fine,' said Dee. 'I've had a little morning sickness, that's all.'

Joe sat down again, his eyes glistening. 'I can't believe it.'

He was on the verge of tears, and she felt the hardness in her stomach melt away. He was a soft man, really. He had huge amounts of love to give.

She got up from her seat and stood by his chair, cradling his head against her stomach as he cried like a child.

60. Don't Know What to Do

Daniel found himself thinking about Maggie at odd times of the day – in the shower first thing in the morning; cycling home from Sainsbury's with his backpack full of groceries; trying to concentrate on *The Times* crossword at the kitchen table. In his mind's eye she appeared unchanged, still a freckle-faced teenager asking on the boat, 'If your life was an Abba song, what would it be?'

She would be a forty-five-year-old woman now and Daniel found it impossible to picture what she might look like. Did she still have the same flaming orange thicket of hair? The same tiny gap between her two front teeth?

Had she married? Had children? Did she still live in the same little town or had she moved away? He couldn't stop himself internally asking questions about her, going back to Maya's email and reading what Maggie had written, as if between the lines he could decipher what had happened to her since that summer in Sligo.

But there was nothing between the lines. It was a straight-up, slightly apologetic email that gave nothing away. At the top of it, almost begging him to click on it and make contact, was her email address.

But Daniel held off. Part of him didn't want his curiosity satiated – he wanted to imagine her as she had been and not be disappointed by the reality of drooping middle age.

Yet when he went to bed at night she flitted through his half-dreams before he dropped off. When he woke up in the morning, she was still on his mind. It was driving him nuts.

He told himself that if he saw her as she really was now, he could forget the mirage. He could let her go again.

So, one Monday morning, after breakfast, he made a decision. He went on to his computer and opened Maya's email. He clicked on Maggie's address. He'd tried to contact her once, years ago, in the days before email and Facebook and instant cyber reconnection. He'd called her parents and left two messages on an answering machine that said, 'Leave a message after the tone', but had no tone, so he couldn't know if his voice was being recorded or not.

It had been during the worst of his depression, when he'd been afraid to emerge from the dark basement flat he'd bought with the first earnings from 'Night Star'. At that point nobody knew or cared about Danny Lane any more, and it was the way Daniel had wanted it, yet his paranoia about being recognised and mobbed had become all-encompassing. His fear of exposure had grown like an incremental rash that he couldn't stop himself scratching until it was red raw.

Jade would knock on the door every now and then, holding Noah's hand, and shout, 'Daniel! I know you're in there!' But Daniel wouldn't reply. In a dizzy haze of weed, he'd tiptoe into the bedroom and hide under the duvet until she'd gone away.

Maggie's parents either hadn't got the phone messages he'd left or just didn't reply, and as quickly as he'd thought of contacting her, Daniel had given up. He'd rolled another spliff and tried to escape into a world where no one made promises and let you down, where no one wanted you for what they could get out of you, where no one ran their car into a wall and left you feeling as if a part of you had been emptied out, that there was a place in your heart that could never be filled again.

In the subject box he wrote: 'Hello from Daniel'. Then he deleted 'from Daniel' and left it just saying, 'Hello'.

> Dear Maggie, it's Daniel Smith here. I got a message
> from a friend of mine called Maya saying you were
> looking for me …

It was hard to know what tone to strike, or what to say, even. Should he suggest meeting up? Should he fill her in on details about his life? Should he ask about hers?

No, he decided, that didn't feel right. Instead he typed:

> If you still want to contact me, this is my email address.
> I hope life is treating you well. Best regards, Daniel

He clicked send before he could change his mind. He was just about to close the laptop when he remembered a song he'd thought of looking up, an Irish singer-songwriter's cover he'd heard of Nirvana's 'Where Did You Sleep Last Night' on the soundtrack to a documentary he'd watched on BBC4 recently. It was bound to be on YouTube.

He opened his web browser and found himself directly on Noah's Facebook page. He must have been using Daniel's laptop last night and forgotten to log off.

It was like coming across someone's diary. An overwhelming desire to read it battled with respect for Noah's privacy. Daniel knew only too well the value of privacy so he brought the computer's cursor to the top of the page so he could log Noah out, but as the cursor moved, his eye stumbled on the word 'Gaylord'.

He lifted his finger off the mousepad and began to read.

There were reams of messages on Noah's wall, all from people with profile pictures that were avatars, showing drawings of villains from superhero comics, with obviously made-up names, like 'John

Destroyer' or 'A. Vengeance'. They'd all written vile variations of the text messages Noah had been sent before, the majority accusing him of molesting little boys.

One message jumped out. It was written by someone who called himself 'The Cleaner': *You sad pervert. We know where you live now.*

Daniel read through the messages again, clicking on the profiles of the people sending them. But the profiles had no photos, no status updates, and no personal information. They were clearly bogus accounts. Yet when he went back into Noah's profile page, he saw that they were all his 'friends'. Daniel didn't have a Facebook account, but he knew that unless you accepted someone's friendship they couldn't write on your wall.

He clicked into Noah's friends list. He had a total of 346, yet in the months he'd been living with Daniel, he had never seen the boy with, or heard him mention, one friend.

'I don't understand,' Daniel said to Noah. 'Explain it to me, will you?'

Noah sat hunched on the sofa, his arms folded and his chin lowered to his chest. 'It's none of your business,' he muttered.

'Why would you accept those people as friends? You know they have it in for you.'

'Because, *duh*, that's what you do, Daniel. It's *Facebook*.'

Daniel shoved down his irritation. 'We have to go to the police, Noah,' he said.

Noah shook his head. His arms squeezed his narrow frame tight.

'So that's it? You're going to let them do this to you? You're going to pretend it's not happening until they make good on the threats?'

Noah said nothing. Then he lifted his head and looked Daniel straight in the eye. 'I could tell you who it is but it wouldn't help. The police can talk to their mums and dads, but it won't make any difference. They'll still get me. And if they know I grassed on them, it'll be ten times worse.'

'You'll have to get rid of that Facebook profile,' Daniel said. Then futility swept over him. As if that was going to do any good.

Noah stood up. From Daniel's vantage point on the sofa, his son now looked like the grown-up, the one who was in control.

'Dad,' Noah said, 'I can shut down my Facebook page. I can get a new phone. I can go to a new school. I can go crying to the police. But in the end they'll get me. That's just the way it is.'

'So you're going to let it happen? You're going to do nothing?'

'No,' said Noah, before going up to his bedroom. 'I know what I have to do.'

61. Lost from the Start

Delia had gained a lot of weight in the ten years since Cassandra's mother's funeral. She tried to disguise it with a shift-like black dress over black leggings, but the difference in her was startling. Her hair, no longer a hennaed bob but peppery grey and shorn short to her head, didn't help.

'Hello,' Delia said. 'Can I help you?'

Cassandra forced a smile. 'Hi, Delia,' she said. 'Is Sam here?'

It took Delia about two slow-motion seconds to gain full recognition. 'Charlie?'

Cassandra blanched. No matter how many times she was called by that name, it still felt like an affront. 'Please,' she said, 'I'd prefer it if you called me Cassandra.'

Delia surveyed her, then said, 'Sam's not here. He's out on a job.'

Cassandra rooted herself to the spot. It had taken all her courage to come here to try to talk to Sam, and she wasn't leaving yet. Despite their differences, they had to decide what to do about their father. 'When will he be home?' she asked.

'I don't know,' Delia replied. 'An hour, maybe. Do you want to come in?'

She led Cassandra through a dim, floral-carpeted hallway. On a table by the stairs there was a picture of the two boys, one of those school shots posed in uniform against a blue background. They'd been three and one the last time Cassandra had met them, Damien running around in his little shirt and tie, Shane glued to Delia's hip. Cassandra wondered if Sam and Delia ever said anything to her nephews about her. If they knew she existed.

Their family kitchen was just the way she remembered it, in disarray. Piles of dirty dishes sat in the sink, a microwave with its door half open revealed what looked like an explosion of tomato sauce inside. Dust particles hung in the bright sunshine streaming through an open window that gave the view of a circular washing-line, strewn with washed-out underwear.

'Sorry,' said Delia, without much conviction. 'The house is in an awful state.'

'Not at all,' Cassandra lied.

There was a lapse in conversation. Then Delia exclaimed, 'Where are my manners? Sit down. I'll put the kettle on.'

Cassandra pulled out a chair and sat at a wooden table, which had white ring-marks all over it. She'd never quite understood Delia's lack of house pride, but she had to admit that there was something oddly homely about the disorder. Having grown up in a house where every mess was vigorously cleaned up within seconds of being made, she liked that Delia wasn't afraid of disorder.

Filling the kettle, Delia gave her the once-over again. 'You look absolutely amazing,' she said.

Cassandra flushed. 'Thank you.'

'No, seriously,' said Delia, as if she'd just been disagreed with. 'You really do.'

Cassandra was momentarily confused, but then she grasped that Delia was voicing something near acceptance. Her sister-in-law had paid her a compliment.

'You look good too,' she said, although it wasn't exactly true.

Delia gave a rueful grin. 'I don't think so,' she said, setting down two mugs on the table. 'We've both changed a hell of a lot.'

Cassandra had a sudden memory of envying Delia when she'd first met her. She'd watched her sister-in-law's ease with her body, the way her hips moved when she danced or how she smoked a cigarette, and wondered if she'd ever be accepted as a woman in the way Delia took so completely and naturally for granted. 'Did Sam tell you I was home?' she asked.

Delia nodded, pouring boiling water on to the teabag in Cassandra's chipped mug. 'I would've called up to see you at your father's, but I didn't want Sam finding out, and there was no guarantee your dad wouldn't say anything … Milk and sugar?'

'Neither,' said Cassandra. 'Does Sam ever talk to you about me?'

Delia heaped three spoons of sugar into her mug and stirred. 'He used to,' she said. 'But then he stopped. He took it very bad, you know.' She sipped some tea and observed Cassandra over the rim of her mug. 'Sometimes I think we all lost a part of Sam when you, well … made the choice to change.'

Cassandra's hackles rose. Here was yet another thing to blame her for, another person negatively affected by her transition. Nobody bothered to try to understand what she had gone through to be true to who she was. All they could think about was themselves.

'I didn't *choose* to become a woman,' she told Delia. 'I was born into the wrong body.'

'I know that,' Delia replied, setting her mug down. 'You did the right thing for yourself, but you have to remember that other people were left behind.'

As Delia said this, they heard a car horn through the window.

'That'll be him,' said Delia, getting to her feet. She plucked Cassandra's half-drunk mug of tea from the table. 'He'll be mad that I let you in.'

Cassandra braced herself as she heard the front door open. There were two men's voices in the hall, a hoot of shared laughter, and then Sam pushed open the kitchen door.

His gaze fell on Cassandra sitting at the table. His smile faded. 'What's *he* doing here?' he asked, looking to Delia.

'I wanted to talk to you,' Cassandra said, as Sam's companion emerged from the hall into the sunlit kitchen.

Her heart plunged.

'Cassandra?' said John, his face a vision of bewilderment.

Sam turned on him. 'It's Charlie,' he said. Then he added, confused and looking from John to Cassandra and back again, 'How do you know my brother?'

62. Mirror of Your Eyes

Daniel had to take off his sunglasses and look around a few times before he spotted her, the lone person sitting at a table for two, a canary yellow scarf tightly wrapped around her head. She saw him at exactly the same time and bolted to her feet, making the table wobble. Putting his shades back on, he took a breath and stepped forward. 'Maggie,' he said, holding out his hand. She didn't take it or reply. Instead she lunged forward, threw her arms around him and hugged.

Daniel patted her back, feeling as if every eye in the room had turned on them.

'You haven't changed a bit,' Maggie gushed, as they sat down, her grin too wide.

Daniel knew this to be untrue, and wished he could say the same for her. The round-faced Maggie he remembered had contracted with age. When she'd hugged him, he'd felt bone through her clothes. Her cheekbones were high underneath pale, translucent skin that was still oddly dotted with freckles, and the cords in her neck stood out like tension wires. Her eyes weren't the same either. The twinkle he remembered was gone, along with her eyebrows.

And then it struck him: she had cancer. That was why her head was covered with a scarf. Her orange hair had fallen out.

'How have you been?' he blurted, and immediately felt like taking it back. He didn't want her to tell him about her illness. Like the hug she'd given him, it would be far too much.

But Maggie said, 'Great. I've been great, and how about you?' Although her voice was chirpy, her eyes were searching.

'Great,' Daniel echoed.

He'd agreed to meet her, telling himself it was a welcome distraction from what was going on with Noah, but he was beginning to regret the decision. The place was full of restaurant noise – chatter and the clatter of cutlery on crockery, a woman laughing at something two tables away, a baby crying in a high-chair, a group of people clinking wine glasses and shouting, 'Cheers!' at a long table near the plate-glass windows that looked out on to crowds strolling towards the London Eye. Daniel had picked the South Bank because he knew it would be distracting. Better to meet her in a busy place than some intimate café. But now he was regretting this decision too. Amid the bustle of the restaurant, the silence at their table doubled.

Maggie interrupted it: 'Tell me everything. How has your whole life been?'

Daniel was struggling with how to reply when he was mercifully interrupted by a waiter in a pristine white shirt and long black apron, asking them if they wanted water while they looked at the menu.

'I'm not eating,' Daniel told him. 'I'll just have a glass of your house white.'

'And mineral water for me,' added Maggie. 'Sparkling.'

The waiter went on his way and she started again: 'How long has it been?'

'Thirty years, next month,' Daniel replied, as if it was an anniversary he kept. He supposed it *was* one, really. The anniversary of losing his virginity. With the person who was sitting opposite him, shaking her probably bald head and marvelling.

'Doesn't time fly?' she was saying.

Daniel nodded and glanced at the exit. She'd grown into a middle-aged woman who trotted out clichés. She'd lost her fire.

The waiter put their glasses of wine and water in front of them and Daniel lifted his. 'To old acquaintance,' he said, before downing a mouthful.

Maggie brought hers to her lips, then put it back on the table without drinking. She gave him a puzzled smile and said, 'Would you mind if I asked you to take off those sunglasses? They're a bit distracting.'

Daniel raised his hand and hesitated. Without them he'd be exposing himself: she'd see what he'd become too. A coward who had opted out of life, without caring how it affected anyone else. A man who had abandoned his own son, and now couldn't even protect him.

'Thank you.' Maggie smiled when he'd folded his sunglasses and put them on the table. Then she hesitated and a flush rose up her neck, as if she'd been the one unmasked. Her fingers went to her forehead and fluttered at the hem of her headscarf. 'I've got cancer,' she said, and gave an embarrassed laugh as if she was apologising for a conspicuous cold sore.

'That's terrible,' Daniel said. He felt unexpectedly sad.

Maggie emitted a little laugh, as if he'd made some sort of joke. 'There are worse things,' she said, looking at the table, her fingers still hovering at her forehead.

Now Daniel experienced a weird stab of irritation, as if her laugh had been at his expense. Was this why she'd gone to the trouble of finding and contacting him? Was she dying and trying to make amends for the things she'd done?

Part of him had agreed to meet because he wanted to ask her why. Why had she ignored all his letters? Why hadn't she written back when he'd sent her the tape of the song he'd written for her? But now he understood he was being pathetically childish. The whole thing had been meaningless. Bringing it up would lend it an importance it had never had in the first place. She was just the first girl he'd had sex with, and that was all. The vague fantasies he'd entertained about her since she'd found him again were just that: fantasies. After this reunion they would go their separate ways and never see each other again.

'What kind of cancer?' he asked, then wondered if he'd been too blunt.

'Breast.'

'And are you okay?' It was a stupid question that sounded even more stupid now that it was out of his mouth.

Maggie was giving him that searching look again. 'I'm as okay as I can be,' she said. 'I don't really want to talk about it, though.'

'Right.' Daniel nodded, relieved not to have to get into the subject any further.

His relief was short-lived. 'So tell me more about you,' Maggie asked. 'What's it like to be rich and famous?'

'I'm neither,' Daniel said. Now he was annoyed again.

'Well, you're the most famous person I know.'

'Yeah, well, that's hardly a big deal.' Daniel knew he sounded bitter, and somehow this made him ashamed, as if he was personally letting her down. As if everything about him was a let-down.

'Have you had a happy life?' Maggie persisted.

Daniel fought the urge to put his sunglasses back on. 'Look,' he said, his throat constricting in a frightening way, 'you said in your email you wanted to ask me something.'

Maggie's glass was halfway to her mouth. She opened it to say something, but shut it again and gave a wan, almost sorrowful smile. 'Do you remember the promise we made on the boat?' she asked.

The only promise he remembered was the one the two of them had made as he was being put on the train back to England that awful day. The one to write to each other.

'On the boat?' he said. 'No.'

'We said that if Abba ever re-formed we'd all get back together to go to their concert.'

So that was what this was about. Her ridiculous Abba fan club. She hadn't changed after all.

Daniel was surprised to find himself laughing. 'Are you asking me to go and see Abba with you?' he said.

Maggie didn't laugh. Her eyes widened in her pale face and she nodded once.

'Have you even got tickets? They sold out in seconds, didn't they?'

Maggie nodded again, still wide-eyed.

'And the others, Dee and Charlie. Are they on board?'

'Yes,' she said. 'Of course.'

'And you definitely have four tickets?'

Now a very familiar spark of gap-toothed, freckled irritation lit up. Daniel watched her smother it.

'Yes,' she said, her face deadly serious again. 'So are you in or out?'

63. Never Again We Two

Walking across the footbridge from the South Bank to Embankment, Maggie cursed herself for lying about the tickets, and about Charlie and Dee being on board. It had happened in a peculiar moment of panic. From the moment Daniel had arrived, she'd felt the undercurrent of his need to slip away. She'd thrown out the lies like fishing lines, to hook him and reel him in.

But Daniel had said he couldn't go to the concert, and wouldn't go further than citing 'family reasons' as his excuse. Maggie had known he was lying, but at first she'd greeted his refusal with an internal sigh of relief, glad that her own lie couldn't be found out. This was followed by a stab of resentment, as if she really *did* have the tickets and he was letting her down.

As they had parted outside the restaurant, he had shaken her hand instead of hugging her and said it was nice to see her again after all these years. Watching him unlock his bicycle and wheel it away towards the London Eye, she'd known they'd probably never meet again.

She'd wanted to run after him but what would have been the point? There was nothing more to say.

When he'd arrived at the restaurant, even though his eyes had been shielded by sunglasses, there was no hiding the disappointment that had dawned on his face. She had been wishing he'd see beyond the cancer, beyond the clumsy middle-aged woman, almost knocking the table over, to the girl she'd once been.

While she had waited for him, having arrived ten minutes early so she'd see him before he saw her, the wish that she'd somehow live up to his memory of her felt crucial. But the moment he'd sat down and ordered his wine, barely able to acknowledge her, she'd known it was a lost cause. There was no going back. She'd become who she was, and it was embarrassing that she wanted this person, whom she really didn't know from Adam, to see her any differently.

When she'd told Daniel he hadn't changed a bit, though, she'd meant it. His hair might have been flecked with the odd silver strand, and when he'd eventually taken off those stupid sunglasses, there were fine crow's feet fanning out from the corners of his eyes, but something exactly like the boy he'd been still hovered about the man.

It was strange. In all the photographs of him when he was at the height of his fame, Maggie couldn't recognise him as the Daniel she'd lain under a tree and made love with, but now in the flesh he was as oddly familiar to her as if she'd seen him every day of her life since that night on the island.

What had happened in the immediate aftermath was still a blur of jumbled memories. Blind shock, as her father had beaten her in the sitting room, with the door shut and her mother standing by it, arms folded. Long periods of crying under her duvet. Dee's voice downstairs at the front door, asking, 'Is Maggie coming out?' A tray with a bowl of half-eaten tomato soup sitting on the chest of drawers. The click of the lock on her bedroom door. Begging her mother to be let out to say goodbye to Daniel.

Standing on the station platform, constrained from saying or doing anything as her parents squeezed up against her from either side. Wanting to break into a run as the train pulled away, to jump on board. Staying absolutely still, watching Daniel's white face as it receded and disappeared.

There were no letters. The last thing he'd said to her on the platform was that he'd write. 'Every day,' he'd promised. But he'd returned to his life and his friends, and he'd forgotten her, pretending, maybe, that what had happened between them hadn't. He had gone back to his sophisticated English life; she was just an orange-haired, freckled girl from the back end of nowhere.

How long had it been between Daniel leaving and Maggie realising she'd missed her period? Before she'd started being sick in the mornings? When she'd arrived with her mother at the clinic in Manchester, the nurse had told her she was ten weeks gone. Maggie could remember the cardigan her mother had insisted she wear for the journey there, with its little red embroidered roses at the collar and cuffs.

'No need to let appearances down,' Mum had said, as they packed their bags.

Maggie could recall that nurse as clear as day too. She was African, her skin reflecting the sunlight streaming in through the clinic's windows, her short hair poking out from beneath her white hat. She'd smiled a lot, explaining to Maggie what would happen, what she should expect afterwards, and gently telling her that she would be fine.

Maggie's mother didn't speak. She'd looked around the clinic, with its pristine grey-linoleum floors, her face pinched, as if she was trying to block out an unpleasant smell. She didn't talk to Maggie much outside the clinic either, not on the boat journey over, or in the bed-and-breakfast room with peeling wallpaper they shared for the two nights they were there. She'd fiddled with her rosary beads and repeated that it was for the best.

'You must pray for the repose of your baby's soul, and for the Lord's forgiveness,' she'd told Maggie, as they waited for the taxi that brought them back from the clinic to the B&B.

It had felt like being bludgeoned with a blunt instrument. Her mother had insisted on all of this, had made the arrangements in the stealth of night so that no one should be the wiser. Yet Maggie was the one who had to pray for repose and forgiveness? She should pray instead that God might forgive her mother, because she knew she never would.

Maggie had tried her best not to feel the tiny baby growing inside her. Not to imagine it. Not to think of it as Daniel's too. She knew her parents were right, that it was for the best, but more than her father beating her in the sitting room – her daddy, who had never raised a hand to her before – it felt like the ultimate punishment.

After they'd got back to their room from the clinic, her mother had knelt and looked with accusing eyes at Maggie above hands locked in prayer. Then Maggie had known that this was the consequence of her having done the worst thing ever. She might swear she'd never forgive her mum, but she was the one who had lied and stolen, and pulled her pants down on the filthy ground, not only allowing but encouraging Daniel to put himself inside her.

This was what happened to bad girls.

Lying underneath the damp B&B's bedclothes, her insides cramping, she'd made a promise to herself. She would try her very best to be good. She would never again make the mistake of losing something she loved through her own badness. And she'd grown to love the baby inside her in the little time they'd had together.

After she'd come home, Dee and Charlie had tried to get the Abba fan club going again, but Maggie hadn't had the heart. She'd drifted away from them deliberately. In the space of two nights and three days away from home, she had grown into a different person. Her friends seemed like aliens. Or maybe she was the one who had become an alien.

She never said anything to anyone about it. Not to Oona, who had stamped her feet and bawled with envy because Maggie had had a holiday with their mother 'in Dublin' and she hadn't. Not to any of her new friends at school, the ones she'd made after she'd begun studying hard and doing well in her exams. Not to William when she'd started dating him or when she'd accepted his marriage proposal, or on their honeymoon in Jersey when she'd had all the opportunity in the world.

As Maggie waited at Embankment for her tube home, she thought of what Daniel might have said if she'd told him in the restaurant about the baby. Would he then have remembered what had been between them?

No. It was better to let the past rest where it belonged. To let Daniel go just as she had had to let his baby go.

As she boarded the Bakerloo-line train and the doors closed behind her, she felt a dull heaviness around her heart. She wished now that she hadn't met him or had the stupid fantasy of going to the Abba concert with him. Then he would never have had the opportunity to see her as she was now.

It had been stupid to imagine he'd see the girl she had once been, because that girl had long disappeared.

64. Present Runs into the Past

'How could you do that to me?' Cassandra cried, after John had slammed the front door behind him. He couldn't get out of the house fast enough.

Sam shot her a venomous look and went over to the sink to pour himself a mug of water. Delia sat at the table, without a word.

'I said, how *could* you?' Cassandra repeated.

Sam turned on her, water dribbling down his chin. 'You were fucking him, weren't you?'

At the table, Delia's mug halted halfway to her mouth. 'Sam,' she warned. 'Don't.'

'Don't *what*? He's my *friend*, for fuck's sake. He *works* with me!'

'And he likes me,' said Cassandra. 'Or at least he used to.'

'Jesus!' Sam spat. 'It turns my stomach. *You* turn my stomach.'

Cassandra gripped the back of the kitchen chair she was standing behind. 'How can you say that to me?' she asked. 'I'm your sister.'

Sam's laugh verged on hysterical. 'Listen to yourself!' he shouted. 'You're a fucking lunatic!'

There had been a time when Cassandra had thought she actually might be a lunatic, or was getting there. When she was a teenager, watching and feeling her body change, she had become so distracted, so unable to cope with the lengthening thing between her legs, the wiry hair sprouting on her chest, the croaked breaking of her voice that she began having little episodes where her head divided in two and she was at once in her body and outside it, watching herself. What she saw was an adolescent boy, but what she was growing into was an adolescent girl.

Before her teenage years it had been easier. When the house was empty she could put on her mother's clothes, belt them around herself to fit as best they could, and pretend. She refused to let anyone cut her hair and secretly gave herself girls' names, trying on fantasies that became childishly real.

But even back then there was a feeling of wrongness. A deep awkwardness. An inherent sense of shame mixed with the absolute certainty from the age of five, when she had first pored over a picture of a female model in her mother's knitting-pattern catalogue, that she was not who she was supposed to be.

As she grew up, the shame, the awkwardness, the wrongness only increased until she felt as if she'd been shut in a tiny pitch-black cell, with only the thinnest chink of light showing underneath its heavy padlocked door. The world was everything beyond that door and although, to all intents and purposes, she seemed to be participating in it, really she was trapped and alone in the darkness, with no way out.

Her divided-in-two episodes became more frequent and she couldn't concentrate on her schoolwork. The only thing that helped her mind stay in one piece was playing soccer. She ploughed everything into it, using the exertion and competition to blindside herself. But in a way it was the worst thing she could have done: who in their right mind would have believed that one half of the school's football-star twins was really a girl inside a body that horrified her to the point of sickness?

Cassandra slumped down at the table opposite Delia. 'It took me so long to accept myself,' she said to her brother. 'Why can't you at least try to accept me too?'

'Accept you?' Sam spat, not moving from his spot by the sink. 'What you did to yourself is disgusting. You were my twin brother, for fuck's sake.'

'But I had to do it, Sam. If I hadn't I would have ended up killing myself.'

Sam stared out of the kitchen window. Beyond him the circular washing-line, dotted with underwear, was slowly revolving in the breeze. When he turned back to Cassandra his expression had changed. He looked like a wounded dog.

'You might as well have done it,' he said, 'because when you did what you did, you died for me.'

Cassandra jumped back to her feet. She wanted to cry, but she wouldn't show him her tears. Not when she'd fought with everything she had, when she'd put herself through so many years of pain and trauma to gain the life she deserved, to be the woman she was.

Her voice went cold. 'Well, you might as well think of me as dead,' she said. 'You won't be seeing me again. Ever.'

Delia ran after Cassandra as she stumbled down the hall, past the photograph of her nephews, to the front door. 'Don't be too hard on him,' she begged.

Cassandra couldn't believe her ears. 'I shouldn't be hard on *him*?' she said, jerking the front door open. 'Weren't you listening in there?'

'You don't get it, do you?' Delia said. 'He's never really got over losing you.'

Cassandra stopped. She looked at Delia and shook her head slowly. 'I'll always be the bad one, as far as you're all concerned,' she said. 'And you know what? I'm glad I came home. At least when I go back I won't spend the rest of my life wondering if my family ever really loved me.'

'Sam does love you,' Delia said. 'I think he loves you so much he can hardly bear it.'

Cassandra laughed, and to herself she sounded sour. 'Come off it, Delia,' she said. 'We both know that's a crock of shit.'

Clicking the door behind her, she took a breath and set off down the garden path. She'd hail a taxi when she got to the main road and go to the hotel where she'd pack her things and get the next train to Dublin. In less than twenty-four hours she could be back in her own world. She'd have left everything and everyone in this pathetic, small-minded town behind. And this time it would be for good.

65. I Was a Fool

Dee had never taken any notice of pregnant women before, but now they were everywhere. Cruising the aisles of supermarkets with their rounded tummies pushed up against the handles of their trolleys, hauling their heavy bodies awkwardly out of chairs in cafés, standing chatting to their friends on the street, one hand resting on their baby bumps ...

In the queue at Boots today she'd wanted to shout to the woman in front of her, who was wearing an expensive royal blue maternity top over white leggings, 'I'm pregnant too!' But she didn't, and the woman didn't turn around, so there was no chance of mutual exchange.

Maybe when it became more visible she'd feel properly part of the Pregnant Ladies Association. It was still so early there were no physical signs, no growth of her stomach, no heaviness in her breasts, no having to go to the loo every five minutes.

Sometimes, she forgot she was pregnant. She loved her reaction when she remembered again – the vibration that ran through her body. It felt as if this was the thing she'd been aiming for all her life, even if she had never really aimed for it. She didn't care about the sickness or the tiredness: the little life growing inside her was worth any amount of pain – even the delivery, which she was looking forward to rather than dreading. Having said that, it seemed so distant she could hardly imagine it happening.

Joe never stopped talking about it. He'd bought a book of Italian names and was trying them out every evening over dinner. 'What about Giovanni? Or Dante?'

'Are there any girls' names in that book?' Dee had asked last night, with a weary smile. It wasn't even eight o'clock but she was ready for bed.

Joe flicked the pages. 'What about Adriana? Or Agata?'

Dee wasn't so keen on the Italian names, but she was indulging him for the time being. When it came nearer the birth she'd start introducing the two names she'd picked out as easily as if they were just waiting in line for her to use them.

Lily for a girl. Dillon for a boy. Lily Dimare. It had a lovely ring to it. So did Dillon Dimare, but for all Joe's focus on the boys' names, Dee had a strong feeling that a girl was growing inside her. A daughter. Lily.

She knew he'd come around to the name, and he'd love a girl just as much as he'd love a boy. Joe was a different man now. He was so gentle with her it sometimes made Dee well up; always making sure she was comfortable, fetching and carrying for her as if she were an invalid. And there was a buoyancy to him that hadn't been there before. She would never have said he was an unhappy man when they had first married, but now she could see that a darkness had lifted. Who knew where that darkness had come from? All Dee could say was that she was glad to be the one who had helped it go away. As each day of her pregnancy passed, she loved and opened herself up to trusting him more.

The house was completely quiet when she opened the front door.

'Joe?' she called, but there was no answer. He was working late this week, trying to secure a distribution deal for a new brand of Chilean wine with a chain of off-licences that were playing hardball.

She dumped her Boots bag on the hall table and, sighing with the satisfaction of being home after a hard day at the office, kicked off her shoes. When she padded into the living room, Joe was sitting on the couch, hunched up with his elbows on his knees.

Dee's heart somersaulted. 'Jesus, you scared the life out of me!' she said. 'Why didn't you answer when I called?'

'Where were you?' Joe asked, his voice low.

'I went shopping after work. I had to get a few things in Boots.'

When he looked at her, she understood she was in danger. His eyes were a glassy black. It was like there was no one behind them.

She turned to go into the kitchen and, trying to keep her voice on an even keel, said, 'I'm dying for a cup of tea. You want one?'

'Where were you?' Joe asked again.

Walking into the hall, Dee said, 'I told you, honey. I had to go shopping.' She resisted an overwhelming urge to run towards the front door and went into the kitchen instead.

It was a mistake.

She was barely through the kitchen door before Joe grabbed her from behind and spun her around.

'You're a fucking liar,' he said, without raising his voice and then he punched the right side of her face so hard that she went hurtling across the room, landing with a hard crack against the sink. She could hardly hear her own scream above the roaring gush of blood inside her head.

Joe advanced on her.

'Don't,' she begged, reaching for her stomach rather than putting her hands out to defend herself. 'Joe … the baby …'

'*Joe! The babeeee!*' He imitated her in the horrible whiny voice he did, and then he grabbed her by the hair, pulling her to her feet. As a bolt of burning pain shot through her skull, Dee had a moment of absolute clarity.

This was the first time he'd ever punched her on the face.

He knew what he was doing. He wasn't going to hit her anywhere that might damage the baby.

Joe was in perfect self-control.

66. Impending Doom

Daniel checked the time at the top of his MacBook screen. It was 15:05, almost an hour before Noah got out of school. He lifted his hand to get Sylvia's attention. She smiled at him and mouthed, 'Another coffee?'

Daniel nodded and smiled in return. He'd have time for just one more before the three-thirty bus.

He'd taken to meeting Noah every day the minute classes ended and accompanying him home, no matter how much Noah protested. And, Christ, did he protest. It was back to the point where the kid was treating him like the enemy at the gates. Barely speaking except to ridicule something Daniel said or did, shooting dagger looks out of the blue for no discernible reason, slamming the door of his bedroom and refusing to come out, no matter how much he was enticed.

But the headmaster had said the school couldn't protect Noah after hours, so what else was Daniel to do? He couldn't believe he hadn't thought of this before. All he had to do was not let Noah out of his sight when he wasn't at school.

'One Americano.' Sylvia smiled, putting a cup and saucer in front of him.

'Thanks,' said Daniel, without looking at her.

She stayed standing by the table. From the corner of his eye, Daniel could see her drumming her fingers on the side of her tray. 'Can I ask you something?' she said.

'Sure,' Daniel said, glancing up at her.

'Are you Danny Lane?'

Daniel stared down at his hands, then raised his eyes to hers again. 'No,' he said, forcing what he hoped was an exasperated smile. 'People are always mistaking me for that guy.'

'Oh,' Sylvia said, grinning back. But she didn't look convinced.

Daniel waited until she had gone back behind the counter and then, without drinking his coffee, put a five-pound note on the table and walked out of the café's front door. It was the last time he'd go there.

Outside on Portobello Road, he brought his face up to meet the afternoon sun and felt again the fleeting sense of isolation that had been dogging him since the day he'd met Maggie. When he'd walked away from her that afternoon, he'd known she'd stood still, watching him. Despite himself, he'd wanted to turn around and go back to her, but he forced himself to keep on wheeling his bike away.

Turn back to her for what? They weren't children any more. He'd refused her offer of a ticket to the Abba concert because of the futility of trying to rekindle the past. Because when she'd laughed at something he'd said towards the end of their meeting, he'd forgotten that she looked ill and disappointed, that she'd grown into a safe, workaday middle-aged woman. It had had a dizzyingly sickening effect on him that had made him want to get away from her.

He walked to the bus stop, pushing her out of his head. With time, he knew, she'd be gone. But for now he'd have to discipline himself to avoid thinking of her.

At the bus stop his phone bleeped four times in rapid succession, to say he had missed calls, which was odd because it hadn't rung while he was in the café where there was usually full coverage. Two were from Noah, and the others were from different blocked numbers. Just as Daniel was about to phone Noah back, one of the blocked numbers rang again.

'Hello?' Daniel answered it, praying it wasn't Joanna Brady or another journalist.

'Hello, is this Mr Daniel Smith?'

'Yes, it is.'

'Mr Smith, this is Constable James Collingwood at Maida Vale Police Station.'

Daniel's stomach pitched. Something had happened to Noah, he knew it.

'I'm calling about your son, Mr Smith. He gave me your number.'

'Is he okay?' said Daniel, his heart hammering.

'Yes,' said the policeman. 'He's fine. But we have him in custody. He was reported for bringing a knife to school.'

'Fuck.' Daniel broke into a run for Ladbroke Grove, where he'd get a cab quickly. 'I'll be there as soon as I can.'

Noah was utterly unapologetic, so Daniel stepped in for him. 'It won't happen again,' he assured the constable.

'It's a very serious offence,' the constable repeated, for the umpteenth time. 'Possession of an offensive weapon with intent to harm.'

Daniel had spent a good fifteen minutes explaining why Noah might have taken the knife to school, about the bullying and the threats on Facebook, but he hadn't got anywhere.

'If we knew the identities of the perpetrators, we might be able to follow up,' the constable said. But Noah refused to divulge them.

While they were waiting for the constable to finish the report paperwork, Daniel phoned the school.

'We look on this very seriously,' the headmaster said. 'Any more offences like this and Noah will have to find another school.'

'What the fuck?' Daniel had half shouted into the phone. 'He's trying to protect himself from a crowd of thugs you can't control, and *he* gets the blame?'

'I'm sure you understand, Mr Smith,' the headmaster replied, his voice level, 'that we can't have students turning up at school carrying dangerous weapons.'

'What the hell were you thinking?' Daniel snapped at Noah, after he'd hung up.

Noah folded his arms and stared straight ahead.

'Answer me!' Daniel barked.

'I didn't do anything with it!' Noah shouted back. 'I only took it just in case.'

Daniel looked at his son. His hair was sprayed into a high candyfloss quiff. Thick black makeup ringed his eyes and his lips bore traces of glitter. Behind him, on the olive green wall of the waiting room, a poster advertised a drug rehabilitation scheme. It featured a picture of a girl with similar panda eyes and dirty-blonde hair, half smiling at the camera with relief. She seemed barely older than Noah, and she was an actress or model, of course, but she looked as though she'd lived a hundred lives. Her eyes were etched with ancient pain.

Could anyone save anyone else? Everyone was destined to be maimed by the world in one way or another. We could either learn from the battle or not. Heal our own scars or let them fester. Even if Daniel was rooted at Noah's side for the rest of his life, trying to shield him from the slings and arrows, there was nothing he could actually do to stop him being shot. What else could he do but hope his son was not fatally wounded?

The constable interrupted Daniel's thoughts by handing him a printed sheet of paper. 'It's a caution,' he explained, and then turned to Noah. 'Don't let it happen again, son, okay?'

Silent and goggle-eyed, Noah nodded.

Daniel sighed and got to his feet. 'Let's go home,' he said.

They were barely out the door of the police station when Daniel clocked the photographer. He was standing behind a blue car at the other side of the street, aiming his camera directly at him and Noah, like a hunter stalking prey.

Without looking left or right for oncoming traffic, Daniel strode across the road. 'Hey, you!' he called. 'What the fuck do you think you're doing?'

The camera fast-clicked a few times as Daniel advanced, his whole being filling with red rage.

The photographer broke into a run.

67. Feeling Blue

It might have been Maggie's last round of chemo, but it was just as difficult to get over, if not more so, than the others. By the following Monday, she was still so drained she was barely able to drink the cup of tea her mother had brought upstairs. She lay back on her pillows and stared at the ceiling, listening to the noise of the radio downstairs, Orlando's laughter occasionally rising above it, Poppy shouting, 'Auntie Oona! Do you want a cup of tea?' Oona's 'Yes, please!' from the back garden. 'Make one for your grandmother too!'

The house was full of sound and movement. Harry had called last night from Thailand, where he was having a holiday before he came back to London on Wednesday. He'd asked Maggie to meet him at Heathrow.

She should have been happy. That was what she'd wanted, wasn't it? Her mother was going back to Ireland at last and now Maggie would be surrounded by her children, doing what she knew she did best – being a mother to them. But lying under her duvet, shivering even though outside a hot July sun was beaming down, she felt utterly bereft.

She squeezed her eyes shut and a picture of Daniel surfaced in the blackness. He was walking away from her with his bicycle on the South Bank, the London Eye turning slowly behind him.

She'd done her best. She'd fought hard to stay positive, to find things to aim towards, but she had been fooling herself. There was no Abba concert, at least not for her. And Daniel was a different person, distant and oblique, so far removed from her life that she might never have met him in the first place.

She might never have lost his baby.

'Mum!' she heard Poppy call on the stairs. 'Can I borrow the car?'

Maggie turned her face into the pillow, unable to muster the strength to reply.

'Mum?' Poppy said, coming into the room. 'Are you awake?'

'Yes,' Maggie mumbled, not opening her eyes.

'Can I borrow the car? Orlando wants to go to Crystal Palace.'

'Yes,' said Maggie.

'Mum?' Poppy sat on the end of the bed. She sounded forlorn all of a sudden. 'Are you okay?'

'I'm fine,' Maggie said.

'Are you sure?'

Maggie could smell her own sour breath. 'Yes. Go ahead and take the car.'

Poppy didn't move. 'Mum?' she repeated, and Maggie heard tears in her voice.

She pulled herself up, the effort causing darts of pain to shoot across her shoulders. 'What's wrong, honey?' she asked.

Poppy rubbed the end of her nose with the sleeve of her baggy grey sweatshirt. 'I'm … I'm …'

'What?'

'Scared.'

Maggie hadn't the energy to open her arms to hug her. 'Scared of what?' she asked. Her tongue felt starched.

'What will I do if you die?' said Poppy, and began to sob.

Maggie lay down again. 'I'm not going to die, Poppy.'

'How do you know that?' Now she sounded indignant.

'Sweetheart,' Maggie sighed, 'I'm tired. I need to get some sleep.'

Poppy stood up. She was still crying, her face scrunched up and inflamed. 'I don't understand,' she said. 'It's like... like the ... *it's* changed you, Mum. I don't even know who you are any more.'

Maggie stared at her, wanting to feel empathy for the pain her daughter was in, but nothing came forth. 'That makes two of us,' she replied, and let her eyes close again.

When she opened them once more, the house was silent. She inched her legs over the side of the bed and put her feet into her slippers. She needed a shower badly, but more insistent was the rumbling in her stomach. It was at least twenty-four hours since she'd eaten.

There was a note on the kitchen table in Oona's perfunctory script. 'We're all going in the car to Crystal Palace. Back at six.'

Maggie buttered some bread and put on the kettle to make a cup of tea. Benny, who had not stayed with her in her room since Orlando's arrival, was snoozing on one of the chairs, warmed by a shaft of sunlight coming through the window, the marmalade fur on his back softly rising and falling. He took a deep breath and let it out as a sleep sigh.

When Maggie's tea was made, she turned on the radio, and sat down at the kitchen table with her plate of buttered bread.

The final verse of 'I Have A Dream' was playing. Maggie had never thought that in her lifetime she'd want to get away from Abba, but with the concert coming the weekend after next, they were on every radio station all the time, Agnetha's and Frida's voices crying out in melancholy unison, making her feel that even trying to live was futile.

'I Have A Dream' was a song that had its whole life stretched out in front of it. A song that believed there was something good in everything and that by sticking to your dream you would somehow reach your destination.

It was bullshit.

'So there you have it!' the DJ said, over the fading chorus. 'Number fourteen in our countdown of the best Abba songs of all time, as voted by you.'

Maggie perked up a little. She wouldn't have put 'I Have A Dream' in the top twenty, even. As far as she was concerned, it was Abba's most saccharine and sentimental song, and not in a good way. Although hardly anyone on the Abbaholics Facebook group shared that view.

'And so we come to the moment we've all been waiting for,' the DJ continued, his voice breathless. 'We're about to phone the winner of our Big Fat Abba competition! Yes, folks, the lucky person who's getting four tickets to see Abba at Stockholm Stadium next Saturday week, four flights to the Swedish capital, two nights in the super-luxurious Absolut Ice Hotel, and ten thousand krona – yes, that's a thousand pounds of spending money!'

Maggie got up to turn off the radio. Listening to this was like rubbing salt into a wound. As Poppy had said, she didn't have a chance in Hell of winning. She'd hear someone else's name announced and then her very last hope would be dead in the water.

But she hesitated.

'We've had a vast number of entries,' said the DJ, stretching the awful moment out, 'more than we've had for any other competition in the history of this radio station!'

On the kitchen chair, Benny woke up with a start. He stretched out a paw, and flexed his claws.

'But only one winner can take it all,' the DJ said. 'And we are dialling that winner's phone number right now ...'

Benny's ears pricked. Upstairs in the bedroom, Maggie's mobile phone began to ring.

68. Ring Ring

With Benny in hot pursuit, Maggie got to the top of the stairs as fast as her legs could take her. She dived for the phone, which was vibrating on the end of the bed, just about to ring out.

'Hello!' she answered, out of breath.

'Is that you, Maggie?' said a woman's voice that was familiar but not immediately identifiable. It was certainly not the radio DJ.

Maggie's heart sank. 'Yes?' she said.

'It's Dee here ... How are you?'

Her tone, Maggie thought, sounded strained and formal, as if she was making a difficult business call. 'Dee!' she exclaimed, attempting to inject some cheerfulness into her own voice and failing miserably. She felt utterly deflated. She tried to think of something else to say, but her mind was still processing the fact that she hadn't won the Abba tickets after all, and it wouldn't connect with her mouth.

'I've been meaning to call you back for so long,' Dee said, and again Maggie heard an odd disconnect in her old friend's voice.

'Are you okay?' she asked.

At the other end of the phone Dee emitted a laugh that sounded artificial. 'Of course I am,' she said.

There was another silence while Maggie tried again to bring herself into the moment, then Dee added, 'How long has it been? I mean, since we saw each other last.'

'Your wedding,' Maggie replied, without hesitation.

She had complained continually to William in the weeks before they had gone to Italy: being forced to go abroad for weddings was unfair, and Dee had only invited her out of duty anyway. They hadn't seen each other since Poppy's first holy communion, for which Dee had come over from Ireland also out of duty, as Poppy's godmother. Dee wanted to be seen doing the right thing.

Despite the professional aura Dee had exuded back then, Maggie could clearly remember her having been drunk – legless – at the end of the barbecue they'd had after the mass, flirting outrageously with Patrick Bird, who had lived next door with his wife. After that, Dee's contact with Poppy had tailed off to sporadic birthday cards and a couple of Christmas presents in the post.

Still, Maggie had enjoyed the Italian wedding, despite her reservations, loving everything about the little medieval town it was held in, with its tiny stone church and the amazing frescos by Botero on the walls, featuring Paradise and the infernos of Hell, with a big fat Madonna and an even fatter, almost comical Lucifer facing each other as Dee and Joe exchanged vows at the altar.

At the reception later on, Maggie and Dee ended up alone together in the hotel's Ladies. Dee had asked her to pull down the zipper on the back of her dress so she could breathe properly, and the two of them had had a fit of the giggles about the wildly inappropriate story the priest had told during his homily, about bouncing Joe up and down on his knee when he was a little boy. Maggie had laughed so hard, she'd wet herself.

'This is just like old times,' Dee had said, wiping away tears of mirth.

Maggie had replied, 'I've missed you so much,' and the laughter had stopped as instantly as it had started.

She'd zipped Dee back up and the two of them had rejoined the wedding party, hardly getting a chance to speak to each other for the rest of the reception.

Maggie had sent a few emails after they'd come home from Italy, and tried to call Dee a couple of times, but there had been no contact in return.

Maggie didn't really blame her. She'd asked her to be Poppy's godmother out of guilt, and only gone to the wedding out of guilt too.

Back when Maggie and her mother had returned from the trip to Manchester, Dee had continued calling to the house every day, but Maggie had refused either to go out or invite her in. Then when Dee had gone back to boarding school she had written every week, like she used to, until eventually she had given up. Maggie had wrestled with wanting to reply and needing to put the part of her life with Dee, Daniel and Charlie in it firmly in the past. She'd turned over a new leaf, and Dee remained on its underside, a reminder of what had happened and the girl Maggie didn't want to be any more.

Now, hearing Dee's voice so oddly strained, obviously needing something but not saying what it was, Maggie realised how rash and wrong she'd been, just throwing away her best friend like that. They'd had such good times together before that night on the island had pulled everything apart.

'Poppy's always talking about you,' she lied, to fill the gap that had emerged in their conversation, then cursed herself for rubbing in Dee's absence from Poppy's life. 'I mean, she remembers you so well,' she added.

'She was such a lovely little girl,' said Dee. Now her voice was congested.

Maggie got the feeling she was crying. 'Are you sure you're okay?' she asked.

'I'm pregnant,' Dee said. She sounded grief-stricken.

'But that's great news,' said Maggie, and stopped. 'Isn't it?'

'Yes,' Dee said. 'It is …' Now she sounded as if she was crying.

'I'm so happy for you,' Maggie tried. 'When are you due?'

Instead of answering Maggie's question, Dee said, 'I've bought my ticket to Stockholm.'

'Pardon?' Maggie said.

'For the Abba fan club reunion. I'm so excited.'

She didn't sound it.

'But Daniel can't come. And I haven't been able to find Charlie ...'

'But you still have the tickets to the concert, right?'

Maggie thought she heard desperation in Dee's voice. 'Well—'

'We could go, just you and me,' Dee interrupted. 'For old times' sake.'

'That would be lovely,' Maggie said, and she meant it, even if she was still avoiding the truth.

'What about a hotel?' Dee said. 'Have you booked one yet?'

Maggie caught her reflection in the mirror on the door of her wardrobe. A middle-aged woman standing alone in her bedroom, her breasts still intact under the faded dressing-gown for a few more weeks only. 'I Have A Dream' was a song about pushing through the darkness. It was about hope in the face of adversity.

'Are you still there?' Dee asked.

'I haven't booked anything,' Maggie replied. 'I was just thinking of checking in somewhere when we got there.'

'Are you *crazy*?' Dee asked, and she sounded just like she had when they used to lie on Maggie's bed and moon over *Abba* magazine while listening to the *Arrival* album on a loop. 'We might have to sleep on the streets at this stage. The whole world is going to Stockholm for that concert.'

'I didn't think of that,' Maggie said, still only half entering the fib she was telling.

'Don't worry,' said Dee. 'I have some contacts in the hotel business who might be able to get something for us.'

'You do?' said Maggie. 'So, we're going, then?' She couldn't quite believe what she was saying.

'Of course we are,' Dee said. She didn't seem so convinced either.

'I can't wait to see them in the flesh,' said Maggie, warming to the idea that it was actually going to happen. Beginning to believe her lie. 'Remember how obsessed we were with Agnetha and Frida?'

'Listen, I have to go,' Dee said, her voice going down a notch. 'I'll email the details of the hotel if I can get one, and my flight times on Friday week. I'm flying direct from Dublin so we can arrange to meet up in Stockholm, okay?'

'Great,' said Maggie. 'And, Dee … I'm really looking forward to seeing you.'

'Me too,' Dee almost whispered.

After they'd hung up, Maggie scooped Benny into her arms. 'I suppose I'd better book a ticket to Stockholm,' she told him, stroking his head as his mouth opened in a wide yawn.

69. Candy from a Baby

Funk 'n' Further's remix of 'How To Be A Man' had become the song of the summer, the one you heard drifting out of every café, filtering through the aisles of the supermarket, belting out of cab radios, filling every possible space in the city where music could be heard. Daniel had taken to ordering his food shopping from Sainsbury's on-line and going out only to collect Noah from school. He left the television off, and listened to Radio 4, where he was sure he would never hear either 'Night Star' or 'How To Be A Man'.

This morning, however, some London Olympics gold-medal winner Daniel had never heard of had picked 'Trailblazer' as one of the discs she'd bring to a desert island. Although it had never been a single, the sportswoman said it was her favourite song on Danny Lane's one and only album; that it brought her back to her childhood and happy times.

Listening to it, Daniel's heart sank. After 'Night Star' and 'How To Be A Man' there were ten more songs on that album for the record company to exploit. He might not be out of the charts for a good year to come. Granted, they were mediocre at best, filler cobbled together quickly with two writers appointed by Vince, but given the right treatment, most of them had catchy enough hooks to chart. With the standard of pop music as it currently was, the remix of a dog barking had every chance of hitting the top spot.

The song the sportswoman had picked as the one she couldn't do without on the island was Abba's 'Dancing Queen'. She had tickets to the big concert, she gushed, before reiterating why the song meant so much to her.

It was a cliché, but Daniel had to agree, the opening bars induced a little trill of joy, no matter how you were feeling. It made him think of how he'd felt about music when he used to write songs in his bedroom and dream of singing them to an audience.

The song played on and he remembered watching Maggie as a teenager, spinning around, like a whirling Dervish, to its chorus, having the time of her life. That had been weeks before they had gone to the island, before anything had happened between them, but he'd wanted to reach out and stop her, to pull her to him and feel her lips touch his, to explore every millimetre of her skin with the tips of his fingers, to memorise her like a blind man learning a love poem in Braille. By heart.

The awkward little meeting with her continued to play on his mind; the feeling of acute isolation kept returning.

The kettle boiled and Daniel filled the cafetière.

He'd told Maya on the phone yesterday, after reluctantly agreeing to go to a final recording session for the new EP, that he'd turned down Maggie's invitation to the concert. She'd let out a loud squeal and said, 'Are you out of your mind? Those tickets are selling for a grand apiece now!'

'It's not for me,' Daniel replied, remembering again Maggie's expression as they'd parted on the South Bank. It had been filled with sorrow.

'Tell her I'll go!' Maya cried. '*Pleeeeease!*'

'I don't think I'll be in contact with her again,' Daniel said.

He was filling his cup from the cafetière when his mobile phone rang on the table and Jade's name appeared on its display.

'Hey,' he answered, and took a sip of coffee. It burned his tongue.

'Have you seen the papers?'

An alarm bell sounded in Daniel's head. 'No,' he said. 'Why?'

'Fuck, Daniel. They've brought Noah into it!'

'Brought Noah into what?'

'You need to go out and buy the papers,' Jade said. 'All of them.'

A scrawny middle-aged woman in a tan woollen beret, the type who baked cakes for church fêtes, walked by as he was parking his bike outside the newsagent's. She hesitated ever so slightly and gave Daniel a noxious glance, as if he'd personally affronted her. He took his helmet off and put his head down, avoiding her even though she'd already walked off.

In the shop the newspapers were laid out on a low shelf beneath a rack of magazines. The first headline that jumped out was 'Blame's On Lane!' Underneath it was written: 'Pop comeback Danny Lane's son in playground knife scandal.'

The *Daily Standard* had: 'Danny's Boy! Police nab son of eighties star Danny Lane in possession of deadly weapon.'

Those were just two of the tabloids. The rest were leading with the story, and each had a variation of the same photograph of Danny and Noah leaving Maida Vale police station. Noah's expression was defiant in every shot and Daniel's whole demeanour exuded guilt.

Daniel had the urge to scoop up every single newspaper in the shop and buy them all, as if he could stop the spread of the story by doing so. But the truth was that people across Britain were sitting down to Saturday breakfast right now, reading about Noah.

His heart hammering so hard it hurt, Daniel picked up the *Standard* and started reading, looking for mentions of bullying or a qualifying quote from the headmaster of Noah's school, anything to give a proper explanation as to why his son had been carrying the knife.

'Do you want to buy that newspaper, sir?' asked the Indian man behind the counter.

Daniel ignored him. The story was told in the most damaging way possible. Yes, there was a quote from the headmaster, but it was skewed to the bias of the article. 'We look very seriously on this kind of thing,' he said. 'Knife crime is a very real problem among our young people today.'

Noah was being held up as an example of how children of the privileged blighted the country. He was being painted as the spoilt kid of a pop star who had gone off the rails. A havoc-wreaker.

'Sir?' said the shopkeeper, and Daniel glanced up at him. He was standing with his arms folded.

Daniel took one copy of every paper, all the tabloids and all the broadsheets, and bundled them on to the counter.

The shopkeeper glanced at the paper on top of the stack, the *Daily Mirror*. 'It's terrible, these kids running around with knives. This country is going to rack and ruin.'

Daniel's nails dug into his palms, but he said nothing. He handed over a twenty-pound note for the papers, avoiding eye contact.

The shopkeeper was bundling the papers into two striped plastic bags when he stopped abruptly. 'Hey,' he said, looking at the photo on one of the front pages and back at Daniel. 'This is you, isn't it? You're that pop star.'

Daniel didn't reply. He reached out to take the bags and left without waiting for his change.

Outside, as he was unlocking his bike, he hoped Noah was still sleeping and blissfully ignorant. The boy was in the habit of turning on his computer first thing every morning, and with Twitter on the go every nano-second, news got around faster than the speed of light.

He might know already that his face was plastered everywhere.

70. See That Girl

Cassandra couldn't stop checking her phone. Every time she picked it up, she hoped to see a missed call from John or a text message she hadn't heard bleep through, even though she'd had the phone with her all the time, on full volume.

But there was nothing.

'Put that stupid phone down!' said Coco, who was working on her makeup at the dressing-table next to Cassandra's. She tilted her head back to apply another layer of mascara to her already thick black eyelashes. 'If he hasn't called by now, I don't think he is going to. It is time to move on, Mama Cass.'

Cassandra knew this to be true, but she couldn't quench the tiny flame of hope that still flickered inside. When she thought about the time they'd spent together, hidden in her hotel room, their eyes locked and their bodies entwined, she knew what had happened between them had been real.

Still, there was no contact from him whatsoever, so she must have been wrong. Maybe the whole thing had been her imagination. He was probably disgusted by her now.

Cassandra's mind went back to Sam's kitchen, and the jumble of expressions on John's face as the truth about her dawned on him. She could recall them almost in slow motion – confusion turning to revelation, turning to disbelief, turning to shock, turning to disappointment, turning to …

She tried to think whether she'd seen revulsion on his face, but now could remember only her own panic as she'd begged, 'Please, John! Let me explain!'

Madam Ovary popped her head round the door and called, 'Five minutes to curtain, ladies!'

In the weeks Cassandra had been away, Madam Ovary had all but usurped her position as queen of the dressing room. There were lots of new things in place, like a little kitchenette, with a microwave and a kettle on a corner of a counter that had previously been stacked with boxes of flyers for Flikkers, and the constant curtain calls, which Madam Ovary delivered with relish.

Cassandra didn't mind. In fact, she couldn't have cared less. Since her return to work, she had been only half concentrating. She lip-synched as she had done almost every night for the past ten years, but her heart was no longer in it. The audience members still gazed up at her as she traversed the stage, marvelling and nudging each other as if to ask how a man could appear to be such a beautiful woman.

Over the years, plenty of them had asked her this question to her face, ignorant of the cringing discomfort it caused. 'It takes a lot of work,' she'd joke with them, batting her false eyelashes for effect. But it wasn't a joke. She'd worked her arse off to become who she was, and she went on working. Beyond the psychotherapy and the surgery, there was the endless diet and exercise, the hours spent in front of the mirror painting herself with miniature brush-strokes so that on the street her womanhood could never be questioned, her provenance never imagined.

Her whole adult life had been an effort to change, to release herself from the chrysalis of her previous body to emerge like a butterfly and display her true colours. She knew she couldn't love herself unless she truly became herself, but until John had slammed Sam's front door behind him, she had never fully appreciated the price she'd have to pay. Her father had rejected her, and so had her brother, but in the loss of John, she understood for the first time that the trade-off for doing what she'd had to do might be loneliness.

For, once the truth came out, who would want to be with her?

'*Madre de Dios*! Stop feeling so sorry for yourself,' Coco exclaimed, pulling what she called her 'Roxy Harte' wig in place. 'You look like a horse, with the long face and the sulking. No more sulking!'

Cassandra blinked away tears. 'Please don't talk to me like that, Coco,' she said. 'You don't understand.'

'I don't understand? Look at me, I'm crying for you!' Coco rubbed her fists at the sides of her eyes, imitating a bawling baby. 'My life is *sooooo* terrible!' she wailed. 'Some guy doesn't want me because I used to have a dick!'

'Don't be so crude,' Cassandra said. 'I'm sitting the next number out. Go on without me.'

Coco pushed her face between Cassandra and the dressing-table mirror, so close that Cassandra could smell onions on her breath. 'So, you used to be a little boy? Big deal! Get over it!'

Cassandra resisted the urge to shove her away. 'You're one to talk!' she shouted. 'Always crying, "I'm a real girl! I'm a real girl!" Well, you're just like me, sweetie. You're a freak of fucking nature!'

Cassandra was thoroughly ashamed of her outburst, but as she packed Coco's things into the three Lidl bags with which the girl had first arrived at the apartment, she tried to justify herself. What had happened in the aftermath was absolutely unacceptable. She could still feel the tingling in her scalp where Coco's nails had dug in and wrenched a handful of her hair. The long scrape on the left side of her neck wasn't as livid now, but it wouldn't go away for a while. It would be a reminder of why Cassandra should never have invited Coco into her life. The girl was a firework with a faulty fuse. Getting too close to her was a bad idea. You never knew when she was going to explode.

Madam Ovary had stood with her hands on her ample hips as Cassandra had stalked out of the dressing room, telling her she was taking the rest of the night off. She'd made noises about not putting up with this kind of behaviour, but Cassandra didn't give a shit. Old Ovary might be lording it over everyone else at Flikkers nowadays, but she had another thing coming if she thought she could try it on with her.

Cassandra pulled open the wardrobe and was confronted by a row of Coco's candy-coloured dresses, their frills protruding. As she reached in to pull out an armful, her mobile phone began to ring in the living room. She dropped the dresses on the floor, their rhinestones clicking on the tiles, and ran to get it.

She was floored by disappointment when she saw Sam's name on the display instead of John's, but then her breath caught. What could her brother be calling her for? Had something happened to their father?

'Sam?' she answered. 'What's wrong?'

'Nothing,' said Sam.

Outside Cassandra could hear a crowd of tourists passing by, shouting and laughing. Her defences rose. 'Why are you calling?' she asked.

'I have a message for you.'

The tourists were still beneath the apartment's balcony. A bottle broke on the pavement and there was more laughter. 'What message?' Cassandra asked.

'A woman called Maggie Behan phoned a while back. She has a ticket for you to the Abba concert in Sweden on Saturday. She said something about a reunion.'

Cassandra's mind tripped back to that long-forgotten morning, and the stillness of the lake as she'd rowed the boat away from the island where they'd all spent the night. 'Did she leave any contact details?' she asked her brother.

After Sam had given her Maggie's number, it was clear that he couldn't wait to hang up. 'Thank you,' Cassandra said to him.

'You're welcome,' he replied, and she thought she'd heard something different in his voice. Then he was gone.

Back in the bedroom, Cassandra picked up Coco's dresses, folded them into a bundle and stuffed them into one of the Lidl bags. She looked at the framed posters on the walls, all from old films starring Marlene Dietrich. *The Blue Angel. Blonde Venus. The Devil is a Woman.*

Her life here was finished; Cassandra knew that now. It was time to stop lip-synching on a stage, half in and half out of her life as a woman. Her mortgage was paid off. She'd sell the apartment and use the money to start again somewhere new, where nobody had any idea of what she'd come from, where there might be a future free of the shackles of the person she once was. A place that was free from Charlie.

But before she finally let go of the past, there was a pilgrimage she wanted to make.

71. *About to Crack*

It had been bucketing down for hours so the air was humid and the tube was stiflingly hot. On the last train of the day, hurtling its way across London from Wood Green, Daniel felt claustrophobic and groggy. The four pints of lager he'd had with Maya and her new session players weren't helping.

'You should come out with us again,' Maya had said, as he was leaving, and he'd found himself giving her a hug.

He'd actually enjoyed himself. As if there was a secret code between musicians, none of them had asked any questions about the newspaper stories, or even identified him as Danny Lane. They had tacitly chosen a sequestered corner of the bar to sit in, where no one might disturb them, and Daniel had begun to relax in their company. It had felt right to be out, to be drinking and talking with other adults about ordinary things. It had felt like what normal should feel like.

The carriage was almost empty and he wondered if he should take off his baseball cap and sunglasses. They were adding to his claustrophobia. But the woman sitting across from him kept glancing his way as if she was sizing him up, ready to pounce. So he kept them on, folded his arms and tucked his chin into his chest, feigning sleep.

The worst of it was that Noah had been recognised on the street too. His candyfloss hair had given away his identity, of course. An old woman, he'd told Jade, had come up to him in the West End and yelled, 'Shame on you, knife killer!' It was the tip of the iceberg, Daniel knew.

As a result Noah had toned down his look. His hair was now a nondescript brown and parted to the side, his clothes were grey and devoid of Lady Gaga slogans. It was what Daniel had wanted him to do all along, to fit in and stop making a target of himself, but now he wished Noah would go back to his original flamboyant self. Everything about him looked defeated. He didn't even do his eye-rolling, gum-popping thing any more. On a few occasions Daniel had deliberately said things that would have made him rise to the bait before, but now the boy just nodded silently. His shoulders had narrowed and the light in his eyes was dulled, and Daniel felt he'd utterly failed him.

He was thankful at least that there was a month of the school holidays to go. By the time Noah went back, maybe the newspaper stories would have been forgotten.

He changed at Baker Street and got a Hammersmith & City line train to Ladbroke Grove. It was packed. Was it his imagination, or were the couple standing by the doors nudging each other and staring at him?

He looked away, but sitting at the other end of the carriage, a man with a suitcase jammed between his knees was openly gazing in Daniel's direction. The Japanese girls opposite him in *Wicked* T-shirts were huddled together and giggling. Then one lifted her head and her eyes, coal black and framed by poker-straight inky hair, rested squarely on him.

Daniel's breathing stopped. The rumble of the train seemed to enter through his feet and make its way into his veins. He was seized by a need to escape, not from the hot, crammed carriage, but from the horrible confines of his own body. It was a feeling he hadn't had in a long time. The bells and whistles that signalled a panic attack.

He shot to his feet, almost overbalancing with the movement of the train. As he reached out to the pole to steady himself, the woman who had been sitting beside him lifted her head and smiled. Her eyes were benign, like those of a sympathiser at a funeral. Behind his sunglasses, Daniel closed his own eyes and tried to internalise her smile, to make it his sole focal point. It was an effort, but visualising it kept him holding to the pole until the train came to the next stop. Although Royal Oak was two stations before his, he got out and stood on the platform for a few minutes, breathing in the damp air, telling himself that the panic had passed until eventually it did. Then, a little unsteadily at first, he set off to walk home in the relative anonymity of the London night.

Before he even opened the front door, he knew that the house was deserted. In the hallway he called out Noah's name, but there was no answer. The kitchen was in darkness. Daniel switched on the light at the wall and called again.

'Noah!'

On the table was a folded-over note, with 'Daniel' written on the top. With a sinking feeling, he opened it and began to read.

Hi Daniel

I've taken Noah home with me. I feel it would be better for him, for the time being. I'm sorry for doing it this way, but I didn't want any arguments. Please don't feel you have to stay away. You're welcome to come and see him any time. I just think this is for the best right now.

Jade was right. If Noah had never come to live with him, his face wouldn't have ended up plastered on the front pages. Instead of properly protecting his son, he'd made him notorious and a million times more vulnerable. He'd been a worse father than his own pathetic father had ever been.

Daniel flicked the light off again. The house was deathly silent. He thought of going out into the streets once more. But he had lost the anonymity he'd fought so hard for and thought he'd gained. There was no escape from Danny Lane.

If only he could go back to a time before Danny Lane, before Vince had seen him busking on the street for food money. Before he had run away from home with nothing, not knowing what awaited him or how to make the right decisions for his future.

He didn't know how long he stood in the dark kitchen before he reached into his pocket and took out his phone.

There was a place he could escape to right now, if he wanted, a place that represented the last time he was truly happy, if it was still on offer.

He began to search for Maggie's number.

72. Rescue Me Now

Harry had morphed into a man since the last time they'd Skyped. Maggie didn't recognise him until he was almost on top of her at the airport, reaching across the barrier in the arrivals hall to embrace her in a bear-hug. His short-back-and-sides had grown out into a leonine mop of curls and a full, rusty-brown beard covered the lower part of his tanned face. He wore a linen tunic-like top the colour of garam masala with a V-neck that revealed a mat of golden hair on his chest, and around his neck dangled an assortment of pendants and crystals on leather thongs. As he'd held Maggie so hard it hurt, she'd thought, *My little boy has turned into a hippie.*

She hadn't noticed the girl standing quietly behind him until he'd let go and turned to take her hand. 'Mum,' he'd said, 'this is Amber. Amber, meet my mum.'

Now Amber was sitting on Maggie's sofa, her knees squeezed together as if she was fending off a predator. Despite the low-cut muslin blouse over her frayed denim cut-offs, her battered Roman sandals and the straight Joni Mitchell hair, parted in the middle, she looked as uptight as a schoolmarm. She insisted on calling Maggie 'Mrs Corcoran'.

On one side of Amber sat an awestruck Orlando with Benny curled up on his lap. On the other was Oona, who kept catching Maggie's eye, as if the two of them were in on some underlying plot.

331

Maggie tried to avoid looking at her mother, who, with Orlando, was also gazing at Amber, but with less admiration. From her vantage point in the armchair at the empty fireplace, Maggie's mother took in Amber's bra-free cleavage and her bare, sun-kissed legs. She looked like a woman who couldn't stop staring at mangled bodies in a traffic accident.

Harry was out in the back garden with Poppy, and the faintest whiff of marijuana was drifting through the sitting-room window.

Maggie wondered if her mother recognised the smell. She had a strong inclination to go out and ask for a puff, but instead put on a sunny smile and said, 'Really?' as Amber came to a pause in the story of how she and Harry had met, which she was recounting as if it was as momentous as the first encounter between Edward and Mrs Simpson.

'And then he winked at me, Mrs Corcoran?' she said, the upward, Australian inflection of the last syllable twanging on Maggie's nerves. 'And I thought, Am I glad I came to this barbie?'

'That must have been lovely for you,' Oona said, meeting Maggie's eye again. It was kind of irritating. Maggie didn't know what her sister thought they were in cahoots about.

Orlando gawked at Amber in open-mouthed admiration and Maggie gave an automatic nod and smile. Her mind went back to Poppy and Harry, smoking weed in the back garden. Were they discussing her? Since Poppy's outburst on Saturday morning she hadn't said two words about how she was feeling. Instead of talking, she spent her time nuzzling Orlando, apparently competing with Benny for his attention.

Since Harry had arrived he hadn't mentioned the cancer, but Maggie kept catching him looking at her with giant anxious eyes, then turning back to Amber as if she was a welcome diversion.

Was Harry intending Amber to stay here? He hadn't said anything to that effect, but her rucksack sitting in the hall didn't appear to be going anywhere soon.

'I'd love to go to Australia.' Orlando beamed. 'It sounds totally sick.'

It sounded like he was using the word 'sick' as a compliment, so Maggie gave another nod of agreement, while her mother added a snort that sounded not unlike revulsion. Orlando was a nice boy, but he had the brain of a newt. She wondered again what her daughter was doing with him. Back when Poppy had done the eleven-plus, her teacher had suggested to Maggie and William that she take a Mensa test when she turned fourteen. Now here she was, dropped out of college, doing nothing with her life and living at home with a guy who'd confessed to Maggie the other day that the only book he'd ever read was *Fifty Shades of Grey*. 'I didn't really get it,' he'd said.

As Amber launched into a detailed explanation of why Sydney was the greatest place on the planet, Maggie's thoughts wandered again. She'd been putting off calling Dee to tell her she didn't have the Abba tickets, but it would have to be done this evening. The concert was fast approaching and it wouldn't be fair to let Dee travel there alone for nothing.

'It's like an outdoor culture, you know?' Amber enthused, looking from Maggie to Maggie's mother and back again. 'Because the sun is always shining, even in, like, the winter?'

Maggie's mother stood up. 'You must be starving,' she said to Amber. 'I'll make some sandwiches.'

'No, honestly?' said Amber. 'I'm not hungry at all?'

'Tea then,' Maggie's mother replied. 'I'll make us all a nice cup of tea.' She disappeared into the kitchen.

'I'll help,' said Oona, giving Maggie a lingering look as she followed.

'Sydney has, like, some of the best beaches in the world?' Amber went on, as if she'd been uninterrupted. 'You'd really love it there, you know, Mrs Corcoran?'

'Will you excuse me for a moment?' Maggie said, getting to her feet.

She walked into the hall and mounted the stairs, heading for the en suite in her bedroom, where she could lock herself away for a few minutes and get some headspace. Maybe have a quiet cry.

She was halfway up the stairs when her mother's voice sounded behind her: 'Margaret. I want a word.'

'Not now, Mum.' Maggie sighed. She knew she was going to complain about Amber's half-naked appearance, and ask if the girl was staying. She was probably going to say something about Orlando too, and the den of morally bankrupt vice and iniquity into which Maggie had let her own home descend.

'I'm leaving for Ireland tomorrow,' her mother persisted. 'There are things that need to be said.'

Maggie turned. Her mother's eyebrows were two fretful question marks. 'What is it?' she asked, feeling weirdly protective all of a sudden.

'Not here,' her mother said. 'We can't talk here.'

For a moment she wondered, with a deadened kind of feeling, if her mum was about to bring up the unspeakable past again. She sat down on the stairs. 'This is as good a place as any,' she said.

Her mother, gripping the banister with her narrow hand, cleared her throat. 'Your father and I ... We think you should—'

She was interrupted by a key turning in the front-door lock.

Over her mother's shoulder Maggie watched William appear. He was carrying a suitcase. She stood up. 'What are you doing here?' she asked.

William jumped. 'I've come to see Harry,' he said.

'He's out in the back garden with Poppy,' Maggie replied, then added, 'Why have you brought your suitcase with you?'

Her mother followed this exchange, her head turning to and fro. 'Hello, William,' she said. There was relief in her voice.

William didn't return the greeting. Instead he gazed up to where Maggie was standing. 'I've decided to come home,' he said. 'For good.'

From inside the sitting room Amber let out a peal of laughter. 'Harry?' she cried. 'Stop that?'

Maggie's eyes wandered past her mother's delighted face and William's entreating eyes to the garden beyond the open front door. All of the pieces in the jigsaw were back in place. Her husband had returned. Her children were laughing in the sitting room. She was surrounded by her family once more.

She felt like barging past William, running down the path into the street and not stopping.

She looked at William again. Both his arms were out as if he were beseeching her to enfold herself in them. 'I'll be down in a minute,' she said, and turned around, making a supreme effort to force down the anxiety that was bubbling up in her chest as she took the rest of the stairs. She shut her bedroom door behind her and leaned against it with her eyes closed.

When she opened them, Benny was there, sitting on the bed, staring at her, his one eye quizzical. A few minutes ago, he'd been asleep on Orlando's knee.

'What am I going to do?' Maggie asked the cat. The answer, she knew, was that she would pull herself together and head back downstairs to do what was expected of her. She was a good daughter. She was a good sister. She was a good wife. She was a good mother. She had been all these things all of her adult life, and she'd been proud of herself for it. Even if sometimes, as she ironed school uniforms and packed lunches, or smiled a perfect hostess's smile at yet another stultifying dinner party for William's colleagues and their wives, she'd felt like an animal caged in a zoo.

In the pocket of her jeans her mobile vibrated. Benny jumped down from the bed and rubbed himself against her calf, purring loudly. Maggie reached down to stroke the top of his head as she awkwardly pulled out the phone.

The name on its display was Daniel Smith.

August 1983
One of Us

As they round the corner of the island, Dee can see a couple of people on the tiny wooden jetty at the edge of Doorly Park. They're standing with their hands on their hips. Are they her father and mother? She can't make them out.

A tiny part of her hopes that at least one of them is there; that they care enough to have been worried out of their minds by her disappearance. But she's not convinced they'd worry at all, or that they'd have noticed she'd gone. Everything she'd once thought about them has been called into question.

She'd only been at the Ursuline for one blissful year before she was sent away. She'd sat beside Maggie for every single class, except the ones where they'd snuck out of the school's side gate by the tennis courts for what Maggie called their 'adventures' downtown. And she'd loved secondary school, the freedom and feeling of being grown-up it gave her. Then, at the end of the last summer holidays, her parents had sat her down and told her she was going to Kylemore Abbey. No matter how much Dee had cried and pleaded to be allowed to stay at home, she had been met with a brick wall. She was going to boarding school, and that was that. It was the best education a girl could get. She should count herself lucky.

She'd cried and begged all the way on that first long drive to Connemara, after her father had packed all her things into the car. In the front seat her parents had sat silent and stoic, like two hunched-over faceless strangers rather than the mother and father who had doted on her from the day she was born, who, she had once believed, adored her more than anyone in the world, when she was a fairytale princess and they were the king and queen of a magic kingdom with just the three of them in it.

When they had finally driven away, leaving her behind at the looming, cold, strange school, she couldn't quite believe it had happened. The princess had been banished. Everything she had once thought was certain had disappeared and she was alone in the dark.

That night, as she had added her own sobs to the muffled sounds of girls crying under rows of dormitory blankets, she'd resolved to make her parents listen to her when she was allowed home for a weekend at the end of the month. She'd go back to her old life of fun and adventure with Maggie. She'd make her mum and dad want her again.

But the same thing happened: her pleading was met with silence. And for the slow journey back to Kylemore this time she was by herself on a freezing, rickety old bus.

Maggie and Daniel are at the front of the boat, with their backs to the jetty, their shoulders leaning towards each other, talking about Daniel's Abba song. From the over-the-top way Maggie's behaving, Dee knows that something happened between them last night. She wonders if they went all the way.

Charlie turns and gives Dee a knowing smile, as if he's thinking about the same thing. Or maybe he's thinking about what happened between him and her, which was not at all like what Dee imagines happened between Maggie and Daniel.

Pushing it out of her mind, she says, 'Let's make a promise. Let's promise that if Abba ever get back together, we'll go to see them.'

She's only saying it to fill space. She'd go to Abba with Maggie in a heartbeat, and maybe with Charlie too, but there's something about Daniel she doesn't like. He's a bit weird. He's got that cool look about him, with the long hair and the battered runners, but it's almost like he's living on a different planet. He hardly gives Dee the time of day, and certainly doesn't look at her in the way she's become used to boys looking at her when she's not in the all-girl confines of Kylemore Abbey, the way Charlie looked at her.

Only Charlie wasn't looking at her that way at all. He was running his eyes all over her for a different reason.

Last night when he'd suggested a walk to the other end of the island, Dee had gone along without question. A little drunk from the wine Maggie had stolen, she'd trilled inside with excitement. At last, she thought, Charlie was going to kiss her. Maybe there'd be more than just kissing.

They'd pushed their way through thickets of trees and thorny brambles, Dee's shoes sinking into the damp, mossy bed of the forest, until they'd come to a little outcrop of rocks on the edge of the lake.

When they'd sat down beside each other on the biggest rock, Dee had thought, This is it, he's going to make a move. But Charlie didn't move at all. Instead he'd stared at the twilit sky, which was streaked with wispy salmon-coloured clouds.

After a while he'd turned to her and, pushing his fringe out of his eyes with one finger, said, 'I want to tell you a secret.'

'Okay,' said Dee. 'Go on.' For some reason she'd felt like giggling.

Behind them in the forest an owl gave a lone hoot and Dee shivered. She didn't really want to stay out all night. It would start turning cold soon.

'We'll make a bargain,' said Charlie. 'I'll tell you my secret, if you tell me yours.'

'What if I don't have a secret?' Dee had wrapped her arms around herself.

'Everyone has a secret.'

Dee had thought about this for a moment. She had hundreds of secrets. 'Okay,' she said, her nerves jangling at the thought of revealing them. 'You go first.'

Charlie had glanced at her, then turned back to the sunset, and Dee had seen that his hands were shaking. 'It's okay,' she said. 'I won't tell anyone, cross my heart and hope to die.'

'I'm not who you think I am,' Charlie had mumbled, still staring into the distance.

Dee had given an involuntary giggle. 'Who are you, then? The spy who loved me?'

Charlie had turned to her, the whites of his eyes clear in the dusky light. 'I'm a girl.'

Dee had giggled again. 'What?'

'I'm serious,' said Charlie, and words had spilled out of him, his deep voice choking. 'You're so lucky. You're so beautiful. I hate my body. I hate myself. I hate myself …'

Dee had put an arm around him. 'Don't say that,' she whispered. 'You're amazing. You're beautiful. Seriously.'

Charlie had shaken his head and sat with his body quietly heaving.

Dee didn't understand – she wasn't sure she wanted to understand – but she knew what it had cost him to tell her. She had lifted her arm from his shoulders and said, 'Do you want to know my secret?'

Charlie had lifted his head and nodded, his eyes swollen, his face streaked wet.

The owl in the forest hooted again as Dee pulled off her sweatshirt. Underneath it she wore a T-shirt with a faded Coca-Cola logo, leaving her arms bare and exposed. She didn't look down as Charlie studied the welted latticework of thin red scars on her white skin, then brought his face up to meet hers.

'Did you do it?' he asked, his eyes pale and frightened.

'Yes,' said Dee, irritated by his stupid question.

'Why?'

'It's hard to explain.'

'Try.'

'It's like I'm invisible. And when I do it, I'm not.'

'What do you mean?'

Dee sighed. 'I don't know,' she said, already wishing she hadn't shown Charlie the scars. He had too many questions, and she felt too exposed, as if she'd torn back her skin and revealed the raw flesh on her bones. Or brought him with her to the tiny bathroom under the eaves of the school's deserted attics, where she slowly and methodically made the incisions, enduring pain that somehow made her feel loved again.

Charlie had gone quiet. Then his arm went around her and he said, 'I promise I won't tell anyone. If you promise not to do it again.'

'I won't,' Dee had vowed, and although she wanted to live up to that promise, she wasn't sure she could.

'Good,' said Charlie.

'I won't tell anyone either,' said Dee. 'I mean, about you being a girl.'

In the fading light, she saw Charlie's teeth in a smile.

'Thank you,' he'd said.

Now in the boat, they're nearing the shore. The people standing on the jetty are not Dee's parents. They're Maggie's.

Part Three
ARRIVAL

73. Old Friends

Dee decided to have just one glass of wine. She hadn't had a drink since she'd been told she was pregnant, but she figured just one would do no harm to the baby, and she badly needed it after the stress of getting here.

She waved her hand to catch the attention of the barman, who was leaning in close to a couple at the other end of the bar and talking in a quiet voice. When he didn't respond, exhausted irritation buzzed in her veins and she called, 'Barman!'

'Can I help you?' he asked, walking towards her. His English diction was studied and he could have been no more than eighteen, all jutting awkwardness in his too-big starched white shirt and bow-tie.

'I'd like a glass of Cabernet Sauvignon,' Dee replied. 'Please.'

Through her sunglasses, she watched him pour the dark ruby liquid into the glass, and when he handed it to her, she swirled it and sniffed. Its deep aroma of berries and spice brought her instantly back to the first time Joe had treated her to a bottle of rare Bordeaux, for which he had paid three hundred euros. It had been their third date, in a cavernous restaurant she'd never been to before, its arched stone alcoves filled with racks and racks of fine wines he'd enthused about, using words like 'body' and 'nose' and 'oak aged'. He'd clinked his glass with Dee's, gazing into her eyes, and she'd sat there open-mouthed, unable to believe her luck at finding this cultured, educated, sexy, solvent, generous single man, with seemingly no baggage. It was almost unheard of.

Now, thanking the barman, she took a sip and let the wine run down her throat. It tasted like relief.

This morning she and Joe had left the house at the usual time, and she'd kissed him goodbye, getting out of the car in the city as if it was just another day. Then she'd gone up to her office, collected the bag she'd stowed there and, without a word to Connie or any of the other staff, had gone back down to the street and hailed a taxi to the airport.

Since he'd punched her face, Joe was keeping an extra special eye on her – leaving her at work, collecting her afterwards, making sure he was almost constantly at her side. He was full of apologies, of course, but something had changed from the usual abasement of the aftermath. He had an animal-like air about him, alert to her every move, corralling her like a sheep dog. Dee wondered if sheep were afraid of sheep dogs, or if they just did what they were told without thinking.

She'd booked her flight to Stockholm in the middle of the night, while Joe was fast asleep, and had bought a weekend hold-all during her lunchbreak one day, stuffing clothes and underwear into her handbag to bring into the office every morning when she went to work.

Dee took another sip of her wine and surveyed the hotel bar and restaurant. It had the air of an Oriental tearoom, with a high gold-painted art-deco ceiling from which enormous, sparkling chandeliers hung at intervals. The walls were lined with incongruous black-and-white photographs of Amazonian-like tribal people, in earlobe and neck-stretching jewellery.

Although the hotel was full to capacity, since she had secured its last four available rooms through her PR contact at the Swedish Tourist Board, the bar was half empty. A few couples were dotted here and there, a clutch of businessmen, a lone woman half out of view, beside a wall of windows that looked out on a little square.

Right now Dee knew Joe would be at his wits' end. She'd turned off her phone before the flight had left Dublin, and hadn't switched it back on. She was here a day before Maggie, Charlie and Daniel, so she didn't need to turn it on until tomorrow when they'd be trying to contact her.

She pictured Joe pulling the house apart for clues, trying to figure out where she'd gone, and felt vaguely sorry for having done this to him, for running away without a word.

Was that what she had done? Run away? She was only here for a weekend. There was no escaping the fact that she'd have to return home on Sunday night. But for now she didn't want to think about it. She wanted to pretend that she had given up her old life for something new, that the blankness she felt in these strange surroundings was how it was going to be from now on. Otherwise, she would have to feel. And if she allowed herself to feel, she might start screaming and not be able to stop.

The woman by the windows turned and looked at her for a few seconds, then went back to her drink.

It was probably the sunglasses that had made her stare. With them on, Dee felt an odd mixture of conspicuous and invisible. She'd had to take them off at Passport Control at Stockholm airport, and the lantern-jawed woman in the glass booth had given her a look with which she'd become familiar. It was at once sympathetic and repulsed, a look that said, 'You poor thing,' and 'How could you be so stupid as to let him do that to you?' It was only a look, though. Nobody ever *said* anything. Not even Connie, who couldn't set her eyes on Dee without welling up.

And Dee said nothing in return. She would not be a woman who walked into doors, but neither would she confide what had happened. Even though the truth was as plain as the bruises on her face, she couldn't bear to admit to it. She felt as if she'd be letting herself down.

The swelling that had welded her left eye shut was almost gone now. Only yellowish-black traces of the bruising remained, but it was still enough to give the game away.

The woman at the window turned to survey Dee again. Even sitting down you could see she was tall. Her streaked blonde hair piled high upon her head, with two curls spiralling down at either side of her face, added to the impression.

Dee averted her eyes and took another sip of her wine – she'd got through almost half already. She wondered if she'd have a hangover tomorrow – she hadn't had a drink since she first suspected she was pregnant. She wanted to be clear-headed. It was thirty years since she'd laid eyes on Daniel, only marginally fewer since she had seen Charlie, and she wanted to give a good impression of herself. The sunglasses, she'd decided, would stay on all weekend, no matter how tempted she was to pull them off. If questioned, she'd say she had an eye infection.

Of all the three, she didn't want Maggie to see her bruises. Maggie with her happy little nuclear family, distant and nice and – what was the word? Smug? No, not smug … Too perfect, maybe. In the handful of times Dee had seen her old friend since she'd married William, Dee had wanted to shake Maggie and shout, 'Wake up!' She'd turned into somebody completely different from the wild, spontaneous, exciting Maggie that Dee had missed so desperately when she was first sent to boarding school. Perfection didn't suit her.

The woman by the window was standing up. She started walking towards the bar. Dee looked beyond her, out of the window to the lit-up square, until the woman was so close, she couldn't be ignored.

'Excuse me,' the woman said. 'You wouldn't happen to be Dee Reddy, would you?'

Dee nodded in mute confirmation. The woman was strikingly beautiful, like a supermodel who'd allowed herself to age appropriately. Her eyes were an odd shade of green – almost yellow, like olives. Suddenly Dee realised she had seen those eyes before.

'I'm Cassandra,' the woman said, holding out a large but oddly dainty hand. 'Cassandra Jones.'

74. Birds of Passage

They were barely through airport security when Maggie brought up the newspaper stories.

Daniel had known it would be just a matter of time, but he'd put his head in the sand, in the vain hope that she wouldn't have read about Noah taking the knife into school, never mind the reams of print that had followed, exploring the personal life Daniel had so successfully shielded from the media until now.

'One of the papers said your son didn't know you when he was younger, that his mother brought him up alone,' Maggie said, as they wound their way through the labyrinth that was Heathrow Terminal 5. 'Is that true?'

Daniel walked faster, fuming as he wheeled his case. She was judging him. As if she was one to judge. She had evolved into a dull woman who nattered on and on about her narrow, suburban life as if, beneath the surface, it was as subtly layered with complexities as an Ibsen play.

Since the moment they'd met at the check-in desk, she had literally not stopped talking, declining to answer his question about her health and filling the space between them instead with stories about her children, her job, her sister, her friends' kids, even her bloody cat.

At the departure gate there was a small WHSmith's concession and he excused himself, saying he wanted to get a newspaper. He needed a bit of space away from her to calm down. She had no fucking right to judge him, but he didn't want the weekend to start with a fight.

As he queued up to pay for the last *Guardian* on the stand he watched from underneath his sunglasses as Maggie took a seat near the flight attendant's desk, her hands wringing in her lap, her gaunt head wrapped in a scarf the colour of pomegranates. She was nervous, he knew. Saying all the wrong things, the way she had when she was a teenager. When he'd first met her she'd irritated him no end. She'd gone from a mouthy girl he wouldn't normally have looked twice at to the centre of his universe without him even noticing it, or even figuring out why.

On the way to the airport, as he'd sat jammed into a window seat on the Paddington Express, he'd had to admit to himself that he was nervous about seeing her again too. After their last meeting he'd understood that the fantasy he'd half entertained, about being with her, was never going to happen and with good reason. The past could not be rekindled because they had so little in common now. They were worlds apart. But, still, in the hours between calling her to say he'd come to Stockholm and now, the fantasy had taken root again.

Maybe she didn't mean to be judgemental. Maybe he should give her the benefit of the doubt. Maybe her life *was* an Ibsen play.

As he paid for his *Guardian*, he tried to look on the bright side. It was still a relief to get away from the house, to be going somewhere completely different. It was funny, but he had had no sense of living without aim before Noah had moved in. Daniel had moved into that house to begin a new life, but now without the boy's presence everything about the place felt derelict.

Plus it might be interesting to meet Dee and Charlie again. Daniel could hazily remember Dee as a bouncy little thing with wide brown eyes who followed Maggie's lead but had her own spiky personality. Charlie was less easy to recall. Even back then there had been something elusive about him. Daniel was curious to see how he'd grown up.

Maggie had held the seat beside her by putting her handbag on it, and as he approached, carrying his paper under his arm, she lifted it off and gave him a drawn smile.

'Look at those two,' she whispered, once he was sitting. 'Aren't they adorable?'

An elderly couple was sitting on the seats opposite, the man sprucely suited, with a checked shirt and a mustard tie, the woman a little less well presented, her fur-collared coat slightly askew on her shoulders. In his lap, the old man held his wife's hand with both of his.

Daniel unfolded the *Guardian* and studied the front page.

'Sorry,' Maggie said. 'I'm talking too much.'

'No,' Daniel replied, without looking at her. 'Not at all.'

'I'm nervous, I suppose,' said Maggie. 'It's a bit strange to be here with you.'

'Don't be nervous,' Daniel said, continuing to scan the lead story. 'I'm not.'

The woman on the airport Tannoy announced that a flight for Düsseldorf was boarding at Gate Twenty-two, her voice striking a perfect balance between languid and urgent.

'I don't believe you,' said Maggie.

Daniel looked up from his paper. 'Honestly, I'm not,' he said, and he wasn't lying. The anxiety he'd felt on the Paddington Express had disappeared.

'Okay,' Maggie said. She lapsed into silence, but not for long. 'It's only human to be nervous, isn't it? I mean, we haven't seen each other in thirty years.'

'We met a couple of weeks ago, remember?' Daniel said, opening the paper to see what was inside.

'I know. But this is different. We're spending quality time together.'

Daniel gave a rueful laugh. 'I'd hardly call waiting around in Heathrow airport quality time,' he said.

'Flight seven seven eight to Stockholm is now boarding at Gate Eighteen,' announced the woman at the flight desk. 'Passengers with disabilities, or with small children, please come to the gate for priority boarding.'

Maggie lifted her bag on to her knee, unzipped it and rummaged inside. 'Did I tell you about my son Harry's girlfriend?' she said. 'She's moving in for a while. With Orlando – he's Poppy's boyfriend – that makes four of them. Honestly, I don't know how I'm going to manage ...'

The old man had risen and was helping his wife to her feet.

'Harry says he and Amber will cook for themselves. They're both vegetarians now. But I know what he's like. I'll be chained to that cooker before you know it ...'

The elderly couple was approaching the flight desk, picking their way through a small mêlée of people with children in buggies. Also pushing to the top of the queue were four women wearing designer shades and carrying ostentatious handbags; they looked like they'd walked off a *Sex and the City* rerun.

Daniel went back to his paper.

Maggie bolted to her feet. 'Alison?' she said, and one woman turned, a Charlotte type, all twin-set and pearls. As she lifted her sunglasses, her jaw dropped.

Maggie pushed through the people with children and past the old couple, until she was standing face to face with Alison, kissing her on the cheek. Daniel couldn't hear the exchange between them, but in the middle of it there were audible gasps from the other three women and Alison was staring at Maggie in bug-eyed shock.

'Well, I never,' one of the women said, as Maggie spun back towards Daniel.

'You can't say things like that to children,' another called, as Maggie took her seat again.

'Too late,' Maggie called, over her shoulder. 'What are you going to do? Shoot me?'

'What was that about?' Daniel asked, as the four women started clucking around each other.

'That's for me to know and you to find out,' Maggie replied, her pale cheeks dotted red, her eyes two firecrackers.

Gone was the over-talkative, ageing housewife, and for a split second Daniel was catapulted back in time.

75. Flying High

Beside Maggie on the plane, squeezed into the middle seat, Daniel was feigning sleep. She was sure of it.

A few rows in front she could see the top of Alison's nut-brown head, turning back and forth as she chatted to the women sitting either side of her.

At first Maggie had been nonplussed when she spotted Alison at the boarding gate.

'What are you doing here?' she'd exclaimed, smiling like a complete idiot.

Alison hadn't replied. She'd just blushed, and looked as if she wanted the ground to swallow her up.

Then the penny dropped.

Alison had got her husband to fix the Abba competition on London FM after all.

'Oh my God. I don't believe it,' Maggie said as Alison squirmed and bit her lip. 'You got those tickets.'

'I know,' cut in one of Alison's friends, beaming like a Cheshire cat in Gucci sunglasses. 'Can you believe it?'

Maggie ignored her. 'How could you?' she'd asked Alison, her voice escalating with each word. 'You knew how desperate I was for those tickets. You knew everything that was going on in my life. And you don't even like Abba!'

Alison had folded her arms and her expression changed, her lips flattening. 'C'mon Maggie. It's not that big a deal, is it?' she'd said. 'Obviously you got tickets anyway.'

'I suppose minding your two horrible brats for two days wasn't such a big deal either?' There was a sharp intake of breath from Alison's gaggle of girlfriends. 'How dare you …' Alison began, but Maggie was only getting into the swing of her tirade. 'And by the way, you should probably know that one of them almost killed himself in Ikea. Practically launched himself from the ceiling. God knows how I even managed to get them back to you in one piece. They're like a pair of … savages!'

The friend with the Gucci sunglasses was now gaping at Alison with her mouth hanging open, as if to say, *You left your precious babies with this raving lunatic?*

Maggie didn't care what she, or anyone, thought. 'By the way,' she said, 'I told them that if they breathed a word about what happened in Ikea, they'd be sent to an orphanage and never see Mummy and Daddy again. Looks like it worked a treat.'

Maggie took her handbag out of the seat pocket to check that the tickets were still inside, which, of course, they were. She hadn't needed Alison's charity after all.

Daniel shifted and turned his head to the other side.

In the airport earlier, he'd been pissed off with her about something. Maybe it was because she'd so hastily avoided his question about her cancer as they'd queued at the check-in desk. But she'd sworn to herself as she'd got out of the car at Departures, waving goodbye to William, that she was going to put the cancer clear out of her mind this weekend. She wouldn't brook any conversation about it.

She should have explained this to Daniel when he'd asked how she was doing, but instead she'd nodded towards a woman in a burqa and told him she just couldn't understand why anyone wanted to dress like that. Then she'd found herself going off on a rant about

Oona, who had arrived this morning insisting that she should come to Stockholm, she'd get a plane ticket at the airport and a ticket to the concert from a tout outside the stadium.

'I mean, honestly,' she'd told Daniel, 'can you imagine what chaos that would have caused?'

She'd figured Daniel would remember how difficult Oona had been when they were all young, but he didn't indicate one way or the other. He'd just given a leaden nod, as if he wasn't really listening.

Then she'd continued blathering on, like a hen on amphetamines, about the ridiculous stories in the press about Daniel's son, about the squat Poppy had been living in, about Harry's trip to Australia – anything to fill the awkward space between them. She couldn't stop herself. At their meeting in the restaurant a few weeks ago, she'd been nervous, but in the context of how she was behaving today, she'd been a picture of composure.

Now that Daniel was pretending to sleep, at least she had to shut the Hell up. She turned to stare out of the window at the little fluffy clouds that stretched into the azure distance, and tried to take some deep, zen-like breaths. The sky above cloud was like the landscape of a different world, silent and unpopulated, a peaceful place where you didn't have to be anything for anyone but yourself.

Daniel distracted her with a light sleep-grunt and she glanced back at him again. He was out for the count, after all, so she allowed herself to linger, taking in the changes to his face, the soft lines on his forehead, the rougher texture of his skin, remembering all at once how truly, madly and deeply she'd been in love with him.

There had been a time when they'd never stopped talking to each other, always hooting with laughter, finding delight in discovering all the things they shared in common. Now she just seemed to irritate him. And, actually, he irritated her in return. Or did he? Maybe she was just being reactionary. Or maybe it annoyed her that he didn't seem to like her any more when – she had to admit it – she so wanted him to.

In the car this morning, as William had driven her towards Heathrow, he'd asked her questions about Daniel. Feeling they were steering into dodgy territory, Maggie had been blasé in her replies. 'He was just a guy who was over from England for the summer we had the Abba fan club,' she'd said. 'Dee fancied him.'

The lie, designed to deflect William from jumping to any conclusions, only served to make her feel guiltier. When she'd told him about the concert reunion he'd said he thought it was a great idea. He was being so nice, lifting her bag into the car, ferrying her to the airport, asking her if she needed any money for the trip.

If only he knew. She'd cleaned five thousand pounds out of his account yesterday morning to pay for the concert tickets she'd miraculously found on ebay. The seller had 100 per cent positive feedback from lots of satisfied clients so she'd clicked on 'Contact Member' and sent him a message, saying she needed four. She'd received a positive reply almost instantly.

The only trouble was she'd have to collect them from the seller outside Deptford Bridge station and they cost £1,250 each, which Maggie didn't have. On her way to Deptford she'd stopped off at a branch of her bank with her photo ID and withdrawn the money, which she'd transferred from William's account to hers on-line.

The seller, who didn't tell her his name, turned out to be an ordinary middle-aged bloke with an anorak and large-framed glasses. 'I'm not an Abba fan,' he'd told her, in a nasal voice, candidly explaining that he'd bought the tickets in bulk to make some money. The entire deal had been researched and done by lunchtime, which made Maggie laugh to herself, considering the hassle she'd gone to in the first place to get them.

'Ladies and gentlemen, we are about to experience some mild turbulence,' a stewardess said, over the Tannoy. 'The captain has switched on the fasten-your-seatbelt sign and we would ask you to refrain from using the toilets until it has been switched off.'

Daniel gave another grunt and opened his eyes. He looked around in confusion and then his eyes alighted on Maggie. 'I must have dozed off,' he said.

Maggie smiled and opened her mouth to apologise to him for earlier – she should have responded to him more positively when he'd asked how she was. But instead she jammed her lips firmly together.

They were in the sky above clouds. She didn't have to be anything for anyone but herself. And it was enough just to be here with Daniel in the moment.

76. Face It Together

According to Cassandra's guidebook, the tiny café sold the best cakes in Stockholm. The place smelt of warm milk, ground cinnamon and nutmeg, and had that Swedish idiosyncrasy of appearing clinical and homely at the same time. Its walls were tiled entirely in hospital white, its counter and tables were shiny, angular white marble, but the cake she'd ordered came on little floral plates that might have come from some mother's kitchen.

'Dee ... Can I ask you a question?' Cassandra said.

Dee nodded as she stirred a sachet of sugar into her macchiato.

'What's with the sunglasses?'

Dee kept stirring. 'What do you mean?' she asked.

'You haven't taken them off. Not once.'

'Is that a problem?'

Cassandra frowned and took a sip of her lemon-grass tea. 'No,' she said. 'I'm just wondering why you keep them on.'

'I have an eye infection,' Dee said, tapping her spoon on the rim of her cup. 'Can I ask *you* a question?'

'Sure,' said Cassandra, keenly aware that the conversation was being steered away from choppy waters. She wished she could get just one look at Dee's eyes. The rest of her had fared well with the years. Her lips still had that pillow-soft pout, her face remained heart-shaped with no sign of gravity pulling her perfectly pointy chin south, and her pocket-sized body was still nicely proportioned, rounded and flat in all the right places. But without seeing her eyes, it was like trying to connect up a dot-to-dot that didn't make a full picture.

Last night, Dee had connected Cassandra's dots in double-quick time.

'Charlie?' she'd said, when Cassandra went up and introduced herself. 'Is that you?'

Cassandra had taken a breath. 'I don't use that name any more,' she'd replied. 'But, yes, it's me.'

Dee's appearance in the hotel's bar had been a surprise. The only connecting flight Cassandra had been able to get from Las Palmas to Stockholm via Charles de Gaulle had been a day before everyone was supposed to meet. It was a stroke of luck that the hotel room booked for her for the weekend was free.

She'd had a room-service dinner sitting on her bed watching *Maid in Manhattan*, with Swedish subtitles that did nothing to disguise Jennifer Lopez's nasal acting talents, but when the food was gone, the evening stretched out in front of her, like a wasteland. The hotel room was fine, with lots of little boutique touches, but it reminded her of the one in Ireland, of the time she'd spent there with John. So she'd done her makeup, put on something presentable and gone downstairs for a drink, in the hope that a bit of people-watching might make her feel less at odds with the world.

At first she hadn't taken any notice of the solitary woman sitting at the bar. But slowly it began to dawn on her that it might be Dee. Even with the sunglasses, there was something recognisable about her. Maybe it was the way she held herself, swirling her wine in her glass, chin in one hand, or the mass of wavy auburn hair falling to her shoulders. In the end, Cassandra took her courage into her hands and went up to introduce herself.

'You look *amazing*.' Dee had gulped.

'Thank you.' Cassandra had smiled, hating the way Dee's jaw was almost in her lap. She'd be going through the same revelation with Maggie and Daniel tomorrow, having signed her email to Maggie with a 'C', rather than go into names and explanations.

There had been an awkward moment, which Cassandra had broken by stretching out both arms and saying, 'Shouldn't we give each other a hug, or something?'

Dee's hug was fluttery. She touched Cassandra on the back with the tips of her fingers and pulled away. 'Are you?' she asked. 'I mean, did you? I mean ...'

Cassandra sat down on the stool next to her and waved to the barman. 'Darling,' she said, 'I'm the real deal. All paid for and certified.' She immediately regretted her tone. This wasn't the dressing room at Flikkers. Even though Dee's eyes weren't visible behind her shades, Cassandra saw that her old friend was staring at her in utter shock. 'Yes,' she explained. 'I've had the operations. I've transitioned.'

While Dee had taken this in, Cassandra had ordered an Absolut citron vodka and tonic. 'Will you have another glass of red?' she'd asked.

Dee shook her head. 'Just a still water.'

When the barman had left them alone again, Dee said, 'I remember.'

'You remember what?' Cassandra asked.

'I remember you telling me that you were a girl. On the island, when we were kids.'

Cassandra took a sip of her drink. In her mind's eye she saw the livid criss-cross of scars on Dee's arms that night. She glanced at Dee's wrist as she brought her glass to her lips. There were no scars to be seen. Then her gaze went back to Dee's sunglasses.

Now, across from Cassandra in the little café, Dee deflected her query about the sunglasses by asking, 'Why did you choose "Cassandra"?'

Cassandra gave a soft laugh and agitated the teabag in her cup.

'Bizarrely enough, it's to do with that morning when we were on the boat, after the night on the island. Remember when Maggie asked us if our lives were an Abba song, which it would be?'

Beneath her sunglasses Dee's full mouth broke out into a smile. 'I remember mine was "Money, Money, Money",' she said. 'God, we were so young.'

'Well, mine was "Cassandra".'

'Was it? I don't remember that.'

'I didn't say so. I kept it to myself.'

Dee put her cup into its saucer. 'So, tell me now,' she said. 'Why is "Cassandra" your Abba song?'

'"Cassandra" is about a girl who could see into the future, but nobody believed her.'

'Okay. How does that make it your song?'

'When I told you I was a girl that night, you didn't believe me.'

Dee shook her head emphatically. 'I *did* believe you,' she said.

'We were fifteen years old, Dee. I'll never forget your face. You were completely baffled! But you know what? In that moment, I saw the future. I knew that some day I would be who I am now.'

'You'd be Cassandra,' said Dee.

Cassandra picked up her teacup with both hands and grinned. 'Plus I liked the name,' she said.

On the table between them, Dee's phone lit up. She grabbed it and stuffed it into her handbag without checking who was calling. 'We'd better get back to the hotel,' she said, zipping the bag closed. 'Maggie and Daniel will be arriving soon.'

Cassandra reached out and touched Dee's wrist. 'Before we go,' she said, 'take off the sunglasses.'

'No,' said Dee.

'Please? Just for one second.'

Dee was still for a moment. Then her shoulders slumped. She reached up and removed the glasses.

Cassandra gasped. The top of her left cheek and under the eyebrow were a mottled yellow and black. To the side of her eye it was clear where the skin had been split open. 'Who did that to you?'

'It doesn't matter,' Dee replied.

'Was it your husband? Does Joe hit you?'

Dee's sunglasses were on again. 'Promise you won't say anything to the others,' she choked out.

Cassandra wanted to cry. 'Dee,' she said, reaching out to take her hand. 'We're far too old for secrets.'

77. We Meet Again

The woman leading the Abba City Walk Tour was dressed up as Frida. She wore a tight burgundy leather coat with a shaggy Shetland fur collar and cuffs, flared jeans and a pair of yellow platforms she was finding it hard to keep her balance on. In the pair of tiny, bejewelled hands that extended from her furry sleeves, she held a picture of Abba standing in the very spot Maggie was now.

In a way it was hard to take in. Agnetha, Björn, Benny and Anni-Frid had always been figures of Maggie's imagination more than anything else, smiling figures on the posters that had lined the walls of her teenage bedroom, not living, breathing human beings.

'In this building, Benny made his first public performance, when he was just eight years old,' the tour guide said, gesturing with one of her little hands towards the medieval building that looked out on to the courtyard where they had gathered for the first stop on the tour. A small crowd – the men dressed in white tie and tails, the women in long gowns – was making its way into the building, as if they were going to an evening event, even though it was only noon.

'There are many occasions in this building, such as the handing out of the Nobel Peace Prize each October,' the guide said, taking in the dressed-up crowd with a sweep of her hand. 'In 1988 Benny was presented with a doctorate in musicology there.'

'Excuse me,' Cassandra interrupted. 'Can you tell us what occasion is going on right now?'

Charlie was called Cassandra now, Maggie kept having to remind herself. She'd made the mistake of calling her Charlie about ten times already.

Glittery seventies makeup on the tour guide's cheeks glinted in the midday sun. 'I'm not really sure,' she said.

Charlie ... No, Cassandra had a look of that blonde Bond girl who had got out of the water in her bikini in the 1960s. In fact, Maggie imagined that in a bikini Cassandra would look better than a Bond girl, given all the work it must have taken to transform her body from that of a man. Her breasts looked bionic.

'Of course, no one really knows exactly when Abba was formed,' the guide was saying. 'Benny once called them a group without a real beginning or a real end ...'

Maggie glanced at Cassandra again. Her personality had changed too: she was no longer the reticent Charlie of their teenage years. Within half an hour of everybody's reacquaintance, she'd asked, as they all sat in the hotel bar, 'Maggie, do you have cancer?'

Truth be told, Maggie was glad it was out in the open. She could explain it and get it over with for the weekend. She'd given a summary description of her treatment so far and told them the chemo was finished. She absolutely didn't want to talk about the surgery, but Cassandra would not be deflected.

'What's the prognosis?' she'd asked, with blunt exactitude. 'Will you need a mastectomy?'

Maggie had nodded mutely, searching Dee's face for a reaction but coming up with nothing. She wished Dee would remove the stupid Jackie-O glasses she was swanning about in. She and Daniel, who hardly took his off either, looked like a pair of gangsters.

Daniel had said nothing, but his sunglasses were on the table and he'd exchanged a glance with Maggie that looked like empathy. She couldn't be sure of it, though.

Cassandra had reached over to put her hand on Maggie's and squeezed. 'It'll be okay, honey,' she'd said. 'I know it will.'

'Yes,' Dee agreed. 'It'll be okay.' She'd sounded so detached she might as well have been in another building.

Maggie had given another silent nod and a resigned smile. She was used to people telling her it would be okay. They knew nothing, of course, but they meant well. Then she had moved the conversation on, asking Daniel whether he'd visited the set of *Glee* when they recorded the 'Night Star' episode. *That* had gone down like a lead balloon.

'Who can tell me what year Abba won the *Eurovision Song Contest*?' the tour guide asked.

Several people in the crowd put their hands up, including Maggie. At the back, a group of Germans – at least, they sounded like Germans – dressed as Abba in shoddy replicas of the infamous cat costumes, were jumping up and down. 'I know! I know!' one of the women was shouting.

'Nineteen seventy-four,' Dee said. Her voice was lifeless.

'That's right.' The guide beamed. 'And who can tell me what song they sang?'

Again the Germans started jumping. '"Vaterloo"!' their token Björn bellowed.

The tour guide nodded, took an iPod out of her bag and started searching through it. 'They sang it in English at the contest,' she said, 'but as we walk to our next stop, we'll listen to the Swedish version.' She plugged the iPod into a speaker in her bag, and the electric guitars that signalled the opening of the song thumped. The Germans whooped and started dancing as everyone took off, following the guide as if she was the Pied Piper.

'Does this go on for much longer?' Dee asked. Beneath her sunglasses, the downturn at the corners of her mouth suggested she was sulking.

'God knows,' Daniel muttered.

When the guide came to a halt outside the Sheraton Hotel, to tell them about a scene from *Abba: The Movie* that had been shot there, Daniel curled his lip, reminding Maggie of a belligerent teenager – Poppy *circa* fourteen. She got irritated with him again, then stopped herself. She needed to get a grip. One minute she was gagging for his attention, the next she wanted to be anywhere other than next to him.

As they ambled away from the Sheraton, the song the tour guide played on her iPod was 'Money, Money, Money'.

'Does anyone mind if I go back to the hotel for a lie-down?' Dee asked, not even noticing her old favourite. 'I can meet you in the lobby this evening, before dinner.'

'You go right ahead, sweetie,' Cassandra said, as if she were counselling a wounded kitten. 'You must be exhausted.'

'I know how you feel,' Maggie sympathised, even though she thought Dee could be making more of an effort, given that she was the one who had pushed the whole trip ahead at the end of the day. 'I used to get so worn out too, especially with Poppy. She was the pregnancy from Hell.'

Although Dee's eyes were hidden, Maggie saw a flash.

'You're pregnant, Dee?' Cassandra asked. She sounded appalled.

'I'll see you back at the hotel,' said Dee, turning to go.

As she stalked away, Daniel shrugged. 'What was that about?' he asked. 'And why won't she take those sunglasses off?'

'Because,' Cassandra replied, 'she has a black eye.'

'How did that happen?' Maggie asked.

Cassandra looked at her like she had ten heads. 'Her husband has been beating the crap out of her,' she said.

'Hello, back there!' the guide shouted from the front of the tour crowd, above the tinny sound of Frida singing about having to leave for Las Vegas or Monaco. 'Keep up! We don't want to lose you!'

78. So Sad, So Quiet

Dee woke to someone pounding on her hotel-room door. The heavy curtains drawn across the windows had acted as blackout blinds and at first, in the darkness, she didn't know where she was. Then her heart stopped.

It was Joe. He'd found out where she'd gone and followed her here.

'Dee?' Cassandra's barely audible voice came from the other side of the door. 'Are you awake?'

Dee lay back on the pillows and breathed out a mixture of relief and disappointment. She hadn't expected to find herself missing Joe as much as she was. She'd been away from him for just over a day yet the yearning was almost physical, grinding her bones down. Still, every time she reached for her phone to call or text him, she managed to stop herself.

Cassandra was knocking on the door again, calling, 'Dee!'

'I'm awake,' Dee called back, dragging herself out of bed. Her limbs felt like iron girders as she trudged across the room. 'What time is it?' she asked, half opening the door. The light from the hallway made her wince.

Cassandra checked a dainty gold watch that was too small for her wrist and said, 'Ten past five.' She stood looking at Dee as if she was waiting for an invitation.

'We're not meeting for dinner until eight, are we?' Dee said.

'That's right,' Cassandra replied. Then she added, 'Can I come in?'

'I suppose so,' said Dee, walking back into the room without holding the door fully open. She wanted to sleep, not make small-talk with Cassandra, who was a complete stranger, if you thought about it.

She got back under the covers anyway, and lay there staring at the ceiling as Cassandra came to sit on the other bed. Normally Dee would have kicked up a fuss at being given a twin room when she was staying alone in a hotel, but this time she was glad there were two narrow single beds. It meant she didn't have to miss Joe's body beside her.

'Why didn't you tell me you were pregnant?' Cassandra asked.

Dee didn't move her gaze from the ceiling. She hadn't really expected Maggie to keep the secret, given that she hadn't said anything about it *being* a secret when she'd told her. She just didn't want to face talking about it right now because it was too overwhelming. If she thought about the baby, she automatically remembered she had to make a decision about whether she could stay with Joe or not, and if she thought about that decision, she felt as if the world was crumbling around her, leaving her to stand on the only rocky outcrop, utterly and finally alone and unloved.

Stockholm had been an attempt at finding limbo. She'd been hoping for a trip down Memory Lane with Maggie, for the distraction of shared, happy memories. But Maggie couldn't play along. Dee had known she had cancer from the moment she had first seen her, although she hadn't guessed that William had left and then come back, and that Maggie's life was less complacently perfect than she'd always let on. Dee wanted to say the right things, to help Maggie in some way, but she couldn't activate the part of herself that empathised. It was like her heart had been switched off.

Cassandra kept trying to switch it on again – yesterday in the little café, and now in the stillness of Dee's dark room. 'What are you going to do?' she asked, when Dee remained tight-lipped.

Dee let her eyelids close, hoping that Cassandra might somehow dematerialise and be gone.

'Dee, honey,' Cassandra said, 'we have to talk about it.'

Dee groaned. 'We?' she said, turning on the pillow to face Cassandra. 'What do you mean, *we*? I don't even know who you are.'

Cassandra's expression was full of unbearable sympathy. She leaned over, touched Dee's shoulder and said, 'I'm your friend.'

Dee shrugged her off. 'Don't touch me,' she said.

Cassandra laid her hands flat on either side of herself on the bed. 'You're depressed,' she said. 'You're not thinking straight.'

Dee shut her eyes again and squeezed her top lip against the bottom one.

'If you want to talk, you know where I am,' Cassandra said.

As Dee heard her open the door to leave the room, she had a sudden urge to cry out, 'Please help me!'

But the door clicked quietly shut and Dee was alone again in the pitch black.

Cassandra leaned against the corridor wall outside Dee's room and took a deep breath. She hadn't wanted to leave Dee alone, but what else could she have done? Sit there and insist that Dee spill her guts, even though it was clear that she wasn't ready to? And what Dee had said was true. They didn't really know each other at all.

She took her key card out of her purse and was walking down the corridor when Daniel came out of his room and she almost ran headlong into him.

'Hey,' he said, moving aside for her.

Cassandra still couldn't get over how little he'd changed. Although he'd seemed like an entirely different person when she'd seen him on

TV during his famous days, it was as if he hadn't grown up. Even though the greasy-haired teenager he'd been had turned into a handsome man, square-jawed and neatly turned out, the hair at the side of his head flecked with silver, he seemed just as unhappy as he had been when he was an adolescent.

She gave him a stiff smile and said, 'Hi,' as she brushed past. When they were teenagers they hadn't really connected. Cassandra couldn't see how it would be any different now.

She was putting her key card into the lock on her door, aware that he hadn't moved from the spot where they'd bumped into each other, when Daniel said, 'Would you like to go for a drink somewhere? In the old town, maybe.'

She saw that he was smiling, or attempting to. 'Why not?' she said, sticking her key card back into her purse. 'You lead the way.'

On the terrace of a bar that gave out on to what seemed to be the old town's main street, given the number of tourists milling around shops with plastic Viking hats in their windows, Cassandra ordered a glass of white wine and Daniel had a Spendrups lager. Almost at once he started talking about his son, telling her how creative he was, particularly in the way he dressed. He didn't impart this information like a proud father. Cassandra got the impression he was trying to tell her something else entirely.

Her thoughts wandered back to Dee, upstairs in her room. She wondered if Dee's husband had known she was pregnant when he'd hit her. But, really, if he knew or not, what was the difference? It was still an untenable situation, as far as Cassandra was concerned.

Dee had been the first person Cassandra had told about herself, sitting on the rocks at the edge of that island so many years ago. It was the first moment at which she had admitted not only to another human being but also to herself who she really was, and Dee had not judged. It was no wonder Cassandra felt so protective now.

As long as she lived, Cassandra would never forget the words

Dee had said to her: 'You're amazing. You're beautiful.' It was the mantra she had used to get over the people who had rejected her throughout the years and to stay strong. In meeting Dee again, she realised that, for all that had happened between her and her father, her and Sam, her and John, it was this mantra she had to remember. *You are amazing. You are beautiful.*

If John didn't want her for who she was, that was his problem, not hers.

'So, tell me about your life,' Daniel said. 'Is it as fantastic as you look?'

Cassandra barely heard him. She was imagining facing John and telling him exactly what he had turned his back on.

79. Take the Future

As he drank from his bottle of lager, Daniel kept surreptitiously checking Cassandra for vestiges of the Charlie he had once known and not finding any. Having said that, his memory of Charlie was sketchy at best. He'd been quiet, Daniel recalled, as if he sat on the outside of life, thoughtfully taking it all in. He hadn't been feminine, though. He'd been a school football star, hadn't he?

Looking at Cassandra now, though, it was hard to believe she had ever been Charlie, ever anything other than the arrestingly beautiful woman she'd become. The delicate way she swirled her wine, the sweep of her pinned-up golden-blonde hair, revealing a ballerina-like neck when she turned to get the barman's attention, the throaty laugh emitted from a mouth that was a perfect Cupid's bow. Earlier, while they were on the Abba walking tour, he couldn't help noticing how men's heads turned automatically as she walked past. It was more than her looks: she exuded pheromones that were exclusively and seductively female.

She was telling him something about her friend – a girl called Coco – in response to him lamenting Noah's latest hairstyle, but he found it hard to listen properly. Her startling green eyes kept catching him – Charlie hadn't had those eyes back in the day, had he? – and he found himself responding to them, with his stomach. There was something about their expression, along with her honeyed voice, that kept giving him the urge to spill his guts. He wanted to tell her everything. He wanted to ask her what he should do to redeem himself as Noah's father. Because, let's face it, he hadn't the first clue.

But at the same time he felt stupid for wanting to confide in her. Why should Cassandra care? He'd only met her again for the first time this morning, and thirty years ago, when they were boys in each other's company, they'd hardly spoken to each other at all.

'I hate bullies,' Cassandra said, out of the blue. She'd broken off her conversation about Coco and gazed out at the river, leaving Daniel to his thoughts.

'Pardon?' Daniel said.

'That's what Dee's husband is. All men who beat their wives are bullies.'

'Maybe she'll leave him,' Daniel said. 'If she has any sense.'

Cassandra took a sip of her wine and shook her head. 'That's the trouble with bullies,' she said. 'They take away your self-confidence. They make you believe you're worthless.'

Daniel swallowed a mouthful of lager and wondered if she'd experienced bullying of her own. He guessed she had. People who were different were always singled out. Like Noah had been. 'Can I ask you something?' he said.

Cassandra blinked her green eyes at him and gave a half-smile. 'Of course,' she replied. But now that Daniel had put it out there, he didn't know what to ask. He didn't know how to say what he needed to say. He concentrated on the bottle he was holding with both hands, rubbing the rim with his thumbs, trying to come up with the words.

'Is it about your son?' Cassandra asked, as if she could read minds.

Daniel nodded. Then he shook his head and gave a pathetically nervous laugh. 'I don't know where to start,' he said.

'Start wherever you think is best.' Cassandra replied.

To his surprise, Daniel found himself beginning at the back of the handball alley at Cardinal Newman, when he was fourteen. He told Cassandra about Philip Ewing, and how he'd said that Daniel's mother had killed herself. 'I never knew if she did or not,' he said, as Cassandra nodded reassuringly, egging him on. 'It's not like she left a note or anything.'

He didn't know why he'd felt he had to tell her that part – he'd never spoken to anyone about it before – but it felt unbelievably good. It was like letting a stopper out. After that, he couldn't stop talking. He told her about the panic attacks that had come with being famous, about the moment he'd left it all behind, about Noah, and how he'd all but pretended his son didn't exist when he was a baby, and how Jade had brought him to live with him, and Noah had run away. It all came tumbling forth. How he'd apprehended the bullies with Noah; how Noah had taken the knife to school, the arrest, the news story, everything. How, in the end, he'd let his son down.

'I don't understand,' Cassandra eventually interrupted. 'How did you let Noah down?'

'I didn't protect him,' said Daniel. After the fervour of telling his story, he was spent.

'It sounds to me like you *couldn't* protect him.'

'Maybe not,' said Daniel. 'But that's not good enough, is it? Because of me, it's been made ten times worse.'

'Because you're famous, you mean?'

'Yes.' Daniel nodded. He hated the word, hated it being attached to who he was, but it was true. Fame had ruined his life, and now it was ruining Noah's.

Cassandra turned to look out of the window once more, and took another tiny sip of her wine. When she turned back to Daniel, she gazed intently into his eyes. 'You can't protect Noah,' she said. 'All children must learn to live in a world where there is hate and intimidation. But you can teach him how to love himself enough not to let the hate win. You can teach him how to value himself.'

'But how do you do that, when your child won't let you?' Daniel said.

Cassandra's eyes glistened. 'You of all people should know,' she said.

80. Night Is Young

'I told you we should have got a taxi!' Dee shouted, although she knew that outside the station there wasn't a cab to be had for love or money. The Abba reunion had turned Stockholm into one big street party.

Inside Central Station it was no less chaotic, as crowds heaved on the concourse, inching towards the platforms with extra trains to the arena. The colour, the noise, the pumped-up excitement reminded her of the crowds at Gay Pride in Dublin. Drag queens dressed up as helium-heeled Agnethas and Fridas, and a few as the characters from *Priscilla, Queen of the Desert*, mingled with cardigan couples in their fifties, trendy teenagers with multiple piercings, and groups of girls with too much makeup, and everyone was singing 'Waterloo' on a loop.

'Hold on to me!' Cassandra called, stretching out to grab Dee's hand. 'I don't want to lose you!'

Ahead of them, Maggie and Daniel were squeezing through the crowds to get into a queue for one of the ticket machines.

'I thought the Scandinavians were supposed to be super-organised,' Dee panted, when she managed to wedge herself in beside Cassandra. 'This is unbelievable.'

'Maybe they didn't expect so many people at the same time,' said Cassandra. 'It's like the whole world's here.'

Dee looked around. It was true: there were people of all nationalities, colours and creeds, shoulder to shoulder, everyone smiling and laughing, despite the crush and chaos. The song had moved on and now they were singing the chorus of 'Thank You For The Music'. The sound of so many voices rising up towards the roof of the station gave her goosebumps.

'Cassandra! Dee! Over here!' Above the heads of a flank of people in front of them, Daniel was waving to them. 'We've got the train tickets!'

But Dee couldn't move. She and Cassandra were jammed between a tattooed couple who looked like extras from a Harley Davidson advert and two tiny Oriental women, who were singing at the tops of their voices.

Cassandra began to sing along. 'C'mon,' she said, nudging Dee with her shoulder. 'Get in the mood.'

Dee couldn't help smiling. Her voice, as she added it to the mix, sounded unsure of itself and weak. When she was a girl, she'd belt out 'Dancing Queen' at the top of her voice in her bedroom with Maggie, both of them using hairbrushes as microphones, preening in the mirror as they pretended to be Agnetha and Frida. Where had that little girl gone? Where was her sparkle?

Last night, in the middle of dinner, she'd finally given up the fight. She'd excused herself from the table and gone to the Ladies, locking herself into a cubicle so she could text Joe in privacy: *I'm in Stockholm,* she'd texted, without a greeting. *Going to see Abba tomorrow night.*

Her phone had rung within seconds of the text being sent, Joe's name lighting up on the display, but she pressed the button to dismiss the call. I'm not ready to talk yet, she texted, leaning against the stall door.

Joe's reply was swift: *I was so worried about u, baby. Why did u go without saying anything? When r u coming home?*

Outside, the bathroom door opened and a pair of heels clicked across the tiled floor. Someone went into the cubicle beside hers.

I'll be home on Sunday night, Dee texted, trying not to make a sound. *We can talk then.*

As she'd flushed the toilet, to make it sound like she had actually used it, Joe's reply bleeped through: *I love u. Always remember that.*

She'd had to stop herself texting *I love you too* in return.

The organisation at the concert was much better than it had been at the station. As the crowds got off the trains and made their way towards the arena, they were filtered by the colour coding on their tickets.

'We're in the purple zone,' Maggie declared, checking the tickets and holding them aloft. 'This way.' She took off through the crowds, following the purple signs, the others trotting behind her.

The expectation hanging in the air was electric. People had been singing Abba songs on the trains, but now an almost awestruck silence had come over the crowd. Maggie kept catching people's eyes, and they all said the same thing: 'We can't quite believe we're here!'

First there would be Roxette to get through, the confirmed support act leaked to the news networks this morning, but then they'd all be watching Abba in the flesh. It was almost hard to believe.

Maggie's phone vibrated in her pocket and she lifted it out, reading as she walked. The message was from William: *Poppy wants to borrow your car to go to Brighton tomorrow. Where are your keys?*

Maggie shoved her phone back into her jeans. Why couldn't Poppy borrow his car? And why was he texting her about it now, when he knew full well she was at the concert?

When he'd called her this afternoon, he'd quizzed her about how much the tickets had cost, and Maggie was sure he'd checked his bank account and the jig was up. She'd given a vague answer with no number involved, but he hadn't pursued it. Instead he'd asked question after question about Stockholm, about how she was feeling, how Dee was, and what it was like seeing Daniel and Charlie again. Maggie was vague. William knew nothing of her past with Daniel, and he didn't need to know.

Eventually she'd lied to him that she was about to go into a subway station and out of range, forcing the conversation to an end.

'Purple-zone tickets here!' called a girl in a black T-shirt and headset. She looked very young, swamped by the crowds.

'Here we go!' Maggie said to Daniel, who had caught up with her and was walking alongside. His eyes were shining with excitement, just like everyone else's.

They waited for Dee and Cassandra, who were a few steps behind, so they were together when Maggie handed the tickets to the girl, who grinned at her and said, 'Hello,' before checking them.

She looked up again, into Maggie's eyes, and back down at the tickets. Her forehead creased.

'I'm sorry,' she said, in perfect English. 'Can you hold on for a moment?' She turned away and said something into the microphone attached to her headset. Maggie exchanged another glance with Daniel.

The girl finished her conversation and turned back with an apologetic smile. 'I'm sorry,' she said, 'but these are not valid tickets.'

81. Win When I Lose

Maggie couldn't stop crying, but her tears weren't out of disappointment or sadness. She was angry. She was so angry, she wanted to kill someone. Preferably the guy on ebay. She didn't care that the lying, cheating prick had ripped her off for five thousand pounds, not as much as she cared anyway about being left standing outside the Friends Arena in the bright fucking Swedish night, while sixty-five thousand people happily inside – including Alison, whom she wanted to murder as well – were listening right now to Roxette belting out 'It Must Have Been Love'.

A few other stragglers were hanging about, hoping for a free concert without the visuals, but the sound coming from the vast mouth of the stadium was so distorted by the time it reached their ears, it was painful. The idea of staying around until Abba came on stage was as enraging as it was frustrating.

Maggie jammed her fingers into her ears. 'I can't believe it!' she wailed again, while Daniel, Dee and Cassandra stood in a semi-circle, staring at her in dismay. Ten minutes ago, after they'd exhausted every avenue and realised there was no way on God's earth they were getting into the concert, Daniel had tried to put his arm around her, but Maggie had shoved him off.

'Get away from me!' she'd screeched. She was livid with him too.

How could he have done what he did? Left her alone to face what she'd had to face, without bothering to write? He'd made her believe he loved her, then flitted off back to England without a care in the world. 'I'll never forgive you!' she'd wanted to scream at him.

The vibration of her phone going off in her pocket distracted her and she plucked it out to see a message from Poppy, saying, *Mum, where are your car keys?*

Explosions of rage went off in her chest like dynamite. 'Fuck! Off!' she roared at the phone and flung it across the forecourt. It fell to the ground with a clatter.

'Maggie,' Cassandra said, her voice as firm as that of a referee in a boxing ring. 'Calm down.'

Ignoring her, Maggie marched back towards the arena's main entrance. She didn't know why. It wasn't as if there was a snowball's chance in Hell of talking her way in. And then she stopped in her tracks and started bawling her eyes out. She turned her red, wet face up to the pale sky and cried to God, 'WHY?'

Why had she been given cancer? Why was she sick when other people – bad people – walked around outrageously healthy? With two fucking breasts. Fury coursed through her veins at the injustice of it. She wanted to get even.

She wanted to get even with William for going off with that compost heap he called a woman, for not being there when she'd needed him most after she had been there for him through thick and thin. She wanted to get even with her father, for hardly deigning to speak to her in thirty years. She wanted to get even with her mother, who'd forced her to have the abortion yet was still passing judgement on her for it, no matter how she pretended not to be.

She wanted to get even with God. If there was a God to get even with.

'Maggie? Honey?'

It was Dee, looking at her with brimming eyes. She'd got rid of the sunglasses and the makeup she'd worn to cover the bruising had worn off a little. Maggie could see a faint tracing of veiny purple just under her eyebrow.

'It's going to be all right,' Dee said. She tentatively put a hand on Maggie's shoulder.

The wave of Maggie's rage peaked and crashed on empty, desolate sands. She sank into Dee. 'How?' she sobbed, her breath catching in her throat. 'How is it ever going to be all right?'

'Do you remember what your Abba song was?' Dee said. 'Back when we had the fan club?'

Maggie nodded against Dee's shoulder, tears and snot bubbling in her nose. '"Head Over Heels",' she said.

'You're the leading lady, Maggie. You push through jungles every day.'

From somewhere in the depths of Maggie's body, a tiny bubble of laughter rose up and burst through her tears. 'I used to sing it when I was locked in my bedroom,' she said, with a sniffle. 'After we stole the boat and went to that island.'

'You'll push through this jungle,' Dee said. 'I know you will.'

Maggie lifted her head and saw that Dee was crying too, tears streaking white lines through the heavy makeup on her cheeks. 'What about you?' she asked, forgetting herself. 'Will you push through your jungle?'

Dee winced. 'I don't know,' she said. '"Head Over Heels" wasn't my song.'

Cassandra and Daniel had drawn close, without saying anything. Even though the sky was still light, Maggie felt as if it was pitch black and they were huddled alone and together, a little island unto themselves on the arena's vast concourse. Her eyes met Daniel's. He was gazing at her.

From inside the arena there came the wave of a massive cheer.

'Oh, God,' Maggie groaned. 'They must be coming onstage.'

'Let's get out of here,' Daniel said, his eyes not leaving hers.

'Oh!' said Cassandra. 'I have an idea!' She zipped open her bag, started rooting in it, then pulled out a piece of paper. 'Somebody handed this to me on the street today,' she said, unfolding it to reveal a flyer with a picture of Abba on the front. 'It's for an Abba karaoke party tonight.'

The piano trill that opened 'Dancing Queen' sounded into the sky and Maggie groaned again. 'I don't think I could cope with a crap karaoke version,' she said.

Dee linked her arm in hers. 'Come on,' she said. 'We'll be together, and it'll be fun.'

Cassandra took her other arm. 'I know what I'm going to sing already.'

82. Sing It Out Loud

As Daniel stood at the bar, trying to catch the barman's attention so he could order another round, he watched Dee and Maggie on the makeshift stage out of the corner of his eye. They were singing 'Angel Eyes' together, which he vaguely remembered from Abba's repertoire, and hamming it up no end, using their hands and exaggerated facial expressions to emote the song's story of love and betrayal. To the side of the stage, Cassandra was whooping along with a bottle of beer in hand.

The bar was the last place you'd expect to find an Abba karaoke night. They'd had to take a train from Solna to town and then the Tunnelbana to get to the suburb it was in, situated slap-bang opposite a still-open Lidl supermarket. A huge sign over the door shouted, 'King of Rock!' and inside the clientele was made up entirely of boys with long hair, faded grey jeans and multiple piercings, and girls with tattooed arms and too much black eye makeup. Nobody was over twenty-five, and all of them looked on the verge of suicidal *ennui*.

Abba were clearly not their cup of beer, and no matter how much the MC goaded them into getting onstage, no one was interested. Which was all the better for Maggie and Cassandra, who hadn't stopped belting out the hits since they'd paid their four-hundred-krona entrance fees and downed a few bottles of Dutch courage. Dee wasn't drinking, but she was singing just as much. The crowd seemed to be tolerating them, in that carefully polite Swedish way, but only just. Underneath the tolerance there was a rumble of aggravation.

Daniel ordered three more bottles of Falcon and a sparkling water for Dee, and was loading them on to the table when Maggie and Dee arrived offstage, arm in arm and laughing, with Cassandra in tow. Maggie and Cassandra, who had both downed three beers already, had the smiley glassy-eyed look of the newly and happily drunk. So did teetotal Dee.

'I'm high on life!' she'd announced to the table, wiping sweat off her brow. It was a complete turnaround from the depressed, downtrodden version of herself she'd been presenting all weekend. Daniel was glad of it. He didn't know how to talk to her about the bruises on her face.

'The MC's taking a break,' Maggie puffed, as she sat down. 'I think he's sick to death of us.' In the muggy heat of the pub, she'd taken off her scarf to reveal a fine coating of golden orange hair on her scalp. If you squinted, her head looked as if it was glowing.

Daniel found himself laughing out loud, as if she'd cracked a singularly hilarious one-liner. He was on his fourth lager too, so he put it down to that.

'When are you going to get up and sing, Daniel?' Cassandra asked, exchanging her empty beer bottle for a full one. 'Or should I say Danny Lane?'

Daniel bristled. 'You know the way you hate being called Charlie?' he said. 'Well, it's the same for me. I hate being called Danny Lane.'

'Point taken,' said Cassandra, with a chastened grimace.

'You know what I don't understand?' Maggie pitched in, pointing her bottle at Cassandra. 'Why did you go to the bother of changing your name? Charlie is one of those names that can be either a boy's or a girl's.'

'It's complicated,' said Cassandra, standing up. 'If you'll excuse me, I'm off to the little girls' room.'

'I'm coming with you,' said Dee, who never stopped going to the toilet.

When they were both gone, the table descended into silence. On the multiple flat screens that hung from the upper reaches of the pub's walls, Abba were singing 'Mamma Mia' with their iconic juxtaposed faces.

'What are you going to do about the guy who sold you the tickets?' Daniel asked, breaking the silence.

Maggie took a swig of beer. 'I don't want to think about it,' she said. 'Not tonight anyway.' With only the orange fuzz on her head, her eyes looked big and vulnerable in her pale face. Daniel was seized with an urge to kiss her. A drunken urge, he reckoned.

The MC, returning to the stage, brought him back to some sober senses.

'*Mina damer och herrar, mesdames et messieurs*, ladies and gentlemen! Welcome back to our karaoke extravaganza, where we're having our very own Abba reunion concert!'

There were a few general grunts from the tattooed and pierced audience, and over the rim of her beer bottle, Maggie gazed at the stage with shining eyes, as if she was enjoying the real reunion.

'Now we are looking for a new singer,' the MC continued. He seemed to cross the stage on air, the silver sequins of his jacket glittering in the light from the television screens. 'You, sir,' he said, pointing to Daniel. 'I think it is time we heard from you.'

Daniel shook his head. 'No way,' he said. How many years was it since he'd last performed by himself, front and centre? How many years was it since he'd vowed he'd never do it again?

He glanced at the stage and the microphone. If he was going to take Cassandra's advice, he'd have to get used to being front and centre once more.

Maggie was looking at him with an unreadable expression, the little vertical line at the top of her nose deepening. 'I really, really want to hear you sing,' she said.

Daniel sighed and put his bottle down. 'Only for you,' he said, getting to his feet.

From the sheet the MC handed him, he chose 'Fernando'. It was the song Maggie had sung to him on the island when they were kids, after she'd pointed out the single star in the sky.

As the flutes faded in with their sad, nostalgic calling, he opened his mouth to deliver the first line and found himself lost. The music took over. The bar, the rock nerds and chicks, the television screens, all disappeared and Daniel was singing only to Maggie.

Her eyes did not move from his as he crooned the words to her.

How could it be that he loved her still? After she had let him down the way she had? After all these years?

83. About to Crack

The bathroom walls were bare brick, painted black with dribbles of silver and gold paint splashed on them, like a Jackson Pollock picture. A chipped mirror ran across one wall above a row of sinks, over which a fluorescent light kept blinking on and off, making it almost impossible for Dee to see what she was doing with her makeup.

'God, that light's annoying,' Cassandra said, from inside one of the cubicles. She flushed the toilet and emerged to stand beside Dee at the mirror.

'Look at us,' she said. 'We're not half bad for our age, are we?'

'Speak for yourself,' Dee said, leaning in close so she could make out whether the dabbing of her foundation was working to hide what remained of the bruising. 'I think I've put on ten years in the last few weeks.'

Cassandra turned a tap on. 'Nonsense,' she smiled. 'You have the skin of a woman half your age.' She washed her hands, then held them under an electric dryer that sounded like a plane landing. She turned back to Dee. 'Here,' she said. 'Let me help you with that.'

She'd done the same earlier on, arriving at Dee's hotel room before they'd left for the concert with a makeup case the size of a weekend carry-all. 'You can't watch Abba through a pair of sunglasses,' she'd insisted, and when Dee had protested that she couldn't cover the bruises no matter how she tried, added, 'Trust me, sweetie. I've had to cover up a lot worse than that in my time.'

Now Cassandra leaned over and gently prodded foundation onto the skin to the side of Dee's eye with the tip of her index finger. Although the spot was still tender, it felt oddly comforting.

'You've a pretty good voice,' Dee said, looking up to the ceiling while Cassandra worked. 'Do you sing in the cabaret show you do back home?'

'I lip-synch,' Cassandra said, squeezing another little dollop of foundation on to her finger. 'It's what drag queens generally do.'

'But you're not a drag queen, are you?'

'Well, technically, no. But I kind of am one, for the job.'

'Oh, I see.'

Cassandra put the lid back on the foundation tube. 'Do you have an eyebrow pencil?' she asked.

Dee pulled her bag open and found one at the bottom of the rubble inside. She handed it over and, as Cassandra went back on the job, said, 'Do you mind if I ask you another question?'

'Shoot,' Cassandra said, smoothing Dee's eyebrow with the flat of her finger.

'Why do you dress up as a drag queen when you say you're a real woman?'

The motion of Cassandra's finger stopped. 'I don't *say* I'm a real woman,' she said, her voice going chilly. 'I am a real woman.'

'I know that,' Dee said. 'Don't get annoyed. I was just wondering. Drag queens are usually guys dressed up as women, aren't they?'

Cassandra leaned back against the sink with her hip. 'It's just a job,' she said. 'I have to earn a living somehow.'

She looked so stricken, Dee regretted broaching the subject. She decided to change tack. 'You never told me how Sam was,' she said. 'Is he still living in Sligo?'

'Yes.'

'Did he get married? Has he any kids?'

'Bloody Hell!' Cassandra snapped. 'What is this? An interrogation?'

'Sorry,' said Dee. She lifted the eyebrow pencil Cassandra had thrown into the sink and put it back in her bag. Cassandra was very interested in other people's lives, but she obviously didn't want to let anyone into hers.

But then Dee changed her mind. 'Why are you so touchy about your name?' she asked. 'About Charlie, I mean.'

'Let's go,' Cassandra replied, taking her own handbag from the sink unit.

'I mean, it's only a name, isn't it?'

Cassandra rounded on her. 'It's *not* only a name,' she said. 'It's everything I hated about myself, everything I fought fucking hard to leave behind. I don't need to be constantly reminded of it.'

'What about the good parts of Charlie, the bits you loved about him?'

'I didn't love anything about Charlie.'

'But you *must* have. I loved you when you were Charlie.'

'And what? You don't love me now?' Cassandra's voice was sour.

'That's not what I'm saying at all,' said Dee. 'I'm just saying that Charlie is part of you. You can't just leave that part of yourself behind and pretend it never existed.'

Cassandra pushed past Dee and made for the door. She'd wrenched it open and was about to walk out, but then she stopped. 'You're a fine one to talk about pretending,' she said. 'You've been pretending all your life. Putting your oh-so-perfect face forward, cutting your arms when no one's looking. Staying with a husband who beats the shit out of you.'

Dee couldn't believe what she was hearing. 'I showed you my arms in confidence,' was all she could manage in reply.

Cassandra squared up to her. 'I know you're going back to Joe,' she said. 'And you know what I think? It's pathetic.'

'You don't know anything,' Dee argued. 'I'm pregnant. It's complicated.'

But the door had closed and Cassandra was gone.

84. One More Toast

The hotel's bar and restaurant had morphed into a club in the hours they'd been away, with music pumping out on to the pavement and queues of half-dressed girls wearing too much makeup being slowly filtered by a pair of black-tie bouncers with the self-importance of Pentagon staff.

'Do you want to try getting in?' Maggie asked Daniel. Even though half an hour ago she'd been on the verge of total wipeout, now the last thing she wanted was to sleep. She felt wired to the moon.

'Not exactly,' Daniel replied, his eyes twinkling. 'But we could go somewhere quieter. We passed a bar that didn't look too hectic around the corner.'

'I'll leave you two to it.' Cassandra smiled. 'This girl needs her beauty sleep.'

Dee had already gone to bed, finding a side-door entrance to the hotel the minute they'd got out of the taxi. Her mood had shifted again, back to black, and before she left she'd kissed everyone goodnight, except Cassandra, which led Maggie to wonder again what had gone on between them in the Ladies at the karaoke bar.

Waving Cassandra goodnight, Maggie half stumbled off the pavement. As she found her balance, Daniel took her arm and linked it in his.

'I'm a bad girl,' she told him, following his lead. 'I shouldn't be drinking, you know. I have a very serious condition.'

'Sometimes it's good to have a blow-out,' Daniel said. 'Sometimes you need it.'

'I know!' Maggie said, in thorough agreement. 'Let's move on to shots!'

Daniel laughed. 'Maybe not that much of a blow-out,' he said.

The pub he brought her to seemed to have been built entirely of glass. It stood in the middle of another square, a kind of shopping precinct with a McDonald's on the corner.

'This is very romantic.' Maggie giggled, as Daniel held the door open for her. 'Maybe we can go for a Big Mac later.'

Inside the minuscule bar a DJ was squeezed into a little booth in the corner, earphones half on, concentrating on his decks, but at least his music was a little mellower than what had been blasting out of the hotel's club. Daniel found them a seat that looked out at McDonald's and went to order two beers.

Watching him lean over the bar, waiting to be served, Maggie wondered what it would be like to sleep with him again. To feel his lean body against hers. To kiss him … But she shook the idea out of her head. That was not going to happen, for all sorts of good reasons.

The problem was, she was too drunk to remember them all.

To shift her thoughts, Maggie took her phone out of her bag. She still hadn't replied to Poppy's message, looking for the car keys, or William's, asking her how the concert had been. She didn't want to tell him there had been no concert, that she'd spent five grand of his money on nothing.

She read William's text again. It was signed off with three Xs. In the car he'd told her he'd be at the airport to collect her when she got home on Sunday night. In the meantime he was bringing Maggie's mother to Stansted for her flight home on Saturday. Seemingly he'd turned back into the old William. Her reliable husband.

When Daniel came back with the beers and sat down beside her, Maggie found herself asking, 'Why didn't you ever write to me?' She jammed her hand over her mouth, as if she could shove the question back in. She hadn't meant it to come out.

Daniel turned to her. 'I did,' he said. 'I wrote every day. For ages.'

'But …' It dawned on her. She'd been locked in her bedroom and had given her mother the letters to post. She'd written one before she was taken to Manchester, telling him everything, and her mother had promised she'd send it. After Maggie had got home and there was nothing from Daniel, she'd stopped writing. It was just one more thing to give up on.

'My mother mustn't have posted the letters,' she said now, the truth of it becoming crystal clear through the fog of alcohol. 'She must have kept yours too.'

Daniel was frowning. 'But why didn't you post the letters yourself?' he asked.

'I was locked in my bedroom,' Maggie said. She looked down into her beer and wondered if now was the right time to tell him. Drunk, in a busy bar, with a DJ playing the Spice Girls.

'You were locked in your room?'

'At first it was as punishment,' Maggie said. She took a breath. 'But then I found out I was pregnant.'

As Daniel sat, his glass frozen in mid-air, Maggie let it all pour out. When she had finished, she felt mostly relieved. She'd never told another human being the story, and she actually felt lighter around her shoulders.

But Daniel was staring at her in silent horror. 'Jesus,' he said.

Maggie sobered up. 'I'm sorry,' she said. 'I shouldn't have told you. Not here.'

Daniel got to his feet. 'Excuse me for a minute,' he said, but didn't move. He sat down again. 'You went through all that alone?' he asked.

'Well, my mother came with me,' Maggie replied. But, thinking about it, she *had* been alone. It wasn't as if her mother had been playing a supportive role.

'Jesus,' Daniel said again. 'I wish …' He reached out and put his hand on Maggie's knee, his touch sending a quickening through her blood.

Maggie waited for him to finish, and then, seeing he was speechless, lifted her beer glass. 'It was for the best,' she said, taking a mouthful. 'I was far too young to have a baby.'

'We were such kids,' Daniel said. 'It's hard to remember what we were like back then.'

'I remember,' Maggie said. 'Everything.'

Daniel stared at her, his eyes soft. 'I sent you a song, you know. On a cassette tape.'

Maggie shrugged. 'My dear mother must have got rid of that too.'

'It was "Night Star". I wrote it for you.'

How could she not have known? The lyrics were all about that night on the island, about what had happened between them. They were the letter she'd never received, played a million times over.

Maggie felt floored with tiredness, as bad as the kind she'd felt during the worst of her chemotherapy days. She wanted to lay her head on the table and fall into oblivion.

'Maggie? Are you all right?' He was watching her closely.

'Can you take me back to the hotel?' Maggie said. 'I'm suddenly very tired.'

85. The Strange Attraction

Joe was waiting for her at the arrivals gate when Dee walked out through the sliding doors, trailing her bag behind her. He was holding up a sign emblazoned with 'Dee Dimare, I Love You!' in black marker. It was at once mortifying and made Dee want to cry.

She flushed as she walked towards him. Her legs were unsteady, so she hesitated and, for the briefest of moments, wondered what in God's name she was doing. She wanted to stumble into his arms. She wanted to be engulfed by him, to find herself warm, secure and safe.

But there was no safety to be had.

'I missed you,' Joe said, when she reached the barrier. His eyes were shining and he was gazing at her helplessly.

It was crazy. At this moment she was the one holding all the cards. She could tell him now that it was over and walk away. She could stay and make him pay for what he had done. Even if he hurt her again, she could go on exacting payment, constantly finding herself returning to the same situation, with him pouring gratitude and love over her until she felt gratified and loved.

It felt so good, his love. She had always wanted to feel the way he made her feel. He had filled the yawning gap inside her. She couldn't properly remember a time before when she'd felt anyone's love, even her own for herself. She'd become accustomed to the boarding school, to its institutional life of unbreakable rules and cemented routines, to the long bus journeys to and fro, and the division of her life between one place and another. She'd made new friends and participated. At exam times she'd put her head down and excelled, remembering that in this world she could rely only on herself and no one else.

After leaving Kylemore Abbey she'd poured herself into college in Dublin, and then into her career. She'd made a success of herself, and she'd taken great pride and comfort in that. But every so often, in the silence of night, alone in her bed, she had allowed herself to see why she was doing it. She had created a life for herself where there was no room for anything else because she didn't want to be turned away ever again.

Then Joe had come along, her knight on a white horse. This complicated, confusing man whom she loved in a way she had never loved anyone before, who loved her back in the same way. When he was violent, even though she was ashamed to admit it to herself, part of her excused it. He wasn't himself when he was hitting her. It was like some stranger had taken over his body. That stranger was not a man who loved her as Joe did.

When it was all over and Joe came back, desperate for her love, it felt like the return of the prodigal husband. For all her protests that she wouldn't take it from him, the millions of times she told herself she hated him, that she was leaving the next time, that she would never again allow him or another man to treat her the way he did, she was overjoyed.

Joe was back. She was safe again.

If someone opened her head and looked inside, they'd certify her as clinically insane. A woman unable to help herself.

A pregnant woman unable to help herself.

'How are you feeling?' Joe asked, as they walked over the ramp towards the airport car park. He'd taken her suitcase, as if wheeling it might be too much for her.

'Exhausted,' Dee said. 'I feel like I could sleep for a week.'

All through the time in Stockholm she'd pretended to herself as much as she possibly could that she wasn't pregnant, and even though she'd had to pee every ten minutes, she'd by and large managed it. Now, with Joe fussing over her, the fact of it began to close in.

When they reached the car and Dee got in, she felt so confined she couldn't keep her seatbelt on. The thing was like an animal trap, pinning her to the seat. Joe began to reverse out of the parking spot and the seatbelt alarm kicked in, its repetitive bing-bing-bing reverberating against the interior of Dee's skull.

'Stop!' she cried, jamming both palms on the dashboard.

Joe glanced at her in confusion, then put the car into first and took off.

'I said stop the car, Joe!'

He jammed on the brakes, jerking Dee forward in sickening motion. She pulled the door open and got out, gulping the exhaust-fume-laden air. She began to walk back blindly towards the lifts.

'Dee! Where are you going?' Joe's voice came from behind her.

She stopped and turned. He was standing beside the car in the middle of the aisle, its hazard lights on.

'Why, Joe?' she cried. 'Why do you hit me?'

He crumpled, holding on to the roof of the car, and she barely heard his reply. 'I don't know,' he said.

Dee started walking back towards him. 'Is it me?' she asked, knowing how utterly pathetic that sounded. Maybe, somehow, it was her fault.

'No,' Joe said, fervently shaking his head. 'No.'

'Then what is it?'

'I don't know what comes over me.'

Dee was standing right beside him now, looking directly into his face. She felt calmer, more in control of herself. 'That's not good enough,' she said. 'If we're going to stay together and bring up a child, you're going to have to do better than that.'

'I will,' Joe replied, meeting her eyes. 'I promise.'

She'd heard similar promises before. At the beginning she'd believed them.

'Did your father hit your mother?' she asked. It was a question that had been on her lips so many times, but for some reason she'd been afraid to ask.

Joe's gaze disconnected from hers. His voice turned bitter. 'When I was a kid, I swore I'd never be like him when I grew up.'

'You can change,' Dee said. 'I know you can.'

In her mind's eye she saw Cassandra. She was sitting on the twin bed in Dee's hotel room, selecting the shade of foundation to cover the bruising from her makeup case. 'You can't make someone change, Dee,' she was saying. 'You can only change yourself.'

Joe was crying, and shaking his head, and she knew that in his life he'd seen more pain than she ever had. Maybe now, in admitting it, he was being given the chance to change himself.

86. This Is Goodbye

Maggie was leaning over to buzz for more painkillers when Daniel walked in carrying a big bunch of white roses.

She winced as she lay back on the pillow, then tried to meet his wide grin.

'How are you feeling?' he asked, pushing the flowers towards her.

'I've been better,' Maggie replied. She didn't think she'd ever felt, or looked, worse. The pain where her flesh had been sliced open was raw and radiated across her chest, up her shoulders and neck into her face and skull, where her brain felt as if shards of glass were lodged inside it. Last night, when she'd woken up after the operation, she'd groggily pulled out the top of her hospital gown to look down at the place where her breast had been. The thick scar that snaked from the centre of her ribcage across the flattened, greyish skin on her chest to the drain under her arm was livid. Its ugliness made her feel sick to her core.

Now, as she pulled herself up in the bed as best she could, cringing as pain darted across her chest again, Daniel's eyes travelled to the empty space under her gown, where her breast had been. His smile faltered.

'Is there a vase I can put these flowers in?' he asked, looking away.

Maggie didn't know or care. 'They're gorgeous, thanks,' she said, wishing he had given her some warning instead of springing on her like this. At least she would have had time to wipe away the sleep that had caked her eyes together and maybe put on a bit of makeup. What had grown back of her hair was pasted against her head like a greasy shroud and her lips were dry and cracked.

'Maybe they'll have a vase at the nurses' station,' she said, trying to buy herself a little time alone so at least she could run her fingers through her hair and pinch some colour into her cheeks, but Daniel didn't budge. He was smiling at her again.

'I've been thinking about Stockholm a lot,' he said, laying the bouquet on the bedside table. He gave a little chuckle. 'In fact, I can't stop thinking about Stockholm.'

If he was a puppy, Maggie thought, he'd be wagging his tail.

Something about it irritated her. Couldn't he see that she was barely out of an operating room where her body had been dissected, where lumps of meat that had once been a living, pulsating part of her had been carved away? She felt as if she'd been utterly changed, as if a piece of her soul had been ripped from her body, along with the offending flesh. She couldn't imagine that he didn't see her alienation, her diminishment.

But he was beaming like a child. A man who had never properly grown up. It occurred to Maggie that he wasn't thinking of her trauma at all. He was only thinking of himself.

Daniel sat on the end of the bed. 'When you're better, maybe we could go back. We barely got to see any of the city, when you think about it.'

Maggie shifted her weight, soreness shooting now from her chest to her abdomen. 'That would be lovely,' she managed to say.

She tried to conjure up the wonderful feeling that had flooded through her when he was holding her outside her hotel-room door that night in Stockholm, but nothing came. 'It was very nice of you to visit me,' she added, wanting him to take the hint and go.

'What else would I do?' he asked. He paused for a moment and then said, 'Maggie … about you and me. I was thinking—'

'Mrs Corcoran,' the ward sister interrupted, putting her head round the door. 'How are we feeling?'

Maggie swallowed. 'If I could have some more painkillers, that would be great,' she said, relieved they would be coming her way at last.

'Let's see,' the sister said, moving to the end of the bed to take up Maggie's chart. 'You've had some this morning already …' She checked the chart and looked at her watch. 'Oh,' she said, and knitted her brow. 'You should have rung for more.'

'I was just about to,' Maggie said.

Daniel watched this exchange, his head turning as if he was at a tennis match.

'I think your wife needs some rest now, Mr Corcoran,' the sister told him.

'Oh, this isn't my husband,' Maggie said quickly. She was seized by a fit of coughing. 'He's just a friend,' she managed to add.

'Well, it's time for you to get a little sleep,' the sister said, attaching the chart to the end of the bed. 'We don't want too many visitors today.'

When she'd left, Daniel stood up. 'She's right, I should go,' he said.

Maggie thought he sounded a little peeved. 'Come another time when I'm in better form,' she said, but she had a feeling Daniel had shut up shop and wasn't listening.

'I hope you feel better soon,' Daniel said, his chin set.

'So do I,' Maggie replied, trying to give a rueful grin but not properly pulling it off.

The door opened again and Maggie's mother appeared. She looked at Daniel and Maggie saw a flicker of recognition pass across her features.

Daniel nodded stiffly to her, then turned back to Maggie. 'Well … goodbye,' he said.

'See you soon,' Maggie replied. Through her pain she felt a stab of loneliness, as if she had said goodbye to him for the last time.

87. My Picture Clear

'Sorry, mate, she's gone to the shops.'

Rob was barring the threshold of Jade's house, beefy legs wide and tattooed arms folded, regarding Daniel as if he was going to refuse him entry.

'I'm not here to see Jade,' Daniel said, remaining polite. 'Is Noah in?'

'He might be. He might not.'

Daniel sighed. 'C'mon, man,' he said. 'Just let me in, will you?'

Rob didn't move. 'Maybe you should come back another time,' he said. 'When Jade's here.'

'Dad?' Noah had appeared behind Rob's shoulder, his pale, narrow face illuminated by the light in the hall. 'Aren't you coming in?'

Rob hesitated, then moved aside to let Daniel past. He grunted and lumbered off to the kitchen, leaving Daniel alone with his son.

'How have you been?' Daniel asked. He knew what he had come to say, but after his experience at the hospital with Maggie he felt shaken and unprepared. He'd known what he'd gone there to say too, but at the end of the day, what would have been the point? Saying three words wasn't going to change anything. She had a husband and a family and no place for him in her life.

Noah shrugged and went into the sitting room, where the TV was on full blast. He'd shaven his head to a number-one buzz cut that gave him the look of a convict.

Daniel followed and took a seat on the edge of the sofa. Noah reached for the remote control and put the television on mute, which Daniel registered as a possible improvement in mood. A week ago, the thing would have been left on at full volume.

'There's something I want to talk to you about,' Daniel said.

Noah kept his eyes on the flickering TV screen, where Ross and Rachel were silently fighting in an old episode of *Friends*.

Daniel cleared his throat and launched in before he could stop himself, like he had at the hospital. 'I was bullied at school too,' he said, the words spilling out. 'It was after my mother died. Some kids said she killed herself, even though I don't think she did. And instead of standing up for myself, or her, I just kept my head down and pretended it wasn't happening …'

He took a breath. Noah was still staring at the television.

'The thing is, Noah, I wasn't like you. I wasn't brave. You don't care what people think. You dress the way you want, and you're the person you are, and even though those arseholes treated you like shit, they couldn't take it away from you. Please, Noah. I don't want you to let them take it away from you.'

'Dad,' said Noah. 'I'm gay.'

Daniel thought for a moment that Noah had deliberately thrown this into the middle of the room, like a teenage grenade. But then he saw his son's face was twisted with anxiety. He had come here with so much to say but now he found himself at another loss. Silence drew out between them and he understood he had to say something quickly before he lost Noah again. Something affirmative.

'That's okay,' he tried.

Noah still looked stricken.

'I mean … well … are you sure?'

Noah nodded, his eyes on the floor.

Knowing Me **Knowing** You

'Well, if you're sure, then it's fine with me. As long as you're happy ...'

The room descended into silence again and Daniel felt as if something was missing, some essential bit he'd left out. Then it came to him.

Three words.

'I love you,' he said. 'You know that, Noah, don't you? I love you exactly the way you are.'

Noah lifted his eyes from the carpet and met Daniel's. 'I know, Dad,' he said, his voice a squeak.

Daniel's heart was ready to burst. He wanted to put his arms around his son, to hold him close. But Noah wasn't giving off any signals that the physical barriers were down. Instead he put his palms on his knees to steady himself. He had come to tell Noah his plan, and now it felt more important than ever.

'I've made a decision, Noah,' he said. 'I'm going to give an interview about what really happened. Why you brought the knife to school in the first place.'

Noah was frowning as Daniel spoke. Somehow he looked more grown-up. 'Are you sure that's what you want to do?' he asked.

'I know it could backfire,' Daniel said, 'but I think it's important to name what's been happening for what it is. And right now the press wants to hear anything I've got to say.'

Noah's frown smoothed out. 'Dad,' he said, 'you sound like a proper grown-up.'

Daniel gave an involuntary laugh. 'So do you,' he said.

'I want to do it with you,' said Noah. 'The interview.'

'I'm not sure that's a good idea,' Daniel said. But Noah looked set on being part of it.

'I'll have a think about it.' Daniel smiled as Jade's voice rang out in the hall.

'I'm home, boys! I've got takeaway!'

403

Noah jumped up from his seat. 'Great,' he said, grinning at Daniel. 'I'm starving!'

Later, after they had all dug into pepperoni pizza, garlic bread and a giant-sized bottle of Coke, and even Rob was at the table, rubbing his belly and looking satisfied, Noah turned to Jade. 'Mum,' he said, 'I'm going to stay at Dad's tonight. My computer's still there and I want to do stuff.'

Jade glanced at Daniel and smiled. 'Of course,' she said. 'Why don't you go and pack yourself a bag?'

As Noah bounded out of the room, Daniel knew that, in his own way, his son had just told him he loved him in return.

88. He Is Your Brother

The shop floor of Sam's Tool Hire smelt of newly laid carpet mingled with furniture polish. The place was almost clinically neat and tidy, like the foyer of a hospital rather than a place where someone might hire a chainsaw. Glossy posters displaying power tools were framed on the pristine white walls, as if they were part of an art exhibition, and behind the gleaming bare counter, Sam held himself in a different way, shoulders back, chin up. He looked confident, a captain on the prow of his very own ship.

Cassandra was struck by the fact that she hadn't seen Sam looking like this since they were kids, when he was the king of the football team and the quarry of every teenage girl in town. 'How are Delia and the boys?' she asked, making another stab at conversation. Since she'd plucked up the courage to walk into the shop, and found Sam alone there, he'd hardly emitted two words.

'Fine,' Sam replied. He went quiet again, then added, as if he was making an extreme effort to find something else to say, 'They're going to Westport, to her mother's, for the weekend.'

'That's nice,' Cassandra said, conjuring up the best smile she could manage. The small-talk was excruciating.

A bell rang to announce the shop door opening and a large, ruddy-faced man, wearing a coat too thick for a warm day and a flat cap walked in. His eyes went straight to Cassandra, running up and down her body, pausing at her breasts. She saw Sam take this in, his expression unreadable.

'Excuse me for a moment,' Sam said to her, as if he was addressing a stranger. He went over to the customer and started dealing with him.

Cassandra watched them talking, their heads inclined towards each other. They looked like the essence of manhood, communicating in a code that might as well have been Swahili, it was so foreign to her. She marvelled, not for the first time, that Sam was her identical twin, that once upon a time they had been one egg in their mother's ovary. This man, and her.

When they were children, everyone called them 'the twins'. Not Charlie and Sam, but 'the twins'. They had been each other's reflection, the mirror they woke up with every day and shut their eyes on every night. What Cassandra had seen in that mirror was her own horror, the body she detested with every fibre of herself made manifest in another human being. But she knew what Sam had seen in the mirror was different. He'd seen himself doubled and made better. He wasn't Sam – he was Sam *and* Charlie.

The last thing he'd said to her that day in his kitchen, before she had gone running back to the Canaries, was that she was dead to him. But it wasn't Cassandra who was dead. It was Charlie. In a way Cassandra had taken Charlie away from Sam, as cleanly and finally as if she had killed him. And in killing Charlie, she'd killed an essential part of Sam's identity.

Reflected in Charlie's eyes, Sam was the leader, the winner – the man. With Charlie gone, the reflection was gone.

The customer gave Cassandra another once-over before he left the shop, the bell ringing again on his way out. As Sam closed the till, Cassandra said, 'I've decided to move home. To take care of Dad.'

Sam heaved a sigh. 'Don't,' he said. 'If you know what's good for you.'

'I do know what's good for me,' Cassandra said. 'I always have.'

'Dad's getting too hard to handle. He's better off in the nursing home.'

'I want to do it, Sam. I really do.'

Sam said nothing for a few seconds, and then he asked, 'What about John?'

Cassandra was taken aback. 'What do you mean?' she said.

'Are you going to start up with John again?'

Even though he'd contacted her about Maggie and the Abba concert, no truce had been called; nothing had changed. Sam was worried that she was going to embarrass him, just as he always was. Cassandra almost told him to mind his own business, but then she saw that he was watching her, not with his usual open hostility but with what seemed like concern.

'I don't think so,' she said. 'I'm probably the last person John wants to see.'

Sam put both hands on the counter. 'I think he'd like it if you called him,' he said.

Cassandra took a breath. Was this the same Sam who had told her she was disgusting and turned his stomach the last time she'd seen him? He seemed awkward and formal, as if he was at some kind of function where he had to be on his best behaviour.

'Sam …' she hadn't planned to tell him – not yet, anyway. 'I'm thinking of changing my name back to Charlie.'

Sam didn't move. His gaze travelled beyond Cassandra's shoulder to the framed posters of power tools at the other end of the room.

'What do you think?' she asked, knowing that it was a lost cause and she really should leave now before he lost his temper.

His gaze returned and he looked her in the eyes for the first time since she'd told him she was going to transition. 'I missed Charlie, you know,' he said. 'For a long time. But I like Cassandra. It suits you better.'

A flush made its way up Cassandra's neck as Sam lifted the counter flap to let himself out. 'I'm going to shut up shop early today,' he said. 'You fancy going for a pint?'

89. All My Cards

Dr Snow's spectacles glinted with the reflection of the fluorescent strip that lit his office. He was beaming as he reached across his desk to take Maggie's hand. 'It's a pleasure for me to give you such positive results, Mrs Corcoran,' he said, shaking it vigorously.

Sitting in the chair beside Maggie, her mother let out a little sob. On Maggie's other side William was throwing relieved glances her way.

She remembered the beginning of this journey, when William had been with Rita and she'd sat in Dr Snow's office alone. She couldn't remember ever seeing her mother cry before.

'So, there aren't any traces of the cancer left?' she asked, feeling oddly divided. On one hand there was the inexpressible relief of a reprieve from Death Row. On the other, she felt as if the air had been let out of her, leaving her flat.

'That's right.' Dr Snow smiled, sitting down. 'It's the best we could possibly hope for in the circumstances.'

'But does that mean it won't come back?' Maggie asked.

'Well, we can't say it's an all-clear for ever. But in the medium to long term, your chances are good. We will, of course, be running checks on you every month for the first six months, and every three months after that. But, really, you should be very happy with the prognosis. We all are.'

Maggie's mother continued to sniffle. 'Thank you, Doctor,' she said. 'We were so afraid we were going to lose her.'

Dr Snow took a tissue out of the box on his desk and handed it over. 'She did very well,' he said. 'Very well indeed.'

While her mother dabbed at her eyes, William reached over and laid his hand on Maggie's, on the arm of her chair. 'We can't thank you enough, Doctor,' he said, and although Maggie agreed, she couldn't say it for herself. She knew it was selfish, but part of her wished she was receiving the news alone.

Or with Daniel.

Before they left Dr Snow's office, Maggie said, 'I feel like giving you a hug, Doctor. Is that allowed?'

His glasses glinted again as he smiled. 'Of course it is.'

She put her arms around him and squeezed tight to show the depth of her gratitude to him and all the people who had helped her fight this thing, who had helped her win the battle. There were no proper words for it.

'Well done,' Dr Snow said, gently patting her back. 'Well done.'

Rather than go straight home, William suggested a champagne lunch in celebration. Although Maggie's bones ached with weariness, and she was sore where the drain under her arm had become infected, she said, 'Why not?'

If anything had to be celebrated, it was the news that you were going to live. All the same, she felt like going home and getting into bed, pulling the covers over her head and crying. Instead of disappearing in the face of such good news, the depression that had been welling up over the past few months was threatening to engulf her.

She was relieved at one moment, despairing the next; sickened, then raging. She decided she was in shock, and that in time she would come to accept this different, one-breasted and possibly sexually redundant version of herself. Right now she wanted to hide and lick her wounds.

In the restaurant, a half-deserted little place full of polished wood and mirrors, William raised a toast. 'To Maggie,' he said. 'Our little fighter.' He was giving her that ever-so-patronising smile again, the same as when he'd told her he didn't mind about her taking the money for the concert tickets.

Maggie's mother clinked her champagne glass with Maggie's and then she took a little sip. 'Oh, my,' she said, with a slight grimace. 'Drinking in the afternoon. What's next?'

Out of the blue, Maggie experienced a flash of fury of such force, she wanted to shake her mother until she broke into pieces on the floor, like an old porcelain doll. 'Why did you keep his letters from me, Mum?' she asked, her voice level.

William stared at her in confusion, as her mother replied, 'Pardon?'

'Daniel,' said Maggie. 'He wrote. Every day. But you let me believe he'd forgotten about me.'

'Daniel?' said William. 'Why are we talking about Daniel?'

'I'll tell you why,' Maggie said. 'When I was fifteen I got pregnant. Daniel was the father. *She* made me have an abortion.'

Maggie's mother gasped. 'Margaret,' she said. 'Please ...'

'Please what, Mum? Please pretend it didn't happen? Shove it all under the carpet and keep up appearances?'

The door of the restaurant opened and a couple walked in, the woman carrying a baby in a papoose.

'Well, I'm sorry,' Maggie said. 'I'm too tired to pretend any more.'

William's face had gone pale. 'Are you serious?'

'Tell him, Mum,' Maggie said. 'Tell him all about it.'

Maggie's mother sat in horrified silence, looking first at Maggie, then at William, and back again.

'You don't know what it was like,' she said eventually. 'You were a wild thing, Maggie. We never knew what was next with you. Can you imagine what it would have been like if you'd had that baby? We wanted to protect you. We did what we thought was best.'

'And then you pretended you'd done nothing at all. And you kept his letters, the only things that could have given me comfort.'

Maggie's mother shook her head slowly. 'They would have brought you no comfort,' she said. 'They would have ruined your life. You were too young for that kind of relationship.'

'My life was ruined anyway.'

'That's not true, Maggie, and you know it.'

'What are you saying?' William interjected. The colour had returned to his face and was high. 'What about me? What about us? Didn't it count for anything?'

'Perhaps you should have asked yourself that before you left for Rita,' Maggie replied.

As a waiter arrived and put their plates of food in front of them, they all went quiet. When he had gone, Maggie's mother had recovered herself enough to say, 'Calm down, Margaret. There's no point in thinking about the past now. About *him*. What's important is that you have a family of your own, and they need you.'

William looked at Maggie's mother and then turned to Maggie, searching her face. 'We do need you,' he said. '*I* need you.'

Maggie lifted her glass and downed her champagne in one gulp. 'William,' she said, never more sure of anything in her life, 'you might need me, but I need you like I need a lump in my other breast.'

90. At the Crossroads

Dee couldn't get back to sleep. She had woken up in the middle of a dream about the baby. It was a little boy and he'd been crying and crying, the flattened-out mewling of a newborn, and she'd wanted to go to him, to pick him up and comfort him. But every room she went into was just an empty box with white-painted walls and a bare wooden floor. She'd tried door after door, as the jagged crying became more and more urgent, drilling into her head and her heart, but her little boy was nowhere to be found.

Fleeting images from the dream drifted into her mind as she lay on the pillow, willing herself to forget it and doze off again. But they still frightened her.

She opened her eyes and reached out to touch Joe, to anchor herself back in the real world. He was lying on his back, snoring softly with his mouth open, the duvet pushed away, his bare, hairy chest rising and falling with a kind of certainty, a rhythm that made him seem at one with the world. She lay looking at him for a few minutes, but memories of the dream were still making her heart race so she decided to get up to make a cup of chamomile tea to calm herself.

The kitchen clock said 5.25 a.m. Dee rolled up the window blind and stood with her mug of tea in both hands, looking at the empty street outside as the sun rose to illuminate it. In the middle of the road, the cat from the house opposite was washing itself. It saw Dee looking at it and sauntered off.

It was comforting watching the little housing estate when it was just coming to life. It was a quiet neighbourhood, really. People kept themselves to themselves. Soon curtains would start opening and the lives that were lived in those houses would start again for another day.

Who knew what those lives were like? It seemed so peaceful out there on the street, but the dreams her neighbours were dreaming right now might be just as disturbed as hers had been. Another woman might be standing in her dressing-gown and slippers, looking out of the window, grappling with what she should do.

She'd followed Joe yesterday. They'd both gone into town in his car, Dee to do some Saturday shopping, Joe to go to his first appointment with the counsellor they'd found for him to see – a guy working out of Trinity College who specialised in dealing with men who were violent in relationships. At the bottom of Grafton Street, Joe had kissed her goodbye and Dee had wished him luck.

'It'll be fine, you'll see,' she'd said, reaching out to straighten his collar.

Something about the way Joe smiled back had jarred. He'd looked like he hadn't a care in the world, as if he was off for a jaunt rather than going to confront the hard truth about himself with a professional for the very first time. As he'd walked away, Dee had stood and watched him. Then, making the decision quickly, she'd allowed some people to go ahead of her so that if he turned around he wouldn't see she was following him.

He had walked past the entrance to Trinity College and around the corner, crossing the junction with Westmoreland Street while the lights were still green, dodging in and out of stalled cars. By the time she got across, she thought she'd lost him, but then, on the corner of

Hawkin's Street, she'd picked up his trail once more. He jaywalked between jammed traffic again and disappeared through the doors of the Screen Cinema.

If she confronted him about it, she'd have to tell him she'd followed him, so instead, in the car on the way home, she'd quizzed him about his visit to the counsellor.

'What was he like?' she asked, and Joe had described a man who sounded perfectly plausible.

'What kinds of things did he ask you?' Joe, drumming his fingers on the steering wheel, had supplied a few details, telling her he'd talked about his childhood and his parents.

'What did you tell him about your childhood?' The question was barely out of her mouth when Joe jammed on the car's brakes and she lurched forcefully forward, the strap of the seatbelt cutting into her chest, hurting her breasts which had started to become tender.

'Jesus fucking Christ!' Joe yelled. 'You nearly made me crash the car, you stupid bitch!'

Tears had leaped to Dee's eyes, and she reached for the door handle. She had an urge to jump out of the car, but it was moving again at a faster pace.

After a minute, Joe had pulled into a loading bay and turned the engine off. In the ensuing hush Dee could hear the thumping of her own heart.

'I'm sorry,' Joe had said eventually, a pleading note entering his voice. 'I shouldn't have reacted like that. It's just that it was very difficult. It's not every day I spill my guts to a counsellor.'

Now, outside the kitchen window, the cat came back into vision again. There was something dangling from its mouth and Dee squinted to get a clearer view. It was a mouse, tail dangling, as the cat walked back to its own garden to do whatever it intended with it.

Dee experienced an instant, overwhelming desire to talk to her mother. The feeling was almost childish, a need to run and find herself comforted and protected in the arms of her constant ally when she was a very little girl, before she was sent to boarding school. The one who had cuddled her, who was always on hand in times of crisis. But it was only five thirty-five in the morning, far too early to disturb her.

As she switched on the kettle for another cup of tea, panic flapped up from her chest to her throat. She had to speak to her mother; she had to speak to her now.

'Hello?' her mother said, when Dee got through. Her voice was barely audible and tentative, as if she was expecting bad news.

'Mum,' Dee said. 'It's me.'

'Dolores. Is something wrong?'

'Yes,' Dee replied, and started to cry. The sound that came out of her was like a howl, a nightmare shriek. She couldn't stop making it. She couldn't speak. She knew that the noise she was making would wake Joe upstairs.

'Dolores?' her mother said. 'What is it, love?' Her voice was fearful.

'He … He …' Dee tried, but she wasn't able to get it out. She couldn't get any breath into her body between sobs. The idea flashed through her head that she was going to die.

Her mother's voice changed from frightened to firm. 'Dolores,' she said. 'Calm down.'

Upstairs there was the creak of a floorboard, the sound of Joe getting up.

Dee stopped crying. 'He beats me, Mum,' she said.

There was silence at the other end of the phone and then her mother said, her voice even and low, 'Leave him, Dolores. Go now. Don't subject your child to that.'

Dee heard the flush of the upstairs toilet and then Joe's feet on the landing.

'I'll call you later, Mum,' she said, and hung up, her mother's voice – 'Leave him, Dolores' – ringing in her ears.

She put her cup beside the sink, pulled her dressing-gown around herself and went to the front door. Opening it, she saw the cat across the road, tossing the dead, or maybe half-alive, mouse between its paws.

She closed the door behind her and got into her car. As she drove away she watched the house recede in the rear-view mirror. Joe had come to stand on the doorstep in his T-shirt and pyjama bottoms.

'Goodbye,' Dee said out loud, and adjusted the mirror so that she couldn't see him any more.

91. Now It's History

When Maggie opened the front door, Daniel was on the doorstep, drenched.

'Hi,' he said, rain trickling from his hair down his bunched-up forehead.

Maggie was speechless, not knowing what to think. It had been almost two weeks since he'd visited her in the hospital. She'd resisted every urge to text or call him. She'd been trying to forget he'd ever existed.

'Can I come in?' he asked.

Maggie stood aside. 'I suppose so,' she said, glad that at least William was out flat hunting and the house was empty. She thought she should get a towel for Daniel so that he could dry himself off. But she decided against it. 'What are you here for?' she asked, not inviting him past the hallway.

Daniel ran a hand through his thick, wet hair. 'I wanted to talk to you,' he said.

Halfway up the stairs Benny was sitting perfectly still, watching them.

'So, talk,' Maggie said.

Daniel's mouth opened, then closed again. He frowned. 'I had it all rehearsed ...' He trailed off.

Maggie was pricked by annoyance at his ineptitude and felt sorry for him at the same time. Maybe if she was with Daniel it would always be this way, she thought. Her feelings would be conflicted and she'd end up the caretaker in every situation, the way she constantly had with William. What she'd thought about Daniel that day in the hospital was true. He was still an inarticulate, immature boy.

'I'm sorry,' Daniel blurted, his frown deepening.

Maggie kept her arms folded. 'Sorry for what?' she asked.

'For disappearing again.'

The words that sprang to Maggie's mind had nothing to do with the last two weeks. 'I waited for you for so long,' she said, unable to hold it in. 'I kept thinking, He'll come back for me some day. But you never did.'

'I wrote to you. You know I did. I never stopped thinking about you.'

'Your grandmother was still in Sligo. You could have come back any time. Remember that day when you were being put on the train to go home? You said you'd never let anyone separate us. I believed it. I believed you.'

Daniel looked at the puddle he was leaving on the floor. 'I thought you didn't want me,' he said, his voice miserable. 'I never got your letters either, remember?'

A lump rose in Maggie's throat. What was the point in rehashing the past? It only brought back the pain. And, at the end of the day, Daniel wasn't to blame.

'It doesn't matter,' she said. 'We were both too young.'

Daniel met her eyes and then his gaze wandered to the pictures of the family on the wall – Harry's graduation, Poppy's communion. He cleared his throat. 'You have this great life that you built for yourself, Maggie. You have your family. But I want you to know that if … if things aren't going okay, or if you need me for anything, anything at all, I'm here.'

On the stairs, Benny got to his feet and walked down to stand next to Maggie. He pushed his head against her calf, purring.

'What I'm trying to say ...' Daniel pressed on. 'What I want to say is ...'

Maggie's eyes filled, although they didn't leave his. She reached out and put one finger against his lips to stop him talking. 'We're different people now,' she said. 'I'm a different person.'

Daniel gave a forlorn nod as she took her hand away and silence stretched out between them. 'I don't expect anything,' he said eventually. 'I just wanted you to know that I'm not going anywhere. I won't disappear again.'

'Thank you,' Maggie said. She knew that what he really wanted her to know was that he loved her, and she could have told him she loved him in return, because she did, with all her heart. But it wasn't as simple as that. She'd put other people first her whole adult life. Once William had moved out, she needed time to find the right way ahead on her own terms. And Daniel was already threatening to steer her off course.

Benny let out a loud miaow and nudged her calf again.

'We could be friends,' Maggie said. 'We could see how that goes.'

Daniel's face brightened. 'Yes.' He nodded. 'Friends.'

Before he went back out into the rain he reached out to hug her for one last time. It felt the same as it had that night outside her hotel room in Stockholm. Like absolute safety and reckless adventure rolled up into one.

August – One Year Later
Thank You for the Music

Daniel switches off the boat's little engine and there is complete silence, only broken by a little dream-whimper from Lily, who's fast asleep, cradled on Cassandra's lap.

'Isn't this beautiful?' Maggie says, as the boat floats on the lake's glassy surface, water lapping gently at its sides. She doesn't remember seeing it like this when she was a kid, the emerald green symmetry of the islands, the angel-hair clouds reflected in banks of blue in water that stretches out and disappears around a sun-dappled corner. A pair of swans glide by in the mid-distance, making the whole scene look like a chocolate-box painting, more perfectly pastoral than nature itself.

This boat is called *Chiquitita*. It came with the whitewashed house that overlooks the lake, and it had a different name. They rechristened it last March when Daniel bought the house, Maggie insisting that, although she'd let go of her addiction to the Abbaholics Facebook group, she'd never let go of Abba.

Over the week Maggie's been visiting, Noah and Daniel have repainted the boat, Noah spending hours rendering its new name in red script on either side of the prow. Yesterday afternoon Maggie, Oona and Poppy watched him working on it through the kitchen window, his tongue jammed against his upper lip in concentration.

He'd taken a calligraphy course at his new school during the term before the summer holidays. Daniel said the place had more art classes in it than you could shake a paintbrush at.

'He's so cute,' Poppy said, and Oona, laughing, replied, 'I don't think you're his type, missy.'

Across the lake the two swans abruptly take off in flight, the deep whirr of their wings reaching the boat through the quiet.

'We ought to be getting home soon,' Dee says. 'I don't want Lily out too late.'

Cassandra cuddles her goddaughter closer. 'You'll be fine for a little while yet, won't you?' she croons.

Dee's a bit over-protective of the baby, Maggie thinks, but it's understandable. It's only now she seems to be recovering little bits of her former humour, hints of the person she used to be. At first, after she left Joe, she was still hiding, always looking over her shoulder for him. He hadn't come after her, though, not to London, where she'd stayed with Maggie and worked remotely for a month. Not to Sligo, where she'd lived with Cassandra and her father for another few weeks before she'd felt safe enough to return to Dublin and a rented house. He'd turned up at the hospital when the baby was born. After that, Dee told him he couldn't see Lily unless he was in psychotherapy, which he would have to prove he was having with receipts and reports. So far, he hasn't filed any with her solicitor.

As if Lily has heard and understood her mother, she gives a little cry in Cassandra's arms, then nods off again. She's a dainty thing, her head a mass of black hair inherited from her father, her heart-shaped face and wide-set eyes, the spitting image of Dee's mother, who dotes on her like there's no tomorrow.

'Just five more minutes,' says Daniel. He loves the silence and solitude of the lake, Maggie knows. He still needs escape, a place where he can be at rest without the world tugging at his sleeves. He'll be touring in America in October again, with the Shoulder to Shoulder campaign.

He says he's still physically sick before he gets onstage, and Maggie has witnessed it, but she knows that he's found the strength in himself that he had all along but never knew how to tap into. When he's centre stage and all those kids are loving him – not because he's Danny Lane but because he's Daniel Smith, who stands up and says, 'We'll stand together in solidarity against bullying' – he's like the leader of a new revolution.

After the American tour, he plans to work with the Shoulder to Shoulder Foundation for one year, then hand it on. He'll settle down to gigging here and there, maybe writing for other people. The little outbuilding behind the whitewashed house has been fitted out as a recording studio, and when she arrived on Monday from England, Maggie heard the strains of his guitar floating out on the breeze.

She'd wanted to come and see her mother anyway, so Daniel's suggestion that they all go to the island for old times' sake had been perfectly timed. Oona had jumped at the chance of a holiday at home and, surprisingly, Poppy had been excited too. It's a bit intense with three generations of women packed into her parents' house, but there's lots of laughter too, which still feels new. Poppy, it turns out, is a dab hand at Scrabble and can beat even her grandmother into submission.

The two swans come flying back and land on the water in a smooth glide. Daniel squints in the sunlight as he smiles at Maggie.

They are here, all four of them, older and maybe a little wiser, but still as wholly and essentially themselves as they were on that morning when a different boat bore them towards their separate lives, towards the events that led to Maggie's life with William. He's settled into his new place now, in Battersea, which is far enough away not to have him on her doorstep the whole time. He still calls her, though, needing her advice about some woman he's dating, or in a panic because he washed his whites and coloureds together and they ran. Maggie suspects it will always be that way with him. She's done with picking up his pieces, though.

'If my life were an Abba song, I think it would be the same as it was when we were here last time,' she says to the assembled company.

'"Head Over Heels",' says Cassandra. 'I remember.'

'Would yours be the same too?' Maggie asks.

'Well, mine was "Cassandra",' Cassandra replies. 'But now I think it would be "Thank You For The Music", because I'm grateful that Abba's music brought us all back together again.'

'I was going to say that!' Dee laughs.

'So?' Cassandra smiles. 'We can have the same song, can't we?'

'I suppose we can.'

Dee turns to Daniel. 'We never found out what yours was in the first place,' she says.

Daniel replies, just as he did that summer, 'Go on, have a guess.'

But, of course, Maggie doesn't have to. The other night, after the dinner party with Cassandra and John, she had asked him what it was while they were washing the dishes.

'"Fernando",' he'd said, without hesitation.

Maggie had laughed. 'Why?' she asked.

'Because when you sang it to me on the island all those years ago, I knew in that moment I loved you and that I always would.'

'There was something in the air that night,' Maggie said.

He'd put the pan he'd been drying on the draining-board, and taken her into his arms, and as he'd kissed her they'd both kept their eyes wide open, taking each other in. Maggie had thought she could stay like that for ever.

Now, as he goes to start the engine on the boat, he gives her a conspiratorial wink. She grins and turns, shielding her eyes from the sun to see if anyone's waiting on the jetty for them.

There's no one.

Acknowledgements

Above all, thanks to my editor, friend and mentor, Ciara Considine, without whom this book would not have been written. Thanks also to Breda Purdue and the staff of Hachette Ireland for their belief in me.

For their help with characterisation and plot I'd like to thank Eilish Kent and Sarah Francis, and for sharing their stories with me, Martina Beagan Greenan and Vanessa Lacey. Also thanks to Maggie Breheny, Anne Gildea, Louise Mitchell, Manny and Cathy O'Hara, John McCarthy, Hazel Orme and Ami Smithson.

Thanks to Patsy and the much missed Nick Fyfe for their hospitality and encouragement in Tuscany, where part of this book was written, and to the wonderful staff and inmates of the Tyrone Guthrie Centre in Newbliss, Co. Monaghan for the same.

And last, but not least, thank you Abba, for the music.

Reading is so much more than the act of moving from page to page. It's the exploration of new worlds; the pursuit of adventure; the forging of friendships; the breaking of hearts; and the chance to begin to live through a new story each time the first sentence is devoured.

We at Hachette Ireland are very passionate about what we read, and what we publish. And we'd love to hear what you think about our books.

If you'd like to let us know, or to find out more about us and our titles, please visit www.hachette.ie or our Facebook page www.facebook.com/hachetteireland, or follow us on Twitter @HachetteIre.